KINTA—
FREEDOM
FIGHTER

The Legend Begins

KIM LOOKE

BALBOA.
PRESS

A DIVISION OF HAY HOUSE

Balboa Press books may be ordered through booksellers or by contacting:

Balboa Press
A Division of Hay House
1663 Liberty Drive
Bloomington, IN 47403
www.balboapress.com.au
1 (877) 407-4847

Because of the dynamic nature of the Internet, any web addresses or
links contained in this book may have changed since publication and
may no longer be valid. The views expressed in this work are solely those
of the author and do not necessarily reflect the views of the publisher,
and the publisher hereby disclaims any responsibility for them.

The author of this book does not dispense medical advice or prescribe the use
of any technique as a form of treatment for physical, emotional, or medical
problems without the advice of a physician, either directly or indirectly. The
intent of the author is only to offer information of a general nature to help you
in your quest for emotional and spiritual well-being. In the event you use any
of the information in this book for yourself, which is your constitutional right,
the author and the publisher assume no responsibility for your actions.

Any people depicted in stock imagery provided by Getty Images are
models, and such images are being used for illustrative purposes only.
Certain stock imagery © Getty Images.

Print information available on the last page.

ISBN: 978-1-5043-1668-2 (sc)
ISBN: 978-1-5043-1669-9 (e)

Balboa Press rev. date: 02/15/2019

After an idyllic early childhood, an innocent young girl is ripped from the safety and security of her family home. She is thrust early into unexpected adult responsibilities by her frightened, concerned parents. Their need to escape from the clutches of evil tyranny threatens the lives of all three.

Along the way, Kinta meets a remarkable, unusual friend. Her new friend joins her on her travels and helps her through the transition from awkward teenager to confident young woman. Eventually, her new friend helps her to discover her true destiny and her first love.

The family stands firm, side-by-side, in the daunting face of abject adversity. They refuse to buckle under immense pressure or to risk compromising their solid values until peace and tranquillity have been restored to their land.

Her journey from a young girl to a new bride and her ultimate freedom takes many twists and turns. Eventually, it allows the unlikely heroine to grow and mature into a strong, courageous young woman, with a fighting warrior spirit, and a solid sense of justice for the people in her life.

Dedication

Dedicated to my wife Joan, who always provides the inspiration to start, and the encouragement and support to finish, in everything that I pursue.

CONTENTS

PART 1

Chapter 1 1
Chapter 2 7
Chapter 3 14
Chapter 4 18
Chapter 5 22
Chapter 6 29
Chapter 7 37
Chapter 8 43
Chapter 9 48
Chapter 10 54
Chapter 11 60
Chapter 12 65
Chapter 13 70
Chapter 14 79
Chapter 15 85

PART 2

Chapter 16 93
Chapter 17 99
Chapter 18 105
Chapter 19 112
Chapter 20 117
Chapter 21 123

Chapter 22 129
Chapter 23 137
Chapter 24 143
Chapter 25 148
Chapter 26 154
Chapter 27 161
Chapter 28 167
Chapter 29 173
Chapter 30 178
Chapter 31 184
Chapter 32 191
Chapter 33 197
Chapter 34 205

PART 3

Chapter 35 217
Chapter 36 224
Chapter 37 232
Chapter 38 238
Chapter 39 244
Chapter 40 250
Chapter 41 257
Chapter 42 264
Chapter 43 270
Chapter 44 275
Chapter 45 281
Chapter 46 288
Chapter 47 294
Chapter 48 301
Chapter 49 307
Chapter 50 313
Chapter 51 320

About the Author 323

PART 1

FLIGHT TO FREEDOM

CHAPTER 1

The dark, ebony mantle of night softly settled like a smoky, black veil over the usually busy seaside village of Bayville. The hustle and bustle of regular daily activity slowly ground to a halt, which sent the exhausted working occupants' home to their families.

Like ever-expanding ripples across a calm lake, twinkling lights from lit candles and lamps suddenly appeared in the open windows of the mud-brick and thatched-roof houses in the sleepy hamlet and slowly spread. Fat, black, rain-laden storm clouds drifted across the face of the thin crescent moon and finally removed any of the faint, pale light it had provided. The night was plunged into full inky darkness as the village's inhabitants settled down for the night.

Suddenly, the blood-curdling howls of hunting dogs closing on their prey split the silence and grew ever louder as three frightened figures huddled like ghostly shadows, hunched in the darkened corner of a concealed laneway. Family friends had secretly informed Aedyn and Catelyn earlier that day that the high priestess had suddenly become aware of Catelyn's special powers, and now they had been running for hours, trying to stay clear of the temple guards and their dogs. Their frightened young daughter, Kinta, crouched cringing in the darkened lane along with her parents, trembling but stoically silent, and drawing strength from their apparent calm in the face of such dire circumstances.

"We simply can't go on any further like this, my love!" gasped

Aedyn. His chest heaved as he attempted to suck the cool refreshing night air into his burning lungs. "You must do whatever is necessary, without using your special powers, to get yourself and Kinta to The Haven!"

"Once you reach there, our friends will be able to help the two of you to find your way through the maze of tunnels to the rendezvous point!" he said, puffing heavily. "I'll attempt to create a diversion, to distract these guards and their dogs, and help buy you enough time to escape!"

"No!" replied Catelyn vehemently, her whole-body trembling, "I won't leave you here alone! We must all make it safely together! I can use my special powers to help us!"

Aedyn was gentle but firm, in his reply. "You cannot use your powers, my love, or they'll be able to track us!" he said, "At the moment, the guards and their dogs only have our scent by which to track us. If you use your special powers, they'll know our location for sure! As I said, I'll create a diversion to allow you and Kinta to make it safely to The Haven!" He paused once more to catch his breath. "You must be strong for her!"

Kinta glanced nervously back and forth between her parents. And, although she was worried sick about their situation, she had complete faith in Catelyn and Aedyn's ability to find a solution.

Aedyn took a long, slow, deep breath to calm himself and attempted to quell his anger at their current situation. "We cannot let the priestess take her!" Aedyn continued passionately, placing his arm around Kinta's shoulders and hugging her close. "We both know what that would mean!"

Slowly, Catelyn closed her eyes and hung her head dejectedly. She knew what her husband was saying was both logically and practically correct. But it took all her courage to accept it and quietly stand. She gazed lovingly down at Aedyn, and her eyes went from his thick dark hair, which was yet to show any grey, across his ruggedly handsome face with a neatly trimmed beard, and down to his broad chest and muscular arms.

Eventually, her eyes came back to rest on Aedyn's dark brown eyes, which usually sparkled with merriment, but tonight they showed his great concern and determination for his family's safety. "Be careful, my love," she whispered in a worried tone and placed her lips gently on her husband's forehead. "I need you to come back to me!"

Aedyn's mouth smiled to relax his wife, but his eyes retained their steely determination. "Don't you worry your pretty head, I can take care of myself," he whispered, chuckling to hide his concern. "Now, be gone with you woman, and have some hot broth waiting for me when I return!"

Playfully he slapped Catelyn on the backside. He placed Kinta's hand in hers and pushed his wife and daughter out into the darkened street. Aedyn strained his eyes to observe them until their dark silhouettes disappeared into the inky blackness.

His heightened awareness, brought on by the impending danger of their situation, had greatly amplified all his senses and he could smell the faint odour of the ocean that carried to him on the light evening breeze.

When he felt they must be far enough away by now, Aedyn rose wearily, turned and slowly moved in the opposite direction, towards the distinct and ominous sound of the barking dogs, knowing that the temple guards would not be far behind them. Stepping carefully, to avoid making the slightest noise that would give away his position too early, Aedyn's face twisted and grimaced in pain as he made his way slowly through the shadowy streets and listened intently for his pursuers.

Earlier that night, he had been struck in the left shoulder by a crossbow bolt from one of the chasing guards. Although it passed straight through without causing too much damage, it had sapped much of his usual strength. He now suffered the full consequences of pain and dizziness through loss of blood, which had soaked through his upper garments and was now drying and causing them to stick to his skin.

As he silently listened, he heard the approaching voices of the guards calling to each other and realised that the dogs were right onto their scent. Now he must delay them at all cost, despite the sadness that gripped him as he realised that he might not see his loved ones again. *I must try to keep our pursuers tied up here for as long as possible!* He thought.

Taking a calming breath, he stepped out into the low flickering light that was cast by the flaming torches of the guards. Aedyn shouted defiantly, "Are you boys and your four-legged lovers looking for me?"

Instantly, the four heavily-armed guards and their two savage dogs turned toward him and rushed forward. The guards showed a sudden urgency and rapidly shouted commands, drawing their swords in an uncoordinated tangle.

The moment the guards released the first of the two dogs from the restraint of its leash, it raced to Aedyn and leapt at him with eyes blazing, sharp white fangs bared, and long drools of saliva hanging from the open mouth. Aedyn deftly sidestepped and swung his massive razor-sharp sword furiously, which severed the dog's head cleanly, sending it flying and spraying blood across the street. The dog's body dropped at his feet and slowly oozed blood across the cobblestones of the small road.

He then kicked out sharply with his right boot at the second lunging, snarling dog, which had leapt up aiming for Aedyn's face. He struck the dog in the chest with such force that it snapped the dog's spine and broke its sternum and ribs. The shattered bones punctured its heart and lungs.

The second dog immediately collapsed onto the cobblestones, moaned pitifully at Aedyn's feet and feebly kicked its front legs several times. Then finally, unable to make a sound or twist its head, the second dog tried to follow Aedyn's movements with eyes that were slowly glazing over.

As both dogs lay quivering in their final spasms of death, Aedyn turned quickly to face the four approaching guards who had hesitantly followed their dogs into the attack. They had now spread themselves into a tight semicircle facing him with their swords drawn.

He was an accomplished swordsman and had gained his extensive experience in constant daily battle against the many thieves and vagabonds that littered the roads and pathways through the forest. On more than one occasion he had fought for his very life against these cut-throat interlopers on his way to and from the city, as he travelled to supply the rebel forces with his secret weapons.

Although his current opponents were poorly trained, Aedyn was injured, and he could already hear other guards arriving to support them. But he was determined to take as many with him as he could to ensure the best possible chance for his family to escape. Aedyn prayed silently that his wife and daughter would make it safely to The Haven. He took great satisfaction in the knowledge that, with the dogs gone, it would now make it so much harder for the guards to find his fleeing family.

The first guard stepped forward breathlessly and, as Aedyn waited, the guard twisted his body and swung his lunging sabre wide, which left his ribs exposed. Quickly, Aedyn thrust forward, taking the guard in the ribs and felt his blade slide between the bones and carry on through the vital organs in the chest cavity. This action caused the lifeless guard to drop his sword and blood to trickle from the corner of his mouth.

With a swift kick of his left foot, Aedyn dislodged the first guard from his sword as a second guard lunged, and Aedyn parried. The clash of their steel blades rang out loudly into the night. He struck out with his other foot and knocked the third guard to the ground. The second guard stepped back quickly to change his angle of attack to the right, trying to catch Aedyn off-guard. The fourth guard was extraordinarily unlucky as he tripped and fell over the third guard in his enthusiasm.

Aedyn tried to follow the second guard's movements with his sword. The fourth guard fell awkwardly and found himself impaled on Aedyn's sword. The fall caught Aedyn by surprise as well and wrenched his sword from his hands.

By now, another large group of guards had arrived and surrounded the rough-house melee. They were acting on orders to take Aedyn alive and were using their fists and heavy sticks to try and subdue Aedyn. Frantically, Aedyn thrashed about, swung with both his fists and tried to dodge the incoming blows from the other guards. Aedyn used all his strength to knock another guard to the ground but, eventually, their sheer numbers overpowered him.

Held to the ground, Aedyn gasped for air as a large hairy arm grasped his neck from behind and began to choke him. Although he had tried valiantly to put up a fight, his efforts were futile. The feeling slowly ebbed from his legs, and everything gradually went black.

He was roughly woken with a slap to the face to find the sharp point of a dagger pushed up against his neck, and a gruff voice muttered, "Where is the woman?"

"She's in a safe place where you and your bitch of a priestess will never find her!" spat Aedyn.

A leather-gloved fist hit Aedyn in the mouth. Immediately, he tasted the sticky sweetness of his blood as he tried to catch his unknown attacker. Aedyn only succeeded in covering his face in the blood that was now flowing freely from his mouth.

"Tell me now, you fool, or you will die!" muttered the gruff voice again.

"Well, my friend," replied Aedyn, as he tried to waste more time. "If, by my death, I can save my family, then so be it! I have never professed to be a genius. Even I know that, if I tell you where she is, I am headed towards the heavens!" he added condescendingly. "So, you can take that dagger and stick it in your arse!"

Quickly the dagger was removed from his neck and thrust into the open crossbow wound in his left shoulder. This harsh action caused Aedyn to shudder and cry out in pain as the last of his strength left his body.

Then, he felt another stabbing pain as a sword pierced his side and he was engulfed in total blackness again.

CHAPTER 2

L oud, boisterous cheers erupted from around the wooden table, as another piece of half-eaten food hurtled across the room. This loud clamour added to the already noisy ambience of the evening's revellers at the Bayview Tavern.

"Great shot, old boy," slurred a drunk off-duty soldier.

"Not such a great shot, with so large a target," replied another.

"Are you debating what a bloody good shot I am?" retorted the first soldier.

"Of course, he is," giggled a third. "Look at the size of the bugger! You could hardly miss him!"

The four drunk and dishevelled soldiers seated at the table had ordered and noisily devoured their meals. They now proceeded to throw the remnants at a large hulking fellow in the corner.

Ox was an enormous bearded man and his head, and his upper body was disproportionately large. He had long, thick, reddish-brown shaggy hair covering most of his massive muscular body. He made a futile effort to look smaller by hunching down at one of the corner tables. Although he was inwardly annoyed at the attention he received from the soldiers, he showed no visible outward sign of his annoyance.

He had silently endured a lifetime of being bullied, jeered at, insulted, and teased. It had been the same from the day he was born, and would no doubt continue until the day he died. Over the years he had found not to react or show his displeasure at another person's behaviour towards him. It would usually just get worse, and he would then have to endure the increased consequences.

So, he just sat there, completely still and frozen to the spot. An expressionless face, sullen and silently brooding, he hoped that they would soon get bored with his lack of response to their barbs and go away.

He was born a huge baby, and his mother had died under excruciating circumstances giving birth to him. Ox's aged grandparents had reluctantly taken him into their care, and by the age of seven, he stood taller than most fully grown men. The elderly couple were utterly unprepared for this extra responsibility and became extremely cruel to Ox. He had taken many a massive beating as a child, often wandering the streets with numerous bruises and contusions on his young growing body.

They had unimaginatively named him Oxalis, then deliberately shortened this to Ox, due to his vast size and the overabundance of thick body hair. Ox's grand-parents had cruelly told him he was too big and stupid to have a real name. Fortunately for Ox, the elderly couple had finally died of old age when he was still a young adolescent.

From that time on, he had lived on in their house. He worked on various itinerant labouring teams that were building new trading routes for the abundant trade emanating from the city. His employment doing daily road-building was physically hard work, and the payment he received for it was just a pittance. However, it was a permanent ongoing job where he could indeed put to work his only physical talent, his enormous strength.

Once again, the guards at their table roared in laughter and slapped each other on the back. A large half-eaten orange narrowly missed hitting Ox's head, but once again he sat silently staring stonily at the floor.

"Yes, that's right!" The soothing, tinkling tones of a sweet young female voice came from right near the front of Ox's table. "You just ignore them, lovey!"

Ox looked up to see a beautiful young woman, with the most intense sparkling blue eyes. She was standing in front of him holding several jugs of ale, and he couldn't believe his luck that she would possibly want to speak with him. She had a slim build, which belied her incredible strength of personality. Thick honey-blond hair hung loosely in long natural ringlets down to her waist and failed to cover her ample breasts. To Ox, the late afternoon sun's golden rays, shining through the large plate-glass windows behind her, made her curly blond hair glow like a halo.

Her name was Madeleine, and she was the daughter and only child of Erwyn, the Tavern owner. Erwyn's ex-wife, Elsbeth, had run off with a soldier and now lived as an itinerant camp-follower, leaving Erwyn to raise his daughter as a single parent.

Although her circumstances had forced her to grow up early, Madeleine had a natural air of kindness about her. Her calming manner made Ox feel instantly comfortable in her presence and time seemed to stand perfectly still. Her flawless complexion and tinkling laughter made her look and sound just like an angel.

Not many people showed Ox kindness. Usually, they just teased him or avoided contact completely. Madeleine smiled at Ox kindly and tilted her head slightly to one side. Her gentle, caring action caused his whole face to light up as she enquired about his needs. "Would you like anything more to eat, lovey?" She smiled kindly. "Or, maybe, just another nice cold ale instead?"

Ox stared dreamily at the seemingly ethereal vision before him, slowly shook his head and thanked the girl as she moved on to the next table. He could not take his eyes off Madeleine. She had blossomed into a beautiful and shapely young woman, and it was evident that she was an experienced Tavern maid already. Ox could tell by the way she artfully dodged the gropes and pinches of the drunken patrons without offending them and still made them all feel welcome.

However, Ox's keen eyes immediately noticed that she deliberately stayed well clear of the soldiers' table. It was as if she instinctively knew that she would be in great trouble if she didn't take care around them. The military diners consisted of a Sergeant and three of his men. All four men were becoming more inebriated the further the night wore on. The Tavern owner Erwyn served the soldiers himself. It was apparent to Erwyn and the other patrons that the men were doing their utmost to impress their superior by puffing their chests out and boasting about all the women they had previously bedded.

The Sergeant, however, was only half listening. His gaze was fixed on Madeleine as she swayed gracefully around the room. Another roar of laughter erupted. This time the youngest soldier got too carried away with his hand gestures and fell over his chair. The Sergeant rose noisily and unsteadily to his feet and called loudly to get Madeleine's attention. "Hey girlie, get over here immediately and help my friend!" He shouted drunkenly at the top of his voice. "He's just fallen over one of your stools and hurt himself!"

To forestall the inevitable, Erwyn rushed quickly to the assistance of the drunken soldier. The soldier had by this time entirely succumbed to his inebriated state and passed out on the floor. He lay there in a pool of his vomit.

The Sergeant grabbed the owner roughly by the scruff of his neck and jerked him roughly to his feet. He slapped him with the back of his hand, then knocked him almost senseless to the ground with his fist. "I didn't ask you to do it," growled the Sergeant menacingly. "I told the girl to get over here!"

The bar instantly turned deathly quiet and sensed trouble. The other patrons slowly stood and left. Madeleine tentatively approached the unconscious soldier and attempted to revive him. "He's too drunk to get up, Sir," she hesitantly replied to the Sergeant.

"Oh well, never mind, stay here with me then!" slurred the Sergeant. He bent and slipped his arm around her slender waist, then lifted her easily up to her feet.

"Please, Sir!" pleaded Madeleine. She attempted to wriggle away from his grasp. "I must attend to things in the kitchen!"

"Rubbish!" The Sergeant grinned menacingly and tightened his grip on her waist. "Everyone else has already gone or is leaving! Why don't you stay here and have some fun with us?" he said suggestively.

Erwyn stood up unsteadily and attempted to protest loudly, only to be knocked down again by the Sergeant's fist. This time he didn't move from where he fell and lay sprawled across the unconscious soldier.

"Don't be shy, girlie," said the Sergeant. His drunken grin had now turned into a lustful stare. "Now, let's get a better look at you!"

With a grunt, he ripped open the front of her blouse and exposed a pair of young, firm, full rounded breasts. The sudden exposure to cold air caused Madeleine's large nipples to stand erect, as she tried in vain to cover herself with her hands. Her face turned a pink flush of embarrassment.

"Hey boys, what do you reckon about these?" drooled the Sergeant. He stared fixedly, as he prodded the exposed breasts with his finger. "Ain't these a mighty fine set of melons?"

The two remaining soldiers looked about themselves uneasily, then darted glances around the room. They did not dare to challenge their superior. Instead, they just giggled nervously and shuffled their feet on the spot.

The Sergeant released his grip slightly on Madeleine's waist and stood back to admire her nakedness. She tried to escape from the crazy look in his eyes and the stink of alcohol on his breath. However, she was not quite quick enough, and her open defiance earned her a slap in the face. "This is a feisty one, boys!" he said.

The Sergeant suddenly spun her around and bent her over roughly, holding her face-down on the table with one hand. Then, in one deft movement with his spare hand, he flipped up the back of her dress and held it in place with both his hands as he restrained Madeleine. His action prevented her from moving and revealed the smooth milky-white skin of her firm round buttocks and long slim legs.

Madeleine struggled frantically with all her strength to twist and squirm her body to escape from the Sergeant's grasp. He was far too strong, and she was firmly trapped and at his complete mercy.

Clumsily, he released one hand and undid the front of his pants. He allowed them to fall around his ankles and exposed his rampant manhood. Then he wedged his boots in between Madeleine's feet and kicked out with his feet, which savagely forced her long legs even wider apart and further exposed the thick mass of dark curls around the open pouting lips of her now prominently displayed womanhood. "I am going to enjoy this one, boys!" he loudly and drunkenly boasted, as he prepared to enter her.

Suddenly, there came the loud rasping, scraping sound of roughly moved furniture followed by a loud meaty thud, as the Sergeant's eyes rolled to the back of his head and his body slumped onto Madeleine's back. He was dead before he slid onto the floor.

The remaining two soldiers were standing fixed to the spot like unmoving statues, riveted to the floor. Ox stood and fumed over the dead Sergeant's body with his massive fists still clenching and unclenching angrily. He had been sitting patiently watching the whole episode from his table.

Although he had not wanted to interfere and bring attention to himself, he couldn't stand by to see the young woman in distress. His usually controlled and suppressed rage had suddenly taken over.

As the first soldier suddenly realised what had happened to the Sergeant, he quickly recovered his wits. He came at Ox with his sword drawn. Ox immediately retaliated to this threat by thrusting out his huge right foot. He did this with such violent force that it struck the soldier in the chest and caused him to fly back across the room without touching the floor.

The soldier flew out through the thick, closed oakwood front door, which smashed and fell from its hinges. The soldier remained in a crumpled unconscious mess on the ground outside.

Having managed to jump out of the way in time to save himself, the third soldier froze. After seeing the sudden demise of his counterpart, he decided that discretion *was* the better part of valour. He quickly grabbed his sword from the table and bolted for the open door, waving his arms and yelling for help at the top of his lungs.

Ox carefully bent down and used his massive hands to pull the back of Madeleine's dress down to protect her modesty. He gently helped Madeleine to get back up from the table. Her feeble efforts to cover her large exposed breasts with her hands were almost useless since the front of the blouse was now in shreds.

Ox reached around behind him and stripped the clean tablecloth off the nearest table. He gently placed it around Madeleine's shoulders to provide some cover. Madeleine snuggled up against his broad chest, and he closed his massive arms around her, prepared to defend her against all the odds. She had never felt so safe and secure in all her life. "Thank you, kind Sir! Please tell me, what is your name?" she whispered up to him.

Ox tenderly used a corner of the tablecloth to wipe the tears from her once joyful face. A broad grin spread across his face, which lit up as he looked down into her thankful eyes. "My name's Ox!" he merely said.

"Ox, my sweet, you must leave now!" Madeleine gently pleaded. "Save yourself before the relief watch gets here!" Her words, however, came too late, as a new troop of armed soldiers with swords drawn suddenly rushed through the door and surrounded them.

CHAPTER 3

Catelyn sighed loudly and slumped down with relief. Time had seemed to stand still. Once again, the sound of patrolling palace guards passed by without incident. She and Kinta had been hiding in the basement cellar of The Haven for several hours, and the tension was becoming almost unbearable.

The Haven was an inn being used to secretly hide and safely transport refugees fleeing out of Skargness under cover of darkness. For the past two years, the high priestess Vylaine and the King's soldiers had been rounding up any person that harboured an inkling of special powers. She was supposedly holding them in the palace dungeons. No one knew why this was happening. The fact that none had ever returned was enough for most to believe the worst and attempt to flee the country.

Catelyn had more powerful unique ability than most. For her family's safety, she chose not to use it other than small sporadic covert healings. While she didn't openly use her powers, the palace guards could not track her.

For many years now, Aedyn had been successfully operating his blacksmith's forge in the little hamlet of Bayville. He had earned an excellent reputation that extended far beyond the city limits. He would sometimes smuggle things at night through the village sewers and up into the Nantgarw Mountains. It was the secret entrance to the city's sewers, located in the basement of The Haven, which they had used to visit the rebels who had taken refuge there. Aedyn and Catelyn had secretly helped hundreds to leave the city for safety. All was well, and their business had prospered.

When Kinta was born, Aedyn was not prepared to spend as much time away from his family. He was acutely aware of the danger that was presented in him not being available to look after Catelyn and Kinta while he was away personally.

Recently, Kinta had joined Catelyn as a teacher in the village school, and between them, they taught the youngest children's classes. Although Kinta had so far never used her special powers, or even showed the slightest interest in doing so, to the experienced eye, it could be seen just by looking at her that she possessed great skills. So far, Aedyn and Catelyn had successfully kept Kinta out of sight of the palace guards. However, if they ever laid eyes on her, Kinta would have been in grave danger.

Catelyn and Kinta crouched at the secret entrance to a long narrow tunnel. The tunnel wound for several hundred dark, unlit paces until it eventually connected to the sewers. They were with Alwan and Sonja, the current owners of The Haven. They knew that the guards would discover The Haven's real purpose this night and they must flee the city before they were captured and tried for treason.

"We must leave shortly! We can't afford to wait any longer for Aedyn!" Catelyn spoke quietly and nervously to Sonja. "I'll have to use my powers to seal the door to the cellar! It'll take the guards quite some time to open it, and that should give us ample time to get outside of the city walls!" she said. "When we get there, we'll find a horse and cart! We must make haste and stick to the planned route!" she continued. "It'll take us a few days longer to get to the rebels, but it'll be a lot safer!"

With no trace of the nervousness she felt inside evident in her voice, Catelyn took Kinta in her arms and hugged her tight. *"Be brave, my sweet!"* she whispered to her daughter.

She then turned to the scared Tavern owners and passed Kinta to them. *"Go now,"* she whispered. They began to shuffle towards the concealed exit. *"As soon as I use my powers to seal this doorway, those guards will be here within minutes! Wait at the cart and don't leave without me! I'll be right behind you! Just do as I have instructed!"* Catelyn gave her instructions confidently.

Quickly Catelyn pushed them through the dark, narrow opening, then stopped to hug and kiss Kinta one more time. She watched silently until the silhouettes of the Tavern owners and her daughter disappeared into the darkness of the tunnel.

Catelyn closed her eyes and, with a look of intense concentration on her face, she began to use her powers, which totally sealed the entrance and temporarily masked the whereabouts of the secret tunnel. Her prediction had been correct. No sooner had she sealed the opening than the guards started to pound on the front door of the inn.

Catelyn stepped backwards slowly into the tunnel and awaited the arrival of the guards. She had only ever used her powers for healing purposes before and, although she knew she could, she had never used her gift in anger. Tonight, however, things might change!

The combination of the rage she felt at separation from her husband, coupled with the fear of what would happen if they caught her daughter, would help her call upon all her powers to thwart any attempt to harm Kinta. Suddenly, the door to the tunnel burst open, and a Sergeant from the temple guards stepped through. Catelyn had not counted on a Sergeant being part of their pursuit party, and he quickly sensed Catelyn's powers and started issuing orders to those following close behind him.

Luckily, Catelyn had prepared herself, and a massive fireball shot from her fingers. The ball of fire struck the Sergeant in the chest and sent him hurtling back through the door, totally engulfed in flames. Catelyn continued to amble slowly and carefully backward as two guards pushed past the flaming Sergeant to get to her.

The guards lunged angrily with their swords aimed at Catelyn's stomach. Surprisingly, the swords never made their mark as Catelyn had cast an invisible force field around her body, and this had caught the guards by complete surprise as their swords became entangled in it.

Gently, Catelyn reached out and touched the tips of the swords and grimaced as a bright blue bolt of energy left her fingers and danced menacingly down the blades. The guards, who still had a grip on their swords, convulsed uncontrollably before falling to the floor in a smouldering mess, which left the rest of the guards mingled in the doorway, not sure of what to do next.

"Get out of my way!" came a voice of command from behind them. The guards immediately stood aside as a short, stocky Corporal stepped into view.

Once again, Catelyn shot a huge fireball down the hallway. This time, however, the Corporal was ready, and he ducked out of the way to let the ball of flame pass by harmlessly. One of the guards standing behind in the massed and mingling group was not as lucky, and his blood-curdling screams of fear and pain could be heard clearly standing out as the other guards tried in vain to extinguish the flames.

Catelyn had started to tire. The protective force field had sapped much of her power, and she could gradually feel it beginning to fall away. The Corporal also sensed this and attempted to immediately launch his counterattack. Catelyn had little strength left but knew that she must quickly ready a decisive blow, or all her efforts so far would have been in vain.

Thinking that Catelyn's power was spent, the Corporal turned to command the guards to rush forward and restrain her, but it was the last thing that he would ever do. Catelyn concentrated, summoned all her available strength and sent an enormous bolt of lightning into the ceiling of the tunnel above her attackers. This colossal explosion caused the roof to collapse from above the guards, covered them and completely blocked off the shaft.

As the dust settled, Catelyn turned and hurriedly headed down the dark tunnel after the other three escapees.

CHAPTER 4

$\mathbb{B}$ alloons, dust, and streamers rose into the warm, fetid air before the balmy autumn breeze, as the parade wound through the dirty streets like a lazy serpent. King Daemon's annual parade occurred every year in the last week of autumn and was held to commemorate the successful planting of the kingdom's crops. This parade was the festival where everyone prayed for plenty of rain in the winter so that the plants would grow prosperously and make for a bountiful harvest.

Skargness's landmass borders are protected on all sides by a natural impenetrable fortress of mighty, towering, permanently snow-capped mountain ranges. Inside these physical barriers, the fertile alluvial soil has been deposited over thousands of years by the annual flooding of the extensive river systems. An expansive network of large rivers crisscrosses the landscape as they flow down from the melting snows.

Vast leafy verdant forests have grown up over time. They now provide a rich source of timber for the small villages that are springing up to support the many farming communities that dot the countryside. Small wagon trains of settlers followed the trappers and hunters when they finally succeeded in crossing the mountain ranges over one hundred years ago.

They have now spread out to take full advantage of the patchwork quilt of rich, lush grasslands to grow their swaying grain crops and raise large herds of animals. Such ample abundance has led to the apparent development of strong trade agreements with the friendly neighbouring border nations of Eshoram, Wachile, and Nantgarw.

Eshoram lies to the east of Skargness, and they have been blessed with a subtropical climate. Their temperate annual weather pattern supports vast orchards of a multitude of fruits, nuts, and berries, which are then subsequently found in the market stalls of all her neighbours. Wachilians in the west have discovered rich veins of precious metals within their mountainous terrain and used the proceeds to develop huge fishing fleets to scour the Great Southern Ocean.

On the other hand, the stone quarries of Nantgarw to the north are considered an essential source of raw materials. They are necessary for the many large construction works that are beginning to take place far and wide throughout this part of the world.

The annual parade was just one of the many festivities involved. For most of the citizens, it was considered the most boring. Many were merely here for the drinking, gambling and the many local produce food stalls that had been set up by the more industrious peasants, to make a quick profit.

The parade's primary purpose was mainly to display the size and might of the King's army. There were numerous VIP carriages dotted throughout the shambling marchers. The wagons held the royal family, high-ranking nobles of the land and a few other wealthy Skargnessian figures.

King Daemon and Queen Seraphina always rode in different carriages. Daemon rode with Vylaine, the high priestess, who in recent times rarely left his side. The young Queen rode with her even younger sister, Lorelei, the Duchess. "This parade is such a damn bore!" muttered the Duchess to her sister. "Although, some of those food stalls smell good!"

"I know it is, my dear!" was Seraphina's reply. "However, my husband is by far the most unpopular King to ever rule this Kingdom! He thinks it would be in his best interest not to cancel this foolish, drunken orgy in case there is a revolt!"

Lorelei chuckled at the thought before replying. "I know I would much rather be participating in the drunken orgies than fattening my rump in this damned carriage," she said. Seraphina laughed at the crude, impudent response. She leaned forward and tenderly embraced her sister, then half-heartedly turned and waved out of the open window.

In the distance, a commotion was occurring in the crowd. "Oh, goody!" exclaimed Lorelei. "It looks like a bit of excitement is coming our way!" It was a rather tall, stout man doing his best to outrun some of the local guardsmen. The man was completely naked and quite obviously intoxicated. The guards would have caught him effortlessly if it were not for the crowd of bystanders. They were cheering him on and doing their utmost to hinder the guards' progress.

"That man is stark naked!" exclaimed Seraphina, as he drew closer to the royal carriage. This comment immediately gained Lorelei's complete attention, and she stuck her head out of the open carriage window to gain a better view. "Oh, my God!" replied Lorelei. "He's hung like a war horse!"

"Lorelei!" gasped the Queen to her young sister. "You're supposed to be a Duchess and a lady!" she said. "Please, try to act like one for a change!"

"Ha!" retorted Lorelei. "I can tell you now if the Duke had a pecker like that, I'd be a lot less ladylike to him than what I am now!" Seraphina tried in vain to look disgusted. However, it had been so long since the King had spent any real intimate time with her that she could not draw her eyes away from the man's ample endowment. She was always highly amused by her sister's constant crudeness and burst into laughter instead.

Suddenly, loud jeers erupted from the crowd as the guards were finally successful in catching their man. "What was all that about?" growled the King from his carriage. "Just some drunken cleric streaking down the street, Sire," replied a guardsman, who was riding alongside the royal carriage.

"Well, make sure he is dragged before me in court tomorrow," grunted the King again. "I want to sentence him personally! He will pay dearly for exposing himself in front of his Queen!" The guard acknowledged and rode off.

"Damn parade," grunted Daemon. "I knew I should have cancelled it!" The King was always worried about his popularity of late. He had found that the best way to gain relief was to attend the court sessions and pass judgment upon those who had strayed from the law.

"You must learn to control yourself, my King," noted Vylaine. "You will do yourself no good by it!"

"Well, it would help if you and your people could find that missing person and her damn husband," retorted Daemon. "For all we know, she is over the border by now!" he continued.

"Oh no," replied Vylaine "She's still in the city! We have stationed guards at all the exits, and they are trapped here! Sooner or later she must use her powers and then we'll have her!"

"Well, I hope so," replied the King. "If she gets across the border, it is going to be that much harder to find them!"

"You must trust me, my love," whispered Vylaine, as her hand slowly slipped down the front of his tunic. "If you can pack our little Queen off to bed when we get back to the palace, I'll do something about calming your nerves!"

The King smiled to himself. The high priestess always covered herself from head to foot permanently in public, but beneath that camouflage, she was the most beautiful woman he had ever seen. This body coverage was Vylaine's personal strategy to ensure only a minimal number of people knew what the priestess looked like. That way, Vylaine could vanish incognito into a crowd if necessary.

She was also not as inhibited as his wife and could always find new ways to make him feel like no other could. He had strayed before and had no problem finding himself a partner. However, some women were intimidated by his title and felt uncomfortable sleeping with him.

Vylaine was not afraid of him! She quite often took full control of their lovemaking sessions. Her acts of boldness always left the King satiated, fulfilled, and happy at the end of each.

Together, they had a plan. Eventually, under Vylaine's guidance, with the help of the Commander and his ever-expanding army, they would invade every neighbouring nation until they all knelt before his banner.

CHAPTER 5

"Silence in the courtroom!" screamed the Lord Chancellor. He banged the large, heavy wooden gavel loudly on the bench in front of him. The crowd dulled to a whisper and dropped to one knee in hushed expectation for the arrival of the royal party. The court usually wasn't a place of interest to the local populace. Only a handful ever bothered to watch the myriad of petty criminals be tried and sentenced before the Lord Chancellor.

The King did not regularly attend, nor did the Queen or high priestess for that matter, leaving those decisions to the court officials. Today, however, all three were in attendance and the courtroom was at its maximum capacity. Everybody was in anticipation for the trial of Skargness's most wanted man, whom authorities knew as Zoran.

He was Skargness's most dangerous and effective assassin. For years, authorities had been trying to capture him, with little success. Then, a bungled assassination attempt on a noble had led him straight into the arms of the local guards. These guards had been tipped off and were waiting for his arrival. His real name was Narchis; however, only a select few knew this name.

"All hail, the King and Queen of Skargness!" screamed the Lord Chancellor. The royal party consisted of Daemon, Seraphina and Vylaine. They entered the court and proceeded gracefully and regally down the centre aisle. When they reached the royal box, the party took their seats. After everyone was comfortably seated, the King nodded to the Lord Chancellor who directed the gallery to be seated.

Whenever the high priestess attended court, she would take charge of proceedings as well as pass sentence on the guilty parties. The Lord Chancellor would perform these duties in her absence, which was most of the time. "Tell me, Lord Chancellor," asked Vylaine. "What sorry soul do we have first up today?"

"We have a cleric by the name of Tyson, Ma'am!" said the Lord Chancellor. "He is charged with drunken behaviour, exposing himself before the royal party in public, and attempting to escape from lawful custody!"

"Bring him in then!" replied Vylaine. Quickly the side doors opened, and the guards brought a rather stout, muscular man before the court. Seraphina's eyes opened full initially, as she recognised the amply endowed man from the parade. Then she promptly narrowed them again as her imagination began to paint pictures in her mind that caused her to wriggle with discomfort in her seat.

"So, cleric," grunted Vylaine. "Explain yourself?"

"Well, m'Lady," replied Tyson, trying his best to look contrite. "It's indeed unfortunate that I suffer from a debilitating mental illness!"

"And what would that be?" inquired Vylaine. Her voice showed curiosity, but very little empathy for his condition.

"It's called 'Blooming Shame'," grinned Tyson mischievously. He looked around cheekily at the crowd in the gallery for their support.

"I have never heard of that ailment before," replied Vylaine. She spoke with a continued tinge of curiosity in her voice.

"Not many people have, m'Lady," said Tyson with a cheeky grin.

"Well, you had better explain the symptoms to me then," stated Vylaine.

"Well, it's a 'Blooming Shame' that when I get pissed, I take all my clothes off, m'Lady!" said Tyson with a chuckle. The courtroom instantly burst into gales of laughter.

"Quiet in the court!" screamed the Lord Chancellor. He slammed his gavel down forcefully onto the table. Slowly the laughter subsided, and he was able to restore order.

"It looks to me like you don't take this court very seriously, cleric!"

accused Vylaine. With a sneer, she turned to the Lord Chancellor. "What is the normal sentence for indecent exposure?" she asked.

"Thirty days in the mines, m'Lady," was the reply.

"Well, Cleric," she scolded, turning back to face Tyson. "Because you've made such a mockery of my courtroom and have exposed yourself in the presence of the Queen, I sentence you to two years in the mines!"

The smile immediately disappeared from Tyson's face, and a repentant look replaced it. "Surely that sentence is a bit harsh for a crime of my nature, m'Lady?" begged the Cleric.

"Oh, I don't think so!" replied Vylaine. "You'll have two years to repent and learn that if you come into this courtroom again with that attitude, then you'll be dealt with accordingly!" She then waved her hand, and the guards dragged him from the courtroom. This harsh action caused Seraphina to feel a little deflated at his departure as the mind pictures continued to play through her imagination.

The next case was that of Zoran. It was a straightforward case, and everyone in the courtroom knew that this man would hang on the gallows. The crowds had gathered in large numbers to catch a glimpse of his face. There had been wanted posters out for years, which offered a reward for his capture. But they had never had a face printed on them because no one had ever seen him in person.

His reputation resulted in him becoming a folk legend among the locals. Mothers would often threaten their children that Zoran would take them away in the night if they misbehaved. Many people thought that this man was not Zoran at all. They thought it was someone else acting as a scapegoat and falsely accused of his crimes as a means of lifting the King's ever-diminishing popularity.

However, it was the real twenty-eight-year-old Zoran that stood before the court. It was not his lack of skill that had gotten him captured, but betrayal from the underground. He had never actually met or gotten to know his biological father. Since his mother was a still-employed whore, his identity could have come from any one of several of her clients.

The wealthy and powerful head of the underground, known as the Gatekeeper, had taken him into his care at an early age. He had initially acted as Narchis's mentor, before eventually adopting Narchis as his son. Although no one apart from a select few knew his identity, if someone wanted a job done then the message would always end up with the Gatekeeper.

No thief or assassin could operate that the Gatekeeper didn't know about it first. He had identified Narchis from an early age as a potential assassin and his instincts were right. Narchis had mastered his trade very quickly, prompting the Gatekeeper to give Narchis his alias as Zoran.

However, Narchis became too powerful, and the Gatekeeper feared that soon he would have to face a challenge from him for the right to be Gatekeeper. Knowing that he would probably lose if such a test had ensued, the Gatekeeper had pondered this problem long and hard. Then, he sent Narchis on a job and had the local guards tipped off.

Narchis now stood forlornly before the courts in the guise as Zoran, awaiting his already predetermined fate. His professional skills and powerful self-discipline were exceptional and, even as the priestess read out his sentence, he was still scanning the room for an avenue of escape.

"For your crimes, this court sentences you to the gallows, where you will hang by the neck until you are dead!" Vylaine announced. "And, to avoid a debacle, this will not be a public execution!" At this, the crowd moaned loudly. They had all been hoping that the hanging would be made a public exhibition as a clear indication of the King's apparent intolerance to crime.

However, the King had already made up his mind and decided that it would not be a public execution. Due to the vast crowd that a performance of this magnitude would attract, this would have become a logistical nightmare.

The group continued to moan loudly and disagreeable as the guards led Narchis from the courtroom. After Narchis's exit, many of the gallery group also left. They would not be waiting to see the remaining trials, which paled into insignificance compared to this one.

"Well, Lord Chancellor, who is next?" asked the priestess.

"His name is Ox, m'Lady!" said the Lord Chancellor.

"With what crime is he charged?" asked Vylaine.

"He is charged with murder, m'Lady," was the Chancellor's response. "He killed an army Sergeant in a drunken brawl over a Tavern girl!"

"Is this true?" Vylaine asked Ox, who didn't respond. He knew unequivocally from the very moment that the Sergeant had collapsed and died, and the guards had caught him, that he would be headed for the gallows, so he remained silent.

"Well then," said Vylaine, "for your crime I sentence you to the gallows, from which you will hang by the neck until you are dead!" Ox stood like a statue, not wishing to show the overwhelming fear that had suddenly gripped him. He had already guessed his fate, yet nothing could prepare him for the dread that he now felt from hearing his sentence.

Suddenly there was a huge commotion and significant disruption from the rear of the courtroom, with guards running from every quarter of the room to attend and a loud wailing from a distressed female. "No, you can't hang him!" came a shrieking voice.

Vylaine erupted, "Who dares interrupt this courtroom?"

"Please, don't hang him," pleaded the voice again, as Madeleine stepped into view. "He didn't murder the Sergeant! He was protecting me from being raped by that animal!"

Vylaine was outraged. "Remove this woman from my courtroom," she screamed. The guards started to drag the weeping woman from the room.

"Stop!" came a loud voice from the royal box. The Queen stood up, and the guards froze in their place.

"I said to take that woman from my courtroom," repeated the enraged priestess. "She had a chance to register as a witness and didn't! She has broken the court rules and will be removed from this courtroom, now!" The confused guards shuffled forward again and started to remove Madeleine from the court.

The Queen's voice bellowed out, "Guards! If you take one more step, I am going to have your heads removed for treason!" Seraphina was furious and shot a menacing look towards an equally angered Vylaine. "How dare you challenge me, priestess!" she threatened

Vylaine. "One more word of insolence out of you, and you will be hanging next to this man on the gallows!"

At this public embarrassment, Vylaine was livid and looked across at Daemon for some intervention. However, the King remained aloof and did not involve himself in the matter, and this infuriated the priestess even further. She knew that Daemon would not let her hang, so she bit back on her lip and let the Queen have her way this time. Vylaine knew that soon her plans would be complete, and the Queen would be gone. Today she would have to eat some humble pie. "Please accept my most humble apology, your Highness," she replied in an apologetic tone and then returned to her chair.

"Explain yourself, young woman?" Seraphina asked, turning back to Madeleine.

"If it pleases you, my Queen," pleaded Madeleine. "This man stopped the drunken Sergeant of the Guard from raping me! He didn't kill that Sergeant on purpose!"

"Why didn't you register as a witness before this trial?" asked Seraphina.

"I tried," cried Madeleine. "But the guards at the registry were the Sergeant's men, and they just laughed at me and told me to go away!"

"Well, my dear, I'll grant you your wish, and I'll not hang this man," said Seraphina. Once again, she stared angrily at the priestess. "However, he has still killed one of my soldiers and, no matter what the circumstances, this is still a grave offence," said the Queen. Seraphina turned back to face Ox. "I, therefore, sentence you to the rest of your life in the mines for your crime!"

Ox showed absolutely no emotion at the Queen's lenience because he knew that he would eventually die in the mines anyway. The only difference is that now his pain and suffering had been prolonged indefinitely. His eyes met Madeleine's across the courtroom in an unspoken exchange. Instantly each knew what the other was thinking. They had begun to share an emotional bond, which was slowly growing much stronger between them. Madeleine was still staring longingly back at Ox as she exited from the court and Ox was driven back to the cells.

Then, completely unexpected, Seraphina ignored all formal royal traditions. She turned on her heel and left the courtroom as well, and on her way stopped before the high priestess's chair. "Be warned, priestess!" she growled. "If you ever dare to cross me again, I'll have your head on the castle wall!"

With that, she stormed from the building.

CHAPTER 6

Daemon had been monarch of Skargness for almost ten years now, ever since his father, King Elwood, had passed away prematurely of a sudden heart attack. Skargness had been a wealthy, prosperous nation when he ascended to the throne. It had been the leading trading nation of the entire region with a massive fleet of merchant ships. It also had numerous specialised workshops and factories, as well as many quality highways, encouraging sizeable foreign trade.

Large numbers of itinerant workers from neighbouring countries regularly roamed the countryside seeking part-time employment. Skargness's army had initially been relatively small but well trained, and its people were content. However, Daemon was not a born leader, and his father's boots had been tough to fill. And, unfortunately, this situation meant he had made many mistakes in his ten-year rule that had made him grossly unpopular with his people.

Through his total ineptitude and complete lack of business skills, he had bungled many trade treaties with his neighbours, which caused much of Skargness's trade income to be irretrievably lost. To counter this loss, he had subsequently introduced an enormous raft of new taxes. Then he raised all the existing taxes and the mooring fees on Skargness's docks. This strategy worked for a short time until the merchants decided to move their ships to the neighbouring nation of Wachile. The mooring fees there were only half of those imposed by Daemon.

However, Daemon's popularity had fallen most when the high priestess arrived at the castle and cast her influence over him. Only a select few people had ever laid eyes on the priestess's beauty. She kept her face and body completely covered whenever in public.

Rumours had quickly spread throughout the land of her great beauty. The King had not only seen this but had been completely smitten and overcome by Vylaine's beauty. Somehow, she had managed to convince Daemon that she and her loyal followers could be of great assistance to his realm. A large temple was constructed for her within the castle complex.

Daemon was lured by her great beauty, as were most men. Vylaine had tried unsuccessfully to use her limited special powers to influence his decisions. She had then relied upon the Kings complete infatuation with her and her many sexual talents. She had slowly inveigled her way into his confidence and become his most trusted royal advisor, and ultimately gained total control. When she decided she wanted something done, or a royal decision made, she would lure him into her bed and slowly coax it out of him. Daemon had just become her puppet.

Her many sexual talents and her alluring promises of world domination had kept Daemon entirely under her spell. It indeed was she who ruled Skargness. Vylaine had no real feelings of love for Daemon at all. She now utterly despised him for the pathetic fool that he had become. Daemon was merely used as the scapegoat for her most cruel and heartless decisions as she siphoned money away from the royal treasury.

She had allowed all the infrastructure in the country to deteriorate to the point of inoperability. Then she had removed all available assistance from the farmers and tradespeople. To add salt to their wounds, she had doubled the taxes and instructed the army to be very harsh on those who either could not or would not, pay on time.

This strategy had almost brought the country to the brink of civil war. The now vast and ever-expanding Skargnessian army was the only thing that had stopped such a fight from taking place. Vylaine was slowly bringing the morale of the people to rock bottom. Daemon, of course, was the one who was blamed for the gross mismanagement of the country, and this is precisely what she had wanted.

Vylaine had carefully kept her great beauty concealed. She was slowly hatching a plan, and her vision was meant to play a significant role in it. World domination was also on her agenda.

However, the King had never been included in these plans. After she had successfully destroyed the economy and made the people of Skargness destitute, the only thing left was to remove the Queen. The people of Skargness had always had a soft spot for their Queen. This strategy is how she planned to gain the throne.

...oooOooo...

Vylaine threw back her head and laughed with glee. The four tortured souls in the cell frothed at the mouth and hammered at the bars with their bare hands, as they raged and fumed. They were extraordinarily agitated and attempted to get through to her. They still appeared human in form but had long ago lost their sanity and any shred of humanity.

Each stood naked and looked as if they hadn't bathed in years, with long dirty hanks of hair. The four of them were at one time each individually sentenced to the gallows, but Vylaine had secretly relocated them. She moved them all to the cell that they now occupied.

Vylaine referred to them as her little Dark Angels, and Dark Angels they were indeed. They had at one time been the country's worst sex offenders. Their crimes were hideous, ranging from murder, and aggravated rape, to indecent acts with children and animals. They were the scourge of society, and Vylaine was utterly fascinated with them. She had saved them from the gallows for her pleasure and entertainment, and housed them in their current cell, from where they had never moved.

Vylaine had slowly, but surely, sent them mad. She would frequently walk past their cell naked, or suggestively massage herself in a provocative manner. That would send the Dark Angels into violent fits of frustration. Their minds now only registered with food, water, and sex. By denying them the latter, she had turned them into nothing more than animals in a human form.

She would quite often bring in one of her man servants or a guard and fornicate in front of the Dark Angel's cell. The large, heavy, cumbersome timber table covered with shackles and straps, where she performed her many tortures and interrogations, had also been located directly in their field of view. Whenever she interrogated her many prisoners, Vylaine would always do it in such a way that she also either tormented or excited the Dark Angels.

The Dark Angels were grossly hideous, and most people were disgusted at just the mere sight of them. However, Vylaine treated them like pets and took great pleasure in tormenting and teasing them. She burst into laughter as she exposed one of her nipples through her cloak. Then she slowly and seductively encircled it with her finger.

This action caused the Angels to instantly go into a frenzy, fighting and biting each other maliciously to get closest to the bars.

Quickly Vylaine put away the offending nipple and then giggled wickedly as the Angels sank back to the floor, whimpering. "Bring her in!" ordered Vylaine. Two guards dragged in a young woman dressed in a long black cloak. "So, my people have finally caught you?" snickered Vylaine.

"Yes, you have," replied the woman. "And, I know the exact response that you want! I also know that, regardless of whatever you do to me, you won't get it!"

"Well, well," replied Vylaine with a smirk. She beckoned to the guards. "It looks like Catelyn's little sister here wants to play hardball!"

Quickly, the guards stripped Anaiel naked and shackled her arms to the table. Then, they pushed her legs back until her feet were beside her ears and strapped them into the leather-lined stirrups at the end of the table. She was now unable to move any part of her body.

Her long blond hair tumbled down around her face since it had been freed from beneath her cloak. Her firm breasts and tight stomach showed no signs of the two children she had raised.

"Tell me, where is your sister?" Vylaine asked in a gentle tone. She had also seductively removed her clothes, folded them neatly and placed them over the back of a chair.

The two beautiful naked bodies being on display caused the Dark Angels to once again come to life. They punched and scratched at each other to gain a better vantage point. "You will not get any information from me, no matter what you do to me!" snarled Anaiel in disgust.

"Is that so?" replied Vylaine. She sprang cat-like from the floor up onto the table, landed hard upon Anaiel and knocked the wind from her with her elbow. She then seductively kissed Anaiel full on the lips and again on the neck. Anaiel shook her head vigorously to escape Vylaine's attention.

With a playful laugh, Vylaine stared at the Angels' cell and proceeded to run her tongue down the full length of Anaiel's naked body, which caused a frenzied response from the cell. The noise increased to a crescendo as Vylaine sunk her teeth hard into the blond tuft of Anaiel's womanhood, causing her to cry out in agony.

Vylaine's face sported an evil grin as she dropped from the table and walked past the cell, just out of reach of the groping Angels' clutches. Her body was precisely the perfection that all women seek, with silky-smooth flawless skin, long, lean, shapely legs and rounded buttocks. Her long raven-black hair hung down over full, ripe breasts, tipped with nipples like small plump grapes.

Her actions were enough to send a sane man slightly mad, let alone the demented souls of the Angels. Vylaine's smile could melt the hardiest man's heart. But, underneath, she was pure evil and not capable of kindness. Everything she did was to disguise some devious intent.

Anaiel then laughed out loud, catching Vylaine by surprise. "I don't hate you, Vylaine!" she said. "I pity you for the foul being you've become, but I'll not hate you!"

The look of smugness instantly left Vylaine's face and was replaced by a black rage. Two years earlier she had discovered how to tap into the unique ability of others. By using the elements of either fear or hate, she could tap into the mind of a person and draw upon their powers for her use.

For two years, she had ordered all the people showing special powers in Skargness rounded up. One by one she had stolen their abilities and their souls. Most of them had only limited skills. Tapping into their frightened souls had been easy. However, Anaiel's sister Catelyn was a very different story. Her skills were far more significant than any of the others that she had encountered and Vylaine wanted them badly.

Vylaine had resolved herself to the fact that Anaiel would not give away Catelyn's location. She also knew that Anaiel was unlikely to fear her, so she was relying on her hatred as the gateway. Anaiel somehow knew this and had transformed her hatred to pity to obstruct Vylaine's intentions. "I beg to differ, my dear! You will hate me!" snarled Vylaine.

She had the guard's release Anaiel from the table and held her in front of the Angels' cell. "Open the door!" she commanded the guards.

Hesitantly, one of the guards unlocked the cell door's lock then stepped back quickly. "Well, Anaiel, my darling," Vylaine whispered into Anaiel's ear. Her tone had once again become deathly calm. "I would like you to meet some friends of mine!" Vylaine slid the bolt open on the door, pulled the door open and, with a thrust, pushed the naked Anaiel into the cell. Then, she slammed the door shut again and watched in fascination as its foul inhabitants instantly fell upon her.

Anaiel's terrified screams engulfed the room and echoed back from the stone walls as the Angels ravenously attacked. The guards turned away in disbelief at what happened before their eyes. Vylaine didn't move a muscle and giggled with glee at the show that took place before her. After a while, she turned to leave the room and again barked orders to the guards. "I don't want her dead! Leave her in there a little while longer, and then I want her removed and put back on the table!"

The guards waited only until the moment the door had clicked closed behind Vylaine. Then, they instantly removed Anaiel from the cell and beat back the Angels harshly with large wooden clubs. Finally, Anaiel again lay strapped back onto the table, still naked but in excruciating pain. The Dark Angels had invaded her body in every imaginable way. Blood poured from every orifice and the many bite marks that now also covered her torso.

Through intense concentration and focus, she was still able to control her mind and channel all her anger from hatred into pity for the dark priestess. She had silently vowed to do this until her eventual death, despite whatever pain Vylaine inflicted upon her.

Vylaine re-entered the room and ordered two of the guards to place their swords into the fireplace. "They will be red hot in a few minutes," she said to Anaiel. "Why don't you save yourself the pain and just tell me where Catelyn is?"

Anaiel did not dare answer. She just lay there in agonised silence, waiting in dreadful anticipation for the pain that would emanate from the swords that now glowed in the fire. Suddenly the door swung open, and two more temple guards came bustling into the room. "How dare you enter my room uninvited!" Vylaine screamed at the intruders.

"I'm sorry, m'Lady," exclaimed one of the guards. "I have some urgent news that I thought you would want to hear immediately!"

"It had better be good," replied Vylaine. "Or else you two will end up like her!" she said. Vylaine pointed towards the beaten form of Anaiel on the table.

"We have captured the fleeing woman and her child just outside the city walls, m'Lady," exclaimed the guards excitedly.

Vylaine shrieked with glee and turned towards Anaiel, who now had a worried look across her face. "Did you hear that my little Angels?" asked Vylaine. She rubbed her hands together vigorously with glee. "It looks like you boys will be in for a special treat shortly!"

"Noooooo!" screamed Anaiel. She tried to grab at Vylaine's arm, although her strength had considerably dwindled, and the massive, fixed shackles restricted any possible movement. Vylaine easily evaded the attempt and turned to look down at Anaiel writhing on the table. The look of pity no longer adorned Anaiel's face, as it now showed pure hatred.

Vylaine reacted instantly, forced her forehead onto Anaiel's and held it firmly in place as she gripped onto Anaiel's hair. Anaiel's body uncontrollably convulsed as she tried in vain to force herself free. Portion by portion, every bit of power drained from her mind and was slowly and painfully transferred to that of the dark priestess.

Eventually, Anaiel's body went limp, and Vylaine raised her head to look in triumph at the corpse of Anaiel now lying on the table. "Throw the body into the cell for my Angels!" said Vylaine to the guards. She turned and headed for the door.

The two guards, who had brought her the news stood before her, still shocked at what had transpired before their eyes. "You men have pleased me," grinned Vylaine. "That was a fine theatrical performance, and you shall be well rewarded!"

Vylaine felt a sudden wave of warmth pass over her as she gloated over the small victory that she had just won and she shuddered in anticipation of the many more to come.

As she left the room, she was in deep thought. *The day would have been a lot better if only we did find that wretched missing Catelyn!* She had now just to remove the Queen and find and destroy Catelyn, and her plan could finally hatch.

CHAPTER 7

"Prepare the prisoners!" The jailer's voice echoed off the walls. The squad of guards entered the hallway of the castle's dungeons and made their way towards Narchis's cell. There were nine people cramped inside the cell, and all of them had been condemned. At the sound of the jailer's voice, they all cowered back towards the rear of the compartment.

All the prisoners except Narchis had hatched a plan together. When the guards opened the gate, the inhabitants of the cell would rush them in a last-ditch effort to escape the gallows. Narchis, however, had decided he would play no part in the attempt. *Fools*, Narchis thought to himself. These men were desperate, and the thought of the gallows had forced them to this futile attempt at escape.

The guards were ready for the rush. As it came, the condemned men were restrained one by one and received a sound beating for their efforts. Narchis knew it would happen, as did the guards. They contended with the same response every week when the condemned cell emptied, and the inhabitants marched to the gallows.

The fruitless disturbance had however given Narchis enough time to remove a nail from one of the wooden arches used to prop up the cell roof. He quickly concealed it under his tongue. Then he stood still as the last guard shackled his arms and legs and added him to the rear of the line of men headed for the gallows.

Slowly the men were marched out of the dark dungeons and up

nine flights of stairs to the outside world. The prisoners instantly covered their eyes as they exited the cells, to stop the sudden burst of sunlight from blinding them.

However, Narchis's eyes adjusted quicker than the others. His training had made him adept at entering brightly lit rooms from the darkness. It was paramount that his eyes adjusted quickly to the light to finish his business and then leave again before getting caught.

Over a hundred and fifty men sat in a large column, three abreast, to the left of the condemned prisoners as they exited. They were all shackled together, awaiting a long ten-day march towards the iron mines in the Nantgarw Mountains, situated on the northern border of Skargness.

In the distance was a large wooden platform with a timber framework, erected over a series of trapdoors. The ropes that hung from the overhead reinforced timber crossbeam formed the gallows to which the condemned men were being marched.

There were only five gallows constructed on the platform. This situation meant the last four people in line would have to watch and wait until the first five had been hanged and the bodies were removed.

Three guards marched the condemned prisoners to the gallows, and all carried crossbows and short swords. Two of the three took great delight as they taunted the third soldier, Aleksi, about a young servant girl. She had taken his fancy, and he looked quite uncomfortable at the taunts.

Aleksi had just that night asked the young girl for her hand in marriage, and this caused great amusement to the other two soldiers. The girl in question was well known around the barracks and had seen the inside of many soldiers' beds. She was Aleksi's first love, and the young man was smitten with this girl who had made him feel extraordinary.

"You do know that they call her Big Barracks Betty?" questioned the first soldier in mock seriousness. The executioner's assistants dragged one of the first five prisoners towards the gallows.

"Why is that?" asked Aleksi.

"Because she has had more soldiers in her than any normal barracks," roared the soldier in laughter. Aleksi was quite visibly angry at the comments made about his new wife-to-be. He stood there and silently fumed as the last of the five ropes was fastened around a prisoner's neck, and the hangman made ready.

Narchis had taken full advantage of the soldier's lack of attention. He had used the nail he recovered from the cell to pick his shackles. They still sat loosely around his arms and legs but could be quickly removed should an opportunity arise.

He had scanned the inside of the barracks from the time his eyes had adjusted to the outside light. All around were stone walls with crossbow-wielding guards on wooden platforms dotted across them. He knew he could quickly climb the walls and escape if it were dark. However, in broad daylight, a half dozen crossbow bolts would strike him down before he could get halfway up the wall.

He continually scanned the walls but could find no lapse in their security. Any ordinary man would have started to panic, but Narchis held his nerve and remained calm. There was no point in doing something desperate that would get him killed. He would continue to try and find a solution and a means of escape right till the very end and, if his luck ran out and he eventually couldn't find one, then he would die on the gallows and not before.

Suddenly, there was a loud, ominous creak, followed by a cracking sound. The doors to the five gallows opened and the necks snapped simultaneously on the first five criminals. Everyone watched in silence as the five bodies now swung freely in the breeze. Every one of them was lifeless, with wet patches around the crutch. Their terminal fear had caused a loss of control of their bodily functions.

The executioner and his staff hastily rushed backwards and forwards across the platform. They removed the bodies one by one and reset the gallows to be ready for its next victims.

In the meantime, the teasing of Aleksi recommenced and broke the momentary silence. "Hey, Aleksi," questioned the first soldier. "How many times have you poked her?"

"None of your business," replied Aleksi in an agitated tone.

"Well, I'll bet you haven't done it as many times as me," laughed the soldier.

"Or me!" giggled the second.

Aleksi was becoming extremely agitated. It was clear that he was having trouble holding his temper, but the teasing soldiers just did not let up. "Shit! I hope she's not pregnant!" exclaimed the first soldier.

"Will be a tough little bugger if she is," laughed the second. "The kid will have the fighting ability of every man within these garrison walls!" Both soldiers burst into hysterical laughter. Aleksi finally lost control and lashed out, hitting the first soldier flush on the nose and then grabbed the second around the throat. Cheers erupted from all over the garrison as a mini-brawl erupted amongst the soldiers.

It lasted for only a few minutes before an officer emerged from one of the garrison huts to order a halt to the melee. "What the hell is going on here?" bellowed the officer.

"Nothing much, Sir," replied one of the soldiers as he dusted himself off. "It's just a friendly disagreement between friends!"

"Well, your friendly disagreement has gotten you confined to barracks and appointed to the night watch for a week," scolded the officer. "Now, do your bloody job and get these three men up onto those gallows!"

An instant look of terror came over the faces of the three soldiers. "For God's sake man, what is the matter now?" quizzed the officer.

"Well, Sir," explained Aleksi nervously and glanced around to the other two soldiers for confirmation before continuing. "There is supposed to be four of them!"

Narchis sat quietly hidden among the columns of men that were destined for the mines. He had deliberately chosen this spot while the soldiers were brawling, and he now sat between two of the shackled men.

The first was named Santeri, and he laughed at the commotion that Narchis's disappearance had caused. "They are going to find you eventually," he snickered to Narchis.

"Maybe they will, and then again, maybe they won't," replied Narchis. He used the nail from under his tongue to pick the metal locks of the shackles of the other man next to him. He constantly ranted incoherently, and it was readily apparent that he had lost his mind. He was about the same height as Narchis and had a long black beard like his.

"Leave him be," said Santeri. "His name is Yezag, and he's not all there!"

"Shut up!" said Narchis. "I can be more helpful to you in the mines than this man will ever be!"

"You are Zoran, aren't you?" asked Santeri.

"Yes!" came Narchis's aggravated reply. "Now help me change into his robe before the guards get here!" Santeri knew that this man would make a handy ally in the mines and that Yezag would be a hindrance to him. He quickly helped Narchis swap into Yezag's robe.

Narchis had just clicked himself into Yezag's shackles when the guards started looking at the front of the line. They then slowly worked their way back. Narchis waited for a short time and then whispered into Yezag's ear. "Be gone with you my friend," he said. "Go home now; it's all over!"

Yezag stood up and stared around him vacantly. "Run, Yezag, run!" came Narchis's voice again. Yezag turned towards the gate and bolted. He shouted at the top of his voice, "I'm free! I'm free!"

Instantly, one of the soldiers pointed at Yezag and screamed, "There he is!" A whirring sound filled the air as crossbow bolts flew from all directions. Yezag stopped in his tracks and reeled around as his body became limp, and he dropped to the ground.

The Officer ran to inspect the body, then called to Aleksi and his two guard companions. "I am going to have you men flogged for this," he scolded. "You are lucky we got this man, or I would have had you hung!" He was furious and could not even dream of the consequences that would have arisen, had this man escaped from his Garrison. "Now get this body in with the others and report back to me," he yelled before storming off.

The three guards stood and shook until finally, Aleksi was the first to speak. "But that's not him…," Aleksi started to say quietly. Instantly he was punched in the stomach by one of the other two guards and dropped to one knee in pain.

"Shut your mouth!" replied one of the other soldiers. "Everyone thinks he's dead! I would rather take a flogging than face the priestess! So, let's get this body in the cart and forget about it!" Aleksi slowly nodded, then rose to his feet to help load Yezag's body into the cart.

Narchis felt relief as the line of men destined for the mines stood up and started to move out of the garrison gate. Santeri had promised to keep his identity a secret, and he was happy that he now had a powerful friend.

Narchis had already identified all the people around him that could have possibly seen the earlier events and knew that, along with Santeri, none of them would make it to the mines alive. He slowly shuffled along with the other prisoners.

CHAPTER 8

$\mathbb{D}$ aemon was deeply worried as he carefully studied the financial report in his hands. Earlier that day he had been forced to send some of his troops to one of the outlying villages, to quell a minor rebellion that had erupted there.

The crops this year had been especially bad. The peasants were suffering, but instead of lowering the taxes to relieve their suffering, Vylaine had convinced Daemon to raise them instead. The extra money raised through the increased taxes had poured into the ever-expanding army. Her strategy was the only thing standing in the way of outright civil war as the destitute citizens suffered.

Daemon looked up as Vylaine entered the room. "Hello, my darling," she whispered. She lifted the edge of the scarf covering her face and kissed him on the cheek.

Daemon frowned and looked back down at the report. "We can't keep taking more and more money from the people! If we take much more, the country will be in economic ruin!" he said.

"Our plans are near to fruition," replied Vylaine with a scowl. "The army is now big enough, and I am prepared to move on Eshoram at any time! The only thing that now stands in our way is your wife!"

A worried look passed over Daemon's face. He instantly tried to hide this, but Vylaine sensed it and slowly slipped her hand down the front of his pants. "The Queen is barren, my love," she said softly. Her hand started to move slowly. "There will be no point in conquering this land, or your neighbours if you don't have an heir to your throne!"

Vylaine's hand started to gain rhythm. "Besides, once you have finished mourning, then we can wed, and I'll give you the son you desire!" Daemon groaned as Vylaine's hand slowed again.

"Just think," whispered Vylaine. "We'll no longer have to sneak around as we do now, and I can please you whenever you wish it!" Vylaine knew how to play Daemon precisely. Many a rash decision had been made while she performed her sexual favours.

As Daemon leaned back expectantly on the soft covers of the bed, Vylaine began to strip away his tunic and pants slowly. As each new area of skin appeared, she covered the area in delicate, sensual kisses. She was careful to ensure that the final area exposed was now the centre of Daemon's focus. He was almost beside himself, as he burned with passion.

Vylaine took Daemon's rigid manhood into her soft, warm mouth and began to move her head up and down slowly. The whole time, her fingertips played gently across the now highly sensitive skin of his chest. It seemed like an eternity, but then she slowly gained momentum. Daemon's body began to shudder, rocked in the ebb and flow of release until his eyes rolled back. He let out a long, loud sigh, then collapsed back onto the bed.

After a while, he looked up at his lover and sighed again, resigned to the fact that he was now expected to deliver. "I'll be visiting some of the neighbouring countries, for the next few months, to discuss the possibility of allying with them!" he sighed. Slowly, he dragged himself up off the bed and pulled on his rumpled tunic and pants. It was always difficult to leave the boudoir of this amazing lover and return to his chambers alone.

However, Daemon could imagine what it would be like once their plans were successful and he became the undisputed ruler of all the surrounding territory. The thought of having Vylaine by his side for the rest of his life was a dominant force. "Make it a quick death!" demanded Daemon. He turned away and left the room.

A victorious smile adorned Vylaine's face as she stood up and walked to the door. "Get me another dress!" she barked at one of the servants. "This one is soiled!"

...oooOooo...

The brilliant white light that had been glowing at the far end of the long dark tunnel in his mind began to fade slowly. In its place came an intense, excruciating pain that wracked his entire body.

Aedyn carefully opened one eye. Without moving a muscle, he slowly surveyed the room that came into view within his field of focus. He judged by the wooden slab walls, thatch roof, and meagre furnishings that it appeared to be a small hut of the kind used by woodcutters when they worked away from home for an extended time. He could only guess that he was somewhere in the forest, outside the city's walls. In the distance, he heard men as they called to each other. One of the voices seemed to have broken away from the main group and was getting closer.

Aedyn tried to sit up but immediately fell back in agony. His breath caught in his throat as his whole left side seemed to explode in pain. He glanced down and noticed that a homemade dressing of moss and Aloe Vera covered his left shoulder and the area just below his left ribs. He was still trying to recover his breath when a leathery brown face peered in through the window.

"So, you've finally decided to join the living again, have you?" asked the face.

"Who are you and where am I?" enquired Aedyn, politely.

"I'm Ezra, the woodcutter, and this is my hut! We're in the forest, just north of Bayville!" Ezra said. "I found you, bleeding like a stuck pig, just outside the city gates! Those animals, the palace guards, had left you to die on the side of the highway! That way it wouldn't look like they were to blame!"

Suddenly, Aedyn was forced to close his eyes, as the fight with the palace guards rushed back to flood his memory. He lay still and prayed quietly that Catelyn and Kinta had made it safely out of the city.

He opened his eyes again and turned his head to look at the man who had saved his life. There was a calm gentleness about Ezra that seemed at complete odds with his occupation. Ezra bent over and gently touched the area of Aedyn's wounds. "You've been off with the Pixies for the past two days! I thought you were gone a couple of times!" he said. "You kept saying 'Catelyn', and I guessed it must be your wife!"

"She is!" said Aedyn. He felt an instant bond with this gentleman of the woods. "My name is Aedyn! If they managed to make it safely out of the city, both Catelyn and my daughter Kinta are headed for the Nantgarw mountains!"

Ezra sauntered over to the fireplace, deep in thought. He dipped a large cooking spoon into the deep blackened pot, lifted the contents, and poured two cups of soup, which he placed on the table. "Were they travelling alone?" asked Ezra quietly. He made his way back to stand beside Aedyn.

"They should have been in a cart, with an older couple, if everything was fine," explained Aedyn.

Ezra placed his large rough, calloused hand on Aedyn's uninjured shoulder. "You must concentrate on getting well fast then, my friend! A party, just as you have described, has already come by this way by horse and cart earlier today!" he said. "They seemed to be headed north but were travelling very slowly and could easily have taken a different route!"

Ezra went on to explain that very little happened in these woods without the usual inhabitants being aware. It was sometimes the only thing that kept them alive.

"Please Ezra, help me to rise!" said Aedyn. "I must be on my way to care for my wife and child!" Aedyn extended his arm, and the old woodcutter clasped it between his rough, brown, calloused hands.

Slowly, painfully, Aedyn eased himself into an upright position and placed his feet upon the cool compressed earthen floor of the hut. Sheer grit and determination allowed him to stand, albeit unsteadily, on his feet for the first time since that fight with the guards.

"You are certainly a strong, brave man, Aedyn, my friend!" said Ezra.

"It is my wife, Catelyn, who is the brave one! If not for her courage, we might all be dead now!" replied Aedyn. "Or, worse still, we may have had to face the high priestess!" Aedyn could not imagine living now without his family. The thought of what might have happened caused a shudder to pass through his body.

"We all know that is worse than death!" agreed Ezra, and a sudden shudder also passed over his old body. "Come, join me for some warm broth!" said Ezra. He helped Aedyn to the small wooden table in the middle of the single room.

Even as he sat down at the table, in the back of his mind Aedyn was already planning his journey to the rebel camp to find his family. He must travel soon, regardless of his wounds. If he didn't arrive by the sixth day, as they had planned, Catelyn would assume him dead. She and Kinta would eventually make their way over the mountains to the safety of Abyssal, a friendly country still several weeks away by horse and cart.

His mind churned at the genuine possibility of him having already missed them, so Aedyn ate fast. Already, with each tasty mouthful, he could feel the strength that slowly returned to his aching body.

CHAPTER 9

O x let out a gentle sigh, as a small ray of sunshine poked through the clouds. For two days, the prisoners had already slowly marched towards the mines. For the whole of that time, it had rained relentlessly and drenched every man to the bone.

At night-time, the prisoners had been made to sleep out in the open on the side of the road, while the soldiers had taken whatever cover there was available and made it their own.

Although all the prisoners had huddled together to beat the cold, there was not much they could do to stop the rain. Many of the weak had already come down with a sickness. Every morning, a handful of those unfortunate prisoners that had not survived the night needed to be buried along the side of the road.

All the prisoners had initially been chained together in groups of six for the trip. Ox's group came from a very mixed origin. On one side was the drunken cleric who had been tried in the courts before him. Although Tyson had played the fool in front of the court, it was quite plain to Ox that this man knew how to look after himself.

Shackled to the other side of Ox was an ex-Skargnessian senior army officer, who looked quite young. Ox surmised that he couldn't have been much over thirty years of age. His name was Azrael. Although he had a youthful appearance, it was apparent by the way he conducted himself that he also would have no trouble making it to the mines in one piece.

There were three others in Ox's group as well. One was a student named Waelon. He looked mightily out of place amongst the common criminals surrounding him.

There was also a farmer named Tomas who was over sixty years old, and he had been one of the most recent prisoners to fall ill. Although the others in the group had helped carry him for the last day, it was apparent that he would not last another night of rain and cold.

The most mysterious member of the group was a dwarf named Aurak, who was short, stocky and muscular, as most dwarfs often are, but he hardly spoke. It was very evident from the scars on his face and the absence of part of his right ear that he had seen his share of life's hardship.

Once again, Ox looked towards the sky. Today, the clouds had cleared fast, and the sun had started to push through. Morale amongst the prisoners had finally begun to improve. For the first time in the trip, they began to talk among themselves.

"Hooray!" exclaimed Waelon. "Those wretched clouds have finally started to clear! Now our trip should get a bit more comfortable!"

"I wouldn't get too thankful if I were you," replied Azrael. "It's late in the afternoon and the sun's low!"

"Yes, but any sun is better than no sun," said Waelon. He stood with his arms outstretched as if to soak up as much as he could.

"Enjoy it while you can!" said Azrael. "There won't be enough of it to dry these cloaks! Without that cloud cover, tonight will be even colder than the last!" The enthusiasm quickly left Waelon at the thought of another cold night in wet clothes.

"Whose turn is it now?" questioned Tyson. He pointed with his chin to the semi-conscious body of Tomas, who draped over his shoulder.

"I think it's mine!" replied Waelon with a whining tone to his voice. Tyson gratefully unloaded Tomas onto his shoulders. Waelon was quite frail, and it was apparent that he was not accustomed to manual labour. He lasted a hundred paces before the weight of Tomas became too much for him. He crumpled to the ground panting.

"You're going to have to gain some more strength in those arms, lad," barked Tyson. "If not, you won't last more than a week in those mines!" Waelon looked annoyed at the comments. He said nothing as Ox picked up Tomas and quickly threw him over his shoulder.

With dusk approaching, the soldiers called the procession of prisoners to a halt. As had happened on the two previous nights, the prisoners did their best to get comfortable and huddle together. However, their efforts were in vain. Azrael was right. The night was the coldest yet, and, in the morning, there was ice on the roads, and a heavy frost hung over the trees.

Their usual ritual as they buried the dead bodies took much longer than average this morning. There was more than the usual number to be disposed of today, and Tomas was one of them. He had not lasted the night. Although there was a little sadness at his departure, most were relieved that they would no longer have to carry him.

The prisoners had started to prepare for their final day's march to the mines as two soldiers approached the group. With them came another prisoner to replace Tomas. "You boys will like this one," laughed one of the soldiers.

"He's jinxed," laughed the other.

"And why would that be?" enquired Azrael. He wasn't that interested in the answer.

"Well," laughed the soldier again. "He's already been in two groups so far! Everyone else that was in them is now buried between here and the garrison!"

Azrael didn't bother to speak further as the new addition to the group was shackled amongst them.

"What's your name?" Tyson asked the new prisoner. "And, I certainly hope that you are not jinxed! We've already had to carry one person for far too long!"

"Well, I don't think you'll need to carry me - I can look after myself," was the reply.

"What about your name?" asked Tyson.

"My name's Narchis," came the surly reply.

"Well then, Narchis," exclaimed Tyson. "Welcome to our humble group!"

Narchis looked around at the group and was pleased. All his new workmates looked healthy and fit. Except for Waelon, and Narchis knew that he wouldn't last long once he got to the mines.

The group travelled for a further day with little trouble. The rain had all but disappeared, and the cloaks that the prisoners were wearing had dried in the sun. This arrangement made travel a lot more comfortable.

It was nearly nightfall again when the convoy of criminals finally arrived at the mines. The guards called them to a halt in the shadows of the enormous mountain that towered over them. The timber entrance to the tunnels was unusually narrow, and only two groups of six could be escorted through at any one time.

Extra guards from the shaft waited there for them. The soldiers performed a formal hand over of prisoners before they retreated to the line of eight small huts. They would enjoy an overnight rest here before they returned to the garrison.

The guards from the mine were much harsher and less tolerant than the soldiers from the previous three days. They regularly wielded their whips and made it known that they were in total charge. Each guard carried a long, plaited leather whip. They cracked their whip unforgivingly over the backs of any workers that were slow to respond or spoke out of turn.

The disgruntled groups of prisoners waited patiently, five minutes apart, before being bustled through the main entrance. It had become quite late by this time. Tyson's group was met with complete darkness as they entered the mines. They were led for quite a distance before one of the guards lit a torch.

Narchis looked cautiously around him from side to side to study his surroundings. They continued quite briskly down the narrow tunnel. There were not many stories of people who had managed to escape from the mines and Narchis could see why.

The tunnel the prisoners tramped down was carved out of the middle of the mountain. Every few hundred paces there was a large, solid iron-barred gate, set securely into the rock. At each gate stood two guards with long spears. The gates were only opened upon the prisoners' arrival and then closed quickly behind them as they passed through.

There were about thirty or forty such gates between the surface and the main living gallery. This location was where Tyson's group of six prisoners eventually came to rest. Not all the prisoners that had marched with them from the garrison were in the same gallery as Tyson and the rest of his group.

During their time in the mines, they discovered that there were many such living galleries. There were thousands of tunnels honeycombed throughout the mountain. Tyson studied the guards intently. He looked for any signs of a lapse of concentration.

The prisoners were moved towards a mass of small fires. The guards were all skilled with their whips. Tyson surmised that, if given the opportunity, they would be equally as competent with the short swords that hung from their belts. Tyson's group had finally stopped at a small fire where a burly guard ordered them to rest. "Get some sleep," he said. "You'll start work in two hours!"

"At least we get fires here," said Waelon, as he tried to get closer to the flames.

"They have to provide fires," replied Aurak. "If they didn't, then everyone would freeze down here, and they would have no one to mine their ore!"

"I wonder how far below the surface we are?" mused Azrael.

"By the look of this level of rock, I would say that we are at least two hundred metres down," answered Aurak, having studied the various rock strata levels they had passed as they marched in from the entrance.

"Have you been in here before?" asked Waelon with a puzzled look.

Tyson laughed loudly. "He's a dwarf, you idiot! They practically live underground!" he said. "Some of them never see daylight in their entire lifetime!"

Waelon frowned and looked around him. "Well, I had better get used to living down here, I suppose! I have a twenty-year sentence to serve! By the looks of all those gates on the way down, we're not supposed to go anywhere!"

"You've got a lot to learn my friend!" Tyson laughed again. "If you can manage the manual labour and stay here for twenty years, without being buried by a rock fall, then miner's sickness will take you way before then!"

"What's miner's sickness?" asked Waelon.

"All the smoke from these coal fires and the dust generated from mining gets into your lungs and will, over time, kill you!" explained Aurak. "Even those who are strong enough to last out their sentence, usually are too sick when they return home to get any work, and they don't last long!"

Waelon swallowed hard. "How do you dwarves last so long then?" he questioned.

"We use wood instead of coal in our fires, spray water to damp the dust when we dig and build fresh air ventilation shafts to the surface along the entire length of the tunnel," explained Aurak. "It takes longer, however, and that's why they don't do it here! They don't care if they lose us because there are always plenty more to come along and take our place."

A harsh voice came from the group next to them. "You lot had better get some sleep!" it said. "Because, believe me, you're going to need it!"

The men in the next group were extremely dark skinned, indicating that they had been in the mines for quite some time. Everyone immediately lay down to get some sleep.

Waelon listened, and, for the first time, he suddenly noticed the number of loud, hacking coughs coming from the groups around him.

CHAPTER 10

Seraphina was furious and steamed with bottled up rage. She had just received word that someone had entered the royal vault. It was set aside exclusively for the secure storage of all the crown jewels and the royal treasury. "Get me the Vault Sergeant!" she screamed at a guard.

She hastily descended the stairs to the bowels of the castle. The Vault Sergeant was already present when Seraphina finally arrived there. "Who opened this vault?" yelled Seraphina.

"Ah, it was me, m'Lady," replied the very worried looking Sergeant.

"Then, explain to me why it was opened?" questioned Seraphina. "Aren't you aware, this vault doesn't open unless either the King or I have personally permitted it?"

"The priestess forced me to open it, m'Lady," was the Sergeant's reply. "She had two of her men hold me with a knife to my throat until I opened it! I would've reported it to the King, m'Lady; however, he's not in the castle!"

"What did that evil bitch want in my vault?" questioned Seraphina.

"She didn't take anything, m'Lady," replied the sergeant. "However, she did try on the Ruler's Crown!"

At this comment, Seraphina froze, then asked, "Who saw her touch the crown?"

"I did, m'Lady," was his reply. "Both of my corporals were present as well," he added.

"Did you see this happen?" Seraphina asked of the two corporals.

They were trying to stay as far removed from the proceedings as possible.

"We did, m'Lady," grunted one of the corporals. "She picked it up, and then tried it on! When she had finished, she placed it on the ground!"

It was high treason for anyone to wear the Ruler's Crown and it was expressly forbidden for it ever to touch the ground. This news would typically have infuriated Seraphina. However, on this occasion, it brought a smile to her face. She turned to the vault sergeant. "Get ten men, Sergeant!" she said. "The priestess has just committed treason against the royal family, and that is punishable by death! I want you to get your men and meet me by the entrance to the temple! We're going to have that bitch's head mounted on the front gate to greet my husband on his return, and we're going to do it this night!"

The sergeant had gathered the ten men as ordered. He waited at the door to the temple when Seraphina arrived. "Break down that door!" she commanded.

The guards kicked and beat on the door until it swung open.

"Scour this temple!" she yelled again. "I'll give ten gold pieces to the man that delivers the priestess back here to me!"

The guards stormed into the temple to search for the high priestess. This situation left Seraphina and the Sergeant to wait alone together at the entrance. "Today will be one of my happiest, Sergeant!" said Seraphina. "I'll finally be rid of that filthy slut that the King calls a priestess! She's no more a priestess than I am an ass!"

Suddenly, a burst of laughter erupted from behind them. Seraphina and the Sergeant snapped around to see Vylaine standing directly behind them. "You may be right about me not being a priestess," she replied. "However, you are a 'Prize Ass' if you think that any of those men will return alive from my temple!"

"Arrest that woman!" demanded Seraphina as she waved her hand in Vylaine's general direction, with her eyes shooting this way and that as she looked for further assistance.

The sergeant moved swiftly towards Vylaine. She stepped back and raised her arms to point at the sergeant. A bright light danced menacingly around her fingers and up her sleeves. As the Sergeant approached, the ball of fire leapt from her fingers and struck him directly in the chest. The sergeant fell to the ground in a fit of spasms.

Seraphina looked horrified as the spasms slowly subsided and his body lay still and limp in the dirt. "You will be made to pay for this!" warned Seraphina.

"I don't think so!" replied Vylaine. "As we speak, your guards lay dead, as is your Sergeant! And, you're about to be taken into the temple! That means that there'll be no witnesses to the fact that any of these events even took place tonight!"

A sudden uneasy feeling came over Seraphina as dark robed figures emerged suddenly and silently from the temple. "You fool!" replied Seraphina. "The King will be home tomorrow, and he'll have you beheaded for treason!"

Once again, Vylaine burst into laughter. "My dear," she replied. "The King has given me his blessing, just to be rid of you! He won't be taking me to the chopping block on his return! I imagine he'll be more intent on taking me to his bed! All I needed was to get you within my grasp, and I knew I could rely on your temper to do that for me!"

Quickly Seraphina turned to run; however, it was too late. The robed figures were too quick for her, and she was silently dragged into the temple.

...oooOooo...

She had stepped tentatively out from the protective darkness of the fetid sewer tunnel. As her eyes had slowly adjusted, Catelyn was just able to see the dark silhouetted shapes of Alwan, Sonja and Kinta as they had huddled together hiding at the back of the covered wagon.

The horse and cart had been almost impossible to see unless you knew exactly where to look. The shadows and reflections created by the rain-laden, cloud-covered sliver of the crescent moon made everything seem a little disjointed.

They had silently climbed aboard, and Alwyn, Sonja and Kinta were secreted inside the covered wagon to protect them from snooping eyes. Then, Catelyn had started the horse moving, and they had slowly trundled out onto the darkened backroads that passed through the rural landscape on their way north.

It was still going to be a long six days and six nights travel to get to the foothills of the Nantgarw Mountains and safety. They would have to do most of their travel during the dark hours to escape possible detection on the highway. The guards had eyes and ears everywhere and would soon have word back to the high priestess if they discovered anyone considered a fugitive.

Their cart had now passed into the protective cover of a small wooded area, just as dawn had broken, and this would provide some measure of safety for a short while. The night had passed slowly. As the sun rose and sparkled through the leaves of the overhead canopy, Catelyn could start to feel the tension easing from her shoulders.

She looked down at Kinta, who lay snuggled up on the seat beside her. She had her head resting on her mother's lap, sleeping soundly. It took all of Catelyn's reserve of strength, and a couple of deep breaths, to stop from crying.

However, one tiny teardrop did eventually escape and wound its way slowly down her cheek. She began to stroke Kinta's forehead gently with the tips of her fingers. She carefully lifted her hair back out of her face and placed it behind her ears. Their daughter was becoming a young woman, and Catelyn and Aedyn had hoped fervently for peaceful security for their family.

In the back of the wagon, Alwan and Sonja sat huddled together and comforted each other. Their heads nodded onto their chests as they strained to stay awake.

The gentle clip-clop of their horse's hooves on the hard road's surface had soothed away some of their concerns. Catelyn allowed the horse to make its own time. There was no point in forcing the pace and exhausting their only means of reaching safety. Besides, the slower they travelled, the more natural it seemed and would attract far less unwanted attention.

Throughout the night, they had stopped only to take an occasional drink from the many swiftly-flowing freshwater streams that flowed through the forest. In the early morning, they had stayed at several locations and gathered some nuts, fruit, and berries from the heavily laden trees that lined their route. That would be their only meal today.

The hot sun that beat down relentlessly through the canvass cover began to heat the inside of the wagon and made it unbearably uncomfortable. Catelyn carefully turned the horse off the main highway and found a small secluded clearing hidden among the dense undergrowth. A gentle, babbling brook ran through the hollow. This shaded location looked like an excellent place to spend some quiet hours until night came, and they could travel again.

Alwan and Sonja settled themselves down for a much-needed snooze. Catelyn and Kinta climbed slowly down from the wagon and made their way over to the edge of the brook. Catelyn sat quietly, leaned back on her arms, and listened to the gurgling sound of the stream. It bubbled gently over her bare feet and the rocks along the riverbank. The icy-cold water soothed her tired feet, and she closed her eyes to relax.

It was so peaceful here in the forest that it was difficult to remember that only last night she had fought for her life in the tunnel under The Haven. Her thoughts immediately turned to Aedyn. The last time she had seen him was when they had made their escape from the guards. Her generous, courageous husband had put his very life on the line to ensure both she and Kinta had got away safely. *I wonder where he is?* She thought. *God, I hope he's safe!*

Suddenly, Kinta's voice broke into her thoughts. "Mama! Mama!" she called. "Look at me!"

Catelyn opened her eyes and sleepily turned her head around to see her daughter. "Yes, my precious?" she asked.

Kinta stood in the middle of the small clearing, her arms outstretched. By her side sat a small fluffy white dog, which calmly looked around as if it were entirely at home. "Look, I have a new little friend to play with now, Mama," Kinta's voice chimed. "I've called her Misty!"

"Where did you find Misty, sweetheart?" asked Catelyn drowsily.

"I just wished for her, and she appeared," answered Kinta sweetly.

"How sweet, darling! Misty will make you a wonderful companion," said Catelyn sleepily. A real weariness started to come over her. *Oh, to have the carefree life of the young!* Thought Catelyn to herself, then she thought no more of it. However, it did lift her spirits to see Kinta so happy with her new friend, despite their current dire circumstances.

Her thoughts drifted back over the last couple of days, and it was like a dream. It was an out-of-body experience over which she had no control. In her mind, fragments and images from the last couple of days played together to form a kaleidoscope of memories. One image slowly overlayed another until finally, she drifted into sleep.

Then, slowly, Catelyn's focus returned. They would need to rest until tonight to recover their strength for the journey ahead. Sleep was difficult for Catelyn as she constantly thought of Aedyn and wondered if he were still alive.

It was too painful to think of life without him. They had married young and still had so many dreams for what they would do with their lives together. For all their sakes, she must remain focused on getting to the assigned place safely. Aedyn could meet her there and, together, they would make a new home for their family.

It was some time mid-afternoon before Catelyn finally drifted off again into a troubled sleep.

CHAPTER 11

Kinta and Misty wandered together along the banks of the little brook. They spent the whole day and enjoyed themselves as they walked and investigated all the little nooks and crannies until they found a quiet secluded area of level grassy ground beside the water.

The overhanging tree branches provided them with shady coverage in which to get to know each other personally. Throughout the long afternoon, Kinta talked non-stop. She shared all her many and various dreams and aspirations with her new little companion. Her voice bubbled and tinkled like the stream that ran beside them.

Kinta spoke of her childhood with Misty. She had vivid memories of being a little girl and helping Catelyn with lots of small tasks. There was always something that needed doing. She and Catelyn had regularly visited Aedyn's blacksmith shop every day. They often took lunch with them, and all three sat and shared the meal.

When Kinta reached school age, she and Catelyn travelled to the village school together. Catelyn had started work as a teacher at the school. Kinta was then in Catelyn's class, and again they spent the day together. All this shared time together created a strong mother-daughter bond.

It was not unusual then for Kinta to wish to work with Catelyn at the village school when she finished her studies. She also began as a teacher and worked with the younger children. Her idyllic world had suddenly disappeared when the family needed to escape from Vylaine's clutches.

The two girls had spent the relaxed day bonding. By the time they were all ready to board the wagon again and move on that evening, they were inseparable and the closest of friends.

...oooOooo...

"I wonder if it's day or night up on top?" questioned Waelon.

"Who cares?" replied Tyson. "I don't think any of us are going to see it for a long time!"

The group had been incarcerated in the mines for over a week now. They had completely lost all track of time. "I suppose you're right," said Waelon. "I have a twenty-year sentence but, because I have no track of time, how will I know when my sentence is up?"

"You'll want to hope someone does," laughed Azrael. "Because I'm sure that if anyone lasts longer than five years in this place, then they will indeed be very fortunate!"

Waelon sat down dejected and despondent. The days were long and tiring. At first, Waelon had trouble keeping up his workload and had relied on the others to aid him. Aurak had adjusted the easiest. His dwarf heritage made him a natural rock miner. He had helped keep Waelon from the guard's whip on numerous occasions.

Tyson and Azrael were both healthy, muscular men. However, it had even taken them a while to get used to the unfamiliar tools involved with mining. Narchis was also slightly awkward with the mining implements. However, his firm, wiry build helped him adjust very quickly.

Ox had spent his entire life working on road gangs and was a master with a pick and hammer. With the aid of his immense strength, he could remove large amounts of rock and ore with one swing of a pick. His only problem was the height of the tunnels. The gallery was the only place where he could stand fully upright. With the constant stooping in the rocky tubes, it would only be a matter of time before he was crippled by back pain.

The mines worked steadily around the clock, with every group doing shifts in the tunnels. At the end of each shift change, the guards would let the returning workers back into the gallery, and then escort the on-going workers out to their allotted areas. The mines were split into over a hundred galleries, and each gallery was responsible for mining its section of the mountain.

Each group was required to attain a certain amount of ore during their work period. If this quota were not met, then the group would stay there until it was. Tyson's group waited patiently for the return of the workers they were to replace.

"I wonder if anyone has escaped from here before?" questioned Waelon.

"I doubt it," replied Aurak. "It would be nigh on impossible to breach all the gates. Even if we managed to get everyone in here to rush at once, the guards would just stand back with their spears. They would pick us all off before we could breach any of the forty-odd gates between here and the surface!"

The sound of footsteps coming from down the tunnel that led to the gate interrupted their conversation suddenly. As the work group came into view, it was apparent that something was wrong. Four figures slowly materialised out of the darkness. One of them had a severe limp, but there was no sign of the other two workers that should have been with the group.

As they approached, the guards barked orders at the men and then opened the gate. The limping worker had a gash in his shin that was deep enough to see the bone. He was incoherent and in a great deal of pain. "Get in," barked one of the guards and the four men entered the gallery. The guard shouted again. This time it was for Tyson's group to start moving towards the work area.

Waelon looked at the limping man in pity. He would receive no medical attention and would still be forced to work the next shift. He would continue working until either his wound became infected and he died, or until his other group members murdered him. They would do this to get a new worker who could help them attain their work quota.

"There's a rock fall in the work area," grunted one of the guards. "You lot will clear it, recover the bodies and then mine your quota!"

The mood of the group suddenly darkened. Their shift would probably be doubled, due to the extra work that would be involved with clearing the rock fall.

At the start of each shift, the group of six would follow the guards to the work area, which was marked by a large iron gate. The guards would let the workgroup in and lock the gate behind them, but the guards would not proceed past the gates for many reasons. The rockfall that now presented itself to the group was one of those reasons.

The mortality rate among the workers was extremely high. There was no way that the guards wanted to be a part of it as often work groups would return to the gallery minus workers. Rock falls were only one of the hazards involved. Often the workers would hit a pocket of poisonous sulphur gas, or a large piece of rock would deflect from a mining implement, which caused injury.

"Holy Mother of Mercy!" exclaimed Tyson. The group approached the rock fall, which stretched from the gate to the work area. It was evident that it was going to take a long time to clear a path. There was no use in complaining to the guards, as it would have fallen on deaf ears.

So, the group started work immediately, knowing that the quicker they finished, the faster they would return to their gallery and sleep. After an hour, they stopped to look at their progress. They had carted over fifty loads of rock from the rock fall so far yet had barely put a dent in the pile of debris in front of them.

Fortunately, however, the guards had also noticed this. Shortly after, another three work groups arrived to provide help as they worked on the pile. The guards had not called the others as an act of kindness, but because the rock fall was slowing ore production. The kingdom's war efforts depended on the ore, so the guards were to make sure that the supply was continuous.

The reason was of little consequence to the group, but at least the help was there. Eventually, the rocks had been cleared, the bodies had been removed, and routine work was recommenced. It had been the hardest day of work that the group had encountered since entering the mines. On their return to the gallery, they collapsed to the ground in near exhaustion.

"There must be an avenue of escape from this pit," sighed Waelon. He tentatively touched one of his many painful blisters.

"I doubt it," replied Aurak "This place has been operating for fifty years, and nobody has found one yet!"

"I suggest we get some sleep, as we don't have much time until our next shift," came an annoyed grunt from Tyson. The clearing of the rock fall had taken a long time. The guards would not take that into account when their next shift arrived.

No sooner had they stopped their conversation than the group all drifted into a deep sleep. It seemed as if they had only been asleep for a minute when someone began shaking Waelon's shoulder and awaked him. He could tell that he had been sleeping for longer though, by the stiffness that had now crept into his muscles. Crouching above him was an old man. "Who, may I ask, are you and what do you want of me old man?" asked Waelon. He was incredibly annoyed at being awoken from his sleep.

Quickly the old man brought his finger to his lips to quiet Waelon. "My name is not important," replied the old man. "What I have to say is! When you start your shift tomorrow, you must tap on the left wall and then head for the mouth of the volcano!"

Waelon could tell that the man had been in the mines for a long time. It was evident by his dark complexion and the way he had to fight the mucus in his throat every time he spoke. "What is your point?" asked Waelon. He was now even more annoyed at being awoken, only to listen to some crazy old man chatter at him.

"If you want to end up like me, then choose to ignore what I tell you," replied the old man, and then he was gone.

Waelon was astounded at how quickly the old man had disappeared. *How odd!* Waelon thought to himself. *I wonder what on earth he meant?* Waelon sat for a minute, as he tried to make some sense from what the old man had told him.

Eventually, he shrugged his shoulders. He dismissed the old man's conversation and drifted back to sleep.

CHAPTER 12

As Aedyn looked back over his shoulder, he could see Ezra still stood in the doorway of his hut. Both men waved farewell like old friends before Aedyn turned back to the path ahead. Hanging at his side was a massive broadsword, courtesy of Ezra. The sword hung proudly in its handmade leather sheath, which was attached to a thick leather strap across his shoulder. Despite Aedyn's protestations that the man had already been overly generous, the woodcutter insisted that all he would ever need is the huge double-bladed axe with which he earned his living.

Rather than follow the main road, Ezra had suggested a different path. It was a more direct route and would help him to make up some time and catch up with Catelyn, as well as keep him from prying eyes. The path was quite hard to see in places. Aedyn had to be very careful not to trip or slip on any of the loose moss-covered stones that littered his path. If he slipped and fell, it might tear open his almost healed wounds, and he could not afford to be bedridden again.

However, Ezra had also explained that Aedyn would need to be most careful when the track made its way through the marshy swamplands, to the north of the forest. After several hours of having worked his way through the clinging undergrowth, Aedyn felt he needed to rest briefly to catch his breath. He sat down on a fallen tree, which lay beside the path.

He noticed that, up ahead, the path had begun to get much harder to determine and the trees had closed in overhead. This intense gloominess made it very difficult to see anything in the dark, gloomy light. However, the thought of seeing Catelyn and Kinta again soon was therapeutic. That was all that Aedyn needed to regain his breath, so he decided against stopping for long after all.

He focused on just putting one foot after the other and continued to push forward. He hoped to eventually find the road north and a sign of the wagon that must have passed through earlier today. Even the pain in his shoulder and side seemed to ease slightly with his renewed focus.

He slowly increased his pace to eat up as much of his remaining journey in the shortest possible time. Every hour or so, Aedyn would haul out the enormous broadsword from its sheath. He would swing it around his body with each arm to try and regain some of his former strength into his upper body. He was very aware that his and his family's lives would still very much depend on his ability to protect them.

Before much longer, the ground underfoot became very soft, and the stinking, fetid mud clung to Aedyn's boots. The sticky clinging mud increased them in size and made it more difficult to maintain his balance. It was also placing a strain on the injury to his side. It caused him to catch his breath whenever it pulled at the wound, which increased his discomfort and tended to slow his progress.

In the increased darkness created by the dense foliage overhead, it had become challenging to notice that the ground underfoot was covered in water. It was slowly getting deeper until it covered Aedyn's leather boots. Aedyn could hear all sorts of noises around him as he made his way carefully through the clinging vines and branches. He paid close attention to the snakes, lizards, and other poisonous creatures that used the trees for a secure habitat.

However, the sudden, and entirely unexpected, grunting, growling, coughing sound as something substantial, splashed and slithered to get out of his path, caused him to stop and take careful stock of where he was and where he could safely place his feet. He suddenly became consciously aware that the water had begun to lap over the tops of his boots. It sloshed around inside, which made walking slower and even more uncomfortable, not to mention unsafe.

Aedyn stared intently up through the thick canopy overhead. He could vaguely make out the sun to his left, which meant he had maintained the right directions given to him by Ezra. *Admittedly, there can't be too much longer before I'm out of this swamp?* He thought. *If Ezra was right, this path should now begin to skirt the western side, and I should come to the drier ground again soon!*

Aedyn pushed on again. It wasn't long before he could feel that the level of water had dropped, which reduced the drag on his feet and the possibility of nasties attacking him.

Eventually, after he had walked half an hour more, he made it onto dry land again. The firmer footing eased the strain on his calves and thigh muscles and allowed him to increase his pace once again.

The dense canopy of thick leaves overhead began to open and let small patches of sunlight through. Bright shafts of light lit up tiny dust motes that floated in the air and illuminated the path in front. Without the clinging slush underfoot, that had previously clogged his boots, Aedyn began to make much better time. He soon came out of the clinging undergrowth and back onto the road northward.

Aedyn finally sat down and sighed loudly with relief on a fallen log. He removed his wet, saturated boots, emptied the muddied water and leaned back to enjoy the warmth of the sun on his face. After a short period had passed, he picked up, shook out and replaced each of the still wet boots onto his now much drier feet.

He walked around to help his feet settle back into the soft leather. Ezra had been perfect in his directions. Aedyn could see the road stretched away to his left and right and began to climb up a small rise. He set off at a brisk pace and hoped to catch up to Catelyn soon.

As the afternoon wore on, Aedyn continued his relentless push among the trees that lined the road. He followed the highway that Catelyn and the others had been using on their way to get to the rebel's camp. From his previous dealings with the rebels, he knew that their complex was only a few days journey from here. If he could maintain this pace, he should catch up with Catelyn by early evening.

After a couple of hours of trudging through the clinging

undergrowth, the winding road had become more overgrown with the foliage from overhanging trees that lined its edges. It, therefore, made clear visibility more than one hundred paces ahead almost impossible.

Nevertheless, with bated breath and rising excitement Aedyn squinted and strained his eyes, as he attempted to make out the details of the wagon he now closed on rapidly. However, because of the cart's closed canvass canopy and the overhanging leafy trees, he could not see any of the people that travelled in the wagon.

Now he was in a bit of a quandary! As much as he wanted to rush up to the wagon and confirm whether Catelyn was riding in it, he also knew that it might contain palace guards. They sometimes travelled incognito along country backroads, dressed in camouflage as peasants and rode in wagons, to spy on the population as they passed.

Eventually, Aedyn decided that he should remain discreet as it would be of no use to Catelyn and Kinta if he wound up dead now. Aedyn eased his way into the undergrowth at the side of the road. Fortunately for him, the wagon only travelled slowly.

It would not take long to make his way through the thick undergrowth until he was ahead of the cart and could confirm who was driving. In his heart, he knew it must be Catelyn. Silently he prayed that it would be!

The tension was so intense that he didn't even feel the scratches to his face and arms from the sharp thorny branches that seemed to snag at his clothing to try and stop him from passing. He focused on making it quickly and safely through to the edge of the scrub at the next bend in the road.

He strained his eyes to see forward through the thick leaves. He could hear the clip-clop of the horse's hooves on the road, but the wagon was no longer visible. So intense was his focus on trying to see the cart through the leaves, he didn't see the edge of the road and stepped out onto the highway. To his relief, there on the front seat of the wagon sat Catelyn and Kinta.

Catelyn immediately stopped the horse as she and Kinta leapt from the wagon and ran toward Aedyn with their arms outstretched.

"My darling, you're alive!" shouted Catelyn. "I've been so worried that something might have happened to you!"

Aedyn could feel the lump rise in his throat, and the moisture started to well in his eyes. He loved his wife and daughter more than life itself. Only now did he realise how close he had come to losing both.

As they rushed into his arms, Aedyn embraced them both. He stood unmoved for what seemed like forever. It was almost beyond his comprehension how much he had been blessed, especially with a family who loved him back with such intensity.

Aedyn looked back up the road toward the wagon. He was surprised to see a small fluffy white dog seated on the front seat.

CHAPTER 13

"I demand that you men unhand me!" screamed Seraphina. The two dark-robed figures held her arms in a firm grip and escorted her forcefully into the bowels of the temple. The temple was a large stone tower, which contained many rooms and was attached to the side of the royal castle. Daemon had built it for the high priestess when she had first come to him some years before.

Vylaine had since added a few secret additions to the temple, which were situated underground. They included many dungeons and rooms where all types of experiments and dark acts were performed. The cell that contained the Dark Angels was also located there.

Daemon was oblivious to the temple additions, as Vylaine had wished it so. Even if Daemon had discovered Vylaine's lair of evil, it probably would not have mattered. He was so taken with her that, with just a small amount of affection, Vylaine could have convinced him that it was for the kingdom's wellbeing.

"I'll not tell you again!" commanded Seraphina. She struggled against the grip of her captors. The dark robed figures ignored her order and continued to drag the furious woman down the stairs.

Eventually, the guards stopped at a small table halfway down a corridor. One of the men picked up a curiously carved metal rod from the table and placed it into a small hole in the wall. He waited for a short time and, on hearing a loud click, began to push on the wall.

It swung back out of the way and revealed a cleverly hidden

doorway that opened into a well-lit room. It was the same room that Anaiel had been brought to some weeks before. Vylaine stood there and waited, completely naked, as the guards hauled Seraphina into the room. There were also two guards already present. From the commotion that emanated from the Angels' cell, it was clear that Vylaine had once again tormented them.

"How dare you greet the Queen of Skargness in such a state of undress!" demanded Seraphina. She had always been in charge and barked orders was the only way she knew how to handle such a situation. However, despite herself, Seraphina could not take her eyes off the vision before her. Vylaine's entire body appeared to be polished white porcelain without a single blemish. Since Vylaine was always covered from head to foot when in public, Seraphina had always just imagined that the high priestess was attractive. But that grossly understated the flawless beauty she beheld.

Vylaine's exquisitely beautiful face was wrinkle free. She had finely chiselled features and high, prominent cheekbones, dark, smouldering eyes and a large mouth with full, pouting, naturally-rosy lips. Unfortunately, her mouth had been permanently set into a sneer.

She had a long, thick, mane of silky raven-black hair, which was plaited and framed her face. It hung down over her voluptuous firm breasts with large bronze nipples and almost reached her tight, slender waist and smooth flat stomach. Vylaine's smoothly-rounded curvaceous hips cradled a dense mass of tight dark pubic curls nestled in her groin. Her pubic hair grew naturally in the shape of a heart and instantly attracted Seraphina's attention.

Beneath the taut, smooth, white, rounded globes of Vylaine's buttocks, a pair of long, slender, shapely legs stretched down to the carefully trimmed and coloured nails of her bare feet. There was no denying the magnificence of this woman.

Vylaine grinned wickedly at the angry woman who stood before her. "Oh, *my Queen*, I am so sorry for offending you," she laughed. "But this is the way your husband prefers me to dress!"

Vylaine suddenly took two quick steps towards Seraphina and grabbed her by the shoulders. She raised her knee swiftly and struck Seraphina a sharp painful blow in the groin. Seraphina buckled forward and screamed in pain as the two guards dragged her back upright.

Vylaine then stepped back and glared at Seraphina. She shouted at the guards. "Get this woman's clothes off her and strap her into my table of pain!"

While Seraphina's clothing was being cut away, she tried desperately to cover herself. She struggled vigorously but in vain against the firm grip of the guards. She had generous, shapely curves because of the lavish royal lifestyle, but small, firm breasts. She was extremely embarrassed by this and always wore loose fitting clothes to hide the fact.

As the last shreds of her clothes fell away from her, two of the guards pushed Seraphina backwards and held her down onto the table by her legs, to prevent her from kicking. The other two guards secured her arms and wrists and locked them firmly into the metal shackles on either side of her head.

Once locked in place, the short lengths of chains combined with the heavy weight of each metal shackle prevented Seraphina from lifting her arms or torso from the table. Her legs were then dragged forcibly apart by all four guards.

Then, they pulled her legs back until they lay alongside her chest and strapped them securely into the second pair of leather-lined metal stirrups. They were firmly mounted on either side at the end of the table right beside the arm shackles. They were designed to prevent any possible movement and held her legs spread so wide apart that the soft, pink flesh of her inner depths was entirely exposed to the occupants of the room.

Once Seraphina was utterly helpless, and entirely at her mercy, Vylaine began to smile a devious smile. She sidled up beside the table and used her fingertips to tweak Seraphina's nipples. They responded instantly, became erect and stood up proudly on her small, firm breasts, which were now covered in tiny goosebumps.

Vylaine turned to face the guards, who had all moved back against the wall and tried desperately to ignore the theatrics being played out before them. "Oh, my goodness!" she exclaimed. She held a finger to her mouth with a look of mock amazement. "I have just discovered that our Queen is a bit sensitive in the breast department!"

"You'll be hung for this!" screamed Seraphina as she struggled in vain against her bonds.

Vylaine laughed out loud, and then struck the back of her hand sharply against Seraphina's right cheek. This action caused Seraphina to let out a cry of both shock and pain at the blow. Despite all her efforts to the contrary, tears began to well up into her eyes. She had wanted to try and remain in control but had never considered being treated this way.

"What you don't realise, is that I'm the one in charge here," explained Vylaine, with a sneer. "I have run this kingdom for years! I also have many influential friends, some of whom are spreading the unfortunate news of your sudden illness, even as we speak!"

Seraphina was furious, and her moist eyes glared at her tormentor. However, she had quickly learned that an outburst would probably mean more pain inflicted upon her, so she remained sullenly silent.

"Do you know what papaya is?" questioned Vylaine. Seraphina shook her head, spilling the teardrops down her face. "It's a tropical fruit!" explained Vylaine. She giggled to herself and went on. "It comes from the plains of Eshoram and is used by the local villagers in times of famine or little food! It's dried and then finely ground and taken by the women, to stop them from falling with child! It's the same plant that the cooks have been placing in your food for the past two years! The King is sick of trying for a son and heir, thinking that you are barren!" Vylaine stated. She stared at Seraphina and looked for a response. "He has given me permission to get rid of you!"

Seraphina's anger suddenly overcame her, and she sobbed loudly. "How could my husband be at all interested in such a vulgar animal as you?" There was a tone of utter disgust in her voice. When she realised what she had done, her body suddenly tensed, as she awaited Vylaine's response.

Vylaine simply laughed. "It's simple, my *Queen,*" she said. She drew out the title mockingly. "I'll show you!"

She then turned to the nearest guard. "Take off your pants!"

she barked. The guard looked puzzled and embarrassed at Vylaine's request. "Do as I say!" ordered Vylaine. "Now!"

Slowly the guard undid his pants and lowered them to the floor. Seraphina turned her head to see what Vylaine was going to do. Vylaine grinned wickedly back at Seraphina, as she flirtatiously swivelled her hips and strutted towards the guard.

She then stopped directly in front of him and playfully kissed him full on the lips. She darted her tongue in and out of his mouth, then dropped to her knees and took him into her mouth.

Seraphina let out a sound of disgust and jerked her eyes away as Vylaine's head started to move rhythmically backward and forward. The young guard was even more surprised than Seraphina. He tried in vain to hide his obvious discomfort and embarrassment.

The distressed look was soon replaced by one of pleasure, though, as Vylaine worked her powers and he groaned noisily. Vylaine had anticipated correctly and knew her actions would both provoke disgust in Seraphina and excite the Angels, both of which she was trying to achieve.

The Angels responded instantly, thrashing about and throwing themselves against the bars in a frenzy, at the sight of Vylaine and the guard. Vylaine continued her act of debauchery on the guard until his breathing increased to a rapid pant. At the moment of climax, he let out a loud yelp of joy.

Suddenly, everything became silent in the room, apart from a loud thud that emanated from the guard. He had lost his legs at the final moment of pleasure and toppled over in a pathetic heap on the floor.

"Get up, you fool!" ordered Vylaine. "Put your pants back on!"

The guard quickly scrambled to his feet and dressed, as Vylaine wiped her mouth and sauntered back towards the table and a very disgusted Seraphina. "Now, that is but a sample of what your pitiful husband sees in me," grinned Vylaine. She playfully ran her tongue around her still moist lips.

Eventually, Vylaine stopped at the end of the table, standing between the wide-open outstretched legs of Seraphina. She cast her eyes over every part of the naked body before her. Suddenly, Vylaine stood upright, turned to the guards and ordered them all out of the room.

As the last guard disappeared and the door slammed shut behind them, she leaned forward and gently massaged Seraphina's breasts and nipples beneath her fingers. Seraphina locked eyes with her.

Vylaine straightened and slowly, sensuously, traced her fingertips down the full length of the sensitive skin on the inside of both legs. She only stopped when her hands reached the thick patch of coarse, dark curls, which framed the open, blooming rose petals of Seraphina's womanhood.

"You are a foul animal!" replied Seraphina shakily. She closed her eyes and tried to catch her breath and stop her heart from racing. "I hope you rot in hell!"

Vylaine ran her fingertips lightly through the thick curls of Seraphina's pubic hair. Then she trailed a finger lightly across her lower abdomen, which caused an involuntary shudder. "I may indeed rot in Hell, but you are not 'Queen' here!" said Vylaine. "Down here, you are merely a puppet to my desires! Many people have passed through these chambers, but very few have lived to tell the story! Now, you will do whatever I say!"

She then stood back slightly. She surveyed Seraphina closely, apparently deep in thought, before suddenly spinning around and making her way to a cupboard on the wall behind.

After opening the cupboard door, she rummaged around inside until she came out with a cut-throat razor, a metal bowl, a small brush, and some soap. Then she part-filled the container with hot water from a kettle on the stove in the guard's kitchen.

She made her way back to stand between Seraphina's open legs again. Vylaine placed the closed razor on the small strip of the table between Seraphina's forced-open legs. She put the soap into the hot water and began lathering a foam with the wiry bristled brush.

Seraphina was baffled as to Vylaine's intentions until she began to use the soap-filled small brush to create a lather of foam in the pubic hair surrounding her exposed womanhood. When there was enough lather in the coarse hair, Vylaine placed the small brush with the soap in the bowl of water and held it in her left hand, then picked up the razor and opened it with her other hand. "Now, if you don't move, you won't get hurt!" she said. Then she leaned down closer between Seraphina's legs to focus on the task at hand.

Seraphina tensed her body at the feel of the cold steel blade against her soft skin. She could feel the skin softly tugged as the sharp blade easily removed the hair. Vylaine continued cutting the hair and rinsing the razor in hot water until every trace of pubic hair had been removed from between Seraphina's legs.

She used a small cotton towel to wipe the area dry and remove any evidence of soap and loose hair. "There now, that's much better!" she said. She lifted the bowl and razor and placed them on the floor under the table.

Then she stood back up and leaned slightly forward. She softly and sensuously traced her long, manicured fingernails from between Seraphina's buttocks and across her now smooth, hairless pubic area. Then, slowly but deliberately, she traced a fingertip down between the wide-open outer lips of her womanhood until she reached the moist opening to Seraphina's vagina and gently inserted two of her fingers.

Involuntarily, Seraphina could feel her nipples rise and become erect again, as small goosebumps stood out on the flesh of her breasts. Her back suddenly arched, and she felt a series of small tremors pass through her entire body, leaving her skin tingling and slightly out of breath. She had never felt like this before. *It must be something to do with being tied up and unable to escape*! She thought to herself. Another shudder began, and her breath caught in her throat.

Lowering her head, but leaving her fingers deep inside Seraphina's vagina, Vylaine gently traced the tip of her tongue lightly across both of Seraphina's already sensitive and aroused breasts and nipples. As Seraphina began to writhe within her restraints, Vylaine moved her fingers slowly in and out.

She dragged her tongue down across her stomach, coming to rest with her mouth covering Seraphina's exposed open womanhood. Suddenly, the fluttering and twitching of the tip of Vylaine's tongue played with Seraphina's highly sensitive erogenous bud. Along with the rhythmic movement of the fingers inside her, this caused a feeling like an electric shock to pass through her.

Despite her best intentions, Seraphina could not restrain herself and began writhing and moaning as she succumbed to the intensely pleasurable sensation. Slowly, Vylaine removed her fingers and began to run her tongue deeper and deeper, until she had penetrated and moistened the entrance to Seraphina's vagina.

Suddenly she stopped and stood up straight, then slowly and carefully inserted two fingers again easily into the moistened opening. She continued to gently plunge and remove the fingers until she was satisfied the entire vagina was adequately lubricated with natural juices.

Then she quickly crossed the room and disappeared into yet another smaller room off to one side, and left Seraphina in a highly aroused state. Vylaine reappeared seconds later from the room with what, at first, appeared to be a long, thick wooden baton. She padded on her bare feet back to between Seraphina's open legs. It was about as thick as her wrist and the length of her forearm.

However, on closer inspection, one end of the baton had been intricately carved and highly polished into the shape of a man's penis. Seraphina quaked at the sight of the enormous phallus before her, and her entire attitude changed instantly, as she wept in fear. "Please, don't touch me with that!" she sobbed to Vylaine.

Vylaine laughed maniacally at Seraphina, who was now hysterically begging for leniency from her. "Oh, hush and be quiet!" commanded Vylaine. "If there's one thing that I can't stand, it's a blubbering woman! Besides, by the time I have finished with you, you will be begging me not to stop!"

Vylaine stepped away, reached up onto a nearby shelf and took down a small tub of wool fat. She used her fingers to extract some from the container and slowly began to rub the wool fat sensuously all over the wooden phallus.

She casually moved back between Seraphina's legs. Once it was suitably lubricated, Vylaine leaned back against Seraphina's restrained right leg and began to rub the tip of the wooden phallus between her own legs. Then she simultaneously used the other hand to stimulate Seraphina's clitoris.

As Seraphina writhed and moaned again in pleasure, Vylaine continued to rub herself with the wooden penis. Inserting it entirely, she caused herself to cry out loud in pleasure as her provocative actions began to cause another stirring within Seraphina that she was unable to suppress.

The Dark Angels were in an uproar and had never been elevated to this state before. The vision as Seraphina writhed on the table and Vylaine stroked herself to arousal with the wooden penis was enough to send them over the edge.

As Vylaine took the phallus from within herself and began to trace it over Seraphina's breasts gently, a glowing tingling sensation began to build between Seraphina's legs. It felt like vibrating hot coals, glowing deep inside her. She could feel her body respond and knew she had no control over where this was going.

The enormous wooden penis travelled slowly down across her stomach and eventually hesitated as it reached the now very moist entrance to her womanhood, as Seraphina quivered in anticipation. Vylaine deliberately waited, then took great delight as she teased her again. She slowly moved it away and rubbed it gently back across her breasts.

The embers began to glow brighter. The feeling of absolute vulnerability felt by Seraphina heightened each erotic sensation. The giant penis began its sensual journey back across her stomach. Eventually, the smoothly polished phallus once again found its way to the sensitive, expectant entrance of the quivering opening of her body. Vylaine began to knead Seraphina's right nipple gently between her fingertips.

Seraphina could feel her whole body begin to pulse again. Vylaine's gentle fingers continued to work on the erect nipple of each of her breasts until, again, her body arched in an involuntary spasm. However, this time Vylaine did not hold back on Seraphina. The giant wooden penis buried itself deep within her and began to plunge in and out, immediately causing wave after wave of trembling orgasmic spasm to wrack her body.

The glowing embers leapt into roaring flames!

CHAPTER 14

"Get up!" came the gruff voice from the guard. He sank his boot into the supine body of each of the sleeping members of the group. Slowly, all six men rose from the ground, as they nursed their already sore muscles from having dug the day before and then slept on the hard ground.

They shuffled towards the main gate, to where a new set of guards would lead them back to the work area. "I hope there isn't another damn rockfall today!" whined Waelon. "I even dreamed of escaping last night," he laughed.

The footsteps of the returning group could be heard as they came from the tunnel. The group waited in anticipation. The returning work detail approached, but they all breathed a sigh of relief as the group came into sight and all six members were present.

"Yes!" Tyson clenched his fist and pumped the air. "Looks like there are no rock falls to be cleared today!"

The spirits of the men were unusually high on this work detail. They laughed and joked with one another all the way to the last iron gate. Once again, the guards let the workers through and locked the gates behind them.

The men all moved towards the work area to start another shift. The group rounded a bend in the tunnel, and the gate and guards disappeared behind them. "Watch out for that rock!" said Aurak. He pointed to a large boulder that protruded from the tunnel roof.

"What's so special about that rock?" asked Tyson.

Aurak once again pointed towards the roof. "Do you see that crack running deeply through the substrate on either side of the boulder?" he asked. The group all nodded, as the crack was quite pronounced. "That boulder is the only thing that holds up the whole roof of this shaft, and, if you disturb it, there will be another rock fall, but this time with us underneath it!" Aurak continued.

Waelon looked puzzled at the boulder, and he couldn't work out why the roof would collapse. However, Aurak was a dwarf and, if he said that the roof would collapse, then Waelon was not going to go near the boulder. The group proceeded to the work area and began work.

For some reason, the digging was more straightforward on this shift, and the group decided to stop and rest a while, as they had nearly attained their quota. "Damn these blisters hurt!" complained Waelon, as he removed some dirt from one of them.

"You're always complaining about something," replied Narchis. "What did you do before they had you thrown in here?"

"I studied shipbuilding at the university," replied Waelon.

"Well, that should help you marvellously down here," laughed Narchis.

"What type of ships will you build if you ever get out of these pits?" asked Tyson.

"Well, if I can find someone to fund my project, then I'll build warships," was Waelon's reply.

"Aha, tools of war!" laughed Tyson, with a grin. "Now that's the type of talk that tickles my fancy," he said.

"But, aren't you a cleric?" questioned Azrael. "Shouldn't you be in a temple praying?"

"And I will be," replied Tyson. "I'll be praying to Mantis, the Goddess of War! My order of clerics studies the art of war and the perfection of it!" Tyson celebrated, with his chest out and a look of pride in his eyes.

"Well, can you fathom a mighty war galley that was armed with catapults?" asked Waelon.

Instantly Tyson burst into laughter. "No wonder they locked you up laddie," he squealed. "Everyone knows that if you fire a catapult on a sea-going vessel, that you will tip her over!"

"Incorrect!" replied Waelon. "Everyone knows that if you fire a catapult on any *existing* sea-going vessel, that she will tip over! It's all in the shape of the hull and the placing of the ballast!"

"Well, master ship-builders for centuries haven't been able to do it, so what makes you think that you can pull it off?" replied Tyson.

"Once again, Tyson, you are incorrect!" was Waelon's reply. "Master ship-builders have been *saying* for centuries that it can't happen! However, not many have attempted to do it! I've come up with a design, but everyone is like you and just laughs! I know my design will work, I must convince someone of it! That is, of course, when, and if, I ever get out of here," he said. His voice tapered off as he began tapping the tunnel wall with his shovel and sending echoes down the tunnel.

"Will you stop that?" complained Narchis. "It's making my ears ring!"

"Sorry!" laughed Waelon. "In my dreams last night, some crazy old man told me to tap the left wall of the tunnel!" He laughed again as he thought of his bizarre dream. "I was hoping that it was some miracle dream and, if I tapped the silly wall, then I might be secretly transported out of this hell hole!"

"You are more likely to bring the roof down on our heads," grumbled Narchis. He was annoyed at everyone's high spirits.

"Wait," laughed Waelon. He walked over to the right side of the tunnel. "The old man in my dreams was a senile old coot; maybe he meant the right wall!"

Jokingly, Waelon tapped his shovel on the right wall and then closed his eyes for a second. On opening them again, he said laughingly, "Nope, that didn't work either!" He sighed sarcastically and threw his shovel on the floor in a mock display of disgust.

"Do that again!" said Aurak. He stood up with a puzzled look on his face.

"Do what again?" asked Waelon.

"Tap the wall again!" replied Aurak.

"Does he have to?" grumbled Narchis. "Why don't we just finish our quota and get back to the gallery?"

"No," said Aurak. He stood up and collected Waelon's shovel from the ground. "Listen!" he said. First, he tapped the right wall and then the left.

"Sounds like you can be just as annoying with a shovel as that idiot," grunted Narchis, pointing at Waelon.

"No," repeated Aurak. "This time listen carefully to the sound the shovel makes on the walls!" Once again, he struck the right wall; then again, he tapped the left.

Narchis listened carefully and then shrugged his shoulders. "Sounds like just an annoying racket to me," he said.

Tyson stood up. "Do it again!" he said.

Once again, Aurak repeated the tapping.

"The left wall gives off a different sound than the right wall," announced Tyson.

"That's because you are sitting closer to the left wall," said Narchis.

"No! He's right," replied Aurak. "The right wall gives a crisper sound because it's solid."

"But, unless I am mistaken," said Narchis sarcastically. "So is the left one!"

"True!" said Aurak. "But somewhere behind it is a hollow space! It may only be a cavern! However, it could also be a natural cave or tunnel, leading to who knows where!"

"It may also be just another mine shaft," said Azrael.

Aurak turned around and started his tapping again. He meticulously tapped the right wall, and back to the left for over a hundred feet. The others followed silently, not knowing what it was that Aurak was doing.

Aurak had spent most of his life underground, and nobody doubted his geological expertise and finely tuned sense of hearing. After a short time, Aurak turned and headed back towards the others.

Then, just before he reached them, he stopped, reached down and placed a small rock next to the wall. "There's a tunnel running parallel with that wall," he said, with a touch of excitement in his voice. "Right here, is the thinnest section of wall,"

"How thin?" questioned Tyson.

"It's hard to tell," replied Aurak. "It could be anywhere from five to fifteen feet!"

"Let's start digging then," cried Waelon. He turned back down the tunnel to retrieve his mattock.

"Wait," said Tyson. "It's getting late, and we need to finish our quota, or else the guards will be down here to check on our progress!"

"There could be only five feet between us and a possible escape route," said Waelon in an excited tone.

"There could also be fifty," said Tyson. "And, if we act too hastily, then we may ruin our chances completely! That is, of course, if that tunnel leads to anywhere in particular!"

"Tyson's right," Azrael said and agreed with Aurak. "That tunnel's not necessarily going to go anywhere! However, we are only going to get one shot at it! If we're going to attempt to dig through this wall and do it properly the first time, then we're going to need a plan! Let's finish our quota and get back to the gallery, and we can discuss it there!"

The rest of the group agreed. They were only going to get one attempt at digging through the walls, and it needed to be planned, as much as possible, to maximise any chance of success. The group returned to the work area and finished their quota.

It seemed a lot easier today, as a faint glimmer of hope had crept into the minds of the men. Aurak's secret tunnel may not lead anywhere, and the guards would probably kill them if they were caught trying to escape. However, it was a chance that each was prepared to take. Once back at the gallery, the men's spirits were high since they had all agreed that the group's escape attempt would need proper planning.

"How will we keep what we're doing from the guards?" asked Waelon.

"It shouldn't be too hard," said Azrael. "The guards will be staying at the gate and will hear our digging! They won't know where we're digging, because we're out of their sight!"

"It depends on the guards," replied Aurak. "Because we'll be closer to them than normal, our digging will sound louder, and an alert guard may pick up on it!"

"Well, it looks like we pray for an incompetent guard then," said Waelon.

"No," said Narchis. "Nobody has ever escaped from these mines!

If we plan to be the first ones to do so, then our plan needs to be workable, no matter what guards happen to be on duty!"

"Narchis is right," agreed Azrael. "We'll only get to try this once, even if it takes days to plan! We must recognise all the obstacles that we can encounter; then we must have a solution to every obstacle before we start our attempt! If we do this, our odds of success will be much greater!"

"I think you're right," interrupted Tyson quietly. He indicated with his hands to keep the sound of their voices hushed. "However, I think the best place to plan it is in the work area and not here! There are too many ears around in this gallery, so we must be discrete! The last thing we want is someone else escaping and the guards sealing off the work area! We all need to get some sleep as well! Tomorrow, we're going to have to make plans and still maintain our quota, without raising the guard's suspicion!"

Everybody agreed, and soon everyone began to drift away to sleep. There was not one who was not dreaming of freedom again.

CHAPTER 15

L ife in Libertas, the rebel camp, was a peaceful, idyllic existence since Laytn, and his wife Maeve, discovered a secret entrance to this valley, and they set up a place for escaping refugees to use on their way to safety over the border. Many people passed through the camp over the previous five years, and this constant stream of displaced persons was not about to slow. In fact, the numbers had recently started to swell.

At any given time, there were usually more than two hundred transient people who spend time at the camp, some of whom were to recover from wounds received in their flight to freedom. And many others just tried to catch their breath and relax before they pushed on to a new life in another country, having lost everything they had gathered throughout their lifetime.

In addition to these transients, there also developed an entire community of permanent inhabitants that decided to settle here and use their many respective trades and skills to aid those passing through.

Laytn stood at the centre of the rough-hewn wooden bridge, which provided the only safe means of passage over as the swiftly flowing mountain stream passed through the hidden valley.

As he looked down along the winding path towards the village Tavern, it was possible to imagine that he was looking at any other village in this part of the country. His mind went back to the time he and Maeve had been running from the temple guards and tried to make their way over the Nantgarw Mountains to freedom. After several days of continuously running and hiding, they were exhausted and still only found themselves in the foothills, unable to continue up through the mountain pass until they had rested.

As the evening approached fast, they turned away from the road they had followed and headed into the trees that lined the highway. They tried to find somewhere safe, where the guards wouldn't see them, that would allow them to rest and recover their strength to move on.

They picked their way slowly between the scrubby trees that tried to slow their progress. The walls of a small ravine rose steeply on either side of the narrow path that they had followed, and it felt like they were closing in.

Eventually, the stone walls of the chasm were so close that they could touch either side as they walked. Suddenly, as they rounded a bend, the path appeared to come to a dead end as there was a sheer rock wall in front of them, and Laytn edged forward carefully, prepared to leap back to safety at the first sign of danger.

As he slowly and tentatively approached the rock wall immediately in front of him, the hand he was using for support against the smooth rockface slipped. He noticed a hidden opening off to the left-hand side, which was impossible to see until you were right up to it as it lay in permanent dark shadow from the overhanging rock face.

Laytn and Maeve nervously entered the dark tunnel, and cautiously followed its winding path back into the heart of the mountain along the twists and turns. They expected at any moment that they might confront a savage wild animal or another person hiding from the authorities.

Suddenly, as they rounded a bend, the tunnel emerged into a beautiful sunlit hidden valley, which stretched back between the steep walls of the Nantgarw Mountains and followed the path of a fast-flowing mountain stream.

Laytn placed his arm around Maeve's shoulders and squeezed her. "I think we've just discovered our new secret home!" he said. Laytn glanced down at Maeve, and her smile lit up her whole face as she leaned her head on Laytn's shoulder and finally relaxed. "Once we get a bridge over that stream and access to the whole valley, then we can develop a village to support those displaced by the priestess!" she had said.

Laytn's mind returned to the present, and his gaze swung slowly to take in the rustic village sitting peacefully before him in the early morning sunlight. White smoke drifted up into the clear blue sky from the chimneys of several of the cabins, standing out in stark contrast to the dark rockface of the steep surrounding cliffs, and carrying with it the unmistakable aroma of burning pine logs.

Down the narrow valley gorge, dense thickly wooded forests of pine trees formed a verdant green border from the cleared land either side of the stream to the base of the cliffs, which rose majestically up into the crystal-clear sky. The sounds of activity and rich aroma of the cooking smells of people beginning another day in the rebel camp, drifted up to him and reminded him that he hadn't eaten yet.

Laytn turned and strolled casually down off the bridge and along the path into the village, and he waved and called his greetings to those he passed along the way to his cabin. He felt an almost paternal love for the pseudo-family he and Maeve had founded within this remote outpost of humanity. *If only there were something, we could do to get our country back from that evil priestess!* He thought. *I'm confident that, if we could find a leader, we could then convince these displaced people to fight for our freedom!*

As he arrived at the door to his cabin, Maeve came out to call him for breakfast. "Oh, you're home already!" she said and turned to go back inside.

Laytn stood for a minute and looked back up the path as if he waited for a leader to appear.

...oooOooo...

The sudden rustle and flap of the canvas cover of the wagon, unexpectedly disturbed by a strong gust of wind, broke the monotony of the regular clip-clop of the horse's hooves on the dusty gravel road.

Aedyn shook his head, rubbed his eyes, and quickly cleared the fogginess and drowsiness brought on by the gentle swaying motion of the wagon. *I must stay alert!* He thought. *The guards may be anywhere!* The thought of being vulnerable, due to his lack of caution, rattled him out of his lethargy.

He sat up straighter on the bench seat and took a firmer grip on the reins. Then he glanced cautiously to each side of the slow-moving cart. Another night had slowly passed. They now fast approached the foothills of the Nantgarw Mountains. The mountains could be seen rising like a massif wall before them. They sat like jagged rows of sharks' teeth across the horizon, through which they must travel to escape their current plight.

Aedyn turned his head slightly to look at Catelyn. She sat hunched up beside him on the box seat of the wagon, and her head rested lightly on his shoulder. The noise of the canvas blowing had disturbed her from a snooze also. Her eyes still had a glazed appearance as she attempted to wake herself from slumber. Aedyn leaned down and kissed her gently on the forehead. *"The sun has been up for a little while now! We need to pull over and seek cover for the daylight hours!"* he said quietly.

Catelyn nodded and raised herself to turn around and look back into the wagon. Kinta and Misty lay curled together, as they slept on a straw mattress in the front of the wagon enclosure. Alwan and Sonja slept soundly, as they cuddled together in the rear, rocked gently with the swaying motion of the wagon.

Catelyn turned back to Aedyn and placed her arm around his waist. *"The others are sleeping already! There's no need to wake them!"* she said. She gently put her head back on his shoulder.

Aedyn gently tugged on the reins, and the horse responded immediately. They turned off the road and entered a clearing surrounded by a grove of trees. He kept them moving slowly around the outside of the glade.

When the wagon faced back toward the road, he brought them to a complete stop under the trees. *"This will give us cover from the sun and any passing traffic and allow us to see anyone that approaches before they can get too close!"* he confided softly in Catelyn.

Aedyn jumped down from the wagon and walked forward to

unharness the horse. When the horse was both hobbled and turned loose to graze, he moved back to the side of the cart to help Catelyn down. "C'mon, my sweet! Let's find a shady place to get some shut-eye!" he said. He took Catelyn's hand and helped her down the steps.

She stepped onto the gravel surface, looked up into Aedyn's face and fluttered her eyelids. "Hey, big boy! I'm not very tired right now! Is there anything else you would rather do instead?" she said seductively and winked at him.

Aedyn slipped his arm around Catelyn's waist and pulled her in tight. "Well, little lady! I'm sure we can find something to keep us occupied while these other folks are sleeping!" he said. They both turned simultaneously and headed for the shade of the trees, arms wrapped around each other's waists like a couple of teenagers.

With the sudden lack of motion of the wagon, Kinta awoke and opened her eyes. She sat up and peered out from under the bottom edge of the canvas cover, which she had lifted slightly. When she saw her parents had settled down on the grass, a relieved Kinta relaxed and settled back down next to Misty. She closed her eyes and, in next to no time, was fast asleep again.

It seemed like no time had passed before Kinta awoke as Misty's roused. Misty stood up on her hind legs to peek out over the front of the wagon. Her ears twitched from side to side and worked to determine the direction from which she had heard something.

Kinta quietly and carefully rose. She peeked out over the bench seat as well. She strained her ears and suddenly realised that she could catch the clip-clop sound of horses' hooves that came from down the road. Misty gave a muffled growl to show her displeasure.

Kinta quickly and quietly climbed out over the bench seat of the wagon and down onto the ground. Then she silently ran over to the grove of trees where her parents still slept soundly. As she gently shook them both, they awoke with a start.

Kinta placed a finger over each of their mouths to indicate not to make a sound. She quietly explained the predicament in which they currently found themselves.

Catelyn immediately jumped up to help Kinta catch the horse and get it back to the front of the wagon. Aedyn sorted out the leather harness straps and began to couple them back into place. It took immense mental effort to stay calm and work carefully and methodically, as they maintained their disguise as itinerant peasant workers, as such impending danger approached.

Fortunately, they were all safely back in the wagon and had slowly moved out onto the road before the unknown horsemen appeared. All occupants of the carriage sat rigidly still and held their breath in nervous anticipation.

As it turned out, they were just three local farmers who had returned from a visit to the early morning markets. A friendly wave and exchange of greetings saw the farmers slowly ride away from their interminably slow wagon.

When they disappeared out of sight around a bend up ahead in the road, the sense of relief within the cart was palpable.

It took quite some time for the bubbling laughter and excited chatter to ease and the tedious monotony of the trip to resume. But not before all the occupants of the wagon had given Misty some huge cuddles and resounding thanks for the early warning alert that she had provided.

After just a couple of days, Misty had already proven to be a vital member of their family unit.

PART 2

FIGHT FOR FREEDOM

CHAPTER 16

It was now seven months since Aedyn, and his family had found their way to Libertas. Laytn's rebel village lay hidden away among the many secret valleys and streams within the Nantgarw Mountains. They were way too rugged for anyone to have explored thoroughly and had remained mostly untouched.

The camouflaged wagon had been a blessing and had not attracted any unwanted attention as they trundled along. The family had travelled up the steeply sloping road through the foothills and up into the mountain pass.

Being a regular visitor to Libertas, Aedyn was familiar with the second secret entrance to the hidden valley. This lay secreted spectacularly behind a screen of removable trees and shrubs on the side of the mountain road. After they had revealed the opening and passed through, Aedyn carefully restored the camouflaged entrance to its original condition.

The wagon had then carried them down into the village proper. Alwyn and Sonja had immediately accepted Laytn's generous offer for them to take over management of the Tavern. They gratefully took up residence in the manager's rooms provided.

The members of Aedyn's family had used their wagon as temporary accommodation while they all worked on building their wooden cabin. They had now settled comfortably into their new home.

When they finished building their cabin up on the raised ground away from the river, Aedyn had established a blacksmith's forge in the main street of the village. He now spent most days there meeting the urgent needs of the itinerant residents.

Since his factory had operated, the reassuring sound of Aedyn's blacksmith's hammer rang out loudly as he beat the white-hot metal into submission and was heard up and down the valley.

Along with Aedyn and Catelyn, several other people had also brought their children with them in their bid to escape. They had now also settled into their comfortable wooden cabins in the hidden valley. These children consisted of babies through to young adolescents. Catelyn, Kinta, and Misty had taken to helping Maeve each day to supervise and teach the children while the adults attempted to get their lives back together.

Today was one of those rare days when Aedyn and Catelyn both had the same day off. It was the first opportunity for a long time that he and Catelyn had found time to spend together without concern for others.

Kinta and Misty were going to spend the day down at the village schoolroom, as they helped to supervise some of the other children in a music class run by Maeve. Since their daughter was about to turn eighteen in a few weeks, it was such a relief to feel safe enough to allow Kinta and Misty to stay with Maeve and help supervise the other children.

This morning, Catelyn had packed a picnic lunch for herself and Aedyn. After they set off together from home as a family, Catelyn and Aedyn stopped and watched Kinta and Misty take a different path. When the two girls had safely reached Maeve's place, then they both turned and headed for the stream.

They ambled along the banks of the river and held hands until they stumbled across a secluded little private clearing. There was a small waterfall that plunged over the edge of the ridge into the pool below. The pool of water beneath the waterfall was crystal clear and sparkled like diamonds, as the sun filtered down through the overhead branches onto its surface before it drained away into a small babbling stream.

For a long while, they just lay there on the grassy bank, as they talked of their future. They stared up at the emerald canopy overhead and then as if by some secret cue, each reached for the other.

What began as a gentle embrace soon turned into a passionate tangle. Aedyn tenderly undid the buttons on Catelyn's blouse and lifted away the fabric to expose her full, firm white breasts. Dark port-wine coloured nipples sat like grapes on the tips. Catelyn's breath began to sound a little heavier, as Aedyn gently ran the tip of his tongue around each of the erect nipples. Her firm breasts rose and fell beneath his touch.

Catelyn tentatively reached her hand down so as not to disturb Aedyn from what he was doing. She slowly released the buckle on Aedyn's belt, then carefully undid the buttons on the front of his pants.

When they fell loose, she moved her hand and slid it down inside his pants to grasp his manhood. It had now grown large and rigid as it pulsed and throbbed within her tender grip.

As she slowly moved her hand backwards and forwards along the length, she could feel the familiar warm glowing sensation begin to grow, deep within her belly and between her legs. She heard Aedyn groan with pleasure.

Slowly, without interrupting each other and as if they followed an unwritten script, each gently removed the remaining clothing from the other. Both the now naked bodies glistened from the dew on the grass.

When she released her grip, Catelyn lay back and spread her arms wide. Her long, wavy, golden-blond hair fell in a pool around her shoulders. She lovingly watched Aedyn as he experienced and enjoyed the total sensuality of their moment together.

Aedyn gently took hold of Catelyn's knees and bent, lifted and tenderly opened her legs. Then he knelt upright between them, but still held lightly onto her knees for support. His gaze travelled slowly down her body, from her blue-green eyes and ruby red lips, past the soft tan lines left by the sun on her upper chest.

His eyes reached the milky-white mounds of her firm breasts capped with now erect dark port-wine nipples. Then, his eyes continued past her tight rippling muscular stomach. The inverted golden triangle of tight blond curls covered her exposed, but now slightly open and inviting womanhood.

Sinking his buttocks onto his heels, he trailed his fingertips down the sensitive skin on the inside of each thigh. He noticed the quiver in Catelyn's stomach muscles as she responded to his touch.

Aedyn used the thumb and index finger of his left hand to open the outer lips of Catelyn's womanhood gently. He held them open, which exposed the highly sensitive bud of her clitoris hidden like a pearl within their recesses.

He then used his right thumb to begin to gently and tenderly massage this erogenous node of nerve fibres. Catelyn visibly relaxed then groaned with pleasure and arched her back slightly. She closed her eyes at the pleasurable sensations he had elicited and could feel herself become receptively moist.

Aedyn followed the obvious visual cues of Catelyn's arousal and gently eased his thumb down into her vagina. It caused an immediate response within Catelyn as she trembled with anticipation.

After several exploratory probes with his thumb, Aedyn decided she was sufficiently moist. He gently inserted both the middle and ring fingers of his right hand deep within her vagina. Then he worked them slowly in and out to relax and thoroughly lubricate her vagina in preparation for what was to follow.

When his fingers were fully inserted, he very gently gripped her clitoris between his fingertips on the inside of her vagina and his thumb on the outside. As he applied some slight pressure, he massaged the bud between them until Catelyn suddenly spasmed in pre-climax.

Aedyn gently removed his moist fingers and leaned his body forward, then took his weight onto his elbows and knees. He took her right breast gently into his mouth and used his tongue to tweak the nipple, while his right hand was busy with her left breast.

Catelyn reached back down between his legs and lightly ran the tips of her fingernails gently back and forth across his swollen scrotum. She felt it tighten and tuck up tightly under his rigid manhood, which pulsed against her wrist.

Then, she tenderly let her hand slide slowly forward and took his throbbing manhood in a firm but gentle grip. It filled her hand and caused a moan to come from Aedyn's busy lips.

Slowly, gently, accurately, despite the urgent need within her, Catelyn positioned the engorged tip of his rigid, throbbing manhood just inside the now readily accessible entrance to her warm, moist vagina. Then she released her guiding grip and placed both hands on his broad muscular back.

Catelyn opened her legs up even more extensive, and further bent her knees to lift her legs and put her feet tightly behind Aedyn's buttocks. It caused her pelvis to rotate up and her body to open even further to receive him.

Aedyn took immediate advantage of the suddenly more natural opening and thrust his enormous fleshy sword all the way up to the hilt. Catelyn's eyes popped open wide in surprise. When he entered her so unexpectedly, her breath was taken away in the passion of the moment. She gasped and struggled to recover, as he filled her body and touched the very core of her being.

Aedyn began to slowly raise and lower his body, pivoting his hips back and forth. His rigid swollen penis moved gently up and down inside along the length of her very moist vagina. His slow plunging rhythm built smoothly to a crescendo.

He kissed Catelyn tenderly on the sensitive skin behind her ears and down her neck. She was already highly aroused, and the coarse hair on his chest further stimulated her sensitive nipples.

Catelyn gently and tenderly ran her fingernails slowly up and down along the length of Aedyn's spine. From the damp hair at the base of his neck to the moist, sweaty cleft of his buttocks. It was as if a raging inferno suddenly erupted within Catelyn's lower belly and between her legs.

Aedyn began to urgently thrust, and she felt wave upon wave of trembling spasm wrack her body, in multiple climaxes of their coupling. However, Aedyn continually pounded his penis into her for what seemed an eternity before she felt his entire body stiffen and shudder in the scalding hot release of his male juices deep within her core.

Eventually, they collapsed together, spent, but unwilling to separate for fear of losing the intimacy of the moment. Catelyn could feel Aedyn's manhood still deep within her, as he lay with his head rested lightly between her breasts and supported his weight on his elbows and knees.

She began to rhythmically contract and release her pelvic muscles along the length of her vagina and drew him into her body even further. He slowly responded until she could feel he grew large within her again.

She could almost stand it no more. It was as if Aedyn seemed to fill her entire body from the inside. He began to move inside her again. She continued her muscular manipulation until, as one, they again both exploded in a passionate release.

This time the throbbing and trembling of their bodies seemed to take forever to subside. Aedyn's manhood was finally spent and eventually shrivelled and shrank, then slipped from within her. They lay together, unmoving, intertwined, their bodies feeling the total exhaustion of a long-distance athlete on completion of a run.

Then, when he had finally regained his breath, Aedyn rose shakily back onto his knees. Catelyn extended her hands out toward him. He took Catelyn's hands into his own.

He gently kissed the back of each of her hands, then slowly stood and carefully helped her to her feet. They continued to hold each other's hands and slowly, silently, walked together into the warm sparkling waters of the waist-deep crystal pool.

They stood together, still naked and warmly embracing each other beneath the cascading, gushing waterfall, as it began to splash over them in a shower of glistening droplets. They clung together, in the tender afterglow of their lovemaking. They could feel the tension of the past few weeks begin to wash slowly away with the cascading waterfall.

CHAPTER 17

$\mathbb{K}$ inta had thoroughly enjoyed the company of the other children at Maeve's music class. She and Misty had both tried to sing to the musical sounds of the children's home-made instruments.

Now it was time for them to both go home. Kinta needed to help Catelyn get the evening meal prepared for their family's main meal of the day. As they walked together happily back through the camp, Kinta chatted endlessly away to herself just like children everywhere have a habit of doing.

Then, seemingly from nowhere, a random thought popped into her mind. "Misty, I wish you could speak so we could talk to each other about the fun things we have been doing today!" she said.

"What would you like me to say?" asked Misty.

Kinta's eyes lit up, and she started to giggle in that little girl way. "Tee hee! I am so glad that we can talk to each other now, Misty!" she chuckled. "It's always more fun to share good times with a friend!"

"We did have a lot of fun today, didn't we?" said Misty. She started wagging her tail with pleasure.

Kinta squatted down close to Misty and spoke quietly and conspiratorially. *"This will be our little secret, just between us, okay Misty?"*

Misty wagged her tail and nodded her head in agreement. The pair headed off together, as they chatted animatedly. Neither one of them could have guessed just how big a role they and their "secret" would play in the future.

...oooOooo...

Tyson lay himself back uncomfortably onto the hard-packed earthen floor of the gallery. One eye covertly opened and studied the others in his group, as he pondered their current situation.

Azrael had been a senior officer in the Skargnessian army, with command of several hundred men and responsibility for several regions across Skargness. It was abundantly clear to Tyson that Azrael was a born leader.

He wondered what he had done that was so bad that he ended up in the mines. He slowly moved his one open eye and shifted his gaze casually across the group, from one to the other. He silently wondered what extraordinary tales each of the other members could tell.

His gaze fell on Ox, who hardly ever spoke, which made it hard to gain information from him. He just seemed to go along with everything that the group decided, whether he agreed with them or not. Narchis often referred to him as a great big faithful dog, which followed your every step and did whatever someone told him. Tyson could see intelligence in Ox's eyes and was at a loss to explain why he chose to hide it.

Aurak was a typical Dwarf of short, solid, stocky build. He seemed to be quite at home in the low tunnels and confined spaces of the mines, but nowadays dwarves were rarely seen in Skargness. On one odd occasion, when a heavily armed wagon train had entered the outer provinces selling gems and gold mined from their mountains, Aurak had been a guard on one of these wagons. He was involved in a Tavern brawl. Unfortunately for him, his antagonist had ended up dead. Aurak had been arrested and thus had ended up in the mines.

However, Narchis and Waelon were the two that worried Tyson the most. Waelon was the type who would act impulsively before thinking, which was how he had ended up in the mines. He was entirely and utterly obsessed with designing the perfect warship.

To finance some of his research, he had secretly stolen some money from the university treasury. However, Waelon was not a thief. He had not premeditated the theft that had resulted in him being captured and sentenced to hard labour for his efforts.

Narchis, on the other hand, was very mysterious. He had told the party that he was a Tavern owner, who had been framed for murder when trying to stop an intruder who had broken into his shop.

Tyson neither believed him nor did he trust him. Narchis had assumed the identity of Yezag from the garrison and, although he had convinced the rest of the group of this, Tyson was not so sure.

Once again, the heavy-footed boots of the guards awakened the group from their fitful slumber and roused them for the long, arduous day ahead. Today, however, the ramshackle group of six was able to be ready to head off for work quicker than usual. They were already silently contemplating the preliminary plans for their possible escape.

Once they had arrived in their group's allocated work area, they had worked extremely hard for several hot, sweaty hours. They quickly attained half their quota for that shift, and then they took a well-earned break to discuss matters that were closer to their hearts.

"What happens if that tunnel turns out to be just another mine shaft?" asked Azrael.

"If it is," replied Narchis, "then it'll also be dotted with those infernal iron gates, and our efforts will have been futile!"

"All the conversations that I have picked up on, from the guards, suggests that this tunnel is to the far left of the mountains and that there are no others to our left," explained Tyson.

"That would explain why our tunnel swings around to the right then," surmised Aurak. "And that makes me more confident that our secret tunnel is not a man-made one."

"Well, let's get planning then," said Waelon, as he leapt enthusiastically to his feet.

The group left the rockface they had been working on and casually strolled back down the tunnel to the place Aurak had marked with a rock the day before. Then, as they arrived at the spot, they instinctively formed a semicircle around the rock marker. "How are we going to dig here, without arousing the suspicion of the guards?" asked Narchis.

"I've been thinking about that!" replied Waelon, with a serious look on his face.

"That would be a change!" sniped Narchis under his breath, but just loud enough to carry to all the group.

Narchis had developed a great dislike for Waelon's boyish stupidity and the fact that he seemed to like the sound of his voice. However, Waelon had developed a thick skin and was impervious to Narchis's taunts. He was indifferent to ridicule, due to his outlandish boat designs.

He frequently just ignored Narchis's constant abuse. "Like I was saying, before being rudely interrupted," continued Waelon. He looked sternly at Narchis and then glanced at each of the others. "All we need to do is keep the ore carts moving! That way, they'll make a constant racket and will mask the closeness of our digging!"

The group stood silently. They pondered and stared at the marker rock while they tried to find fault with Waelon's suggestion, but eventually, they all agreed that they couldn't see any. Even Narchis was unusually impressed. A show of hands unanimously decided that someone would always be moving an ore cart in the tunnel, while digging was underway.

"What happens if the wall turns out to be thicker than expected and the guards wonder why we're taking so long to attain our quota and come to inspect?" asked Tyson.

The group sat down and thought long and hard, wondering if they could come up with a solution to this very perplexing question. They knew that, until they had an answer to that question, the escape attempt could not take place.

Each member scratched their head and pondered on it for over ten minutes before Azrael finally spoke. "Let's think it over while we dig!" he said.

The group immediately agreed, as the quota needed to be met to stop the guards wielding their whips. As each member dug, he pondered over the problem with little success.

The group had nearly attained its shift quota when Ox got his pick stuck in the roof, which was a common problem that Ox quite often encountered. It was due to his enormous height and the relatively low ceilings in the mining tunnels.

Today, however, the implement was jammed harder than usual, which caused Ox to swing his whole body's weight on the handle to dislodge it. "Careful, Ox," yelled Aurak. "Or you'll bring the whole roof down on our heads!"

Ox eased back on the handle and gently prised the tool from its hole in the tunnel roof, looking carefully at the ceiling as he did so.

"That's it!" exclaimed Waelon, in a fit of sudden excitement.

"That's what?" retorted Narchis.

"Aurak's rock!" replied Waelon.

"Ye Gods, man," said Narchis, in anguish. "Do you ever speak in plain language?"

"It's simple," squealed Waelon. He quickly made his way back to the area that Aurak had marked with the rock. The others followed along behind him. They glanced at each other in a puzzled fashion.

When they arrived there, Waelon stood with a smug look on his face and pointed to the roof. Instantly, it dawned upon everyone else what it was that had made him so excited. Waelon was pointing to the rock that Aurak had bought to everyone's attention two days prior. "I say we dig until we are nearly due to finish our shift, and then collapse the roof!" said Waelon.

"Brilliant!" replied Aurak. "The rock fall will gain us extra time if needed! If we take the rock from the front of the tunnel and fill it in behind us, then the clearance team may even miss our tunnel all together!"

"That's possible," concluded Azrael. "However, the guards will eventually find out due to the lack of bodies!"

"There is something else you have missed," added Narchis.

"And what would that be?" replied Waelon, in a smug tone. He looked at Narchis with triumph in his eyes.

"There are six of us here, but only five will make it to the surface if we ever managed to pull that off!" Narchis explained.

Waelon looked puzzled. "Our plan is next to foolproof," he said. "Why won't we all make it?"

"Well," replied Narchis, in his usual sarcastic tone. "If we do manage to fool the guards, and Aurak's mystery tunnel turns out to be an escape route and not just a volcanic cavern, then there will only be five people with their freedom because someone is going to have to remove that damned rock!" The excitement and jubilation felt by all took a sudden downward turn at Narchis's comments.

Damn him! Waelon thought. It was just like Narchis to find the worst in everything. What made the situation even worse, was that Narchis was right. The rock that would bring down the roof of the tunnel was situated some twenty paces away from the thinnest part of the wall. It would take minimal effort to move; any one of them could accomplish the task.

It was quite clear, however, that whoever that person was, they would not be joining the others in the escape tunnel as they wouldn't make it back in time before the roof collapsed.

CHAPTER  18

Aedyn and Catelyn held hands and strolled together back into the camp complex. In the gentle warmth of late afternoon, they could hear a commotion that came from the main building. The sound of raised voices was most unusual in this facility. As they drew nearer, the voice of Laytn was heard over all others. He was extremely agitated and vented his fury to all those present that would listen.

Vylaine had discovered the missing guards at The Haven following Catelyn's successful escape. She had begun systematic destruction of the outlying villages in search of Catelyn. "We must make a stand!" shouted Laytn. "Unless we get rid of the high priestess, she will eventually destroy our entire country!"

Aedyn and Catelyn quietly entered the back of the room and watched the crowd as they became more and more agitated from Laytn's comments. The feeling in the room was quickly beginning to turn nasty.

Aedyn stepped out into the centre of the place and held up both hands to the crowd to silence them. The people in the camp very highly respected him. Slowly but surely the noise decreased, and they sat back waiting expectantly.

Aedyn began, "If we are to rid our country of the high priestess, then we must also consider removing the King! He has allowed her to rule in his stead for so long that I doubt if King Daemon truly knows what she controls and what still belongs to him! The high priestess has built up the King's army until it is so large in numbers that it struggles to finance its activities without constantly increasing the taxes on the people!"

The murmurs of agreement among the crowd began to grow in volume. Aedyn's reputation among them was such that they now hung on his every word, eagerly waiting to see what solution he would propose.

Aedyn waited for a short period to allow the crowd to settle again before he went on. "The only way to achieve what we desire is to attack the heart of the problem!" he said. "We must infiltrate the temple of the high priestess and destroy her and her followers before the army knows what has happened! And, it is essential that we also know the whereabouts of the King during all of this! He will need to be kept away from the temple for long enough to allow our plans to come to fruition!"

The crowd began to get excited now, as they could see the possibility of having their country returned to some order. It was also apparent that, in Aedyn, they had found a leader capable of showing them the way to success.

Aedyn concluded his address by saying, "It is vitally important to have a plan! I'll sit down with some of the other leaders here tomorrow, and together we'll determine the best approach! If we rush into this, we'll only achieve failure, and all will come to naught with the high priestess!"

The atmosphere in the room had become electric. Each of the people in the room could feel an excitement building at the thought of being personally involved in the salvation of their country. "And, now you must go home and begin to prepare for a fight for freedom to regain our land!" he said.

It took a while for the buzz of conversation to die down and the crowd to disperse. Slowly and surely, the rebels headed home to their huts to dream of what was to happen soon.

Laytn grasped Aedyn by the hand and started shaking it vigorously. "Aedyn, thank you!" he said. "At last we have a leader who's prepared to do what is needed! Skargness will be forever in your debt!"

Initially, Aedyn was a little taken aback by the unbridled raw emotion shown by Laytn but understood why he felt that way. Each of the people that had passed through Laytn's camp over the last few years had lost either family members or their homes, or both, as the high priestess had rolled out her secret plan for domination.

Aedyn glanced around the room at the expectant faces of the handful of rough, tough-looking men who remained behind. They were all very experienced warriors who had a long history of fighting against the system to try and survive.

Each of these men also had access to many loyal followers who would also be prepared to lay down their lives, if necessary. They stood for the success of any cause led by them, and it was by common consent that each of these warriors also chose to follow Aedyn with equal loyalty.

Aedyn drew a long deep breath, shrugged his shoulders, and accepted the inevitable; he was *their* chosen leader. From bitter previous personal experience, he knew that before too long, they would all feel that unique bond of brotherhood experienced by those who have put their lives on the line and fought together for a common cause.

...oooOooo...

The choking dust cloud hung heavy, suspended in the warm cloying air. The ceaseless noisy sounds of their digging continued relentlessly into the late afternoon, and the end of their allocated shift quickly approached.

They had each taken it in turns to push the unexpectedly heavy ore cart up and down the tunnel. It created the noisy diversion required to keep from raising the guards' suspicions.

Ox was the one who finally broke through into the tunnel. His immense strength had eventually made short work of the solid rock face, which was all that stood between them and freedom.

"Ha! Ox, you've done it!" yelled Tyson, over the noise of the ore cart.

Immediately, the others began to work frantically on the small opening that had appeared. Sunlight could be seen shining through the hole in the wall, and this was enough to give their spirits a real boost.

Before too long, the slowly enlarged hole was sufficiently large enough for at least Aurak to climb through. He hunched up his body into a small ball, clambered into the small fissure and disappeared.

Several minutes later he reappeared with an enormous smile on his face. "It leads straight out through the side of the mountain!" Aurak said. He tried to contain his excitement.

All six stood there and looked at one another for what seemed like ages, as they tried to comprehend what they had achieved, but it was only a minute or two. Suddenly, as a group, they realised that their precious freedom was just the other side of that small jagged opening. Immediately, they began to attack the rock with a renewed frenzy of activity.

The noise of their tools striking the rock sounded like music to their ears. The deep rumble of the ore cart provided a bass backing to the orchestra of their efforts. Slowly but surely, the hole increased in size until it was apparent that even Ox could fit through.

Now came the tricky part!

They had to shift the rock that held the roof together without being trapped themselves. Ox did not say a word as he sat down and silently began to tear the legs off his trousers and turned them into twine strips. He then plaited the pieces into a cloth rope and used the cord to lash the handles of two shovels together.

The others just sat and watched, fascinated, as he continued to work quietly. "Make me some more rope!" said Ox, with a firmness in his voice that surprised even him. Instantly, as if struck by an electric shock, the others leapt into action and began to convert their clothing into plaited cloth rope until, eventually, the lengths of cloth rope totalled about ten arm lengths.

Ox tied one end of the cable to the handles of the shovels and wedged the shovels between the floor of the tunnel and where the rock jutted from the roof.

Then, they tied the other end of the rope to the ore cart, which was now on the other side of the shovels. As soon as the other five had all made it safely through into the opening, Ox gave the ore cart an enormous shove and ran for the entrance.

He had just crawled into the cavern on the other side when there came an ear-piercing roar from the tunnel behind him. The entire shaft of the mine had collapsed, effectively closing off any chance of the guards ever finding their escape route.

All six men stood in the mouth of the cave and looked out at the sun setting in the distance. The air smelled sweet, and it felt like an invisible weight had been lifted from their shoulders. However, they could not help feeling that something else was going to happen shortly to bond them even closer together.

...oooOooo...

As the sun rose slowly through the mist of early morning, Waelon sat and leaned against the trunk of a tree. He watched as the flames of their little smokeless campfire flickered in the light air.

He could not believe how fresh the air smelled as he remembered the stale, dank air they had breathed in the mines. He looked across the small clearing to where the others were still sleeping and saw Ox turn onto his side.

Ox smiled as he stretched his colossal body awake. Suddenly the smile on Ox's face began to fade as he glanced around at the others still sleeping. "How can they continue to sleep when there is so much that needs doing?" Ox asked quietly. "I'm so excited about being free that I just want to do everything at once, just in case it doesn't last!"

"It all depends upon whether you have exceeded the endurance capacity of your body," replied Waelon. "Some men are capable of sleeping, even in the thick of battle! Do you have a woman waiting for you at home, Ox?"

"I met a girl called Madeleine just before they took me away and locked me up," explained Ox. "I would like to go back and see her again soon!"

"You'll get your chance to see Madeleine again, Ox," said Waelon. "But first we must be sure that we don't get caught again! And, that will require us to quickly put some considerable distance between us and those accursed mines, in case the guards raise the alarm, and they come looking."

Narchis's eyes came slightly open. As he lay there quietly listening to the two men talk, he was grateful that he had found this group of men with which to team up. He knew deep down in his heart that it could have been so much different if he had been stuck together in a team with men who had already given up on life.

Slowly the others started to stir, and Narchis stood up and began to collect wood for the fire. He had started to feel hungry, and his eyes darted around as he looked for something to eat. In the undergrowth, he could hear birds and small animals but was not sure how he could catch them with his bare hands.

He came back to the clearing with an armload of branches and began to break them into short lengths suitable for the fire. "Does anybody know how to catch those little critters in the bushes?" Narchis asked.

"There's a village just down the road a short way," said Tyson. He began to pile the wood on the fire. "If you can forget your belly for a little while, we'll get something to eat when we get there!" The morning air was still fresh and crisp. The men sat close together around the fire and warmed their hands as they discussed their plans for that day.

They were suddenly startled by the sound of men shouting and women screaming. It seemed to come from the direction of the nearby village about which Tyson had spoken.

They quickly extinguished the fire and packed up the clearing, then brushed the ground with a branch to remove all trace of them ever having been there. It would not be wise to advertise the fact that the prisoners' bodies weren't buried under the rubble of the collapsed mine.

Like shadows, they disappeared into the surrounding scrub and began to move in the direction of the noise. It wasn't long before they suddenly came to the sharp rocky edge of a steep ridge.

When they peeked over the edge, they could see down into the village below them in the valley. It was immediately evident that many people were running backwards and forwards between the river and the hamlet. They were trying to carry enough water to extinguish the many fires that were burning.

In total contrast to the villagers trying to save their houses, soldiers rushed from hut to hut and set each thatched roof on fire. This dichotomy added to the confusion in the scene below.

It did not take long before the entire village was nothing more than a smoking, smouldering ruin. Once it was evident to the soldiers' satisfaction that the town had been destroyed, they began to round up the previous inhabitants and move on down the dusty track to the next hamlet.

As they stood there and watched the scene play out below them, the escapees suddenly became aware that they were not alone.

Silently, from out of the bushes, emerged a circle of armed men who surrounded them, and prevented their escape. From their lack of uniforms, it was apparent that these were not ordinary soldiers. "Who are you and where are you from?" asked the large bearded one, who appeared to be their leader. "Judging by the clothes you're wearing; you must be from the mines?"

Narchis was very careful in how he responded, as it would not be wise to get offside with these men. "We were with the mines until two days ago," he said. "There was an unfortunate accident, and the shaft collapsed, leaving us with nowhere to go but out of the tunnel that led to these woods! Now, please explain, who are you?"

"We are hiding in a secret valley just up the way a little," the large bearded man explained. "It seems that we're all escapees from the tyranny of the high priestess! If you would like to join us, then we'll take you back with us to meet our leader! Aedyn is going to lead us in an uprising against the high priestess! Those of us who cannot live with the oppression she has brought upon our people will reclaim our land by whatever means is necessary!"

There was an upbeat air of expectancy about the newly freed escapees as they made their way back through the bush to the secret valley. Each of them was trying to keep pace with their racing thoughts.

CHAPTER 19

Aedyn drew a long, deep breath and held it, then exhaled slowly. He reached for the front door handle and opened the door to his hut, then called out to say goodbye to the three girls inside. "Happy Eighteenth Birthday, Kinta!" he yelled back inside. "We'll celebrate tonight!"

Time in the rebel camp had passed quickly. He was worried that maybe they needed to become a little more strategic in their approach. Deep in thought, he stepped out through the front door of his hut and strolled down the path toward his blacksmith's workshop. *There must be some way that we can turn the tide in our favour?* He thought.

As he wandered along the path, focussed entirely and distracted by his thoughts, Aedyn didn't even notice that the first signs had appeared that winter had passed. Spring had arrived as wildflowers had erupted into carpets of colour and stretched out in all directions across the floor of the valley.

When he reached his workshop, Aedyn slipped the bolt and opened the large wooden front doors. It let the warm early-morning sunshine into the dark space as he made his way over to the forge, which now lay cold. He pulled aside yesterday's coals, then Aedyn made a small clearing in the bottom of the forge. He prepared a bundle of wood shavings and tinder.

From his many years of practice, it only took a couple of strikes with the flint to get a small glow. Then, he gently blew it into a glowing ember. He placed a pre-arranged bunch of little sticks and split timber over the ember to build a fire. Then, it only took one shovelful of coal to get the fire started.

Aedyn slowly and methodically pumped his foot up and down on the bellows, which were attached to the base of the forge. Soon the coals glowed brightly, and the flames crackled and roared.

Then, he reached up to the wall behind him and took down the leather apron that was hung on a nearby wooden peg. He placed the loop over his head and fixed the ties around his waist.

Now, he was ready for work.

At the rear of his foundry workshop, Aedyn had secreted various pieces of steel, for which he had individual plans. If they were going to form a rebel army, there would be a need for many weapons. He selected a piece of steel, which he had previously cut to the required length.

Then he used his metal pincers to place it into the heart of the forge, where it immediately started to heat up and glow red. He pumped the bellows vigorously up and down. It instantly created an intensely hot and roaring flame, which caused the piece of metal to change quickly from red hot to white hot.

Aedyn immediately grabbed the glowing metal with his pincers and removed it from the forge. Then he placed it onto his anvil, where he started to beat it into shape with a heavy hand-held hammer. After several minutes, the metal began to cool and become harder with which to work. Once again, Aedyn shifted the metal back into the forge and started to reheat it back to white hot.

This cycle was repeated many times until the metal had taken the rough shape of a sword and was ready to be sharpened and shaped on a whetstone. Then, the metal was placed to one side to cool slowly, and the cycle was started again with another piece.

Aedyn worked methodically through the morning before he took a short break to enjoy a cup of tea and some food. Catelyn had brought his meals over on her way to help Maeve with the children.

He sat in the warm morning sunshine on a wooden bench situated outside his forge and enjoyed his morning snack when Laytn joined him on his return from a scouting party.

"Hi, Aedyn! Based upon that large pile of sword blanks, you certainly look like you've been busy this morning!" Laytn said with a chuckle.

"Hi, Laytn! Grab a seat! To what do I owe the pleasure of your visit?" Aedyn asked and turned his head to greet his visitor.

Laytn settled himself down onto the bench seat opposite Aedyn and made himself comfortable. "The soldiers are getting far more aggressive in their torching of the villages!" he said. "We found another village that was razed this morning!"

Aedyn sat deep in thought with his head in his hands, rubbed his chin and his eyes almost glazed over as he pondered the severe situation. *"There must be something that we can do, to cease this senseless destruction!"* he said, almost to himself.

Laytn leaned forward and gently placed his hand on Aedyn's shoulder. "My friend, you seem to have much to trouble your head!" he said. "So, I think I'll leave you in peace!"

Aedyn refocused his gaze on Laytn and looked almost apologetic as he replied. "I'm sorry, Laytn!" he said. "It's just that it saddens me deeply to think that Vylaine will not stop until there is nothing left of our homeland!"

Laytn stood and looked fondly at the man he saw as leading them to freedom. "Aedyn, my friend, it causes me great pain to see you so troubled!" he said and turned for the door.

...oooOooo...

"Get me the Captain of the Palace Guard!" Vylaine's voice rang out over the cobble-stoned courtyard. Her order immediately caused a small commotion from within the barracks at the far side of the courtyard.

Within minutes, a greying, obese soldier appeared and ran to where Vylaine fumed. He came to an abrupt halt, two paces in front of her, and snapped to attention, as he awaited her orders. "I am concerned that these rebels are becoming too confident," Vylaine fumed. "You are to begin burning the villages until somebody tells you where they are hidden!"

"Yes, m'Lady!" replied Captain Stratgii. He spun on his heels, began to run back to the barracks, and barked orders as he ran. The guards immediately began to tumble out of the building and form ranks in the courtyard. Many of them were still trying to finish getting dressed as they fumbled with the buttons on their tunics. Eventually, the commotion began to settle as the soldiers stood stiffly to attention and awaited the command that would set them on their way.

From within the stables could be heard the excited snorting of horses as they were being prepared for travel. Each of the officers would ride a horse to allow them to travel up and down the ranks of soldiers quickly while they were on the march.

A fleet of large heavy carts was also being pulled out of their garages and connected to waiting teams of massive shire draught horses. This convoy would be used to carry the heavy loads of camp support materials and food rations required for a sustained period of activity away from the castle until the troops were able to return to their barracks.

Slowly but surely, the large convoy began to take shape. With lots of noise from shouted commands and cracked whips, the entire living organism began to move slowly out through the stone gateway.

All the while, Vylaine paced backwards and forwards across the courtyard, planning the strategy of her next move. She only left and went back inside the palace when the last soldier had cleared the gates, and the convoy began to wind its way out into the countryside.

The rumble of the large metal wheels on the carts as they travelled along the gravel road, and the sounds of the officers as they yelled at the soldiers, could be heard for some time, even after they disappeared out of sight around the bend.

Vylaine ran upstairs to the tower balcony and watched the dust of the procession as it drifted slowly into the air along the path the soldiers had taken. She could feel a quiver of excitement run through her body as the thrill of the chase began to stir within her.

As she leaned against the edge of the parapet and gazed out over the green tops of the trees, the dust and noise of the convoy slowly disappeared over the ridge. Within her mind's eye, Vylaine could already see the captives being dragged before her as they begged her for mercy. She began to chuckle from deep in her belly, and slowly it got louder until finally she rocked with laughter and tears rolled down her face.

When she finally regained some composure, she turned and went back inside. But the flush of excitement remained in her cheeks for some time after. *I must go down to the dungeon and visit Seraphina!* She thought to herself. *I'm sure my Angels would enjoy seeing me again! It's been quite some time since I was able to get down there and provide pleasure for my pets!*

Vylaine muttered inane ramblings to herself as she began to make her way down the winding staircase that led to the underground chambers. Already her mind had started to think of the many ways in which she could continue to keep Seraphina in a constant state of emotional turmoil. She could already feel her female parts become moist in anticipation.

The deep sensual pleasure that Vylaine could induce from within the Queen was always at conflict with the intense hatred felt for the priestess. It was this pleasure and pain contradiction that Vylaine exploited to break the will of Seraphina and force her capitulation to Vylaine's wishes.

"Not much longer now my little pretty…" Vylaine muttered as she approached the entrance to the dungeon.

CHAPTER 20

$\mathbb{A}$ s Seraphina lay there with her eyes still tightly closed, she could hear the rustle and scuffle of the Dark Angels as they started their day. She had learned over the past couple of weeks that her naked body would not excite them as much while they thought she was asleep.

It was difficult to remain still and pretend to be asleep when her body constantly ached from being restrained in the shackles and stirrups of the table. She would give anything to be able to stretch out her arms and legs and breathe in the fresh air from outside.

The cold dungeon in which she had spent the last few weeks was damp and smelled terribly of mildew. Also, this combined with the horrible stench that emanated from the Dark Angel's cell, which had never been cleaned.

Seraphina slowly opened one eye just enough to be able to see what was happening in the room. Even though the lights remained dimmed from the evening shift, she could see that the Dark Angels were hunched down over their food trough and, for the moment, were distracted.

By ever so slowly turning her head from one side to the other, she could scan the entire room. Everything was as it had been the night before when she had finally drifted off to sleep.

A kaleidoscope of emotions tumbled through her head. It caused Seraphina to feel slightly dizzy and highlighted her empty stomach and dry mouth. *It has been so humiliating, to be captured and made a prisoner in my own castle!* She thought. *Why didn't I wait for Daemon's return, instead of rushing down to the vault?*

The intense anger strongly tempered this feeling of frustrated inability to control her circumstances that she felt at the betrayal by her husband, and the bitter hatred she felt for her captor, Vylaine. However, she was now mentally becoming accustomed to being naked and restrained in such a manner that it seemed her very soul was exposed to all in the room. Her new mental toughness meant it no longer bothered her.

In the far corner, two guards played cards to occupy their time until Vylaine would visit again later in the day. They had not noticed that Seraphina had awoken and continued to speak quietly between themselves of the events that had occurred during the past few days. "Did you hear about the recent explosion at the mines?" asked one.

"Yeah, I heard that there were six prisoners killed in the rockfall, but their bodies are still unable to be found!" the other responded. "The entire shaft collapsed on that side of the mountain and left the area too unstable to occupy!"

"Guards cleared the remaining prisoners out of the collapsed gallery, and they've shifted their operations to the other side of the mountain, which seems to be more stable!" said the first guard.

"By the way, I've heard that the rebels have become more active in the past week!" the other replied. "They've elected a strong new leader and their activities seem to be very effective in slowing down the advance of the campaign."

Seraphina slowly and gently shifted her weight from one side of her body to the other to get the blood to flow again and remove the numbness from her back. She was fortunate that nobody saw or heard her move and she could resume her pretence of sleep.

Behind her tightly closed eyes, her mind returned to its endless search for answers as she plotted and planned her escape, and eventually her ultimate revenge against Vylaine.

...oooOooo...

In the middle of the road, beside the burnt remains of the convoy of carts, lay the broken-open empty boxes. It was all that remained of the confiscated blankets and food that had been spirited away to Libertas by a group of rebels acting as porters.

Aedyn's band of rebels had successfully struck again. This strategy was part of the newly revised guerrilla tactics they had adopted to bring confusion to the army and impede the supply of stores to the soldiers at the front.

Laytn cast one last glance down the length of the road in front of them to ensure that everything worthwhile had been collected and no evidence remained. Then he swung away and disappeared into the forest with the rest of his rebel scouting party.

They travelled quietly and quickly along the path through the undergrowth until the scout in front suddenly stopped and raised his hand. Instantly, the men froze and waited for a signal from the scout to say that it was clear to proceed again.

The scout held up four fingers and made a walking motion with two fingers, which indicated that there were four men on foot in front of them. Then he indicated that these four men were headed directly towards where they were.

Laytn spread his arms out wide and motioned to the sides. Without a sound, the scouting party melted into the forest on either side of the path and waited for the four men to appear.

Within a couple of minutes, four young woodcutters appeared. They laughed at something that one of them had said, then disappeared down the path, completely unaware of the many eyes that watched them go. Laytn slowly and carefully held up his right arm and waved forward.

Again, without a sound, the scouting party emerged from the forest and continued silently on their way back to the camp. They were one of several scouting parties out that day. They had a deadline to be back in their village by evening to report the results of the day's activities before the planning session that night.

Before they had travelled another thirty minutes, they came to the busy main road that leads to the palace. Again, the scout held up his hand, which immediately brought the scouting party to a halt.

Laytn could hear the noise of a massive convoy of heavy carts as it travelled along the road and the shouted commands and tramp of many boots. He guessed that there was a large contingent of soldiers that accompanied this convoy. Laytn raised his arms and quietly signalled to the others in the scouting party, and they silently blended into the scrub while he crept forward to join the scout.

From behind their screen of bushes, he could see Vylaine's convoy as it made its way slowly out into the countryside. It was by far the most massive convoy he had ever seen. It indicated Vylaine's cruel intention to destroy everything in her way as she vented her fury and frustration in not being able to find the rebel force.

As he slowly re-counted the number of carts and soldiers to ensure accuracy for his report to Aedyn, Laytn could not help but think that this must leave the garrison back at the palace almost empty. Laytn could not help but smile to himself as he realised that this might be the first real mistake that Vylaine had made in her careful plan to gain personal control of Skargness.

He waited the few minutes that it took for the last of the large, slow-moving convoy to disappear around the bend before he quietly called up the rest of his scouting party from their various hiding places. After sending two of the men to accompany the convoy from under cover of the forest, he sent another pair to watch the entrance to the palace in case troops started to return in large numbers.

Then, he and the remaining members of the scouting party headed immediately back to their hidden camp to tell Aedyn of this fantastic turn of events.

...oooOooo...

Aedyn had spent many days as he pondered the optimal path for the covert guerrilla tactics of their limited resources and personnel to have the maximum impact against the much stronger force of Vylaine's army. *What's Vylaine hoping to achieve?* He thought. The thought continued to go around and around in his head, even as he pounded the hot metal into submission.

Then, suddenly, like a bolt from the blue, he had an inspiration.

He placed the hot piece of metal on the ground to cool and put down his massive hammer. He sat down at a bench and started to jot down his ideas on a piece of paper and soon scribbled furiously.

Coincidentally, Laytn had also chosen just that moment to visit Aedyn at his blacksmith's workshop to discuss the agenda for their Leader's Meeting that night. But Laytn's brow furrowed, and he stopped dead in his tracks as he saw Aedyn frantically try to capture all his thoughts on the paper in front of him.

Just then, Aedyn sat back to review his handiwork. When he glanced around the workshop, he noticed Laytn who stood and waited in the entrance. "Come in, Laytn!" he said. "I have some things I wish to discuss with you before we go to tonight's meeting!"

Laytn relaxed and joined Aedyn at the bench. Then he glanced down at the numerous sheets of paper that were covered in notes and sketched diagrams and lay scattered across the bench top. "You have been busy, haven't you?" Laytn laughed.

Aedyn smiled back, but his reply was solemn as he bent his head and started to gather his notes. He spoke with conviction of the thoughts that tumbled around in his head. "My friend, I think I have finally figured out Vylaine's strategy!" he said. "She's using the troops to bring fear and doubt to the people in the villages and then plundering their possessions and food to drive them out of their homes! What if we could beat her at her own game?"

He glanced up, then quickly back down and continued. "We already know where the troop convoys are and where they are headed! Imagine their disappointment if they arrived in the village to find it deserted and every house had been cleaned out of everything inside?"

Aedyn lifted his head again to look at Laytn's reaction, but he was pleased to see the huge beaming smile on his face, and they both laughed out loud. The sound of their laughter bounced off the walls and added to the noise. "We can use our scout teams to stay one step ahead of the convoys and warn the villagers before they arrive! Then we can guide the villagers back here to Libertas to assist in the running of the village! Their skills and numbers will be essential if we are to successfully take this fight to the castle and attack the evil within. And, let's face it, we can use all the help we can get!"

Aedyn hesitated momentarily to ensure he had covered all his explanation, then relaxed, sat back in his seat and gazed into Laytn's eyes. "Now Laytn, what brings you to my humble workshop today?" he finally asked.

Laytn proceeded to explain the situation he had discovered both at the castle and during their daily scouting routine. The conversation eventually ended when both men stood simultaneously and regarded each other with deep, genuine mutual respect; no words were necessary. The two friends slapped each other on the back and agreed that tonight's meeting would bring a renewed spirit back to the team.

Then Aedyn resumed his seat at the bench and continued to pore over the details of his strategy, looking for any visible signs of failure. Seeing the apparent passion and commitment displayed by Aedyn, Laytn headed back outside with a new spring in his step and a smile on his face that a team of surgeons would have difficulty removing.

CHAPTER 21

$\mathbb{C}$ atelyn couldn't help herself and continuously laughed out loud at the sight of Kinta and Misty, as the two of them ran like a white blur through the trees along the edge of the pathway.

"Misty enjoys it when we take our walks together, Mama!" called Kinta, as the two ran past again.

Catelyn could not contain her amusement, or her immense love, as she watched her daughter and the small white dog having so much fun. Now, in the months since they had left Bayville, Kinta had suddenly grown up so quickly. Her body already showed that she had blossomed, filled out, and become a young woman.

It seems like just yesterday that she was my baby girl! She thought. Catelyn was mainly determined to spend as much time as possible together with her, now that she had transitioned from childhood to adulthood, and to guide Kinta through these next couple of formative years.

And, it was equally essential to both Catelyn and Aedyn that Kinta had not lost the opportunity to enjoy her childhood and be rushed into early adulthood by their circumstances. *I remember when Anaiel and I were about the same age as Kinta is now!* She mused. *We relied so much on our Mama to help us through the transition to becoming a woman!*

Catelyn lay outstretched on a blanket, with her eyes almost closed and enjoyed the peace and serenity of a clear blue sky and warm sunshine. She thoughtfully reminisced on her younger days.

Suddenly, as if from deep within her psyche, a critical probing thought urgently tried to get her attention. Eventually, she relented and pondered the question this proposed. *When was the last time that I had my monthly cycle?* She thought.

Catelyn spent some time recollecting and counted back in her mind through the various weekly activities and events that had occurred since she could remember the last time with certainty. *I'm sure the last time was a few weeks before Aedyn, and I went on our picnic … and that was about two months ago!*

The sudden dawning realisation that she and Aedyn were going to have another child struck her like a bolt from the blue. It caused Catelyn to unconsciously and involuntarily place both her hands tenderly on her lower abdomen.

She mused on the situation that they currently faced and weighed up whether to tell Aedyn and Kinta her fantastic news. Her decision came as no surprise to Catelyn, as she knew the practical nature of her personality. *I'll keep this to myself for the moment and make my choice later, once we have a clear idea of what our future will be!* She thought.

"Mama! Mama!" came Kinta's urgent voice from a distance. "Come quickly!" The sound of Kinta's voice suddenly roused her from her quiet personal thoughts and reverie. Catelyn looked up to find out what could be the possible source of so much excitement.

"Come and look, Mama!" Kinta called, "Misty and I have found a secret passageway!" Kinta and Misty could be heard as they noisily moved through the undergrowth in the distance, but they were unable to be seen from where Catelyn sat. She carefully stood, packed up the blanket and her few possessions, then made her way slowly in the direction of Kinta's voice.

Along the edge of the tree line, she saw the deep wheel-rutted remains of a worn gravel path, which had of recent times been entirely overgrown with weeds but, at some earlier time, had been a busy thoroughfare. She made her way between the tangled overhanging tree branches, careful to avoid the many stinging and scratching thorns that attempted to block her way, Catelyn followed the track until she came upon Kinta and Misty.

Kinta rushed forward, took her hand and began to excitedly lead her through the dense foliage toward the cliff face. Misty wagged her tail and ran back and forth as she tried to hurry them both along.

Almost hidden entirely from view behind a thick screen of shrubs, vines, and thick bushes emerged the entrance to a large tunnel, which appeared practically capable of allowing a large wagon to pass comfortably through. The three intrepid explorers cautiously entered the shaft through the overhanging green screen.

As they probed forward, they encountered zero visibility, with dark, oppressive blackness, and the sticky, clinging feel of many thick spider webs that stretched across the void in front of them. Even though the tunnel had remained unused for some considerable time, the air inside was heavy and stagnant but didn't have that dank, musty smell that often comes from long periods of vacancy.

Catelyn had an uneasy feeling and quietly, but firmly, turned the eager exploration party around. To her immediate relief, they all made their way back out into the bright sunshine and clean, fresh air.

She made a sharp mental note of the entrance location and decided to leave the complete exploration of the tunnel to Aedyn and his men. Her only sense of responsibility was to the absolute safety of the two excited, bubbling and chattering charges within her care, and the recent tiny budding new-life deep within her body.

Who knew where this tunnel could lead...?

...oooOooo...

Vylaine listened with zero interest to the Sergeant's report as his voice continued to drone on and on with nothing of substance. Eventually, her patience snapped. She could handle no more and shouted, "Get out of here!"

In one motion, the Sergeant snapped to attention and spun on his heels, then he ran at full speed from the room before she could utter another word.

Vylaine sat back in the seat and closed her eyes. Random, haphazard thoughts continued to pass through her mind. She was both confused and bemused by the lack of results from her soldiers. They continued to report their activities, but she still had nothing to show for this. *Why do we have no prisoners to interrogate?* She wondered why her plans had failed to bear her the fruit she had anticipated so eagerly.

Before too long, the warm afternoon, combined with the sticky humidity in the room, caused her eyes to droop and she reluctantly nodded off to sleep.

...oooOooo...

Slowly and silently Aedyn, Aurak, Ox and five other substantial men with swords crept forward and continued to make their way further and further into the inky black tunnel, as they stuck close together for mutual protection.

They used hand-held flaming torches to light the way and clear the thick tangle of spider webs that clung to them and blocked their path. The group had already rounded several bends and inched their way along long stretches of the dark, dusty passageway.

As they got further into the blackness, the familiar smell of humid, stale air was surprisingly missing. Ever since Catelyn had told him about the secret tunnel, Aedyn had felt this might be an important discovery. He squinted his eyes and tried to get them to focus in the dim light.

As they turned another corner, up ahead, he could make out the faint shape of the tunnel walls, draped in thick curtains of spider webs that crawled with large hairy arachnids. Aedyn could feel his heart as it thumped in his chest with anticipation, as he tentatively edged closer and closer to the next upcoming bend.

As he glanced cautiously behind, Aedyn squinted his eyes to adjust to the dim flickering light of the torches. He could make out the squat silhouetted shape of Aurak within an arm's reach, framed by the giant hunched silhouette of Ox further behind. He was unable to see anything of the remaining five members of his team and immediately became concerned.

Aedyn hesitated, then stopped and waited for the group to bunch up tightly again, then reached back with his right hand and silently motioned for Aurak to come even closer. *"Try not to disturb anything, so nobody will know we have been here!"* he whispered into Aurak's ear. *"But, be prepared for anything! Pass it on to Ox and the others!"*

Aurak nodded and touched Aedyn lightly on the arm to let him know that he understood. Once again, the tightly bunched team of men began their painfully slow progress along the dark murky rockface, as they hugged the damp tunnel wall. Being unsighted in the oppressive gloom, Aedyn felt the sticky silk of the unavoidable spider webs on his face and arms. He rubbed silently, but vigorously, to remove any unwanted crawling hitchhikers.

When the team had finally reached the next bend, Aedyn could faintly make out the muted glow of daylight from much, much further up the tunnel, around another corner. With the faint light as a backdrop, it made it easier to see that the shaft ahead was empty immediately in front of them.

They edged forward again with a little more haste, eager to see where this led. With all the warriors crouched over to avoid the sticky, clinging spider webs, the team continued their difficult, painful, back-breaking progress and timidly approached the next bend in the tunnel.

Aedyn cautiously peeked his head around the corner, and he could see bright sunbeams of daylight that filtered through an opening in the far rockface and a thick screen of green foliage that covered it. After their extended time of having explored in the complete darkness of the tunnel, the sudden brightness of the brilliant sunlight hurt their still unaccustomed eyes. It took some time before they could make out the details of their surroundings.

Once their eyes had finally adjusted from the darkness, they were able to discern subtleties, such as the tiny dust motes that floated in the disturbed air and caught in the spotlight of a sunbeam, and the green mossy growth around the edges of the opening in the rockface.

Other than an occasional faintly-audible sound that penetrated the glowing verdant curtain, they were utterly alone in the rock-strewn, web covered, subterranean shaft. Since there was no apparent danger now, the team of explorers stood upright and stretched their aching backs.

Then, Aedyn carefully and quietly walked over to the screened opening, and gently eased aside several of the creepers and vines that formed a green cover. He was immediately amazed at the sight that met his eyes. Completely hidden from view, or the knowledge of anyone outside, by a combination of thick leafy shrubs and clinging lantana vines, the tunnel opened out onto the steep side of a sheer cliff.

As he peeked through the camouflage provided by the concealing plants, Aedyn gazed open-mouthed in amazement at the royal palace that stood immediately above them and stretched up into the azure blue of the sky.

When he recovered from his initial shock, Aedyn motioned Aurak closer and whispered to him. *"I'm going to need your extensive expertise and advice on mining!"* he said. *"How difficult would it be to dig a connecting shaft, large enough to accommodate several squads of armed men, through the wall of this tunnel?"*

Aurak ran the sensitive fingertips of his expert hand slowly and gently over the rough surface of the rock, leaned across and sniffed the wall before he snapped off a small sample and placed it on his tongue.

Then he closed his eyes and gently stroked his beard as he cautiously mulled over the information from his senses for a couple of minutes before he finally reached his decision and turned back to Aedyn. *"The task you ask would be simple, as the walls are of soft chalky sandstone!"* he solemnly announced in a subdued gruff whisper. *"The only difficulty will be in totally suppressing the noise of our digging!"* Aurak gazed expectantly up into Aedyn's usually expressive face, to determine his immediate reaction to this news.

Aedyn's face remained entirely passive, as he again surveyed his surroundings and mulled and cogitated the expert information that he had been presented. Then, ever so slowly, a huge grin lit up the features of Aedyn's face. *"Thank you, Aurak, my friend, since this tunnel lies immediately underneath the royal palace, I think we have just found our covert means of entering undetected!"* he whispered, with a chuckle.

Normally staid and thoughtful, Aurak's face beamed as he smiled back. *"It would be my honour and pleasure to assist you in this matter, Sir!"* he said quietly.

The team of intrepid explorers promptly turned about and swiftly, but quietly, made their way back up their newly found tunnel to their secluded valley. Aedyn had already begun to plan how they could maximise the benefit of this wonderful stroke of luck.

CHAPTER 22

S eraphina lay there completely naked, maintained her silence and remained perfectly still, as she faced the hand-hewn rock wall. She had curled tightly into the foetal position to protect what she could of her modesty.

She lay on top of the single rough horsehair blanket that covered the cot in the corner of her small cell. The coarse material of the rug still annoyed her super-sensitive skin, and was far too itchy and uncomfortable to bear, when she had tried earlier to cover herself.

Vylaine had become utterly bored with having her prisoner strapped continuously to the table, so Seraphina had now been moved to one of the cells on the opposite side of the room to the Dark Angels. It allowed a still naked Seraphina to at least maintain some sense of personal modesty between her regular visits to the 'table of pain' as she suffered through Vylaine's sexual ministrations.

She had already learned from her own recent harsh personal experience that the Dark Angels would only stay calm and unaffected by her nudity, while she remained completely motionless.

All the while, Vylaine wracked her brain, as she tried to think of how best to use Seraphina's current situation to her advantage. The two head-strong women were always at loggerheads with each other in an endless battle of wits and wills.

Ever an eternal optimist, Seraphina never ceased to plan her revenge for when she eventually gained her freedom from Vylaine's incarceration. She closed her eyes and hugged her knees tightly to her chest. She spent every waking moment trying to imagine in her mind, in vivid living colour, all the unthinkable atrocities and punishments she could, and hopefully would eventually be able to inflict on Vylaine. *She will rue the day she was born!* She thought.

Suddenly, her eyes shot wide open in surprise as an almost inaudible faint sound penetrated the solitude of her cell and rattled her out of her usual retrospection. *Oh my God! Was that the sound of digging?*

The thought erupted within her head, and she immediately clamped her hands over her mouth to prevent any noise escaping her lips. Fortunately, this small movement remained unnoticed across the room.

Seraphina tightly closed her eyes again and focussed so intently as she listened, that she could hear her thumping pulse pounding in her ears. The sound of her heartbeat in her chest seemed so enormously loud to her that she was concerned that other people in the dungeon would hear and come to see what had caused the disturbance. *There! I'm sure I heard it again!* The thought thumped in her head.

Once again, the faintly muffled sound of metal as it struck against rock reached her ears from somewhere behind her. Ever so agonisingly slowly, Seraphina gently stretched out the long, lean limbs of her naked body and gently rolled over to face the opposite wall.

She held her breath and immediately froze mid-movement, for an insufferably long moment, when the cot gave a small squeak as she moved her position.

Fortunately, the muffled sound didn't carry outside her cell, and she could gradually relax the unbearable tension from her body and focus on listening for another sound of digging.

It didn't take long before, once again, the faintest sound carried to her strained ears. Seraphina's mind frantically worked overtime, as she attempted to orientate exactly where the digging was taking place. However, it was confusing as the sound seemed to be coming from inside the mountain upon which the palace stands. *How could that possibly be?* She thought.

Seraphina had lived her whole life in Skargness and had never heard of any caves or tunnels in the mountain under the royal palace.

And, why would somebody try to dig under the castle? She thought. *As far as I know, there's nothing of value there anyway!*

She lay perfectly still with her eyes closed and held her breath, then strained her ears to try and hear another sound of digging, despite the constant background noises that came from the Dark Angels. It only took a little while, but she wasn't disappointed. The faintest of sounds brought an immediate smile to her face and the tingle of goosebumps over her bare skin.

Seraphina was so focused on the possibilities and excited at the prospect of what might be the reason behind the digging noises, that she completely forgot about the itchy rug that she lay on. She slowly eased her way over onto her back and lay there with her eyes closed, then she tried to imagine who might be trying to tunnel under the palace. Her imagination ran riot as she considered the various possibilities and struggled to come to grips with the reason why.

...oooOooo...

Kinta and Misty sat quietly together on their picnic blanket, as they enjoyed the peaceful solitude. They stared vacantly at the little waterfall that cascaded over the lip of the escarpment overhead and splashed down into the glittering pool at their feet.

The little waterfall provided the only source of water for the bubbling stream, which became a small tributary into the main river through the valley. It gently bubbled and gurgled over the rocks that attempted to bar its way.

They had discovered this peaceful little hollow during one of their many walks through the valley. Kinta and Misty had covered much of the area within the secret valley, from the rocky dead-end at the furthest point and all the way to the secret opening near the highway. They had even crawled through tiny fissures in the rocks along the sides and giggled as they hid from everyone else's view.

It always felt so secure and peaceful to be able to get away from everyone else. The two girls could share some quiet time here together, without having to worry whether anyone overheard what they were speaking about regarding any little personal adventures together or their plans.

The burning hot sun's fireball hung suspended in a bright blue cloudless sky. Even the frazzled birds had sought shelter in the comforting shade of the surrounding leafy trees. It had been quite a while since they had enough spare time available to use the waterfall and pool for swimming.

Their private, secluded little clearing lay behind a screen of thick, dense, prickly vines, bushes, and thorns, interspersed with large leafy trees. It prevented anybody else from approaching either unseen or unheard and afforded them a shady retreat. Conveniently, the little waterfall flowed continuously throughout the warmer weather, which was due to the melting of the snow higher up the mountains and provided them with constant cooling refreshment.

A very relaxed Kinta lay back, sighed and placed her hands behind her head. She closed her eyes to enjoy the remainder of the peaceful, idyllic afternoon. She and Misty had worked with Catelyn and Maeve today at the school. They always enjoyed spending time with young children, and both girls enjoyed helping.

But they still tried to make it out to their hidden waterfall at least once a week to enjoy each other's company as they discussed their ongoing plans. Kinta felt heavy drowsiness settle in her eyes. She had just started to doze in the quiet, peaceful ambience of the hollow.

Suddenly, Misty turned to face Kinta and broke the silence. "I think it may be best to let Mama and Papa in on our little secret!" she said. Then she sat back and waited for this to have its effect. It didn't take too long before the comment filtered through the haze of sleep. Her best friend finally began to stir.

Kinta's eyes slowly opened from her drowsy sleep as she tried to focus, then they suddenly widened with surprise, and her head snapped around quickly to look at Misty. "Whatever for?" she asked. She sat up on the blanket and rubbed her eyes as she tried to clear her head after being shocked into waking so rapidly.

Misty was slow to respond to Kinta's question but, when she did, it was with a considered tone in her voice. "I overheard some of the random conversations around the camp from the new arrivals! I have a strong feeling that we may both be instrumental participants when the retaliatory campaign against the priestess begins in earnest!" she said. "Things seem to be escalating quite rapidly now, and we could provide a secret shock weapon to our team's attack. However, we *will* need to coordinate our activities with Papa and his plans."

Kinta listened attentively, then playfully placed her right index finger up to her cheek, raised her eyebrows and thought long and hard before she replied. She instinctively knew that Misty was right, but she had wanted to delay having to reveal their secret for as long as possible.

She had anticipated that this situation would eventually arise, but she knew that their previously carefree existence would end abruptly once their secret was shared with others. "In that case, we'll tell them tonight" she slowly said.

A sudden gleam of mischief sparkled in Kinta's dark ebony eyes and a broad grin spread slowly across her face. She reached her hands down and began to slowly release her leather belt. "I'm going in for our final secret swim before we head back home!" said Kinta.

She quickly stood up, then reached behind and fumbled with her fingers as she carefully undid the little cloth-covered buttons on the back of her dress. Once the buttons were all unfastened, she grasped the neckline of her dress between her fingertips, raised her toned, tanned, lean muscular arms and began to shake and shimmy her whole body. This action caused her clothing to ride up her body, and she hurriedly removed her dress over her head. Then she gently lay it out on their blanket to keep dry.

As she glanced up at her friend, after she had finally finished undressing, Misty immediately noticed the little blond downy tufts of hair that had grown in Kinta's armpits and the V-shaped patch of tight blond curly pubic hair between her legs.

It came as a complete surprise as Kinta had now completely changed from the last time they had swum here. She suddenly realised that, along with her young pert, firm, rounded breasts and swollen rose-petal pink nipples, Kinta had changed from being a young girl and had now become a woman.

Her previously slim shape was also much more rounded, where

shapely hips and curves had now emerged. Her new shapely figure was in complete contrast to her washboard-flat abdominal muscles and long toned muscular legs.

Misty sadly realised that the innocence of childhood had passed quickly. Her friend was now an adult but currently still caught in the constant confusion of changes to her body that she didn't fully understand.

A now completely-naked Kinta suddenly giggled and made a surprise dash for the water. The firm round white globes of her buttocks and young breasts bounced and jiggled jauntily with every movement. "The last one in is a rotten egg!" she said. She laughed over her shoulder as she splashed into the edge of the cooling pool.

Misty instantly leapt up off the blanket and bounded after her. The two of them plunged into the waist-deep water together and disappeared beneath the sparkling surface.

...oooOooo...

Ox grabbed the cloth from his back pocket and wiped the beads of sweat from his face. He stepped back away from the pock-marked rockface, lowered his pick and admired their work so far.

He and Aurak had commenced digging an access tunnel from the main shaft that Kinta and Misty had discovered and now attempted to reach their planned access point into the castle. Aedyn had informed them about this last week. It was an 'out-of-body' experience to be back in a rock tunnel again after all the efforts they had gone to only a few short weeks ago to escape. Somehow though, they both felt it made a huge difference to be able to contribute to the effort in a constructive way and were extremely proud to have been asked.

Ox leaned his aching back against the nearest rough-hewn rock wall and felt the cold stone through his damp shirt. He once again wiped the enormous beads of sweat from his forehead with the rag. "Aurak, honestly, did you think we'd be digging rock tunnels again after we expended so much effort and finally got out of that mine?" he asked.

"No way!" Aurak said chuckling. "However, it also feels good to do something worthwhile, after all the kindness these people have shown us!"

Ox slowly nodded his head in agreement, squinted his eyes and glanced back down the dimly lit rock passage toward the main shaft. He tried to estimate just exactly how far they had managed to dig so far. "If we continue at this pace, it should only take us another week or so to be underneath the main building," he said. "Then we can begin the dangerous task of digging up into the enemy's castle."

Aurak shook his shaggy head and muttered in disbelief. "I can't believe we are even thinking of doing this!" he said. Then he stopped, took a deep breath and stood up straight to look up into Ox's face. "No! That's not true! I know exactly why we're doing this!" he said. And, with that, he spun around to face the rock wall again and began to shovel the loose debris that lay around on the floor with renewed vigour.

"Yes, my friend!" said Ox, "You and I are going to provide a secret strategic point of access for our warriors to the heart of evil that currently controls this land!"

Aurak chuckled merrily while his whole body shook with the effort. He began to sing an old dwarf song he had learned as a young man, as his busy shovel clanged away in time with the tune.

"With my shovel and my pick,
To my digging, I will stick,
And, later I will pause as we take stock.

Then, we'll wash away the soil,
And, continue with our toil,
Oh, we will make a passage through this rock."

Ox smiled and closed his eyes as he listened to Aurak sing, then contemplated his future, as he imagined a time soon when he could be with Madeleine once again. In his mind, he could still feel the soft warmth of her body as he held her close.

Then his anger started to swell at the thought of their current situation. He reached down and grabbed the leather bucket of water that they used to soften the rockface and reduce the dust, as well as deaden the noise of digging. Ox emptied the contents of the bucket over the coarse-grained sandstone, threw it to one side and grasped the handle of the pick. Then, with a deep growl that surprised Aurak and made him look up quickly, Ox lunged forward and attacked the rock face as a demon possessed.

Aurak went back to his singing. *Youngsters*! He thought and chuckled as he picked up the discarded bucket and filled it with water again, then he placed it back within reach of Ox as he worked on the rockface. He leaned down and picked up his discarded shovel and continued to remove the crumbled pieces of broken sandstone that littered the floor and proceeded to rain down because of Ox's desperate labours.

The two grossly disparate men had always worked very well together, as they formed an extremely efficient team. Between them, they had already dug their underground access tunnel below the castle for more than twenty paces through the soft sandstone. And, they had made it high enough for a squad of men to stand upright in comfort if they carried weapons, as Aedyn had explicitly requested.

Everything seemed to be progressing well, so far!

CHAPTER 23

Narchis consciously slowed his breathing rate and stood perfectly still in the deep black shadows of the small dark wall alcove where he was dressed all in black from head to toe. If you didn't know he was there, he was completely invisible to all who passed.

His professional skills had made him the obvious choice to sneak into the palace. He was tasked to bring back an understanding of the internal layout. This information would be essential for their successful mission to capture the high priestess and restore the kingdom to peace. Fortunately, nobody had seen him as he made his way around the various levels of the building. Now he was at the lowest level and looking for an escape route.

Suddenly, his pulse began to quicken as he saw the high priestess make her way briskly down the narrow passageway directly toward him. She appeared to be in high spirits with her head-to-toe loose clothing, including the veil that covered her face and head, that streamed out behind as she walked. Then, to his complete surprise, she stopped abruptly, pivoted on her toes and turned to face the blank wall about three paces from his hiding spot.

She glanced around suspiciously, up and down the passageway, before she carefully slipped her hand into a secret pocket in her gown and quickly removed it. Vylaine's hand held a thin, shiny metal rod. She inserted it into a small mysterious hole in the wall, which immediately caused part of the wall to begin to slide back and revealed a hidden passageway into the depths beyond.

As Vylaine entered through the secret portal in the wall, she again checked left and right to ensure that nobody had watched her. Then she reached back and removed the metal rod, which caused the wall to slide back into place, and erased any evidence of its existence.

Narchis slowly and quietly let out his breath, without moving a muscle, still not entirely sure he believed what he had just seen. He suddenly realised he had held his breath since Vylaine had appeared in the passage. After he listened carefully and checked to ensure that he could see nobody else, Narchis slowly eased himself out of his small hiding place.

He soundlessly crept along the passage to the point where he had last seen Vylaine disappear into the wall. As he ran his sharp, trained eyes and sensitive fingertips over the stone surface, Narchis noticed the small round hole.

It was almost invisible to the naked eye unless you knew exactly where to look for it. He measured the size of the hole by carefully inserting the tip of the little finger on his right hand and mentally noted how far he added his finger.

Then, like a shadow, he disappeared out of the building and headed for the secret tunnel they were using to dig their way into the palace. *If we continue too much further, we'll break through into that secret room!* He thought. *And, that might not be wise!*

...oooOooo...

Misty and Kinta simultaneously turned their heads and looked at each other knowingly. Both always instinctively and instantly knew what the other was thinking. They had covertly watched the ongoing preparations and fight training sessions for the upcoming battle for the last few weeks from the cover of some trees on the edge of the valley.

Misty then adapted these training lessons used by the warriors so they could fit them into Kinta's training program. This strategy was part of their plan to assist her in preparation for helping Papa during the attack on the palace.

They had called into their secret observation point on their way home from the waterfall. This secret location and their scheduled stop were always the perfect time of day to watch the warriors in training. The warriors practised their thrust and parry with their swords, target practice with their archery, and various attack formations.

Both girls cogitated over the many concerns that they had pondered over the past weeks. Kinta spoke first. "If we're to be fully involved in this upcoming battle, my parents will need to know that we'll both be safe! Otherwise, we may not be permitted to help!" she said.

Misty smiled, as she sensed her young friend's concern and she already had the solution. "Don't be afraid," she said. "I'm quite capable of looking after myself!" Suddenly the small fluffy white dog was replaced by a huge snarling snow-white wolf with fangs bared and saliva drooling. This scary image caused Kinta to jump back in fright instinctively. Then, in the blink of an eye, the wolf was gone again, and Misty was back as herself. Misty began to chuckle. "I hope I get the same reaction next time I have to change!" she giggled.

Then, Kinta laughed as well. "Okay, so we don't have to worry about you!" she said.

Her pounding heart finally began to slow again after her fright. "And, I think I know how I can feel more secure as well! Which will assist me in convincing Mama and Papa as well!" she said. Kinta went on to explain her plans for a leather-lined, lightweight, metal helmet, and an armour-plated vest made of thick leather and small overlaid plates of metal.

She also described a close-fitting soft leather suit and matching boots, to protect her upper body, arms, and legs. "I've always been a fine shot with the longbow and arrows, and that is a weapon light enough to allow us to move freely!" she said. "Now, I just need to make my weapons and find someone who can prepare my armour!" she said.

Kinta thought that she would need to approach her father to make her list of items as he was the only person she knew that could make something so complex. Misty smiled and knew the answer already.

She moved around until she sat immediately in front of Kinta and looked into her eyes. "Kinta, you just need to focus your mind on what you have just described!" she said softly, as she encouraged her friend.

"You will be surprised at just how powerful the mind can be when trained properly! It will just take some time to develop your true faith in your already inherent abilities fully!"

Kinta hesitated briefly, then closed her eyes and saw in her mind the vision she had. To her utter amazement, she immediately wore the lightweight helmet, heavy armour-plated vest, light leather suit, and soft boots. And, in her hands was the most exceptional longbow and quiver of arrows she had ever seen.

Kinta eagerly placed the quiver of arrows on her back and carefully adjusted the straps until the shafts were comfortably within reach over her shoulder. Then, as she pulled an arrow from its receptacle, it was instantly replaced by another, thereby ensuring the supply of weapons would never be exhausted.

The two girls spent the next hour practising with Kinta's new longbow and arrows until they were finally confident with the results she was getting. They also spent time and exercised Kinta's lightning outfit changes. With the blink of an eye, she could quickly change from her pretty dress and sandals to her battle armour and weapons, and then back again.

These were skills that would greatly benefit their impact on any plans made in the future. It didn't take long before both girls were thoroughly delighted with current developments. Since the afternoon was coming to an end, they were about to leave when they saw Aedyn and Laytn run into the tunnel.

"Well, my 'giant wolf in sheep's clothing' friend, aren't you full of little surprises!" Kinta giggled. "Now, we need to obtain my parent's permission! And, I think I know just how!"

Together, the two young warriors laughed, then turned and headed for the tunnel. Little did they know just how much they would change things.

...oooOooo...

Aedyn and Laytn could not believe their luck as they looked out of the tunnel opening and down through the greenery. They had created a small gap and could see out onto the road far below. When the scouts had come running back into camp and told them that Vylaine was leaving the palace, they had to see it with their own eyes.

Both men had run all the way, and they now huffed and puffed noisily to catch their breath. The carriage that bore the high priestess could still just be seen, as it made its way between the trees on its way to the coast.

They looked at each other and smiled, as they knew that things had finally begun to escalate and would soon come to a head. Out of the corner of his eye, Aedyn saw a slight movement behind him in the tunnel.

He spun around and reached quickly for his sword, but he was surprised to see Kinta and Misty standing there quietly together. He wondered how they had managed to sneak up behind them without being heard. "Sweetheart, you gave me a surprise!" he said tenderly.

His heart rate started to come back down slowly. Kinta stepped forward and gently took Aedyn's hand, while Misty shuffled forward to stay with her. "Papa, we'd like to help!" she said and looked calmly into Aedyn's eyes.

Aedyn raised his eyebrows and quickly glanced around at Laytn, who held out his hands. Then he shrugged his shoulders and rolled his eyes, as he indicated he had no idea of where this was going. "Who is 'we'?" Aedyn asked cautiously. "And, how will 'we' help?"

Kinta kept a firm, but gentle hold of Aedyn's hand then turned and started to lead him and Laytn quietly back out of the tunnel. "Papa, there are some critical things that Misty and I need to explain to you urgently!" she began.

Aedyn turned around and caught Laytn's eye again, raised his eyebrows and winked. "Oh, really?" he asked. He tried desperately to keep the smirk out of his voice.

Kinta stopped suddenly and turned to face her father. "Yes, Papa!" she said firmly. "We're very serious!" Misty decided it was time to let Aedyn know their plan for both girls to assist in the battles ahead. "Papa, we may both look small, timid, and weak, but first impressions can be deceptive!" she said. "We just might be the most powerful and effective weapons you have!"

In the blink of an eye, Misty morphed into a colossal growling snow-white polar bear. Kinta changed from his sweet young daughter into a fearsome armed and armoured warrior with an arrow notched and her longbow drawn.

"Whoa!" Aedyn shouted in surprise, and both he and Laytn jumped backwards in shock. By the time their feet had touched the ground, Kinta and Misty had just vanished. Aedyn felt a light tap on his shoulder and spun around in fright, knowing there was nobody else in the tunnel.

Behind him stood Kinta, as she smiled and stood sweetly again in her pretty dress, and a tiny white mouse sat on her shoulder. Suddenly, they had Aedyn's complete attention, as the initial shock of hearing Misty speak had passed. "Oh, *really*!" he said, in a far more serious tone.

Then, the two men trailed along closely behind Kinta and Misty and listened attentively as the two girls explained how things would now work. They were still slightly dazed as the two girls led them out of the tunnel and back towards the village, as they quietly explained their plans as they went.

CHAPTER 24

Ox arched his back, flexed his massive arms and swung the point of the enormous steel pick back hard against the rock face with all his strength. The wall exploded into a shower of rock pieces that rained down onto the tunnel floor.

Since they didn't know how long Vylaine was going to be away, they had to move as fast as possible. Large pieces of chipped stone continued to rain down from the rock face of the tunnel with every swing of Ox's huge custom-made pick. Despite his extensive experience and endurance, Aurak had begun to tire from all the shovelling needed to keep the floor cleared.

Suddenly, with an unexpectedly dull thud, Ox's pick broke through the rock face as a small hole appeared. When Ox placed his large eye up to the hole and peered in through the small aperture, he was shocked to see a familiar looking woman lay naked on the cot across the room. She looked straight back at him, eyes wide open in shock at the unexpected invasion of her privacy.

Although she had lost considerable weight during her incarceration, Ox instantly recognised the woman as Queen Seraphina. His concern immediately became aroused that she might remember him and send them back to the mines.

However, his sense of honour and duty convinced him to continue to break down the wall and free his Queen from the evil clutches of the priestess. Ox attacked the wall again with renewed vigour, and he soon had a large enough opening into the rock wall through which both he and Aurak could squeeze.

As the two men crawled tentatively into the confines of the small room and cautiously searched the area for any danger, Seraphina defensively curled herself into a ball to protect her modesty. When they looked out into the remainder of the dungeon, they realised that no guards were currently present as they were off having a meal break.

Ox quickly took off his vast sweaty shirt, held out his arm and lowered his eyes, then he passed it to Seraphina. "Your Majesty!" he said. He and Aurak turned their backs in a gentlemanly gesture to allow Seraphina the privacy to dress, mindful of the noises starting to emanate from the other side of the dungeon as the Dark Angels began to rouse.

Despite the muddy smears across the front and large damp patches of sweat under the arms, Seraphina gratefully slipped into the offered garment with pleasure. "Thank you! Thank you! Thank you!" she said softly and joyfully.

As Seraphina stood up from the bed in her bare feet, the large shirt hung down below her knees, and the ends of the sleeves extended way below her hands. "I don't know, or for that matter even care, how you came to be here to rescue me, but I will be eternally thankful to you both!" she managed to get out before she broke down and sobbed.

"We're here to save you, overthrow the evil high priestess, and return our land to peace," said Ox. "Now, Your Majesty, you must follow me quickly, and we'll take you to safety!" he said. Ox turned and took her arm to support her before he carefully helped Seraphina into the narrow rocky tunnel. She was so relieved to have something to cover her nakedness finally, and someone to help her escape from Vylaine's cruel clutches. Seraphina clung to Ox's arm like a helpless little girl.

Aurak scuttled back behind them through the opening in the wall and made sure there was enough light for them to return to the camp through the tunnel. Then, as Ox disappeared with Seraphina along the underground passage, he turned and stared at the gaping hole in the wall. *We're going to have to do something about this hole, or our secret camp is at risk!* He thought.

He began to mix some water from his drinking flask with the powdered rock laying around on the floor, to use it as a mortar to patch up the hole in the wall. *In a couple of hours, it should be dry, and no one will be any the wiser unless they know exactly where to strike the wall!* He thought. *However, I'm genuinely concerned at the length of time it'll take me to complete this task!*

Suddenly, he sensed a presence behind him and turned to see Kinta and Misty who stood there silently and watched his efforts. Aurak's heart skipped a beat as he realised the danger they were all in if someone discovered these youngsters. *"Please, Miss Kinta, you and Misty must leave immediately and allow me to seal this gaping hole before anyone else arrives!"* he whispered, urgently.

Kinta closed her eyes and held out her hands to gently touch the rock walls on either side of the narrow tunnel. Aurak heard a strange noise and spun around to see that the gaping hole into Seraphina's cell, which he and Ox had taken so long to create, had been completely sealed and restored to its original condition.

"Now, we can all leave!" said Kinta. She giggled, as she and Misty turned and started to skip back down the tunnel.

Aurak shook his head, turned and followed as they headed for the camp. His mouth still gaped wide open in amazement at what he had just seen.

...oooOooo...

Vylaine stood still on the sandy shore. She stared forlornly at the small dhow sailing boat, as the lateen sail filled with wind and leaned into the breeze as it started to gather speed to exit the harbour rapidly. She couldn't believe that, despite her best efforts to convince them otherwise, the delegates from Wachile, Eshoram, and Nantgarw couldn't, or most likely wouldn't, agree to an alliance with her.

In fact, they had all laughed at her!

The little sailing boat was now travelling quite fast, with a long foaming wake creaming out behind. It silently approached the rock wall entrance to spirit away the uncooperative delegates. She had offered each of them abundant riches, threatened them with sanctions and invasion, even offered herself; every option that she could consider, but to no avail.

Despite her best efforts to cajole them, embarrass them, even belittle them, they had expressed no interest to partner with her in the destruction and pillage of Skargness, as she stripped it bare. *They will most definitely regret this!* She thought angrily. She scowled at the back of the boat as it quickly disappeared.

Then, she flicked the thick braided cord of her long, glossy, plaited black hair back over her shoulder and spun on her heel. Vylaine replaced the scarf over her face and head to cover her identity, then strode briskly back to the royal carriage to begin the long dusty journey back to the palace.

The coachmen closed the door behind her as she settled into the soft leather seat. Then they moved off and gathered pace quickly.

...oooOooo...

Kinta was still a little perplexed as she tried to get her head around this whole new experience of Misty being able to change into anything that the situation warranted. Her parents now knew and accepted that Misty was more than just her pet.

When they had discussed their plans to conduct a daily reconnaissance mission with Aedyn this morning and obtained his permission, Misty had morphed into an enormous golden eagle, with large round black eyes and long sharp golden beak and claws.

They had left to begin their first mission after they finished a hearty breakfast. Kinta now sat up precariously on her back, with her arms and legs clasped tightly around Misty's large feathery neck.

She leaned forward slightly to escape the large flapping wings. She had worn her full leather armoured outfit and boots but had also included a thick fleece-lined leather jacket and woollen gloves. Kinta's clothing choice was to protect against the bitterly cold temperatures at the heights at which they now travelled, and now she was very grateful for those choices.

They now flew very high over the countryside and made giant lazy looping circles through the air, as they observed troop numbers, movements, and positions to report back to Aedyn. From the ground, they appeared to be just another sizeable predatory bird looking for prey.

Suddenly, way down below them, Kinta noticed a large cloud of dust that rose from a carriage which passed along the main road to the palace and hung suspended in the warm afternoon air through the trees.

She leaned forward to speak with Misty, and they flared out and settled gently onto a ragged rocky peak, high above the valley floor. "Look Misty, if I'm not mistaken, that's the evil bitch returning to the palace in her carriage!" said Kinta. She pointed to the dust cloud way down below.

Misty turned her head back to answer Kinta so her voice wouldn't be lost to the blustery, forceful wind as the thermals rushed up the rockface and ruffled the feathers on her chest and neck. "We must be swift in our mission today then, so we can get this information back promptly to our camp and advise Papa before tonight's War Council meeting!" she said.

Kinta leaned herself forward and tightened her grip around the large feathery neck again. Misty gathered herself up and launched herself off the rocky peak. Then her vast golden wings began to slowly beat faster until she extended them out entirely into a glide. The sharp jagged rock face went past in a blur. Kinta felt the icy cold wind as it blasted into her face and clung on tightly as they dropped swiftly through the air and quickly gathered speed.

Suddenly, Misty felt the extremely sensitive feathers at the very tip of her right wing being gently ruffled by the updraught of a significant rising thermal and turned into the lifting airstream. Immediately, they began to spiral up again into the cold, clear mountain air. They gathered altitude rapidly as they turned toward the mountains in the north and followed the carriage back along the dusty road towards the palace.

At the same time as the priestess's carriage arrived at the palace gates, they passed silently over the top of the palace. Then Mist and Kinta dropped into the hidden valley behind the mountain and entered Libertas.

CHAPTER 25

Narchis squinted and strained his eyes to peer out through the dense verdant foliage of the vines and creepers that covered the opening of the tunnel. He conducted his daily observations of activities in the valley below them.

In the valley below the royal palace that stretched away to the sea, he could make out the faint white plumes of smoke that rose into the crystal-clear blue sky from the burnt remains of the razed villages in the distance. He could also see the dense clouds of dust that billowed out from behind the horses, carts, and boots of the soldiers, as they slowly made their way and trudged along the open country roads to the next village. *Once again, our warriors have ensured that the soldiers have been deprived of their captives and spoils!* He thought. *I wonder how much longer before Vylaine decides to change this useless strategy that she is pursuing?*

Then, suddenly, Narchis caught the glint of sunlight as it reflected off gilded metal. As he shifted his focus, he could see the royal carriage as it made its way out of the forest below and started the short, curved climb up the gentle rise to the castle entrance. He knew that King Daemon was still meant to be away for some time yet while he visited the neighbouring countries, so it could only be Vylaine as she returned from her visit to Bayville.

This situation might be the window of opportunity for which they had waited. Slowly, to ensure he made no noise or sudden movement,

Narchis eased away from the tunnel opening and started back towards the camp.

...oooOooo...

Aedyn sat there quietly and leaned forward, as he mentally focused and listened intently to Seraphina while she sat demurely on his large, soft couch. Her head hung down onto her chest, shoulders slumped forward, and hands clasped loosely together in her lap.

She had spent the past hour to explain in lurid, minute detail, and in between frequent sobs, the mind-numbing, spirit-sapping, harrowing ordeal she had recently been through at Vylaine's hands. The specifics caused Aedyn to wince at the absolute and unmitigated evil of Vylaine.

At Aedyn's gentle insistence, Catelyn had willingly joined them on the couch. She now sat with one arm draped around Seraphina's drooped shoulders, using her other hand to gently stroke her hair and comfort her as she held her hand.

The more of the incredibly mentally disturbed tale that he heard, the more Aedyn fumed and raged inwardly. He silently vowed that Vylaine would be made to pay dearly for all the horrible things that she had done to the innocent people she had dragged into her dungeon for her own needs.

"...And, I'm absolutely certain that, if your wonderful men hadn't arrived when they did, I'd still be laying naked in that awful place, terrified and dreading her return!" said Seraphina. Another small tear escaped and trickled down her face.

Aedyn reached out and took Seraphina's small delicate hand in one of his large rough, calloused hands. Then he slowly leaned forward and used the tips of the fingers on his other hand to gently lift her chin and gaze into her eyes. "I can personally guarantee, you're absolutely safe from Vylaine now!" he said, reassuringly. "And, you may be pleased to know, we're almost ready to begin a retaliatory operation to take back our land!"

Seraphina quickly sat back, bolt upright, as she drew immense inner comfort from Aedyn's reassuring words and Catelyn's comforting arm. She hurriedly wiped away her errant tears on the back of her other spare hand. "Please, just call me Sera!" she said. Seraphina smiled with a force that surprised even herself. "And, please just let me know if there is anything at all that I can do to be of personal assistance!"

Aedyn sat back sharply, dropped Seraphina's hand in surprise, and began to chuckle heartily at the sudden change in Seraphina's demeanour now that she could finally accept that she was in safe hands. "Well, Sera!" said Aedyn, as he smiled broadly. "Since you've asked so very nicely, we really do need to know the layout of the palace complex a little better for our planning, if you please?"

Seraphina smiled warmly back, reached forward and again gripped Aedyn's hand tightly. Then, as she looked deeply into his eyes, Seraphina knew that what was there seemed like a very safe place where she could feel comfortable just to be herself. "It'll be my pleasure, kind Sir!" she said and giggled like a teenage girl.

Now that she needed no further encouragement, and as she tried desperately to please her new-found friends, Seraphina began to describe again in minute detail, the various levels, towers and wings that had been added slowly over the years since the original castle was built on the site.

"...And, the final officially sanctioned addition to the buildings was the supposed Temple that Vylaine added when she came to stay!" she concluded. "It was Vylaine who was responsible for the construction of the secret dungeons beneath the Temple complex!" she said, as she fumed angrily. "I now know, from personal experience, that this structure was simply to provide a covert location for that evil bitch to keep her disgusting Dark Angel pets, torture innocent souls and practice her black magic!" Seraphina sat slowly back, closed her eyes tightly and shuddered uncontrollably at the recent vivid memory.

Aedyn leaned forward, tenderly retook her hand into his and gave it a gentle squeeze. "Thank you so much, Sera! That detailed information will be critical to our success over the next few days!" he said soothingly. "Now, you can just relax and try to forget what you've had to endure for the past few weeks!"

Catelyn used both arms to hug Seraphina's shoulders as Seraphina gently squeezed Aedyn's hand. With her other hand, Seraphina reached up and gripped Catelyn's forearm, to also thank her for the caring support she had provided. "Thank you, both of you, from the bottom of my heart!" she said. Emotion quivered in her voice. "I can never truly remember anybody really caring for '*just me*'!" she explained. "Just caring for '*who*' I am, and not for '*what*' I am!"

Aedyn carefully used his spare hand to release Seraphina's hand tenderly from his. Then he placed her hand back gently into her lap and leaned back into his seat. "Sera, this may be your first real chance just to be 'you'!" he said warmly. "I can assure you; you can totally relax in the knowledge that you are among true friends who deeply care for you and will protect you from all danger!"

Seraphina gripped Catelyn's forearm with both her hands and turned to look deeply into her eyes. "Catelyn, please promise that you'll tell me if, and when, I get out of line?" she pleaded. "I'm getting to like who I am when I'm with the two of you, and I don't want to go back to being who I was!"

Catelyn slowly stood up, took Seraphina's hand into hers and helped her to rise. Then, she placed her hands lightly upon Seraphina's shoulders, gazed directly into her eyes and spoke gently. "Sera, I promise to be the best friend you could ever have!" she said tenderly with emotion. "One whom you will be proud to call your friend and will keep you honest to yourself!"

Then, the two women embraced warmly, as they squeezed each other tightly for several minutes before they broke apart, then each dabbed gently at the drops of moisture that had begun to form in their eyes.

Aedyn stood and tenderly placed his strong, muscular arms around the shoulders of both women, turned them carefully around and gently steered them towards the door. "Okay, Ladies!" he said and chuckled. "Please, allow me to take you both down to the Tavern for something to eat and a celebratory drink!"

"Now, that sounds like fun!" the two women answered together, simultaneously. Then all three began to laugh and headed off down the path towards the Tavern, locked together arm-in-arm.

...oooOooo...

Frustration had gradually begun to take its damaging toll on both him and his men. Captain Stratgii, the Captain of the House Guard, could not believe his eyes as his men started to return empty-handed once again.

It was the third such village in the past couple of weeks that his squad had entered. To their complete surprise, they found them totally empty with no signs of the previous habitation left behind to indicate anyone had ever lived there, adult or child.

It was as if someone had just snapped their fingers and every single person, including everything they had owned, had just merely disappeared into thin air. He was really beginning to dread to have to report this constant lack of results to the high priestess.

As he squatted down carefully onto his beefy haunches, then slowly and deliberately stroked his heavily bearded chin, the Captain cogitated and deeply pondered the many possible reasons behind this. *Where can they possibly have gone?* He thought. He questioned and reflected on every move and decision recently made, as his Corporal returned and stood rigidly to attention in front of him, *And, how can we possibly have missed them?*

"Captain, there's absolutely nothing here!" said his Corporal, as he shook his head in total disbelief. "We've searched every building and can't even find evidence that anyone has ever lived here! Even more mysterious, Sir, there is absolutely no sign of any tracks leading into or away from the village, either! Surely they can't just have simply vanished into thin air!"

The Captain stood up slowly and turned to the Corporal. "Follow me!" he said brusquely.

The two men began to stroll from house to house and look carefully for any possible sign of occupation. But, after several identical empty shells, the Captain suddenly spun on his heels and headed for his horse.

"Get everyone back into the wagons!" he shouted to the Corporal. "We're heading out to the next village immediately!"

There was one single thought that persisted. What on earth am I going to tell the high priestess?

CHAPTER 26

"C'mon folks, let's speed things along!" shouted Laytn at the top of his voice. "It's time to hit the trail quickly and quietly before the soldiers arrive!" The hustle and bustle of activity had reached fever pitch as both rebel warriors and villagers hurried back and forth.

They carried everything from furniture, clothing, food items, even children's toys, as they rapidly vacated the houses. And, around and among all this activity, young children laughed and ran after each other in the air of excitement.

Laytn carefully cast his trained and experienced eyes across the entire length of the ragged convoy of makeshift wagons. They were laden until they overflowed with the heaped contents of the villagers' huts.

Everything that they owned had been salvaged and stacked into the wagons. It was to allow for a much speedier relocation to Libertas for the villagers and to frustrate the soldiers further. "Let's get those first few fully loaded wagons moving!" he shouted to the front of the convoy.

Suddenly, there was a rapidly ramped-up increase in the ambient audible level of noise and swirling clouds of dust. Bullock whips cracked, oxen bellowed, and drivers began to yell and curse at their teams to get them to move. The displaced and disgruntled villagers formed up into small grouped gatherings of families and friends. Then they trailed along on foot beside the wagons, which held all their belongings.

Across the whole convoy hung an abject air of despair as the vacated village began to rapidly empty. Choking clouds of dust, kicked up by the straining oxen, began to swirl around the wagon wheels. Children suddenly realised what had happened and started to cry at having to leave the comfort of their homes.

Then, the muffled sounds of frantic activity began to subside slowly, as the last of the villagers and wagons disappeared out of sight. They were quietly led away to Libertas by Aedyn's men via secret tracks through the forest.

Meanwhile, Laytn's team of trained men were bustling as they attempted to eliminate all apparent signs of their movements. They began at the huts and slowly worked their way into the forest, and gently brushed the soft, dusty ground with leafy tree branches. Then, as silent as a mouse, they also vanished into the surrounding scrub. Apart from a few faint wisps of dust, that persistently hung in the air, there was no evidence that anyone had ever inhabited this once thriving village.

After one final cursory glance, Laytn smiled broadly with satisfaction, then turned and followed his men into the trees.

...oooOooo...

Vylaine smiled smugly to herself. She imagined the intense pleasure she would soon get as she continued to push Seraphina to the limits of her mental stability. Then she carefully inserted the particular metal rod into the hole in the wall and watched the secret panel slide open.

The well-hidden wall slid slowly back with a low rumble and revealed the portal to pleasure and pain. Vylaine stepped through into the entrance to the cold dungeon. "Hello, my little Angels!" she called.

She slipped seductively out of her covering clothes and threw them over the back of the nearest chair before she continued naked into the room. The noise of the Dark Angels as they stirred brought another smile to her face. Vylaine always enjoyed coming down here and provoke them into action.

As she excitedly entered the main chamber, Vylaine glanced around quickly and was soon satisfied that nothing visible appeared to have changed since her last visit. *I love coming down here, away from all the hassles outside!* She thought. She slowly padded across the stone floor and enjoyed the feel of the cold stone on her bare feet.

As she silently approached Seraphina's small solitary cell, Vylaine could feel that familiar sense of personal power over another person. Tiny goosebumps of pleasure suddenly appeared on her arms. She slid back the large heavy metal bolt that locked the sizeable heavy metal door to the cell and smiled as she stepped through the doorway.

Then, suddenly, it felt like someone had physically slapped her as Seraphina had just vanished without a trace.

"Guards!" she screamed at the top of her voice. "Get in here immediately!"

As the sound of running boots began to approach, Vylaine slumped to the floor and stared at the vacant cell. The small cot, with its coarse horse-hair blanket that still covered it, stood against the wall where she had last seen Seraphina as she lay naked and vulnerable.

Completely baffled, Vylaine cast her eyes slowly and carefully around the room, as she scoured every possible detail. Everything seemed unchanged, even down to the small spider webs in the corners of the ceiling.

Then, two guards suddenly appeared behind her in the doorway. They cautiously entered the cell, paused and stood close together as they waited for Vylaine's expected reaction.

...oooOooo...

Catelyn sat quietly in her kitchen. She rested her elbows on the table top with her chin in her hands and stared hard at the piece of paper in front of her. Silently, she contemplated the long, complicated list of instructions that Aedyn had given her.

She had volunteered to assist in whatever capacity possible. Catelyn had been tasked to build and train various teams of women, from the displaced villagers that had come to Libertas. It was necessary to continue to function as a village to support the warriors.

Catelyn concentrated and mentally noted down all the necessary components and requirements of the many various tasks for which she would need to develop teams. Each team of approximately ten women would be held responsible for learning and performing one of the many functions necessary to leave all the men available for military missions.

"Bakery, kitchen, laundry, stables, vegetable gardens…!"

Suddenly, her thoughts were interrupted by a knock on the front door, followed by the sound as the door opened, and soft footsteps approached as Seraphina entered the kitchen. "Can I help, please, please, please?" begged Seraphina. She leaned down and placed her hand gently on Catelyn's shoulder. "I've had more than enough of my share of sitting around doing nothing! I *do* want to be able to personally contribute, in a worthwhile way, to our success!" she said. Then she dropped her chin, tilted her head slightly, raised her eyebrows, and looked out through the top of her eyes in a pleading manner.

Catelyn relaxed, looked up and smiled warmly, then placed a hand over the top of Seraphina's, which was still on her shoulder. "But of course, you can help me, Sera!" she said. She gave Seraphina's hand a gentle rub.

Seraphina slid down beside Catelyn. She briefly touched the back of her hand against Catelyn's cheek in a warm, friendly gesture. "I do value your friendship, Catelyn!" she said. "I truly don't remember the last *real* friend I had!"

Catelyn turned and took Seraphina's hand down from her shoulder. She held it tenderly between both of her own hands and looked warmly into her eyes. "Sera, I am blessed and consider myself very honoured to call you my friend!" she said with emotion. "And, you're more than welcome to join me and assist in planning for this important task! God knows I can use all the help I can get!" She chuckled and looked back down at the list of tasks in her hand.

The two of them smiled and amiably chatted as they turned back to the task at hand. Then, both girls settled down to some serious planning, before they called on the others.

…oooOooo…

Slowly, silently, as he edged himself along sideways, Ox eased his huge body down the narrow vacant lane between the closed buildings off Bayville's main street. He slipped quietly in through the back door of the Tavern.

Immediately, his nose could smell the strong biting aroma of lye soap. Erwyn and Madeleine had used it to scrub down the long wooden tables and bench seats. It was to remove the stains and discolouration from last night's trade. Since it was still very early in the morning, and the Tavern was not open for business yet, Ox knew that there would be no one inside but Erwyn and his daughter Madeleine as they made things ready to open.

Once he was entirely inside the kitchen, he held his breath and stood perfectly still. He silently watched over and through the open bar counter and paid attention to ensure everything was as he had expected. Ox was pleased to see that the large oakwood door at the entrance had been repaired again.

It brought a tender smile to his face as he remembered the last time, he had seen Madeleine here. Erwyn and Madeleine busied themselves in the main dining area with their usual and much-practised routine as they set the clean plates and cutlery into place.

Ox tiptoed slowly and silently across the kitchen. He was extremely quiet for such a large man, but Ox made sure not to startle either of them. He quietly opened the service door and eased his way through into the dining area.

Ox slowly put his finger to his mouth. He was still cautious not to make any sudden moves that would frighten them and raise the alarm. "Shhhhh!" he said, quietly. Erwyn jumped with initial fright. He looked up quickly at the soft sound of Ox's voice.

He immediately froze on the spot at the impressive, frightening sight of the enormous man who stood only a few paces away. Then, he remembered the incident when Ox had saved his precious daughter Madeleine from the filthy clutches of the lecherous Sergeant. He immediately relaxed, and a broad smile spread across his relieved face.

Initially, Madeleine's jaw dropped, and her heart skipped a beat. But she immediately rushed into Ox's arms and wrapped her arms around his ample waist, then squeezed him tightly with her face buried into Ox's chest. She slowly turned her face up to gaze into his eyes. "How did you get here?" she said. Moisture gathered in her eyes at the memory of his capture. "I thought I had seen the last of you when they took you away to the mines!"

Ox's face spontaneously lit up. He smiled down at the beautiful young shining face pressed up against him. Tenderly, he reached down and wiped away an errant escaped teardrop with his fingertip. "No matter how hard they may have tried, they could never keep me from you!" he said. Then, he wrapped his massive arms around her shoulders and squeezed her tightly, which Madeleine returned willingly.

Erwyn completely relaxed after he recovered his composure and took the few paces to reach Ox's side. Then, he reached out and placed his hand on Ox's colossal forearm. "Thank you, my boy!" he said. "How can I ever thank you enough for saving my daughter Madeleine from that animal?"

Ox's face blushed slightly with embarrassment at the heartfelt compliment. He hung his head and shuffled his feet on the hard-packed earthen floor. "Sir, under the circumstances, it was no more than any other gentleman would have done!" said Ox modestly. He looked up and gazed pleadingly into Erwyn's eyes. "However, Sir, I have a personal request for you," he added.

"Anything, my boy!" said Erwyn, as he looked up expectantly.

Ox took a deep breath and stood up straight. He silently prayed that he hadn't misjudged the Tavern owner's appreciation and loyalty. "Sir, I have a safe place where you and Madeleine can come and join me and the others who have escaped from the soldiers and the high priestess!" he said. "But we must leave right now before you have any customers!"

"Please, Papa, can we go with Ox?" pleaded Madeleine. "Our business is drying up rapidly since the soldiers have boycotted our service! We need to do something to survive, in case another soldier decides to try his luck! Or, even worse still, the evil priestess decides to level Bayville in vengeance!"

Erwyn sighed resignedly. He nodded his head slowly in agreement, and his whole body shuddered as he contemplated their fate if Vylaine decided to exact her vengeance upon the people of Bayville. Then, the three of them moved quickly and quietly into the meagre living quarters at the very rear of the building.

They began to quickly gather their possessions and clothing. There was not a lot to pack as they had lived a simple life in the Tavern since Erwyn's wife had run away. Ox helped Madeleine to pack her few possessions into a large travel bag.

Then, he lifted the loosely packed bag onto his massive shoulder and took Madeleine's hand. They walked together into Erwyn's small room just as he was closing his travel bag. "Do you have everything that you need now, Sir?" asked Ox.

"My boy, I have everything that I truly need standing beside you and holding your hand! Everything else is just incidental!" Erwyn replied emotionally. Moisture had welled in his eyes at the thought of closing the Tavern, which was his last grip on some stability. He cast his eyes slowly around the room as if trying to capture some of the memories. "Okay, let's make our hasty escape before we are unable to take this opportunity!"

The two men walked out into the lane with Madeleine between them and headed quickly into the surrounding bush behind the street. They disappeared and made their way towards freedom.

CHAPTER 27

$\mathbb{M}$ isty had morphed into a large white horse this morning. Kinta rode her bareback, dressed in her full battle armour and longbow, wholly absorbed as the parade of soldiers and wagons passed in front of her.

The two girls were completely invisible and stood still beneath a sizeable leafy tree beside the dusty road. They watched as the convoy passed slowly by on their way towards the village of Rocky Heights. There were a general mumble and mutter of discontent among the soldiers that regarded their displeasure at the lack of tangible results.

They passed slowly on their way to the next site, which was being covertly overheard by Kinta and Misty. A large choking cloud of finely powdered dust hung suspended in the unmoving air and settled on everything along both sides of the road. It included the two invisible observers as they stood back under cover of the trees.

As the last of the soldiers and wagons passed slowly out of sight around the bend, Misty and Kinta turned slowly and made their way quietly into the surrounding scrub. They were careful not to disturb any of the dust-coated branches and leave a tell-tale indication of their passing.

The dark sky overhead had rapidly filled with huge thunderheads and black storm clouds. They lit up regularly with bright flashes of lightning, which made the air thick with humidity and charged with electricity.

Kinta rubbed her hand gently along the length of Misty's neck, and gently removed the thick coating of powdered dust that clogged her mane and leaned her upper body forward to speak quietly into her ears. "So far, everything that we've seen and heard indicates that things are already coming to a head!" she said. "The soldiers are becoming more frustrated by Papa's tactics, and this is making Vylaine angrier!"

Misty shook her sizeable white head and shaggy mane and whinnied quietly. "That's what worries me … Vylaine becomes unpredictable when she's angry!" she said. "I think it's time to up the ante!"

With that, the two girls began their meandering trip back home. They strolled along the hidden back trails to Veritas that they had followed on their way to intercept the convoy. Kinta's personally designed light-weight warrior outfit included a pair of thin, skin-tight, soft leather pants, and her legs straddled Misty's bare back caused the material of her pants to pull up tightly into her crutch.

It formed a virtual second skin across her sensitive female parts. Misty's slowly ambling walking gait caused a regular constant back and forth rocking motion of Kinta's hips. The subsequent continuous rubbing of her thinly covered sensitive crutch against the bony ridge of Misty's spine could be felt through the soft leather pants.

After several pleasurable minutes of this regular rocking motion, Kinta noticed an unusual, but not unpleasant, warm tingling sensation began to develop between her legs and spread quickly up into her lower belly. She gently leaned her upper body slightly forward to apply more focused pressure to her super sensitive crutch from the bony ridge of Misty's horse backbone. Instantly, she had to suddenly bite her lip to prevent a soft moan escaping as the intensely focused point of pleasure in her groin heightened immediately.

As the continuous pleasurable stimulation to her now highly aroused female parts continued, Kinta began to feel an unfamiliar warm sticky moistness develop within her. When she glanced down quickly, she saw an emerging damp patch in the crutch of her soft tight leather pants.

Then, suddenly, and entirely beyond her control, Kinta experienced the shuddering spasm of her first orgasmic release. It caused her back to arch involuntarily and her legs to suddenly clamp down tightly around Misty's girth. Misty thought she merely wanted to go faster and responded accordingly.

The sudden increased change in pace made Kinta clamp down firmer again with her legs. The increased gait and constant rubbing caused multiple orgasms to continue for quite some time along the trails.

Kinta's self-awareness had indeed awakened today, and she felt slightly flushed and pleasantly exhausted. They finally arrived back at Libertas, and she climbed off Misty's back and changed back into her dress.

However, when she alighted from Misty, her legs were still a little shaky and felt like they consisted of jelly. The short walk back to the Tavern to report to Aedyn today was slower than usual.

...oooOooo...

Aedyn closed his eyes to avoid the blinding flash of lightning that cracked across the summer sky. Immediately afterwards, what followed was a massive clap of thunder that exploded overhead and rolled away down the valley.

The sudden summer storm had come up very quickly and would probably disappear just as quickly. It was normal for this time of year, but the raw violence never ceased to amaze Aedyn. Dark, ominous clouds had rapidly built overhead all afternoon and had closed in over the valley. It caused the sunlight to disappear virtually and brought apparent early nightfall.

Then, suddenly, the skies opened, and huge drops of rain began to fall with a fury, which drove into his face and body with a force that made Aedyn sprint the final few steps to the cover of the Tavern. Once inside, he shook the raindrops from his hair and clothes. He made his way through the warmly welcoming crowd, as he headed towards the back of the room.

Just then, Narchis sidled up beside him out of the shadows at the side of the room. The slightest hint of a smile, that unfortunately appeared as almost a grimace of pain on Narchis's face was a clear and obvious indicator that he bore good news and couldn't wait to pass it on. "Aedyn, Sir, the evil priestess is arriving at the palace as we speak," he said out of the corner of his mouth.

He always spoke without moving his lips, and so quietly that Aedyn had to lean closer and concentrate on catching the words. "I have just come from the secret tunnel, and her carriage had just cleared the woods down below!" Narchis added. "She should be back inside the palace by now!"

As the two men finished whispering together, Aedyn reached his destination at the back of the room. He turned to face Narchis, to extend his thanks for the covertly gathered intelligence. Aedyn glanced around quickly in every direction, but Narchis had vanished and was now invisible.

Although his face showed surprise initially, Aedyn then relaxed and broke into a broad grin as he anticipated the next stage of their strategy. "*Thank you, Narchis! That information is much appreciated!*" he said quietly and conspiratorially to himself.

Aedyn found an empty table in a discretely secluded corner, where he plopped himself down in a chair with his back to the wall. From there, he could keep an eye on the comings and goings of the patrons. *We are now just a couple of days away from launching our offensive!* He thought. *Let's pray that nothing arises to interfere with our plans!*

He was roused from his thoughts by a beautiful young blond woman who stood in front of his table. She wore the unofficial Tavern maid's uniform of frilly, sleeveless, v-fronted white top, with a dark skirt and white apron. She held a full frosty tankard of cold frothy ale and waited for him to notice her.

She appeared to be about the same age as Kinta but had physically matured earlier. Despite her slim body, she comfortably and curvaceously filled out the uniform, and she seemed trained and familiar in the role of Tavern maid.

Aedyn smiled warmly and nodded his acknowledgement of her presence. He wondered how recently she had arrived at Libertas since he didn't recognise her as one of their regular Tavern maids.

The young woman stepped forward and placed the beer mug gently but firmly onto the table in front of Aedyn. Then she curtsied and introduced herself. "Excuse me, Sir!" she said quietly and bashfully. "My name is Madeleine, and I arrived today with my Papa and Ox! We owned and ran the Bayville Tavern until today! Ox has arranged for my Papa and me to work here at this Tavern, and that's my Papa behind the bar!" she added. Madeleine pointed at the bar, then blushed and slightly tilted her head. "Ox insisted that I deliver the tankard in person and introduce myself!"

"In that case, I'm delighted to meet you, Madeleine!" said Aedyn. He smiled and extended his hand. Madeleine blushed enormously at the unexpected friendly gesture. She reached forward and timidly shook Aedyn's hand. This warm reassurance was enough to suppress her anxiety, and she smiled warmly back. "Welcome to Libertas, and please thank Ox for the cold refreshing ale!" said Aedyn.

Suddenly, there was a considerable commotion in the crowded room. Kinta and Misty entered through the front door and tried to make their way hastily towards the back, where he was seated. Immediately, the level of ambient background noise in the room quickly rose to a disorderly din. Everyone left their seats and rushed to intercept them as they tried to say their welcome to their two favourite youngsters.

Madeleine excused herself politely from Aedyn's presence, then turned on her heel. She thankfully used the distraction as her welcome cover to escape quickly back to the other side of the room. Then she promptly collected another order from the bar to deliver to the crowded tables.

Laughing, waving, and chatting cheerily and effortlessly with everyone as they passed, Kinta and Misty finally managed to cross the room and reached Aedyn's table, where they sat down in the chairs opposite him. "Good evening, Papa!" Kinta greeted him. Misty jumped up onto the bench seat beside her. She stood on her hind legs with her front legs on the edge of the table so that she could see Aedyn. "Misty and I have much to report!"

Aedyn smiled his warm welcome to them both and leaned forward to speak softly. *"Good evening to you both, my young intrepid scouts! What news do you bring me tonight?"* he asked quietly.

Kinta took a deep breath and whispered her reply. *"Papa, the evil bitch, has returned to her palace!"* she said quietly. *"But, more importantly, all deployed army troops are now at very distant positions near our country's borders, which means it will take the maximum time for them to possibly return to assist!"*

Aedyn leaned back in his seat, and his shoulders slightly sagged as he relaxed visibly before he replied to this heart-warming news. *"That is indeed great news! I am very proud of both of you girls and the scouting work you have done for us!"* he said. *"I cannot thank you enough for the huge effort you have both put in over the past couple of weeks! I definitely would not feel as comfortable in launching our offensive, without knowing that information!"*

He glanced up at the bar and indicated for two cold, refreshing drinks for the girls. Then the three of them chatted easily about the day's events while they waited for their drinks to arrive.

CHAPTER 28

Vylaine sat quietly and listened as the thunder rolled overhead outside and she stared into the crackling yellow flames in the fireplace. The summer storm had made the air oppressively humid in the stone-walled rooms of the castle.

However, the heavy rainfall outside made it impossible to seek relief in the fresh air as she usually chose. It added to and fuelled her bad temper as she considered the various military options that were still available to her. *I cannot afford to attack any of my neighbouring countries yet, or I'll leave no protection here at home!* She thought. *On the other hand, I have already invited them in to help me overthrow the rebels from within, and they have refused!*

The cozy warmth in the room and the hypnotic flicker of the flames made her sleepy. It caused her chin to drop onto her chest, and her tired eyes began to sag closed slowly. *I wish Daemon would return so that I could discuss this with him!* She thought to herself. *My only workable solution is to use my forces to scour the country and find the rebels so that we can destroy them once and for all!*

Her drowsiness had made cognitive thought nigh on impossible, but she had persisted regardless. She sat back and pondered her chosen solution for some considerable time before she finally rose. As she stood, the sound of the heavy rainfall outside suddenly ceased. The sudden absolute silence was almost deafening.

Then she stretched her arms back over her head, stood up, and headed for the stone staircase that leads to the upper reaches of the castle. "I desperately need to get some fresh air!" she said out loud to herself. She slowly began to climb the long spiral stone staircase.

...oooOooo...

It was as if someone had deliberately drawn back the close-at-hand dark concealing curtains. The light balmy breeze blew the last scattered remnants of the sultry storm clouds away, and the dazzling carpet of twinkling stars emerged. Madeleine snuggled up closer to Ox, and leaned her head against his chest, as he placed his massive arm around her shoulders.

They sat cuddled close together as they looked up at the glittering black canopy. The ebony night sky looked like a soft black velvet sheet covered with millions of tiny sparkling diamonds. Each glittered with an inner fire and resembled a frozen veil of fireflies. *"Compared to other nights, there are so many stars visible tonight that it looks like they won't all fit into the sky!"* whispered Madeleine. *"It's such a beautiful night …"* Her voice trailed off as if she had no words to describe the glorious vista overhead.

Just then, a brilliant shooting star blazed right across the sky with a flash. It left a bright shower of sparks before suddenly it blinked out. "Go ahead! Make a wish!" said Ox gently and squeezed Madeleine's shoulders.

Madeleine closed her eyes and concentrated for a minute. "I wish I may, I wish I might have my wish come true tonight!" she said and snuggled up closer still.

Ox turned his head to look down into the upturned face of Madeleine. His heart felt as if it would burst open, like a ripe melon. "My sweet, if it's at all within my power, I'll do whatever is necessary to make your wish come true!" he said gently.

"I know!" said Madeleine emotionally and picked up his huge hand in both of hers, then she placed it in her lap. "And, that's why I love you so much, my darling!"

They both continued to sit there with their separate thoughts, but one thing was abundantly clear. These two were very much in love!

...oooOooo...

Misty stretched herself out, lounged languidly on the blanket at the very foot of their shared bed and lovingly watched, as Kinta slept on soundly with the peaceful innocence sometimes only reserved for and found in the youth.

A cloud of soft, fluffy, golden curls frothed out onto her pillow. It framed Kinta's angelic face and formed a halo in the silver moonlit beams that streamed in through the window and added to the overall image of her wholesomeness.

Her chest rose and fell gently and rhythmically with her breathing. The firm round mounds of Kinta's young breasts tugged and strained at the flimsy nightdress and created mayhem within the material. Her recently developed nipples stood up proud and erect in the slight chill of the night air.

Kinta's long, lean, coltish-legs lay fully outstretched and almost reached all the way down to where Misty lay. It seemed like it wouldn't be too much longer before there wasn't room enough for them both on the bed. Misty shuffled up the bed until she could snuggle beside Kinta's back for warmth against the cold.

In the crystal-clear clarity of Misty's mind's eye, she could already envision the great and heroic deeds that her beautiful young friend, Kinta, would perform in the future, as the rest of her life unfolded. *Sleep well, my pretty princess!* Misty thought. *We need you all grown up and healthy so your true destiny can be fulfilled!*

Then, as she slowly closed her tired, drooping eyes, Misty allowed herself to relax and drift away into the unfettered, untroubled sleep of the pure at heart.

...oooOooo...

In the dark, ebony, blackness of pre-dawn, Aedyn picked his way slowly along the narrow, slippery path, up the steep rocky cliff.

He had chosen this time so he would not be seen from the castle battlements and windows beneath him.

Each step had to be exceptionally carefully selected, and his foot placed down precisely. He didn't want to slip on the damp mossy ground or disturb the small loose rocks and cause them to tumble noisily down onto the roof of the castle below.

On several especially tricky occasions, Aedyn specifically stopped himself, paused and then carefully leaned down to delicately and deliberately remove a small stick or loose stone. It could have caused him to slip if it had moved under his feet.

Eventually, after several gruelling hours, he reached the place he and Laytn had selected the previous day. From here he should be able to see and hear any activity below him in the castle grounds, but without being seen himself.

After he had adequately ensured that this position would work, Aedyn settled his weary body gently back into a shallow hollow between the rocks. Then he shuffled the location of his arms and legs until he became comfortable for his extended stay. The irregularly-shaped, different-coloured, dusty stripes and smudges, placed on his khaki-coloured clothes by Azrael, acted as active camouflage. It allowed him to blend inconspicuously into the background. From even a relatively short distance, Aedyn was virtually invisible as he sat completely motionless among the rocky recesses on the narrow ledge that overlooked the royal castle, which was immediately below him.

Overhead, the bright, cloudless sky slowly changed colour from purple to pink and through to orange. The sun eventually peeked out from below the eastern horizon off in the distance and painted everything in a golden glow. His proposed plan was to spend all the available daylight hours as he observed staff movements within the castle grounds below.

It was aimed to help him to determine the approximate number of inhabitants and the schedules they regularly followed. It was vitally important to have the best knowledge possible before they launched their assault on the high priestess. If he could determine the usual routines, such as staff shift changeover times, it would allow for more accurate timing of the battle that would shortly ensue.

He drew in a long, deep breath and held it. Eventually, Aedyn exhaled slowly, as he tried to erase the images from his head of what would, or could, happen if they remained unprepared when they launched their offensive.

Although he had heartily laughed yesterday afternoon when Narchis had given him a straw hat with various small branches woven into it, Aedyn had now begun to understand the real merit in wearing it as the sun started to seriously heat up. Besides, although it added to his already effective camouflage, he would be forever grateful later in the long hot day for the cool shade and protection for his face it had already begun to provide.

The day slowly wore on and, from the vital information he had gathered, Aedyn was sufficiently satisfied that he had been in the perfect position to see all the activities below. As he gazed down onto the giant stony edifice below, the sporadic comings and goings across the smooth stone walkways kept him interested.

But, up until now, he still hadn't seen Vylaine. Aedyn was cautiously concerned that, if he didn't get to see Vylaine, he couldn't be sure exactly what her daily schedule was, or where she was most likely to be at any time of the day.

Then, on perfect cue, as if she had read his mind, Vylaine eventually emerged from the Western Tower and made her way out onto the battlements that overlooked the vast valley below the royal palace. Aedyn could smell the acrid smoke in the air from the remains of several nearby villages. He felt the anger rise in his throat like hot bile. But he fought to hold it back and control his breath so he could hear anything that may be said.

To his absolute disappointment, Vylaine didn't make a single sound. She slowly padded barefoot across the stone surface before she stopped and removed the large scarf that covered her face and head. Then, she merely stood there stock still, like a statue carved from stone. She had her bare arms outstretched and long unbraided black hair that blew freely in the breeze, as she stared into the distance.

Suddenly curious, Aedyn shifted his gaze and looked down into the valley in the direction that Vylaine continued to stare. At various points along the base of the bordering mountains on each side of the valley, the smoky tendrils still drifted up into the clear blue sky and were a sombre reminder of yesterday's attacks.

In that very moment, Aedyn knew without a shadow of a doubt that it was his ultimate responsibility alone, and he could be held personally accountable, to ensure the removal of Vylaine. It was the only course open to him, which would then allow peace and stability to return to the land.

As he glared down at his raven-haired nemesis, Vylaine suddenly spun on her heel and headed back into the Western Tower, as she wrapped the large scarf around her head and face as she walked. Aedyn continued to stare long and hard at the place where she had disappeared. Then, once again, he settled back into mundane activity as he counted the details of staff movements.

CHAPTER 29

The delightfully delicious aromatic aroma of hearty and healthy soup bubbled and brewed in a large black metal pot, which hung over a crackling fireplace in the hearth. It was all-pervasive, and the smell reached out far beyond the cloistered confines of the small wooden hut.

After spending the day on the side of the mountain exposed to the elements, motionless and unable to move, Aedyn's appetite seemed almost insatiable. He was extremely grateful for their timely invitation to join Seraphina this evening.

Seraphina reached in and sprinkled a handful of fresh basil into the bubbling brew, courtesy of Catelyn's garden. She gave the mixture a slow, gentle stir before she replaced the heavy metal lid onto the pot and turned back to face her guests. "Thank you, Catelyn!" she said. "I'll be eternally grateful that you were able to teach me how to cook such delicious food!"

"It's my pleasure!" Catelyn said. She laughed, then glanced up to watch Seraphina. "We couldn't allow you to starve, could we?" she chuckled.

Aedyn grinned broadly, reached down and took Catelyn's hand tenderly into his. Then he placed his other arm lovingly around her shoulders. "Sera, you will be quite the Domestic Goddess before long, if you continue to learn all these new skills from Catelyn!" he said and chuckled.

Seraphina and Catelyn looked knowingly at each other and giggled. Then Catelyn gave Aedyn's hand a little squeeze, turned and looked up seductively into his face. "It's not just Sera learning from me!" she explained. "We've both been exchanging lots of girly information during our time together! It's been a bit of an eye-opener for both of us!" The two women giggled together conspiratorially again.

Kinta and Misty glanced at each other, rolled their eyes and shrugged. Then they settled down close together on a mat on the floor.

Seraphina came back over from the fireplace and sat down on an armchair that faced Aedyn and Catelyn on the couch. "I'm so glad we could all get together tonight because I've been thinking long and hard about our situation!" she said. It was her way of opening the serious conversation she had wanted to have for a couple of days now. "I wanted the opportunity to openly and freely explain my decision, when we were all together, as I think it's important that you all know exactly how I feel, in here!" she went on, and patted her chest.

Seraphina glanced briefly at each of her special guests in turn, and then she leaned forward in her seat. She took Aedyn's hand gently in hers and looked directly into his eyes as she spoke with raw, unbridled passion. "I know, without a shadow of a doubt, that I would still be trapped in that cell as Vylaine's plaything, or worse still, dead now if you hadn't arranged for my rescue!" she said.

Aedyn made as if to speak. But Catelyn placed her hand gently on his arm and indicated for him to allow Seraphina to finish.

Moisture welled up into Seraphina's eyes. A large teardrop escaped and slid slowly down her face, which she made no effort to wipe away. "After *many* days of careful and thoughtful deliberation, I have decided to abdicate the throne ... and I would like you, Aedyn, to take over the monarchy and leadership of our country!" she continued.

The emotion of her decision was evident on her face. "I have absolutely no doubt that you and your amazing band of rebels will be victorious in the upcoming battle!" she said. "And, I also know that I don't want Daemon to regain the throne, regardless of the outcome! During my incarceration at the hands of Vylaine, I gained some wonderful insight into my strengths and weaknesses, and now I know categorically that I'm not suited for that role!"

She went on. "I've seen your natural leadership qualities and, *I believe*, there's nobody better suited than you to take the reins and rebuild our country back to its former glory again!" she continued. "And, please don't argue with me, my dearest Aedyn, as my mind has now been completely made up!" she said firmly. She settled back into the seat and began to dab gently at her eyes.

From being slightly distracted as she stroked Misty's fur, Kinta's head snapped sharply around to look up lovingly at her father, and she felt her heart almost burst with pride as she fully realised what Seraphina had just said.

Aedyn turned to look at Catelyn, and they exchanged a knowing look. He instantly knew what to say as he turned back to Seraphina and smiled, paused and drew a deep breath before he answered. "I speak for all of us when I say *we* would be honoured to accept your decision, Seraphina!" he said. He extended his arms to include his entire family group. "However, I feel it's strategically important that we keep this just between ourselves until this whole Vylaine mess has been dealt with fully!"

Seraphina relaxed as she smiled. She leaned forward and took both Aedyn's and Catelyn's hands into hers. "I agree!" she said. She pulled them both towards her and kissed each of them on the cheek. "Now, let me give you each some of that delicious soup!" she laughed with relief. She stood to begin to prepare the table for their meal.

Kinta and Misty turned and looked at each other with a huge grin. Kinta scrunched up her nose and hunched her shoulders slightly, as young girls have been known to do when showing suppressed excitement.

...oooOooo...

The clang of the many metal swords upon other metal swords, and the constant whine, zing and thump of arrows, were almost drowned out by the shouts and grunts of men's voices. They rang out loud across the valley as they vigorously practised their fighting skills.

From their elevated position on top of a large rock, Aedyn and Azrael cast their experienced eyes across the writhing field of bodies. They looked for any visible signs of weakness that might spell disaster to their planned offensive.

It was definitely dangerous work and not considered a game!

The more realistic they made this practice, the more likely they were to survive the battles that lay ahead of them. Aedyn had asked Azrael to use his previous soldier's background to prepare a training regime and assist with the training. "Compared to where they began, our warriors are becoming so good at combat fighting, I'm pleased they're now on our side and not against us!" chuckled Azrael. He spoke without taking his eyes off the activities in front of him.

Aedyn smiled and said, "We don't want them hurting each other at practice though!" He turned to nod to the man who stood behind him. The man promptly raised a ram's horn to his lips and blew a loud reverberating sound, which echoed out across the valley and brought all the activity to a halt. The tension of battle was immediately gone, and instantly the whole mood changed as the combatants lowered their weapons. The sound of combat became laughter and friendly banter.

Aedyn addressed the men passionately as they gathered around the base of the rock upon which he stood. "I'm very proud to have you as friends, my warrior brothers!" he said "And, over the next few days and weeks, we'll be fighting for our lives and the freedom of our country! I would gladly give my life for you and this cause!" he continued. "However, with you by my side, I know without a doubt that we'll succeed in removing the high priestess and releasing her hold on our land!"

The men erupted into spontaneous cheers and waved their weapons into the air. Then, they slowly dissipated and moved off toward their huts and the chance to relax for a few hours before their lives would change forever.

...oooOooo...

Vylaine stood serenely on the very edge of the stone battlements. She held onto the nearest parapet to support herself, and to stop the dizziness brought on by vertigo. She stared off into the far distance. She always thoroughly enjoyed it when she came up here alone for the fresh air, and the peace and tranquillity it provided after the hustle and bustle of everyday palace life.

Besides, it also allowed her to see the entire lay of the land in the basin of the verdant valley below. It stretched out like a carpet all the way to the thin blue ribbon of the ocean on the far horizon to the South. At several different locations, spotted randomly across the valley, greyish-white smoke rose into the crisp, clear air and became small, wind-blown clouds that drifted across the blue sky overhead.

Vylaine smiled as she realised the smoke was a tell-tale indication that her soldiers were continuing to harass and pursue the villagers, as she had ordered. But then her face took on a quizzical look as she became confused. *I wonder why the soldiers aren't reporting more successes? There is constant evidence of their endeavours in the smoke rising daily! Admittedly, we should have a greater reward for all this effort?*

Slowly, her thoughts turned to more pressing matters. *Whatever happened to Seraphina? How can she have just vanished into thin air?*

Vylaine's face twisted into a grim look as she pondered the perplexing questions. *Should I bring the Palace Guard soldiers home to find her, or continue pursuing the villagers?*

Finding no immediate solution, she shrugged her shoulders, turned and headed back into the tower to start the long climb again down the spiral stone staircase.

CHAPTER 30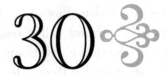

Seraphina sighed, then sauntered across the living room and slumped down into Catelyn's sofa seat. She started to explain the concerns that had been going around in her head for the past few days. "Ever since I was released from my cell, and was brought here to Libertas, I have been worried about Vylaine taking reprisals by capturing my sister or other aristocratic family members!" she said.

At the mere thought of what Vylaine might do to these innocent people, her eyes began to well up with moisture, and a small tear escaped and slowly made its way down her cheek. "I'm not sure I could live with myself if somebody harmed them because of me!" she said and sobbed softly.

Catelyn's heart melted, and she tenderly reached out. She gently took Seraphina's hand in hers, and then she bent forward to look closely into the sad eyes of her friend. "Sera, my dear, you shouldn't worry yourself with these terrible thoughts!" Catelyn said softly. "I'm certain that Aedyn already has plans in place to prevent this from happening!"

Seraphina sniffed and wiped tentatively at her face with her small linen handkerchief to remove the escaping teardrops.

"Now, let me give you a hug!" said Catelyn and gently took her friend into her arms and squeezed comfortingly. Just then, the front door burst open. Misty and Kinta came laughing, skipping and giggling into the room without a single care in the world, as only the young can do in a time of crisis.

...oooOooo...

Aedyn looked up into Ox's huge eyes and placed his hand gently on the big man's massive forearm. The giant man had been humbled by the thoughtful, incredible gift from this fantastic leader.

Ox stood stock still, as he smiled silently, and was just stunned. He admired the incredible talent and amazing, impressive artistry that must have gone into the making of the enormous steel broadsword. With its leather-bound handle, it almost looked like a toothpick in his giant hands. He suddenly shifted his massive weight from one foot to the other and swung the large steel blade viciously. It caused the razor-sharp edge to loudly whistle as it sliced through the air while he tested its balance.

As the adrenaline rushed through his body, a vast booming chuckle developed and then erupted from deep within Ox's barrel chest. It echoed loudly around the whole area as it bounced off the surrounding cliff faces, and he turned to face Aedyn. "Thank you, Aedyn, Sir!" he said. "Now, with this amazing weapon, I truly feel like I can be a *real* warrior standing by your side!"

Aedyn laughed easily, then stepped forward three paces to stand beside Ox. He playfully slapped his giant friend on the back as a show of their comradeship. "You are most welcome my trusted *warrior* friend!" he said. His voice showed some real emotion. "For me 'tis but a simple gift to a great friend! But I'm sure this is something that you will treasure well, and use wisely, as we move forward into the next chapter of our lives!"

Ox effortlessly lifted the huge weapon single-handed over his head. He used the fingers of his other hand to initially place the tip of the blade into the correct position before he slid it silently down and snicked it into place.

His magnificent steel sword now hung in its new heavy leather sheath, which he now wore proudly on his bulging back with the heavy leather straps crossed on his muscular chest. No other man in all the land could even lift the mighty steel blade.

After several successful practices, he could draw and replace the sword and used only one hand with ease. It felt comfortable when locked into its place in the sheath on his back.

"Ox, my great friend, I trust you with my very life, but there is some slight selfishness to my gift!" he said smiling. "Whenever I, or any of my family, leave the relative safety of our hidden valley, I want you and your new sword there beside us as our protector!"

The colossal man visibly puffed up and swelled his chest, then snapped his feet sharply together as he stood rigidly to attention. He slapped his monstrous right fist into a salute on his broad chest. "It'll be my honour and privilege, Sir!" he said. He attempted to look serious and professional, but with the slightest trace of a smile that played at the corners of his mouth.

...oooOooo...

Aedyn squinted his eyes almost closed and raised his hand in front of his face to shield against the bright glare from the recently risen sun. Then he peered out over the calm glistening waters of Bayville's natural harbour towards the rocky entrance.

He had ridden his horse very hard overnight, as he travelled under the discrete cover of darkness to meet the Wachilian Emissary. He would arrive early today, covertly hidden as a crew member on one of their larger, cleaner, off-shore fishing boats.

The two men were to meet for the first time today, and they were going to discuss the possibility of using the many vessels of the Wachilian fishing fleet to help Aedyn's rebel forces escape to safety overseas. It was in the unlikely event that the uprising didn't go according to plan.

Aedyn had the utmost confidence that he and his team had considered every possible contingency during their planning. Although their Plan A was flawless, he wanted a Plan B for security, just in case. The small sheltered cove, in which he now waited patiently, had a large jagged, rocky overhang that extended far out over the small sandy beach. It prevented anyone from being able to see him from above as he paced back and forth along the soft damp sand.

He had taken some considerable time to draw a map by hand, which showed the details of how and where to find the secret cove within the natural harbour. Then he enclosed the map with a note of introduction and invitation that he sent to the Emissary. He now stood in their chosen meeting place.

Aedyn had nervously paced backwards and forwards, up and down the damp, narrow, sandy shore since he had arrived at first light this morning. Now he waited patiently for the Wachilian vessel to appear through the rocky entrance to the harbour and the planned meeting to take place.

Suddenly, as it appeared out of the early morning rising sun, the large white lateen sail of a dhow fishing boat appeared at the entrance to the natural harbour and slipped quietly inside the rocky walls. That was where the large fishing boat slowly glided to a stop as the crew worked quickly and professionally to drop its sails. It now sat and rocked gently, anchored just inside the harbour entrance.

Aedyn kneeled on the soft, damp beach sand and focussed excitedly through his brass telescope. He saw nine of the figures climb into a longboat, eight of them that appeared to be regular sailors. The eight sailors took up the oars to start to row in his direction. The ninth man was a well-dressed, bearded man who sat sternly in the aft end with one hand on the tiller.

Aedyn closed his eyes tightly and slowly lowered the telescope. Then he took a long breath to calm his nerves. He suddenly realised that he had now reached the absolute point of no return. To stay here meant he was committed to an agreement that they made from the time when the rowboat arrived at his secret cove. If this next conversation took place with the Wachilian Emissary, there would be no way to turn back the plans that would already be in motion.

Slowly, but surely, the longboat made its way steadily around the farthest edge of the harbour, while the oars rose and fell, as they gently dipped into the calm, still water. Then it slipped silently and unseen into the hidden cove.

The well-dressed, dignified looking man, with greying hair and a large beard, stepped from the front of the boat as it beached. He walked stiffly up the sandy shore, seemingly unaware of the spreading damp patches on the legs of his trousers. "You must be Aedyn!" he said. He warmly smiled as he approached, then he stuck out his hand in greeting.

Aedyn grasped his guest's hand firmly and responded eagerly. "Good morning, Mr Emissary!" he said. "Welcome to Skargness ... I'm just disappointed it isn't under better circumstances!"

"Please, call me Kieran! All my friends do!" said the Emissary. He gripped Aedyn's hand firmly. Then the two men shook hands, and each of them was instantly aware of the significance of their meeting.

They walked back up the beach away from the water's edge and found a couple of large rocks upon which to settle down. Then they began to discuss the real reason for their meeting while the eight men dressed as sailors stood guard.

Slowly but surely a strong bond of trust was forged between the two leaders of men. "Aedyn, I'm not sure if you know, but Vylaine held a meeting here in Bayville a couple of days ago, with representatives from all your surrounding neighbours!" the Emissary said. "She invited our armies into Skargness to assist in the capture of your rebel band!" he said, with a broad smile and a chuckle. "Unfortunately for Vylaine, she couldn't get anyone to agree!"

Aedyn smiled broadly at the thought of what Vylaine's reaction to this would have been. He became serious again quickly when he realised that this was probably also the reason for the ramped-up activity by the army in the past couple of days. "Thank you for letting me know!" he said, with a small chuckle. "It's a relief to know that we still have friends that will stand by us in our time of need!"

Eventually, after they had spent several long, rewarding hours of detailed strategic planning and discussed their various options, the talks finally came to an end. The two men shook hands again, this time as firm friends.

Aedyn stood and watched as the so-called sailors carefully assisted Kieran to climb safely back into the longboat, without getting any wetter than he already was. Then, they began their slow, arduous journey to row back to the fishing boat.

He remained there on the narrow beach, completely secreted out of sight under the overhanging ledge, while the fishermen rowed slowly and methodically back around the outside of the harbour, so as not to attract attention to themselves. When the longboat full of men eventually arrived back beside the vessel, and everyone was safely back onboard the fishing boat, there was an immediate frantic burst of activity by all.

As he thought back over the discussions of the last couple of hours, he watched admiringly as the disguised deckhands quickly and efficiently raised and set the two large lateen sails and pulled up the heavy anchor. Then the fishing boat slipped silently back out of the harbour and left only a white, foamy, creaming wake to show here it had been.

After all traces of the boat had finally disappeared, Aedyn climbed slowly and carefully back up the rocky path to where his horse waited silently amongst a grove of trees. He continuously checked as he rose up the steps for anyone who may have recognised him.

After he mounted up, he pulled his cloak closed tightly around his shoulders and the hood up over his head to hide his face. Then, with a subtle dig of his heels, they began the long journey back to Libertas and the start of the next phase of their operations.

CHAPTER 31

Kinta drew an arrow from her quiver without having taken her eyes off the target. She carefully notched the shaft onto the drawstring of her massive longbow and slowly eased it back. The many hours of practice had strengthened her lean arm muscles to the point where this was now effortless.

She took careful aim at the distant target, which was made from a piece of paper attached to a straw block. It was mounted at chest height on a tree about thirty paces away from where she and Misty stood. Concentric circles had been drawn on the paper, with the bullseye being in the very centre.

She had taught herself to control her breath and slow her heart rate consciously, so the tip of the arrow didn't move as she stared along the shaft. Now she attempted to judge the speed and direction of the lightly gusting breeze that puffed gently into her face.

She gently released her grip on the arrow. Then she watched as it flew swiftly, and with deadly accuracy, and landed in the exact centre of the target, right alongside another three bolts already there from previous shots.

"You're very accurate with the bow and arrow now!" said Misty. She was very excited and wagged her tail vigorously as she supported her friend. "However, all your target practice so far has been done while you were standing still!" she said. "Now, I think it's time you began to learn how to be just as accurate when either you're moving, or the target is moving!"

"You're right, as always!" Kinta agreed and chuckled. The two of them immediately began to revise their existing training program, to incorporate a range of new advanced skills. The current single target was quickly replaced by multiple targets that hung from different lengths of rope. Each was suspended from various height tree branches, which Misty tugged randomly to keep them swinging at different speeds from side to side.

For the next few busy training hours, Kinta continued to fire her arrows rapidly at each of the now mobile targets, without having missed the bullseye once. She did this while she ran directly at the mark, as well as across in front from either side and fired over her shoulders as she ran away. Then, as an added level of difficulty and increased distraction, she began having to leap high into the air. It was to avoid Misty trying to grab at her feet, as she continued to run and fire from different angles. But, regardless of how amazingly complex they made the situation, Kinta continued to find the bullseye with every single arrow she released.

At the end of their long tiring day of concentrated training, the two extremely close friends made their way back towards home. They were delighted with their progress but exhausted from all their activity.

...oooOooo...

After a long and detailed planning discussion between Aedyn, Laytn, Seraphina, and Catelyn, a list of the few remaining loyal and trustworthy members among the nobles was prepared. Laytn was given specific instructions and personal responsibility for their collection and safe passage back to Libertas.

Next day, they set off with a small, specially-selected band of heavily-armed men. They were secreted into two huge wagons, which were then carefully camouflaged as gypsy tinker vans. The men were carefully chosen for their stealth, ability at camouflage, and exceptional skills with multiple weapons. It would be essential for this exercise if they were to remain undiscovered.

During last night's meeting, the plan had been devised to methodically go from house to house and collect the occupants and their essential belongings and secrete them within the two camouflaged wagons for the return trip. The stealth and cunning that would be required to complete the task successfully, and tick off every name on the list, without having created any suspicion from casual observers, meant that there could be no rushing the process.

The small convoy had slowly plodded inconspicuously down out of the mountain pass. The wagons immediately eased off the main road onto the smaller back roads and fresh tracks across the rural countryside. Laytn's overall strategic intention was to maintain a discrete profile for the convoy. They needed to attract as little attention as possible and, by mid-morning, they had eventually reached their first objective.

From his recent memory of many trips down along the valley floor, he had immediately chosen the closest shady grove of large trees on the valley floor. Laytn had immediately seen this as a possible potential rendezvous point for their return.

He pulled back on the reins and brought the team of horses on the lead wagon to a halt. Then, he handed the reins to the man beside him on the bench seat. Laytn leapt down and made his way casually back to where Azrael sat dressed as a gypsy and perched on the wooden seat of the second wagon. "This is where we'll meet again in two days, Azrael!" he said. He indicated the grove of trees with a wave of his hands.

Azrael climbed down to join Laytn. They went carefully over their allocated lists of names again and precisely ensured that each knew who they were responsible for collecting without duplication of effort. It was going to be their only chance to safely and successfully spirit these chosen few loyal nobles away to Libertas, out of the long-ranging reach of Vylaine's spiteful vengeance.

When both men were satisfied that they each knew and understood their role, they shook hands to wish each other well. Then they made their way slowly back to their respective wagons. As Laytn climbed back up onto the wooden bench seat, he tugged the hood of his jacket back up over his head to conceal his face.

Then he took back the long leather reins, gave them a flick and started the wagon moving slowly forward again. A glance over his shoulder, as he moved out from under the trees and onto the road eastward, confirmed that Azrael had taken his wagon load of men on the agreed westward path. It was the last time they would see each other until they met again under the grove of trees when their task was complete.

While they trundled along through the rustic countryside, Laytn couldn't help but notice the massive collateral damage that had already been done by the soldiers in their attempt to locate the rebel forces. He observed vacant farmhouses with their thatch roof burnt away and the walls charred and blackened from the ensuing smoke and flames.

Even the animal holding pens, which had invariably been constructed from stout hand-cut timber poles, had been burnt and destroyed. All the farmer's stock had been confiscated and taken away to be held by the army as future meat supplies for the soldiers.

The further into the countryside they travelled, the more they observed the damage inflicted upon the innocent population, and the angrier he became. He vowed to speak urgently with Aedyn about seeking his nomination as the new Lord Chancellor, upon their victorious return from their mission to bring down the priestess.

Laytn felt wholly consumed with hatred for the high priestess, at the senseless destruction that Vylaine had wrought upon their country. She had recklessly and ruthlessly inflicted her vengeance upon the population as she pursued their rebel band, and he now couldn't wait to commence retaliation activities.

Up ahead he noticed a large stone chateau concealed among a grove of substantial shady beech trees, with a large stone entrance gateway that opened out onto their current dirt road. He knew from his discussion with Seraphina last night that this was the home of Duchess Lorelei, her sister.

They turned off the main road and went in through the ornate stonework opening of the gateway. Laytn maintained the slow pace to continue anonymity and forestall any suspicions by casual observers. They made their way along a smaller tree-lined driveway towards Lorelei's chateau.

Before long, it opened onto a circular path around a large fountain and gardens at the front of the house. Finally, they arrived at a large ornate front entrance porch. Laytn halted the wagon, pulled on the handbrake and tied the leather reins loosely around the wooden kickboard before he alighted from the cart.

He glanced around for any signs of life and began to make his way up the half dozen stone steps to the enormous hand-carved wooden front doors. Then he knocked loudly and waited for a reply from inside, which didn't come.

He waited for several minutes and then rapped again, even louder this time. But there was still no response. He called out Lorelei's name, and the sound of his voice seemed to echo around and around endlessly inside the seemingly empty chateau for ages.

Laytn turned and made his way back slowly down the stone steps and climbed up onto the front seat of the wagon. He untied the long leather reins from the kickboard and gave them a flick, which started the cart moving slowly forward again.

He turned off the circular driveway and took the access road around the side of the building. Then he made his way slowly back towards a small group of rustic outbuildings. They were used to house the staff that managed the fields and animals supported by the chateau.

One white-washed, thatch-roofed building stood a little separated from the others. It had several holding pens for the milking cows attached to one side. Laytn steered the wagon over to the front of that building and parked, then tied up the reins to the kickboard again before he alighted. "Hello!" called Laytn. He knocked loudly on the front door. "Is there anyone at home?"

After a couple of minutes, a young blond woman with an ashen face devoid of all colour and dressed in peasant-style milk-maid clothing tentatively answered the door. She opened it carefully a small way and peeked out through the gap. "Who's asking?" she said. She spoke so softly that Laytn almost didn't hear.

"My name's Laytn!" he responded in a low voice. "I come seeking the mistress from this chateau with a message from her sister, Queen Seraphina!"

"Are you from the Palace Staff?" she asked. She had still not opened the door any further and not showed Laytn her curiosity or concern.

"No, I'm not!" said Laytn firmly. "I come representing a revolutionary force determined to overthrow the evil high priestess, Vylaine! Queen Seraphina has escaped from Vylaine's clutches and joined our forces but is now concerned for the safety of her sister Lorelei if Vylaine retaliates!" Laytn explained. "Are you able to tell me where I might find Lorelei?"

"How can I be certain that you are who you say?" she asked with no apparent concern.

"Seraphina pre-empted this question and expected that it was what you would have asked!" said Laytn. He quickly realised the woman's identity. "She said to tell you that her sister Lorelei has a small birthmark, in the shape of a heart, on her left hip!"

There was a short silent pause as the blond woman considered all that he had said. Then she visibly slumped with relief before his eyes and almost stumbled as she opened the door fully. "I am Lorelei!" she said. She collapsed into his arms and began to shake. "Thank God you've found me before Vylaine's minions!"

Laytn held Lorelei gently in his arms and supported her until she could recover her composure. It only took a relatively short time considering the exceptional circumstances of their meeting. "It's not safe to stay here any longer than is necessary!" Laytn said soothingly. Lorelei stood up straighter and politely extricated herself from his supportive embrace. "Do you have much in the way of clothing or valuable items that you wish to save and take with you?" he asked.

"I've been living here and hiding out as a milk-maid for the last several weeks, since my husband suffered a fatal heart attack, and everything I own and wish to take is here with me in a single chest!" she responded. Some colour had finally begun to show in her face again.

"Then, we must leave immediately!" Laytn said. "Come with me now, and I'll help you into my wagon, while my men collect your chest and stow it onboard!" Laytn placed his arm around Lorelei's shoulders and steered her out to the back of the wagon. Then he assisted her as she climbed up the three wooden steps and stepped in through the flaps of canvass at the rear of the canopy.

Meanwhile, two of the men from inside the canopy climbed out through the front opening and went quickly inside the small cabin. They picked up the single wooden chest from inside the separate bedroom and carried it out to the wagon. There it was stowed on a carrying rack underneath and tied securely into place.

When the chest had safely been stowed, and everyone was back safely onboard, Laytn climbed back up onto the front wooden seat. He untied the long leather reins, then released the handbrake.

Then he started the wagon moving slowly forward again with a gentle flick of the reins. He kept the horses turning until they were headed back down the driveway towards the large stone gateway.

As they exited the property and turned back onto the main road, headed towards the next aristocratic estate on their list, everyone on board visibly relaxed and began to introduce themselves to Lorelei. The low-frequency rhythmic rumble of the metal wheels on the surface of the gravel road muffled the quiet tones of their conversation. The wagon full of men and Lorelei rolled on down the way to the next chateau.

...Two days later, their mission was complete.

The two large disguised wagons, loaded down with people and possessions, had arrived safely back at the rendezvous point without incident. And, after re-checking their lists for the umpteenth time to ensure nobody was forgotten, Laytn and Azrael had set off again in convoy back along the seldom used trails.

Laytn was immensely satisfied with the result of their mission, as their convoy made its way safely back into Libertas, just as the sun set over the mountains and painted the sky with a myriad of colours.

All rescued male members on the list had gladly volunteered to assist in the inevitable uprising actively and had immediately been assigned to fighting groups. The female members were all allocated to various camp teams.

CHAPTER 32

Captain Stratgii, Captain of the Palace Guard, brought his horse to a stop, then closed his eyes and took in a couple of calming breaths to quell his rapidly rising anger.

Then he twisted in his saddle and cast his eyes over the scenery in front of him. He had become more and more frustrated as the campaign continued to produce zero results, despite the best efforts of his weary men. It was having a negative impact on everyone involved.

Captain Stratgii surveyed the surrounding area on either side of the road they were travelling. He noticed a large open clearing along one side, which looked like it might suit his purpose. His men were bone tired and needed some downtime to raise their spirits and allow them to continue to follow Vylaine's fruitless orders. Otherwise, he may start to have a rebellion among the troops.

"HALT!" His shouted command rang out and was echoed up and down the column by the other officers in his troop. "We'll bivouac here for the night!" he said. He alighted from his horse and passed the reins to the Corporal, who remained still mounted beside him.

The column of men and wagons slowly dispersed off the dusty thoroughfare. They began to form an instant campsite on the side of the road, as only the military can, in a drill they had rehearsed and practised many times before.

"Officers and Sergeants will meet with me in one hour, in the marquee!" the Captain said to his Second in Charge, Lieutenant

Joseph. The Lieutenant had just arrived from the rear of the column and immediately saluted. "Yes, Sir!" said the Lieutenant. He promptly saluted again, then instantly spun his horse around and rode off to inform the others.

Captain Stratgii made his way slowly on foot along the lines and chatted randomly to some of the men. They had already unpacked their bedrolls from their backpacks and started to prepare their evening meals from their rations. He wanted to make sure the weary men were all comfortable. Then he made his way into his tent and sat down on the edge of his camp stretcher, as he felt the tension begin to ease and his body starts to relax. His back and leg muscles ached from the many days of long hours in the saddle. He had looked forward to an early night tonight, which was beginning to look further and further from becoming a reality.

Still fully dressed in his uniform, he lay slowly back and stretched his heavy body out on the thin mattress of the camp stretcher. Then he closed his eyes to rest until it was time to go to his meeting.

One hour later, the officers and sergeants had all gathered in the Headquarters marquee. It had conveniently been situated near the Captain's tent, and he could hear the low buzz of their voices. Although their conversation was hushed, it was still vociferously animated. They argued back and forth and vented their mutual frustration with each other before their Commanding Officer arrived.

Captain Stratgii dragged himself up off his camp stretcher and brushed some creases from his uniform. Then he exited his tent and appeared at the entrance to the marquee, from where he marched to his position at the front of the gathering.

"Atten…Shun!" yelled the Second in Charge and saluted sharply. There was a single sharp noise as all present rose to their feet. They snapped to attention simultaneously, stood rigidly and waited for their next command.

"Thank you! Stand easy!" said the Captain and the men relaxed slightly. "Thank for your patience, gentlemen!" he began. He kept his voice calm and measured as he spoke. "We've all had a long and thoroughly frustrating campaign, with little to show for the many weeks on the road!" he continued. "I'll be leaving Lieutenant Joseph in charge, while I return to the castle tomorrow morning to lodge my report for this week and get further orders! Hopefully, God willing, I'll be back by this time tomorrow evening, with some idea of how long this fruitless campaign is to continue!"

There was a low mutter of voices that agreed with him as the assembled men suddenly realised that Captain Stratgii also shared their frustrated opinion of their mission.

"Now, gentlemen, we all need to get some decent sleep tonight, and allow the weary men to have some well-earned downtime until my return tomorrow evening!" said Captain Stratgii. He stood up straight and glanced at Lieutenant Joseph.

"Atten…Shun!" yelled Lieutenant Joseph, as he took the visual cue and saluted sharply. The assembled men snapped back rigidly to attention. The Captain turned and made his way out of the marquee and back to his tent. Then they in turn dispersed into the night and their shelters.

He removed his boots and uniform and hung them carefully on a hook to one side of the central tent pole. Then he lay back on his camp stretcher and thought long and hard about their current situation. *We've been chewing dust and tramping these roads for weeks now, but still, we've made no real progress in capturing the villagers!* He pondered. *As much as I don't wish the villagers harm, I must report something to the priestess! How I hope this was just a bad dream, and I would wake up with it over!* The recurrent thought kept going around in his mind until he grew weary.

Then he closed his eyes and rolled over and pulled the blanket up to keep warm during the cold night.

…oooOooo…

Meanwhile, entirely and covertly concealed from view, and hidden in the undergrowth just outside the marquee, Azrael had overheard all the conversations that took place within and needed to get the information back to Aedyn.

He waited until all noise inside the marquee had abated entirely, then slipped away quietly into the surrounding undergrowth and recovered his horse. He rubbed his hand gently along its neck and shoulder, being careful not to startle it and alert the soldiers. *This information is essential!*" he thought. *What I have just overheard, may be the trigger to change Vylaine's tactics!*

He led the horse silently through the trees until he could quietly mount up and ride swiftly back to camp. Besides, it has undoubtedly increased the urgency for our attack on the palace to commence! He thought. I'm so glad Aedyn decided to have me shadow this convoy!

He settled himself down lower onto his galloping horse's neck and clung on tightly, as the low hanging branches overhead whipped past his head and an occasional bunch of leaves hit him in the face.

There was a genuine danger of being knocked off his horse if one of those thicker branches struck him at this break-neck speed. It was one time he was extremely grateful for the surefootedness of his mount.

...oooOooo...

Seraphina sat and held her sister Lorelei's hand tenderly in hers, as they spoke softly together. They had caught up on recent events while they enjoyed a cup of tea in the cozy sitting room of their wooden cabin. Lorelei had arrived in the wagons with the other aristocrats from Laytn and Azrael's mission. She was both delighted and enormously relieved to see Seraphina already safely here in camp.

The sisters had hugged each other tightly and cried openly for some time when they were first reunited. They had now recovered and moved in together into Seraphina's cabin where both women had settled comfortably into camp routine. "I'm so grateful for Aedyn and his team of volunteer warriors!" said Lorelei.

Raw emotion caused her voice to tremble slightly. "Without their help, I would still be in hiding as a milk-maid, after my husband's death, and you would still be in the clutches of that evil bitch, Vylaine! I can't possibly imagine how I could have, or would have, survived if our positions had been reversed and that bitch Vylaine had *me* in her grasp!" Lorelei continued passionately and shuddered at the possibility.

Seraphina gently squeezed her sister's hand for reassurance, then placed the extended fingers of her other hand under Lorelei's chin and gently lifted her face to look directly into her eyes. "There's something else you need to know!" she said quietly. She stared intensely into Lorelei's eyes. "And, you're sworn to absolute secrecy and may never discuss what I'm about to tell you with anyone other than myself until I give you permission!"

"Honestly, Sera, I swear!" said Lorelei. She held her hand over her heart and was utterly taken aback by Seraphina's sudden seriousness.

Seraphina leaned forward conspiratorially until both their heads were side-by-side and her lips were right beside Lorelei's ear. She began to speak softly but firmly, and with implied authority. *"I've already spoken discretely with Aedyn and Catelyn and advised them that I'll be abdicating the throne!"* she whispered.

Lorelei's eyes widened, and she sat up sharply in surprise. Seraphina squeezed her hand and held up her other index finger to her lips, to prevent Lorelei from speaking. *"I've also advised them that I'll be passing the throne to Aedyn, and I've asked him to lead the nation of Skargness forward into the future personally!"* she continued.

Lorelei kept her silence. She slowly and quietly nodded her agreement with Seraphina's decision. *"This is all very confidential, and we have all agreed to not announce this decision publicly until after the successful conclusion to our impending uprising against Vylaine!"* Seraphina said softly and squeezed Lorelei's hand again.

"And, what's to become of both of us?" asked Lorelei tremulously. She choked back a sob as moisture began to well into her eyes.

"Aedyn has suggested that we each take the title of 'Duchess' and assume the role of advisors to the new King and Queen!" said Seraphina. *"Lorelei, I'm truly sorry that I didn't get the chance to discuss this with you first, but I wasn't sure if I would ever get to see you again! I wanted this arrangement agreed, understood and securely in place, before the next, and possibly final, stage of fighting commenced!"* she continued.

Lorelei leaned forward to hug her big sister. "Sera, I'm ever so proud of you and the strong, confident, mature person you've become!" Lorelei said. She no longer felt the need to whisper. "I'm also very proud to be your sister!"

The two women embraced warmly, then sat back to enjoy their cup of tea. Suddenly, Seraphina began to chuckle, which slowly got louder and stronger until her whole body shook with laughter. Lorelei's face took on a quizzical puzzled look, as she wondered what had suddenly caused her sister's mirth.

Seraphina slowly regained her composure. "Lorelei, as your much-loved older sister, I have a delightful surprise for you!" she said. She still smiled at the thoughts that had triggered her response. "Do you remember the extremely well-endowed naked man who ran past our carriage during the recent parade?" she asked.

Lorelei's sudden wide-open eyes immediately showed that she did. "Yes, of course!" she giggled. "How could I forget that when he is endowed like a stallion? But, why do you ask?" she asked and smiled. She raised one eyebrow and tilted her head slightly to one side.

"Well, ...!" Seraphina paused, to create the impact she desired. "His name's Tyson, and I've invited him here to join us both for dinner tomorrow night!" she said. She quickly raised her hand to cover her mouth as if she had surprised herself at the words that had escaped.

Lorelei fell backwards in a mock faint, then immediately jumped up and embraced her sister. "Sera, I'm not quite sure what that bitch Vylaine has done to you, but you are the best sister ever!" she chuckled.

The two women held hands and giggled like a couple of young girls. They began to plan in detail how they would entertain Tyson, and in turn be 'entertained' by him, during his visit. Some of the exotic, and often erotic, suggestions caused both sisters to double over with laughter and struggle to breathe as their girly, sibling conversation continued long into the night.

CHAPTER 33

Aedyn stepped slowly, but deliberately, up onto the small raised dais at the front of the meeting hall. He slowly turned his head and cast his gaze around the room at the flushed expectant faces that watched him. This evening, all the current occupants of the camp, men, women, and children, had gathered in the meeting hall to hear his announcement. The responsibility he felt for the faces that looked back at him was a sobering moment.

All their immediate futures and the very future of Skargness depended upon the success or failure of the actions that resulted from their next decisions over the next couple of days and the ensuing results. "My friends, and fellow warriors!" he began. He stopped until the general drum of conversation had settled, and an immediate hush fell over the room.

Aedyn glanced down at the front row and saw Catelyn, Kinta, and Misty seated beside Seraphina, Lorelei, Laytn, and Maeve. Their faces all glowed with intense pride at his courage and leadership.

He felt a nervous tightness begin to grip his chest, and a lump formed in his throat. He came to suddenly realise that his announcement tonight could be the precursor to actions that deeply affected those that he loved more than life itself.

He locked eyes discretely with Catelyn, who gave him a covert reassuring nod to show her support. He began to smile and winked back, as he felt his confidence soar and his belief in their strategic planning gave him the strength to move forward.

Aedyn lifted his head slightly and caught the eye of Ox. He stood with Madeleine and Erwyn at the very back of the room because there wasn't a vacant seat in the auditorium that was large enough to fit him. Ox dipped his head politely and touched his forehead with two fingers on his right hand as a salute to acknowledge his leadership.

Aedyn politely returned the gesture of greeting, then used that as the trigger to start to speak again. "Our limited resources have, thus far, successfully conducted a protracted guerrilla campaign against the full military might of Vylaine's forces!" he began. He spoke slowly and articulated clearly. "Most importantly, we have limited our losses to an absolute minimum and still made a real nuisance of ourselves!" he said.

His voice had increased in volume as he warmed to the subject. "However, the time has finally come to launch a full assault on the palace and overthrow this evil tyranny!" A huge roar of approval erupted from the audience like a clap of thunder. As one, they leapt to their feet and raised their fists in the air as a salute to their leader.

Aedyn waited patiently for the noise to slowly decrease and the occupants of the room to once again be seated before he tried speaking again. "We must all use our faith, and our utmost belief in our just and noble cause, to give every one of us the emotional strength to push forward in our endeavour to rid Skargness of the tyranny imposed by the evil bitch, Vylaine!" he continued enthusiastically.

He stretched out his arms to encompass every person in the room. "And, I thank you all from the bottom of my heart, for the wholehearted and unselfish support you have each given to both myself and this valiant effort!" he continued. "Tomorrow morning, all Squad Leaders will report to this room at first light for their final orders and confirmation of our strategic planning! Now, my friends, in conclusion, I want you all to go home and spend some quality time with your families and loved ones before the uncertainty of tomorrow is altogether too swiftly upon us!" he concluded.

The room suddenly filled with a generally raised hubbub of activity as the occupants stood up noisily and started to file outside and make their way home. Some were still deeply engrossed in conversation about Aedyn's speech and the possible ramifications of tomorrow's battle.

Aedyn stepped carefully down from the dais. He closed his eyes and drew in and exhaled a calming breath, at the realisation of what they were all facing tomorrow.

Then, he opened his eyes and looked up. Suddenly he was met and completely surprised, by Seraphina's warm embrace as she rushed into his arms. *"Thank you, Aedyn, I'm now certain our country is in the very best hands possible!"* she whispered into his ear before she rested her head on his chest and squeezed him tightly.

"Thank you, Sera!" Aedyn whispered back and returned her warm embrace. He glanced up at Catelyn and Kinta and saw their faces beamed with pride.

...oooOooo...

Erwyn, Madeleine and Ox still talked animatedly about the evening's events and the content of Aedyn's address when they arrived back at their hut and made their way inside. While Madeleine immediately went straight ahead into the kitchen, to prepare their evening meal, Ox took Erwyn aside in the living room. "Sir, I very much love your daughter, Madeleine, and I ask you for your blessing and her hand in marriage," he said calmly and quietly. It wasn't straightforward considering the emotions that played through him.

"Ox, you are truly the son for which I have long prayed!" Erwyn replied. Moisture began to build in his eyes. "If Madeleine agrees to your proposal, I'll willingly give you my daughter's hand and wish you and she a long and prosperous life together!"

Ox and Erwyn embraced with strong emotion before Ox broke away and eagerly made his way into the kitchen. He crept up quietly behind Madeleine and placed his huge hands gently around her waist. Then, he leaned forward and kissed her gently on the top of her head.

Startled by surprise, Madeleine turned quickly within his grasp and looked up into his face, which shone like a beacon with his love for her. Without saying a word, Ox slowly sank onto one knee and held Madeleine's hands within his, as he held her gaze. "Madeleine, my love, neither of us knows what will come after we go into battle tomorrow!" he said.

His boundless love gave him the courage and strength to continue. "But, right now, tonight, I only know that I would be proud and honoured to enter that battle as your husband and protector! Please, Madeleine, would you do me the honour of accepting my marriage proposal and becoming my wife?" he asked.

Tears built quickly in Madeleine's eyes and spilled out onto her face as she gently squeezed Ox's huge hands and caught her breath. She tried hard to recover her composure sufficiently to respond. "Ox, my precious, you are my reason for living!" she said. She bent down slightly and kissed him passionately on the lips. "You have given my life purpose! Of course, I accept!"

Ox promptly stood up and lifted Madeleine into a warm embrace. He spun her around on the spot as he clutched her tightly to his chest. Madeleine lifted her face, then laughed loudly and turned in the general direction of the kitchen doorway. "Papa, come quickly, we're to be married!" she yelled excitedly.

Erwyn hurried into the room just as Ox placed Madeleine carefully back down onto the floor and then all three joined in an embrace. "I give you both my deepest blessing and thank you for making me the happiest man alive!" he said. There was a strong quiver of emotion in his voice, and his eyes became moist and misted over. "Now, we must hurry and find Tyson, the cleric, to perform the ceremony before morning!" he said, always the efficient organiser.

Madeleine made a great show theatrically, but gently, as she broke free from the two favourite men in her life. She stood back with her hands on her hips in mock anger. "If you think that I'll be wed tonight, without taking the time to change my clothes or do something with my hair, then you are both sadly mistaken!" she said and continued to feign anger but smiled broadly. "Ox, my sweet, please go to Aedyn's cabin and politely ask Kinta and Misty to both be my bridesmaids!" said Madeleine, and her face glowed. "Then, please escort them safely back to our cabin to help me prepare and then, and only then, fetch the cleric!"

Then, with a great flourish of the skirts of her dress, she spun on her heel and seemed to float across the floor literally. She headed for her room with a huge glowing smile still spread across her face.

Ox threw his massive hands up in the air and turned to face Erwyn with a quizzical look upon his face. "We haven't even been wed yet and, already, she's giving me orders!" he said. Then, he burst out and laughed heartily as he headed for the door, and Erwyn also roared with laughter.

...oooOooo...

Tyson knocked gently on the cabin door with the knuckles of his right hand and stood back politely. He made sure he stayed visible within the flickering light cast by the lantern, which was mounted beside the door. After a couple of minutes, which seemed like an eternity to Tyson, the door cracked opened slightly, and Seraphina peeked out. Then she immediately opened the door fully and stepped out to welcome him to their cabin as she extended her hand.

Tyson straightened himself up, held out his hand nervously, and took Seraphina's small hand gently into his. Then he bowed from the waist and kissed her hand gently on the back. "Good evening, Your Majesty!" he said apprehensively.

"Please, Tyson, call me Sera!" she said. She smiled warmly and took their guest firmly by the hand before she gently guided him in through the front door, glanced around to ensure nobody watched them and closed it behind them. "Thank you so much for joining us this evening!" she continued. "Lorelei and I have been greatly looking forward to your company all day!"

As Seraphina began to lead Tyson down the short passageway of the cabin, his face beamed. "Thank you, Sera!" he said and began to feel a little more comfortable in the presence of his Queen. "I'm grateful to you both for inviting me over!"

The tantalising smell of a roast meal as it cooked wafted throughout the cabin and Tyson's mouth immediately began to flood with saliva, which made it very difficult for him to speak. As a single man, his usual evening fare was simple cold leftovers from the community

Mess Hall, which he secreted out in his pockets after he had attended breakfast in the morning. The mind-numbing thought of both a hot, cooked meal and the delightful company of *two* beautiful women, *in the same night*, was almost beyond the limited capacity of his imagination to fathom.

Seraphina led Tyson by the hand into the front sitting room and joined Lorelei. She was dressed seductively in a low-cut gown and seated in a comfortable chair, and she stood for the formal introductions. "Lorelei, this is Tyson!" said Seraphina, who stood slightly behind Tyson. "And, Tyson, this is my sister, Lorelei!"

Tyson reached out and gently took Lorelei's hand, which she had extended. He bent down with a ramrod straight back to kiss the back of her hand tenderly and held the contact with his lips for a little longer than usual. "It is indeed my great pleasure to finally meet you, Lorelei!" said Tyson. He straightened to gaze into her sapphire blue eyes and beamed his broadest smile.

"The pleasure is all mine, Tyson!" said Lorelei. She was unable to stop the pink flush of both excitement and embarrassment that coloured her neck and cheeks as she had an immediate, and somewhat unfortunate, flashback to the image of a naked Tyson.

However, precisely then, there was a loud knock on the front door of the cabin. Standing behind Tyson, Seraphina discretely rolled her eyes to Lorelei in exasperation at the intrusion, then politely excused herself to go and answer the front door.

When she opened the door, Seraphina was much surprised to see that it was the massive figure of Ox who stood in the circle of lamplight on their front porch.

Ox shuffled his feet and wrung his hands with utter embarrassment at his late intrusion on her privacy. "I'm truly very sorry to disturb you this evening, Your Majesty!" stammered Ox. "Is Tyson the cleric here?" he quickly continued. The words tumbled out in his embarrassment. "Madeleine and I wish to be married tonight, before tomorrow's battle, and I, therefore, seek Tyson's immediate services!"

"Congratulations, Ox, I'm very happy for both of you!" said Seraphina. She turned to go and fetch Tyson from inside. "Madeleine is a fortunate young woman indeed!"

As she reached the front room, Tyson had said his polite and gentlemanly farewells to Lorelei, having already overheard the entire conversation from the front door and he had pre-empted his immediate departure.

"Tyson, it would seem your services are urgently required elsewhere this evening!" said Seraphina. She placed her arm around Lorelei's shoulders and squeezed gently to show she understood her sister's obvious disappointment.

Tyson held out both his hands, palms uppermost, in the universal expression of futility. Then he extended his arms forward and reached for both Lorelei's and Seraphina's hands. "What else can one do when one's popularity exceeds one's availability?" he said and chuckled, then bent from the waist.

Tyson gently kissed the back of each hand in a flourishing gesture of farewell to his hostesses. "I must beg your utmost forgiveness, ladies, and ask that I may take a rain check on tonight's invitation?" he said, as he straightened.

Lorelei smiled and continued to hold Tyson's hand gently but firmly, as she began to stroll beside him out to the door. There she stopped and leaned forward and gave him a polite kiss on the side of his cheek. "Tyson, you are more than welcome to come around again, just as soon as you have a vacancy in your busy agenda!" she said and mocked all seriousness before she giggled at her joke.

As he took his leave from Lorelei, she waved the tips of her fingers, on the one hand, to say farewell at the front door. Tyson turned around and faced the giant figure of Ox. "Ox, I believe congratulations are in order?" he said, as he took Ox by the elbow and led him back toward Erwyn's cabin. Both men enjoyed a spirited conversation about Ox's forthcoming nuptials as Lorelei watched them disappear slowly into the darkness of the night.

She felt a little flushed and lightheaded as her heart raced, then she closed the door and turned and began to walk back inside to join her sister. *Don't be silly, Lorelei!* She thought. *I feel like a young girl on her first date!*

As Lorelei re-entered the front room again, she went to her sister, and Seraphina reached out without having made a sound and enveloped her in a warm embrace. Then, after a couple of minutes, Seraphina broke the silence. "It's finally time for both of us to find some true happiness, with someone who loves us because of *who* we are and not *what* we are!" she said.

They each looked silently and knowingly into the other's eyes for several long minutes, before they reluctantly broke their embrace and headed for the kitchen. "I'm starving! That roast is not going to waste! Let's eat!" said Lorelei and the two of them began to laugh.

CHAPTER 34

When they finally arrived back at Erwyn's cabin, Ox and Tyson were pleasantly surprised to find preparations well and truly underway. Erwyn and Aedyn had cleared and cleaned the sitting room to make room for the wedding ceremony to take place. Catelyn had quickly prepared some snacks in the kitchen for after the service.

Madeleine was still firmly ensconced in her locked bedroom with Kinta and Misty, who had been escorted over by Aedyn and Catelyn, as they put the finishing touches in place for Madeleine to be ready for the most important day of her life. "I love your gorgeous hair, Madi!" Kinta enthused. She brushed through the long natural blond ringlets that hung down to Madeleine's waist and now glowed like burnished gold threads.

"Thank you, Kinta!" Madeleine replied. "However, it's such a chore having to brush it every night to get rid of the tangles!"

"Maybe that's a task you can ask Ox to do for you now?" Kinta giggled. "And, in return, you could offer to brush his beard for him!" All three girls laughed heartily at the suggestion.

Then Madeleine reached around behind her and carefully undid her buttons on the dress she currently wore. She allowed it to fall freely down around her ankles before she stepped out of it without any embarrassment. Then Madeleine picked it up and hung it up behind the door.

As she turned back around to face them, Kinta couldn't help

but admire Madeleine's figure. She quickly compared herself with Madeleine's full rounded white breasts capped with large rose-pink nipples, her narrow waist, and soft mature curves, with a thick dark thatch of pubic hair nestled in her groin and her long, lean legs.

Madeleine quickly crossed the room and bent over a large wooden chest, which exposed the tufts of dark pubic hair that surrounded her womanhood, which was now clearly visible below the firm rounded globes of her buttocks.

Then she carefully unlocked and opened the lid of the chest and began to search through the contents and finally removed a beautiful, hand-embroidered white silk wedding gown.

When she turned back around again, she held the dress up in front of her. Kinta and Misty could see the moisture begin to well in her eyes as the emotion of finally being able to use the wedding gown she had so painstakingly created was released and her face was aglow with happiness.

"Oh, Madi, did you make the dress, it's gorgeous!" Kinta said, and Misty nodded her agreement. "Now, let's get you into that wedding gown quickly so you can go out there and get married, and then Ox can get you back out of it again tonight!" The three girls laughed again.

Madeleine lowered the gown and stepped carefully into it. Then Kinta assisted her to get the gown gently up and into place over her curves and to fasten the many silk-covered buttons up the back. "Would you like me to braid your hair and put it up for you, Madi, or would you prefer to have it left down?" Kinta asked.

"Thank you, Kinta, if you could braid it, that would be wonderful because it will be so much easier to manage!" said Madeleine. She plopped herself down on the edge of the bed in front of where Kinta was seated and with her back to her.

Kinta shuffled herself forward until her legs sat snuggly on either side of Madeleine's hips with Misty, who snuggled up close against her thigh and admired their handiwork. Then she began the long and tedious task as she gathered up Madeleine's long golden locks and twisted and plaited them into place until there was only a single long thick braid.

Then, she and Madeleine wound the long single braid around and around upon itself until it wound itself up into a tight braided bun on top of Madeleine's head, and there they used hairpins to keep it firmly in place.

To complete their final preparations, Madeleine used a hand mirror and dusted her face with a faint coat of powder, and applied some colour to her eyelids, cheeks, and lips.

She then stood and carefully checked her overall image in the full-length mirror mounted on the wall of her bedroom. "How do you think I look, Kinta?" Madeleine asked and sought a second opinion as she turned herself slowly from side to side. She spent some time to check each side's profile carefully, then rotated herself slowly several times to check the whole image.

"Madi, you are a beautiful bride, and Ox is the luckiest man alive!" Kinta enthused. "But we had better get you out there soon, or there won't be enough night left for you to get married, or to enjoy the pleasurable benefits afterwards!"

"Kinta!" Madeleine said. She was initially slightly shocked at the not-so-subtle suggestion, but then the girls all laughed together again conspiratorially. With that, Kinta shuffled herself forward even further until she could stand up onto the floor.

Then she picked up Misty off the bed and placed her on the floor. The three girls all made their way out into the living room to start the ceremony.

Ox stood there utterly speechless, as he waited for her, all dressed up in his most elegant outfit. His eyes opened very wide with both pleasure and surprise when he saw just how amazingly beautiful Madeleine looked tonight. "Oh, Madeleine, you are looking gorgeous this evening!" said Catelyn, who admired Madeleine with a peek around from behind Ox's large body as the three girls came out of the bedroom together.

"My darling, you look amazing and thank you so much for the effort to which you've gone, but I love you so much I would've married you in your work uniform!" said Ox. He finally found his voice again and held out his hand to take Madeleine's as she walked towards him.

The bride and groom walked through together into the sitting room, as they stared intensely into each other's eyes. They were followed closely by Catelyn, Kinta, and Misty, and joined Erwyn, Tyson and Aedyn, who stood together and chatted quietly about manly things.

Tyson stepped away and stood by himself. Ox and Madeleine walked up and stood together directly in front of him, then they faced each other and held hands. The rest of the guests gathered around carefully in a semi-circle.

"My friends, we're gathered here tonight, in the sight of their dearest friends as true witnesses to their love, for the special celebration of marriage between Ox and Madeleine!" said Tyson. "Due to the late hour, and with due consideration for the special circumstances in which we find ourselves, I will keep this brief, but you will be no less bound!" he continued. "Ox, do you take Madeleine to be your wife, etc. etc.!"

"I certainly do!" said Ox and smiled at his beautiful bride.

"Madeleine, do you take Ox to be your husband, etc. etc.!" Tyson continued.

"I most certainly do!" said Madeleine and smiled back at Ox.

"You have both individually and together declared your love before these witnesses! Therefore, by the power vested in me by the State of Skargness, I declare you to now be husband and wife!" said Tyson. "Ox, you may kiss your bride!"

Ox leaned forward from the waist and Madeleine stood up on her very tiptoes to allow their lips to meet and they were able to kiss each other. Then Ox picked up Madeleine and whirled her around as they embraced each other tightly.

At the same time, everyone else in the room clapped loudly and cheered as the two newlyweds celebrated. Then Kinta reached into her pocket and pulled out the handful of rice she had secreted in there earlier and threw it over the couple for good luck. "Congratulations, Ox and Madi!" was the chorus from all present.

Ox finally placed Madeleine down on the floor again and turned to the others while he still held his new wife's hand. "Thank you, all of you, this has been such a special evening, I'm sure we'll look back on it fondly for many years to come!" he said and held out his other hand

and placed it around the shoulders of Tyson. "And, a special thank you to you, my friend!" said Ox, as he turned to face Tyson directly. "For coming here tonight at such short notice and leaving your previous appointment!"

"You're most welcome, Ox, and sincere congratulations to you and Madeleine on your wedding night!" said Tyson. "However, now that you two are hitched, I'm going back to my earlier appointment, if you don't mind?"

"By all means, my friend!" said Ox, and laughed heartily. With that, Tyson kissed Madeleine on the cheek and shook Ox's hand before he disappeared rapidly out the front door.

Erwyn made a little speech and welcomed Ox formally into the family, then he thanked Aedyn and his family who had come over at such short notice. Then everyone moved back through to the dining area to continue the celebration and enjoy some wine and snacks.

Finally, as the table cleared rapidly of food, the guests all stood around and chatted amiably. Aedyn tapped a knife lightly against a crystal glass, which caused it to ring out like a metal bell, and he quickly gained everybody's attention. "My friends, I now propose a toast to the Bride and Groom! To Ox and Madelaine!" he said and held his drink up in the air until everyone else had responded. "Ox and Madeleine!" they all said together loudly.

"Thank you, Aedyn! Congratulations again to Ox and Madeleine, but it is getting late, and we all have some urgent business to attend to in the morning!" Erwyn said. "Let's call it a night and allow the newlyweds to have some time together before we are needed tomorrow!" With that, Erwyn shuffled them all out the front door and took himself off to bed.

Ox and Madeleine retired to Ox's room since it had an enormous bed and would comfortably accommodate both. They closed the door behind them, and Ox sat down on the edge of the bed and held out his arms as Madeleine walked up and wrapped her arms around his massive neck. She kissed him passionately on the mouth as he closed his arms around her in a warm embrace. "Welcome to my room, my darling wife!" said Ox when their lips finally parted. "I love you so much, and I have prayed daily for this moment!"

"I love you dearly also, my darling husband!" said Madeleine, as she gently nestled her head down onto Ox's shoulder. "Now, could you please help me to undo those many wretched buttons at the back of my gown?" Then, she turned slowly around within his arms and waited patiently for Ox to use his clumsy fingers to undo each of the tiny silk-covered buttons down the back and allow the gown to come loose from around her body.

Finally, Madeleine allowed the gown to slide slowly down until it lay crumpled around her ankles on the floor, then she stepped out of it and hung it up over the back of a chair across the other side of the room. When she turned back around, Madeleine had a cheeky grin on her face.

She stood there near the chair and held eye contact with Ox while she adopted several provocative poses that presented her curvaceous body proudly to her beaming new husband. "I know that you have already seen some parts of me before, under very different circumstances, but I just wanted to show you that what you see now is *all* that I bring, and I willingly offer this all to you, with all of my love!" Madeleine said warmly and walked quickly back into Ox's arms. "Now, let's get you out of your clothes so I can see what you bring to me!" she chuckled.

Ox slid his hands slowly down the back of her warm naked body and cupped the firm globes of her buttocks, then drew her in close. Madeleine began to undo the large buttons down the front of his shirt.

Ox stood up and carefully removed the large shirt when she had finished the task and placed it on the foot of the bed. Then Madeleine slowly and carefully undid the buckle on his belt and the buttons on the front of his large trousers, which allowed them to slide down to the floor and left him standing completely naked before her. "Oh my God, my darling, it's a good thing the female body is designed to be flexible enough to accommodate the birth of a baby!" said Madeleine as she admired his body.

Her eyes were wide open in surprise as she beheld the entire spectacle of him, with every part in perfect proportion. Ox's rampant manhood stood up proudly in front of his body. It was as long as her forearm and as thick as her wrist and pulsed in anticipation as she joined him.

They lay down on the huge bed together. Madeleine was pleasantly surprised to find that, despite his massive size, Ox was indeed a gentle giant and incredibly tender and sensitive in his touch.

He gently stroked his fingertips across her stomach and up across her chest, taking each of her breasts into his mouth and sucking each one softly while tweaking her nipples with his lips and the tip of his tongue. Then, while he continued to fondle her breasts, he slowly ran his hand down to between her open legs and found the nerve centre of her erogenous zone within the small firm bud at the upper part of her womanhood and began to massage it gently.

She immediately began to feel the warm tingling buzz within her loins, and it had already started to spread up into her lower belly, as she writhed and squirmed on the bed in pleasure and Ox continued to stimulate her arousal. Madeleine felt his sizeable middle finger move a little lower until he found her now moist vagina entrance and inserted his finger tenderly. Then, he began to move it slowly and gently in and out, which caused her body to naturally lubricate quickly to accommodate him.

She could feel her body quiver as it responded instantly to his tender ministrations and cautiously reached her hand down to find his manhood, which throbbed and pulsed. She placed her hand around its circumference and began to stroke up and down, which caused Ox to gasp with pleasure.

Madeleine raised her knees and lay them flat down against the bed, which opened her legs up very wide and allowed Ox to carefully roll over in between her legs and support himself using his knees and elbows. Then she lifted her feet and placed them up behind his buttocks.

It rotated her hips and placed the warm moist entrance to her vagina in direct contact with the enormous swollen head of Ox's penis. She held him tenderly and guided him carefully into place until she felt him begin to poke at the opening and slowly gain some entry to her body.

There was some slight resistance to his entry as he continued to nudge away. Then, suddenly, Madeleine felt a small sharp pain, and a slight tearing sensation as the full rigid length of him slid down deep inside her. She gasped at the initial impression of being completely full and tensed up slightly. But then she relaxed and enjoyed the pleasurable feeling of being able to feel her husband deep within her body.

Then he began to slide in and out along the full length of his manhood as he gathered momentum. Madeleine quickly rose through the various levels of arousal towards a crescendo, which arrived suddenly as her back arched and her entire body shuddered in the spasms of orgasmic release. And then, simultaneously, she felt Ox's body also stiffen and begin to quiver as he climaxed and flooded her internally with a scalding hot massive gush of male juices.

She clung on tightly around his massive body and found intense pleasure as she felt him still inside her and he pulsed gently with the aftershocks of his climax.

Then, when he finally shrank down and slipped out, Ox rolled over onto his back beside her and Madelaine snuggled up close beside him with her head resting on his massive chest. She took his sizeable flaccid manhood into her hand and cradled it, which is precisely how they awoke early the next morning.

"Good morning, my darling husband!" said Madeleine softly, huskily, upon her having awakened. She gazed up into his eyes and started to move her hand slowly and lovingly along the length of his phallus, which had expanded again quickly and now stood up and throbbed.

"Good morning to you, my darling wife!" replied Ox, as his breath caught in his throat. He carefully helped Madeleine to slide up onto the top of his supine body's belly, and then she carefully wriggled down until she felt the swollen head of his rigid manhood engage with the warm moist entrance to her body and guided him inside. This time he slid quickly, easily and entirely inside until he nudged against the very core of her soul.

She moaned with pleasure at the sensation of fullness, as her husband completely filled her body. Then they began to slowly increase the tempo of their horizontal tango until they both shuddered in climax together and she felt his scalding hot juices flooding inside her again as she collapsed down onto his chest.

Suddenly, Ox remembered today's main event and the Leaders'

Meeting he was meant to attend at first light. He apologised profusely as he slipped carefully out of his wife and placed her gently down onto the bed. Then, he rolled out of bed and quickly dressed into his battle-ready clothing before he kissed her goodbye tenderly and rushed out the front door.

Madeleine was a little nonplussed at his hasty exit but understood the enormous responsibility that rested on her husband's massive shoulders as they began the battle for recovery of their nation from the evil high priestess.

...oooOooo...

Tyson arrived breathless at the girl's cabin door. He saw the lamp still burned on the front porch, so he knocked gently on the wooden door, then stood back and prayed that the girls hadn't just gone to bed and forgotten the lamp.

The front door cracked open slightly, and Seraphina peeked out, curious as to who could be their visitor at such a late hour. Then, when she saw Tyson, she pulled the door open quickly and stepped out to welcome him inside again. "I'm sorry for the late hour, Sera, but I came again as soon as I was able to get away after marrying Ox and Madeleine!" he said.

"Well, Tyson, this is such a pleasant surprise!" said Seraphina and reached out to take Tyson's hand. "Come inside and join us for a meal!" She led Tyson in through the front door and closed it behind them. Then they walked down the passageway to the kitchen and dining area to meet up with Lorelei. "Look, Lorelei, guess who I found standing outside our front door?" she asked, as they entered the room.

Lorelei turned around to see who could have knocked at such a late hour. "Oh, hi Tyson, I thought you'd gone for the night when you had to leave earlier!" said Lorelei and smiled broadly. "Would you like to eat still, please let me get you some food?"

"Yes, please Lorelei!" he answered. "And, my sincere apologies for the hasty exit earlier, but the newlyweds are now celebrating with their friends!"

"It's no problem!" Lorelei responded. "These things happen sometimes, and often at very unusual times!"

They all laughed together comfortably. Seraphina grabbed some cutlery from a drawer and placed it on the table, as she set an extra place for Tyson in addition to the two positions already set. Lorelei removed the roast from the oven and put it on a wooden carving block on the table. "Would you be so kind as to carve the meat for us, please Tyson?" asked Lorelei, and turned to get some clean plates out of a cupboard.

"Of course, it's the least I can do after my late arrival!" he said and chuckled. "A tardy guest is usually an unfed guest!"

Once again, they all laughed. The jovial atmosphere continued throughout the meal and set the tone for a delightful evening by all as the conversation flowed back and forth freely.

When it was time for Tyson to leave, he thanked the girls for their invitation and said goodbye to Seraphina, who remained in the kitchen to commence the clean-up. Lorelei held his hand and walked him out to the front porch.

"Thank you again, Lorelei, it was an enjoyable evening, and I'm sorry I had to duck out earlier!" said Tyson softly. He turned to take Lorelei's other hand as well and looked deeply into her eyes. "Tonight was much appreciated!"

Saying nothing, Lorelei maintained eye contact. She stepped forward and leaned her face up, then rose up onto her toes and kissed Tyson warmly on the mouth. He passionately responded as he opened his mouth, wrapped his arms around her and took her into a tight embrace.

After several long minutes of passionate petting, their lips parted. Lorelei leaned her head tenderly onto Tyson's chest as they continued to cuddle each other, slightly breathless. They both knew that tonight was to be but the first of many nights ahead for them.

PART 3

FREEDOM FOUND

CHAPTER 35

Laytn glanced down and marked off Ox's name on the sheet of paper in front of him at the round table, as the enormous final Squad Leader hurriedly entered and took the last vacant seat. "Okay, Aedyn, we are now all present!" Laytn said quietly, then turned expectantly toward Aedyn.

Aedyn looked up from his notes and placed them in front of him on the table. His eyes moved to each person in turn, as he worked his way around the table from his left, held their gaze briefly and nodded in respect before he moved to the next. Eventually, his gaze came to rest on Kinta, seated at his right-hand side in her full battledress. His heart skipped a beat as he thought how quickly she had grown up and become a young woman.

"Gentlemen, and Kinta, welcome!" he said. His tone immediately conveyed his concern for their welfare. "There is no need for me to spend more valuable time explaining both the strategic importance and the utmost danger of our next mission!" he explained.

"You're each here because you're trusted as leaders to make decisions, where necessary, for your Squad's safety, but to stay to our objectives and the timing of the plan!" he continued. "We received accurate information last night that the Captain of the Palace Guards is frustrated at getting no results and is to return to the palace today for further orders! My genuine concern is that this will probably make

Vylaine very upset and change her tactics, which will once again place us at the disadvantage of not knowing her plans!"

"Predictably, I expect Vylaine to meet with the Captain upstairs, in the Throne Room, as she has always done in the past!" he went on. "This will be to our advantage and her detriment, as she will be exactly where we want her, unable to escape, except through the only opening in the room!"

Aedyn paused, to allow the men to grasp the significance of what he had just said. There was a general mutter of approval and understanding before all attention turned once more to Aedyn. "As soon as the Captain enters the palace and is therefore unable to escape and call up reinforcements, we'll spring the trap! Two squads of archers will be hidden on the rocky ledge above the palace, to prevent anyone using the battlements!"

"At the same time, Laytn will move his six squads of mixed archers and swordsmen out of the cover of trees, on either side of the entrance, and assemble at the gates!" Aedyn continued. "And, Azrael and I will take Kinta and Misty, with a squad of archers and Ox's squad of swordsmen, through the tunnel entrance to the dungeon, where we'll make our way up through the palace to the Throne Room! Narchis will initially accompany us through the tunnel with a small band of archers for support! Then, they will move swiftly through the palace to the gates, which they will open and allow Laytn to enter!"

"Laytn's team will then move methodically through the palace and subdue any resistance, which will free us up to ascend the stairs swiftly!" he concluded.

Aedyn sat back in his seat and took a slow, deep breath, then held it for a couple of seconds before he exhaled slowly. "My dear friends, we may have each travelled a different path to get to this point, but, from this moment forth, we are all of a sole purpose … the capture of Vylaine and Daemon and the end of tyranny within our land!" he said. "Please convey my thanks and trust to your men, as you go now and assemble them in preparation for our battle!"

Aedyn and Laytn spent the next few minutes and allocated specific roles and responsibilities to each of the Squad Leaders, to ensure that each knew their battle plans before he sent them out to gather their men.

Kinta excused herself politely from the two men and went quickly to meet Misty for some quiet personal time together with her best friend before the battle began in a couple of hours.

The two men embraced and wished each other well before they parted and returned to their cabins. Each knew instinctively that he and his friends would willingly give their lives, if necessary, to ensure the success of their mission.

...oooOooo...

Upon arrival back at his cabin, Aedyn was pleased to see that Catelyn had read his note, and had complied with his request to gather Maeve, Seraphina and Lorelei with her as the female leaders of Libertas. They all sat around the kitchen table as they enjoyed a cup of tea together.

"Good morning, Ladies!" he said, as he seated himself at the table with them. "If, ... no, I'm sorry, ... I mean, *when* all goes well today, our time here at Libertas will finally come to an end, and we'll be free to return to our homes! I have every confidence that our mission will be successful but, as Catelyn well knows, I always like to have a little insurance as a backup to our strategic planning!" he continued.

"As a precaution, I would like to ask you, ladies, to please organise some of the women into a First Aid Squad, equipped with medical provisions from the hospital, and position them in the main tunnel!" he said. "This will allow them to provide immediate medical assistance to anyone injured during our mission!"

Seraphina spoke first, as she placed her hand gently on Aedyn's forearm and voiced precisely what the others thought. "A brilliant idea, Aedyn!" she said and glanced around at the other women for their nods of agreement before she continued. "We're all just pleased that we can be of useful assistance!"

...oooOooo...

Narchis peered out through the green vines that covered the

tunnel entrance and studied the tree-lined road below that leads up to the palace entrance, as his trained eyes searched urgently for any sign that something was amiss.

In the grey half-light of predawn, Narchis's critical eyes had barely noticed the slight rustle of the occasional tree's foliage, as Laytn and his men had silently eased into position on either side of the entrance like wraiths. However, he was confident that nobody else in the royal palace above, or any casual observers that passed by, could have, or would have, noticed anything untoward.

Suddenly, he caught a glimpse of a moving carriage leave the cover of the woods below and make for the palace entrance. As he strained his eyes, he could make out the unmistakable identity of the single passenger, King Daemon.

Narchis guessed correctly that the unplanned return of Daemon meant that the royal carriage would not have been prepared to meet him at the pier on his arrival, and a thin smile played at the corners of his mouth as he imagined the huge surprise to be given to Daemon a little later in the day. *You have no idea!* He thought and chuckled to himself.

He watched, silently and motionless, as the carriage drew up to the gate and deposited Daemon at the entrance to his castle, then the gate immediately opened, and Daemon entered and disappeared inside.

Time seemed to stand still for him while Narchis waited the next hour and a half until Captain Stratgii arrived and entered the gate, then he turned and quietly made his way back up the tunnel to meet Aedyn and the rest of the underground raiding party.

...oooOooo...

Aedyn could feel his heart thump loudly in his chest. He quietly made his way through the tunnel, then he glanced around at Kinta and Misty, and the rest of the men packed in tightly behind. His chest swelled with pride, and he choked back a lump in his throat at the sight of the strong young woman warrior beside him.

Until recently, she had been his little daughter, and the golden curls that peeked out from around the edges of her helmet still gave her an air of innocence. But, Aedyn knew the mighty strength of character and determination that Kinta had developed since his family was torn from their home and cast into this fight for survival.

They rounded the final corner in the main tunnel, and he could make out the shadowy silhouette of Narchis as he came toward them. He wore his usual black clothing from head to foot and was almost invisible. Aedyn raised his hand, and his party halted immediately behind him.

Narchis suddenly appeared clearly visible out of the dim light and stopped immediately in front of Aedyn, raised one hand to his forehead in salute. *"You will not believe what has just happened!"* he said. He spoke so quietly that Aedyn struggled to hear him correctly and merely raised his eyebrows in response.

Narchis continued in a hushed whisper. *"We have successfully captured two birds in our trap!"* said Narchis. *"King Daemon and the Captain of the Palace Guard are now both safely ensconced inside the royal castle with the evil high priestess!"*

A look of puzzlement flickered briefly across Aedyn's face. Then, it was immediately replaced by a broad knowing smile, as he suddenly realised what must have happened. *"Thank you, Narchis!"* he said quietly. *"You are indeed the bearer of great news! It is indeed a great omen that our mission is meant to succeed!"* he continued.

"Indeed!" said Narchis. He stepped politely to one side to allow the raiding party through.

However, before anyone else had time to move, Kinta and Misty both stepped forward and spun around to face Aedyn. She was the picture-perfect image of a fierce, nimble warrior, with her shining armour, longbow, and quiver full of arrows. "Papa, please allow me to lead the way into the narrow tunnel, and I'll prepare our entry!" she said, gently but firmly. Aedyn's chest swelled with pride at how remarkably mature Kinta had become in the last couple of months.

Without another word, Kinta and Misty turned and led the way. They made their way through the narrow stone tube to the rock face. Upon arrival, Kinta turned to face her father and the body of fierce fighting men who stood behind him. "Once I have created the opening, we must move quickly to maintain the element of surprise!"

she said, as she assumed control. "However, I have a couple of small surprises to assist us to reach our objectives safely!"

Kinta reached out and gently touched Narchis on the arm. He immediately became invisible to the eye and was shocked when he suddenly couldn't see his body. He immediately realised his advantage when he had to make his way quickly to the main gate. *"Thank you, Miss Kinta!"* he said quietly. She then gently touched the arm of each of the archers in Narchis's party, and they also disappeared. "You're welcome, Narchis!" said Kinta.

She turned again to face Aedyn and the men. "And now, for the finishing touch!" she said. Kinta raised her hands towards the raiding party, whereby each man, including Kinta, began to glow with a bright blue throbbing light around their body. "This is a protective shield, to ensure we don't come to any harm!" said Kinta. Then, she smiled in self-satisfaction at her efforts.

Kinta turned and placed her hands softly on the stone walls of the tunnel. There was a sudden sharp gasp of amazement from the men, as the rockface peeled away and created an opening large enough for them to quickly walk through into the underground dungeon.

"Now!" she said, "Our mission begins! Stay close, don't bunch up, don't make a noise! We must maintain the element of surprise!"

...oooOooo...

Vylaine had carefully studied the many and varied geographic contour wall-maps in the Throne Room. She had attempted to discover the secret hideout of the rebels and could hardly believe her eyes at just how complex the terrain was to decipher.

Suddenly, Daemon had thumped up the stone staircase and strode briskly into the Throne Room, which had surprised her. Vylaine had recovered quickly from her shock and rushed into Daemon's arms. "Oh, Daemon, I'm so glad you're back!" she said. "I've missed having you here! I know, I know! I usually try to take charge of everything, but, sometimes it's good to have someone else to bounce ideas off, or to present a different perspective!"

Initially, Daemon was a little taken aback with Vylaine's apparent slight lapse in confidence. He was used to having her as his rock, to lean on when he felt shaken. "Okay, so tell me what you've been up to while I was away?" said Daemon. He tried frantically to collect his thoughts, "It sounds like you've been busy! More importantly, is there anything happening that should concern me?" he continued.

Vylaine took a moment to recover her composure before she stood back and explained to Daemon. "I've been trying to find those damned rebels, but, all to no avail!" she said, angrily. "Unfortunately, despite everything that I've tried, they continue to keep harassing the convoys and causing untold losses of the stores I send out to the soldiers! I'm at a complete loss as to how to stop them!" Vylaine slumped back into a chair and waited expectantly for Daemon's advice.

Daemon took a long deep breath and sat down in a chair that faced Vylaine and waited, as he deliberately took his time before he spoke. "Now that I'm back, this is something we can work on together!" he said. He leaned forward with his head bowed and reached out to take Vylaine's hands.

His brain worked overtime to try to piece together the situation. "I've been doing my utmost to attempt to gather allies from our overseas trading partners!" he explained. "However, they have all been afflicted with the general downturn in trade caused by the persistent global warm weather and cannot afford to join our cause!"

Vylaine gripped his hands firmly, which caused Daemon to lift his eyes to hers. "There's no need to beat up on yourself!" she said. "I met discretely with the Emissaries from each of our immediate neighbours earlier this week and, despite making them some *very* attractive offers, achieved no better result! It seems we are in this on our own and must find a solution from within Skargness!" she said and smiled wryly.

Just at that moment, there was a polite knock on the door, and Captain Stratgii snapped to attention in their doorway and saluted sharply.

CHAPTER 36

L aytn's eyes already ached as he strained to see through the small gaps in the foliage of the trees to maintain his watch on the main gate. He waited patiently for the first sign of it opening. His men crouched among the trees on both sides of the road and stayed hidden with him ready to spring forward immediately upon his signal.

They had made their way silently out of the safety of Libertas and secreted themselves into this strategic location while the sun had not yet risen. And, they had slowly watched as the sky changed colour from grey through pink and then to orange before the glowing orb of the sun peeked its head over the horizon. It seemed to take forever before it started to climb into the clear blue sky overhead.

It wasn't too long before the bone-chilling cold of the early pre-dawn was slowly eased as the sun's warmth began to gradually take effect. As the morning progressed in silent stillness, the weight of their battle armour and the heat from the sun slowly became oppressive. Every member of Laytn's team was drenched in sweat and had become lethargic from inactivity.

Suddenly, the enormous front gate quietly started to swing open. Laytn stiffly leapt to his feet. He launched himself at the opening portal, and his men rose as one to follow him silently into the castle. As they passed swiftly through the massive gate, Laytn was surprised that he couldn't see anyone there that could have opened it. But he did notice a couple of guards tied up and they looked subdued against one wall.

Laytn paused briefly, just inside the gate, to post a squad of swordsmen and a squad of archers to guard it. He was almost caught entirely off guard when the invisible Narchis spoke right beside his ear. "Go, Laytn, we have this covered now!" said Narchis with an uncharacteristic chuckle.

Once every member of Laytn's troop was safely inside, Narchis and his team immediately closed the gate behind them. It prevented anyone inside the palace grounds from escaping and raising the alarm.

As he quickly recovered his senses, Laytn immediately sent two squads of swordsmen across the courtyard to the barracks and livery stables to flush out and round up any off-duty soldiers.

Then, he took Narchis and the rest of his men with him and set off at a sprint up the passageway. He was headed for the staircase that led upstairs to the Throne Room.

...oooOooo...

As they burst their way into the dungeon, Aedyn watched Kinta and Misty glide effortlessly over the floor and make their way out the secret sliding door, which Narchis's group had left open on their way to the gate. It took all his resolve not to shout out, and his heart soared with pride as his amazing daughter led them into battle.

He paused briefly and glanced across the dungeon to where the Dark Angels stood silently at the bars of their cell, totally confused at the intruders in their usual space. In front of their cell stood a large ominous-looking heavy wooden table, complete with many metal shackles and stirrups.

Aedyn suddenly had a graphic mental image of some of the things Seraphina had told him in confidence about her time in here. *Oh, my God!* he thought and caught his breath. Only the need to maintain absolute silence, and keep the element of surprise, allowed him to sprint after Kinta without venting his fury.

The entire squad ran on silently through the passageway and began to quickly climb the stone staircase toward the upper reaches of the castle proper. To muffle any sound of their movement through the palace, each member of the party had wrapped their sandals in sheepskin. Even their sword scabbards and arrow quivers were bound in linen cloth to prevent a squeak out of the worked leather during their progress up the stairs.

Without having stopped, Aedyn glanced to his right and could see straight down the long passageway, which leads from the foyer to the main gate, and the gate had begun to swing slowly open. Just before he returned his eyes forward again, he caught a brief glimpse of Laytn's large party of heavily armed men as they emerged from the trees that lined the road. They silently headed for the open gate with their weapons raised.

Almost there! Just a few more stairs! He thought. He wiped the back of his hand across his brow and sucked vast gulps of air into his already burning chest from the heavy, physically taxing exertion of the climb. He increased his pace slightly, and he caught up with Kinta just as she and Misty entered the Throne Room, with her longbow drawn and an arrow notched and ready to launch.

Caught completely off guard by the surprise and silent swiftness of their entry, Captain Stratgii leapt to his feet to face the intruders. He had his hand on the gilded hilt and attempted to draw his sword.

In a flash, Misty morphed into a massive white lion and launched herself. She knocked the Captain to the floor and pinned him down with an enormous paw on his chest and his sword arm in her mouth. She also glared menacingly at Daemon, and her yellow eyes blazed. A rumbling spine-chilling roar erupted from deep within her belly. He stood frozen to the spot in mortal fear.

Having recovered quickly from the shock of the intrusion, Vylaine jumped to her feet and started to raise her hands to incant a spell. Kinta swiftly released two arrows. They struck Vylaine in each shoulder and caused her to fall backwards in shock. She curled into a foetal ball to protect herself.

The arrows immediately disappeared, without leaving a wound, but Vylaine found herself locked in glowing blue manacles and leg chains around her wrists and ankles, which ultimately prevented her from being able to move at all.

The supporting warriors came charging into the Throne Room. They surrounded the captured trio, just as Kinta placed each of the other prisoners in a set of glowing blue manacles and leg chains to restrain them.

Aedyn became overjoyed at the remarkable success of the mission. He knew in his heart that Kinta was the secret weapon that had ensured its success.

...oooOooo...

Seraphina, Lorelei, and Catelyn looked at each other and tentatively smiled. Each tried to reassure the other that all would go well during the invasion of the palace, but none of them honestly felt that way inside. "Sera, I'm really anxious for Kinta!" said Catelyn. She choked back a stifled sob, then reached out her hand and gently held Seraphina's arm.

"I'm sure that she and Misty will be fine!" Seraphina said. Then, she placed her hand over Catelyn's and gently squeezed.

"Aedyn won't let anything happen to them!" said Lorelei, as she moved in closer.

"I really appreciate you both for being here to support me, at this terrible time!" Catelyn said. She leaned forward and placed her head on Seraphina's shoulder for comfort. Seraphina and Lorelei both placed their arms around Catelyn's shoulders and encircled her in an embrace. "That's what true good friends are for!" they said together, simultaneously. "Just like you were there for me earlier!" said Seraphina.

Suddenly, after a quick unanswered knock on the front door, Maeve bustled into the room all excitedly. The three girls all turned their head towards her expectantly. "Ladies, I've just received confirmed news that the fighting is officially over!" Maeve blurted out, as she tried to catch her breath from having run all the way here. "Absolutely no lives were lost, and Daemon and Vylaine were both captured and restrained!"

"Oh, thank God!" said Catelyn and her entire body sagged as she felt relief wash over her. The two sisters supported Catelyn with an arm around each shoulder and helped to get her across the room and seated into a comfortable chair. "Why don't I go and make us all a nice cup of tea?" said Lorelei. She hurried off into the kitchen.

Determined not to leave their friend's side, Seraphina sat down on one arm of Catelyn's chair, and Maeve sat down on the other, and each held one of her hands.

"Sera, you should go to Aedyn and get closure on your past life while this is all still fresh!" said Catelyn, as she looked up at Seraphina.

Seraphina looked at Catelyn and was amazed at the kind thoughtfulness of her friend, even in such trying personal circumstances. "You're right!" she said and stood to hurry out the door. "Thank you, Catelyn!"

...oooOooo...

Aedyn felt as though his chest struggled to contain his heart, which was swollen with pride for his daughter as he walked with his arm around Kinta's shoulder. Misty strutted along beside them, having morphed back into herself, as they made their way slowly down the stone staircase and back towards the dungeon.

Several paces in front of them, the three prisoners shuffled slowly along in their restraining metal manacles, shackles and leg chains. They carefully made their way downstairs, so they didn't slip and fall, surrounded by Aedyn's men. As they reached the bottom of the stone staircase, the group moved as one body towards the still-open stone secret sliding door, which was their only portal back into Vylaine's former 'dungeon of terror'.

Once inside the dungeon, Aedyn raised his hand and brought the group to a halt. Then, he politely asked Kinta to turn around and face him. "Honey, I'm very proud of you, and the citizens of Skargness will be eternally grateful for your contribution to our successful mission!" he said tenderly, "However, now I think it's imperative for you and Misty to return home and show Mama that you are both okay!"

"Of course, Papa!" said Kinta, as she hugged Aedyn tightly around the waist. "However, there's just one more thing I need to do before I leave!" she said. She straightened up, just as Seraphina entered the dungeon through the hole in the wall of her old cell and gave an involuntary shudder.

Kinta smiled and waved a greeting to Seraphina. Then, she turned to face Vylaine across the room, raised her right hand and pointed at the former high priestess with her extended index finger. "Since you're not of worthy character, you're no longer permitted to enjoy the benefits of the powers you have stolen!" she said.

A pencil-thin, intensely-blue beam left her finger and painted the priestess in blue light, which caused Vylaine to crumple and slump to the floor. Kinta and Misty immediately turned, and both headed briskly out through the opening into the tunnel, then disappeared from their view and left everyone in the room stunned.

Aedyn recovered his composure and walked over to where Captain Stratgii stood. Then, he reached out with the master key, removed the restraints and released him. "Captain, unfortunately, you were caught up in Vylaine's evil plan and had to follow her crazy orders!" he said. "I'm releasing you into the care of Commander Azrael, and the two of you are free to go!"

The two soldiers turned and walked together out through the open sliding door. They headed for the stables as Captain Stratgii rubbed his wrists and tried to get the blood to flow through them again.

Aedyn turned and paused momentarily, as he stood on the spot and waited for Seraphina to cross the room and join him. When she arrived, she placed her hand on his arm for support. They both strolled across to stop in front of Daemon and Vylaine, who had recovered enough to raise herself onto one elbow with a sarcastic look upon her face.

Once there, Aedyn stood perfectly still and took a calming breath. As he looked at Vylaine, he deliberately quelled his anger to suppress the emotion from his next words. "You are two of the most horrible human beings ever to draw breath!" he said, slowly. "And, Vylaine, your evil plan could have come to fruition in any other land, where the people's love of country and fair play is not as strong as here within Skargness!"

Aedyn turned his head to face Seraphina. He nodded and indicated that it was her turn to speak. Seraphina's eyes narrowed, and muted anger made her voice tremble when she spoke. "Now, you evil bitch, you'll experience firsthand the fear you instilled in those, for whom you should have shown respect!" she said.

Rosy-red colour rose up her neck and into her face as she remembered her time in the dungeon. Then she turned sharply to face Aedyn's men, as anger started to raise her voice. "Remove her clothes and throw her in the cell with those animals of hers!" Two warriors stepped forward and grasped Vylaine by the arms, despite her violent struggles. They lifted her to her feet and held her in position with her metal restraints still in place.

Then, Ox stepped forward!

With a couple of swift, deft strokes from his huge razor-sharp sword, Vylaine's clothing instantly fell to the floor, leaving her to stand completely naked. "Noooooo!" she screamed, absolutely terrified. The men held her under the arms, then hurled her through the quickly opened and closed cell door. The Dark Angels suddenly snapped out of their shocked stupor and launched themselves viciously at their new cellmate.

Aedyn and Seraphina, along with the others in the room, stood frozen to the spot, with eyes staring and mouth agape. They were unable to drag their gaze away from the writhing, twisting orgy that took place before them. Vylaine's initially strong efforts to hold off her attackers slowly weakened. She eventually succumbed and lay still and lifeless, a victim of her debauchery.

Suddenly, her entire body began to vibrate and hum eerily, as it emitted wispy tendrils of white smoke. It caused the Dark Angels to leap back, as they clutched at each other and cringed together into a corner of the cell in fright.

Then, spontaneously, she erupted into intense blue-white flames. Within a couple of minutes, Vylaine became a pile of grey-white ash that eventually disappeared and left just a dark smudge on the floor. All this time, the occupants of the dungeon stood stunned and speechless, with the shock of what they had just witnessed.

Then, Aedyn took a deep breath and shook his head to clear it. He turned away from the macabre scene on the cell floor to face Daemon. "And, as for you, you deserve a similar fate to your partner in crime!" he said. "Your moral weakness, lack of integrity, and inability to keep your pecker in your pants, could have destroyed our country!" he said, as he once again tried to restrain his emotion. "However, instead, you will remain incarcerated here, in a cell, until our new judicial system determines your fate!"

Ox lifted his massive arms, reached over his shoulder and sheathed his enormous sword before he stepped forward and unlocked the cell door next to the Dark Angels. Two warriors took Daemon by the arms, led him into the cell and released the manacles from his wrists and ankles. Daemon turned and moved over to the cot beside the wall, where he sat down and watched the warriors exit his cell.

They locked the heavy metal-barred door behind themselves. Then the two warriors moved across the dungeon and closed the sliding wall before they returned to stand to attention on either side of the tunnel entrance.

"Sera are you ready to leave?" Aedyn asked Seraphina quietly, as he took her gently by the elbow.

"Almost!" Seraphina paused, as if in thought, then answered quickly. *"But I'll only be a minute!"* She walked briskly across the room and disappeared briefly into a small room on the other wall. Then she hurried back out as she clutched something wrapped in a cloth, which was placed in the pocket of her dress as she re-joined Aedyn.

Then, she quickly reached up onto the shelf over Aedyn's head and hurriedly grabbed down a small tub of wool fat, which also went into her pocket, before she offered her elbow for Aedyn to support her again. *"Now, I'm ready!"* she said quietly, and stared straight ahead towards the tunnel, with a broad grin that spread slowly across her face.

"Even though you don't deserve it, you will still be treated fairly!" Aedyn said over his shoulder to Daemon. He turned and walked out into the tunnel with Seraphina on his arm. But he was still left slightly confused by the strange assortment of items she had collected from the dungeon and the smug smile she continued to wear.

CHAPTER 37

$\mathbb{A}$zrael and Captain Stratgii strolled together across the courtyard. They headed for the now secured stables, to collect the Captain's horse and allow him to return to his waiting men. "Sir, I'm greatly relieved that the madness can finally end!" said the Captain.

"Yes, I agree," answered Azrael, "Far too much damage has already occurred to our country and its people! It'll be essential to provide a long healing time, to allow Skargness to recover effectively!" he continued. "As the new Commander of the Armed Forces, I'll be counting on your total support to help me restructure the army and take us forward into lasting peace!"

Captain Stratgii quickly halted and snapped to attention. He spun on his heel to face Azrael as he saluted, but he immediately winced at the pain that shot through his saluting arm, where Misty had held him. "Sir," he said, shakily. "It'll be my honour and privilege to work for you!"

Azrael crisply returned the salute, then visibly relaxed and placed his hand on the Captain's shoulder. "Captain Stratgii, I am very impressed at your extraordinary ability to diligently follow the crazy orders of Vylaine, without actually bringing harm to any of our citizens!" he said. "Skargness needs men like you, with character and integrity, to lead our country back from the terrible place it has been! Together, you and I now have an enormous and very urgent task to perform!" Azrael said. He left his hand on the Captain's shoulder, then began to walk on towards the barracks across the courtyard.

Captain Stratgii turned and fell into step beside Azrael, and he intently listened as they approached the waiting horse and groom.

"Please, Captain, return safely and quickly to your troops, and begin to take responsibility for rounding up the entire army personally!" Azrael continued. He looked up as Captain Stratgii mounted his horse. "Bring our men home and, together, we'll finally begin the rational process of disbandment! I'll begin preparations for a temporary camp, on the plains below the palace, where we'll begin the restructure ... bring the men back to here!" he continued.

Captain Stratgii sat upright in the saddle, snapped another painful salute to his Commander, and began to head his horse for the re-opened gates of the palace.

"I've already begun discussions with Aedyn concerning a transitional training program to assist our soldiers to learn a trade after their discharge from the Army!" Azrael called after him. "Skargness has less need for soldiers and a great need for people of the trades to take us forward into peace and prosperity!" Azrael continued his explanation of the plans to move forward into the peaceful future.

Captain Stratgii smiled as he nudged the horse into a canter. *At last, I finally have a feeling of real purpose and direction to my life! And, leadership I can be proud and honoured to follow!* He thought happily, then carefully adjusted himself to the horse's gait.

...oooOooo...

Catelyn still held Kinta tightly in a loving embrace, with Misty at their feet. Aedyn finally entered their cabin, and the look of grim, puzzled determination on his face dissolved quickly into a huge grin when he finally saw all his family safe at home. "I'm now completely satisfied that we made the correct decision on our timing!" he said and walked briskly towards them. "We could not have predicted a better outcome!"

"I'm so proud of my three heroes!" Catelyn said, and she glowed with pride as she reached out her arms to envelope her husband into their cuddle. Aedyn wrapped his strong arms around the two women and exhaled slowly with relief that it was finally all over. They could now begin the long, slow process of getting their lives and their country back into order. *I'm so glad Kinta and Misty were not there at the end to see the demise of Vylaine!* He thought.

"Our daughter, Kinta, and Misty are the true heroes!" he said. His voice tinged with emotion as he looked down at Kinta. "Kinta and Misty led the entire battle from the front and are the true reason for our success! I've seen grown men crumble with less courage in battle!"

"Sweetheart, we are both very proud of you!" said Catelyn and squeezed her daughter even tighter. "You've grown up so much in the relatively short time we've been here at Libertas!" she said, as her voice quivered with emotion. "You're not our little girl anymore! Now, you're a strong young woman with the courage of a lion!"

"Hey! I thought I was the only lion in this family!" said Misty loudly and everybody laughed with relief.

"I finally feel like I've found my true purpose in life!" Kinta said as she stood up straighter and looked her parents in the eye. Her bubbly, youthful exuberance was super infectious, and the four of them clung together tightly, as they celebrated and acknowledged their tremendous growth as a family.

...oooOooo...

Erwyn gazed lovingly at Ox and Madeleine. The newlyweds sat with their arms and legs entwined, cuddled together on the couch across the room from him. He felt satisfied, knowing his daughter was utterly besotted with her new husband and her love shone from her eyes as she gazed up into Ox's face. *I'm truly blessed to have gained a son, without losing my daughter in the process!* He thought.

He watched Ox gently lift Madeleine's face and kiss her tenderly on the lips. Madeleine then reached up and lovingly raised her hand and placed her palm flat on Ox's cheek, as she snuggled her face against his chest. "Ox, my son, you have certainly made this old man's life complete, with the love you have given to Madeleine!" said Erwyn from across the room.

Ox reluctantly dragged his eyes away from Madeleine's face and looked up to where Erwyn sat across the room in his comfy chair.

"Papa, it's me who is the lucky one! Now, I truly have a family that I can love, that will also love me in return!" he said. "This is the first time in my life that I feel like I truly belong somewhere!"

Ox leaned forward, and Madeleine separated herself from him as he stood and addressed them both. "I am also the bearer of good news for our family!" he said, as a smile crept across his face. "Aedyn has selected me as the Head of his Personal Guards, which will require us all to live within the palace compound! But, equally, as exciting, I have negotiated for the two of you to be equal Heads of the Palace Staff, responsible for all the catering, cleaning and any entertaining staff within the palace!" he continued.

Erwyn felt moisture well in his eyes, and a small teardrop broke the banks and trickled down his face.

...oooOooo...

Aedyn stood proudly dressed in his new formal attire, tall and ramrod straight beside the dais. He gazed proudly at Catelyn, Kinta, and Misty, who stood beside him.

He lifted his gaze slightly to take in the royal families from Wachile, Eshoram, and Nantgarw. Then, he looked out across the sea of smiling faces. He could hardly contain his emotions, as he remembered all that they had been through in the last few months. He glanced around at Laytn and remembered the first time they had met when he and his family had arrived at the rebel camp hidden in the secret valley.

But today, in his new role as the Lord Chancellor, his friend Laytn had a crucial, and personally satisfying, task to perform. He stood beside Seraphina, who was seated upon the throne on the dais. She wore the jewel-encrusted golden Ruler's Crown upon her head. "Your Majesty," he said, loudly and dramatically for the entire gathered throng to hear. "Now that we no longer have a King, do you accept full responsibility and assume the role as Ruler of our land?"

There was a long, drawn-out pause for dramatic effect before Seraphina finally stood up. She looked directly into Laytn's eyes, carefully lifted and removed the Ruler's Crown from her head, then very carefully passed it to Laytn. "I have carefully considered all that would be required to do as you have asked and find that I would be unable to fulfil the responsibilities of that role!" she said, with an emotional tremor in her voice.

Seraphina raised her face and held out her hands beseechingly to the assembled crowd. "Therefore, people of Skargness, it is with a sad and heavy heart that I must abdicate my role as Ruler! However, I happily nominate my replacement ... Aedyn, Leader of our Freedom Movement and Defender of our Land!" she continued loudly.

An immediate hush fell over the entire crowd. Not a soul stirred, as they waited with bated breath in silent anticipation. Seraphina turned and stepped carefully down from the side of the dais. Then she stopped right beside the edge of the dais and turned back to look across at Aedyn. A cheeky, conspiratorial grin played at the corners of her mouth. She caught Aedyn's eye and gave him a discrete wink. It caused him to wrinkle his nose and purse his lips to prevent himself from smiling during this serious occasion.

Laytn slowly and reverently raised the Ruler's Crown high above his head. He held it out in the general direction of the vast massed crowd. "People of Skargness," he implored loudly. "Do you endorse this nomination?" A tremendous thundering roar erupted from the crowd. The noise continued with their fists raised in salute to the one man they knew was responsible for leading their country to freedom.

It was precisely the response he had expected. Slowly, the deafeningly loud noise of the throbbing crowd began to decrease. A huge grin spread across Laytn's face. He turned to face his leader and best friend Aedyn, who stood beside the dais. He was the man Laytn had prayed would arrive at Libertas to lead them to victory.

It was the very pomp and ceremony he had missed from his former life. The moment he had dreamed of every waking moment, during the entire time of their exile in the hidden valley, was about to come true. "Where is this man, Aedyn, Leader of our Freedom Movement and Defender of our Land?" he called in a booming voice. "Show me the man that shall be King!"

Aedyn glanced across the platform and caught Seraphina's eye. She beamed, winked, and discretely nodded to show her full approval.

Then, he nodded back his understanding and stepped up onto the dais. He took a couple of paces forward until he stood directly in front of Laytn. Then he smiled, turned and made a single step forward and held his hands out to the crowd. "I am that man, Aedyn!" he thundered and placed his open right hand over his heart. "And, I gratefully accept your hearty endorsement, and will gladly assume the heavy mantle of responsibility for taking our land forward into the future!"

Laytn stepped forward. He gently raised and placed the Ruler's Crown on Aedyn's head with all the formal pomp of ceremony that the task deserved. Then, he took a step back to stand to one side of the new King before he turned and faced the crowd.

"Long live, King Aedyn!" Laytn shouted with passion. Once more, the crowd erupted into cheering!

Aedyn stepped forward to the very front of the dais to address the crowd. The people's great love and immense respect for this man simply added fuel to their enthusiasm. They began to chant his name, and the noise reached previously unheard proportions.

He waited patiently for the uproar to slowly die down before he attempted to speak. "Since you, the people of our fine country, have blessed me with this role, I have some pleasing announcements to make as your new King!" he said.

Aedyn glowed with the pride he felt for the moral courage and strength of purpose of his people. "Firstly, the former King will be brought before our court and tried for treason against our land!" Aedyn explained. "He will be judged before our new Lord Chancellor, Laytn, by a jury of your peers, which shall be selected by *you* and, as *your* chosen representatives, and this jury shall determine his guilt or innocence!"

A huge cheer erupted again …

Then, Aedyn paused and drew a calming breath. He was personally anxious to hear the crowd's response to his next proclamation. "Finally, as your King, I decree that from this time forward, our country will henceforth be called Libertas, the Land of the Free!"

This time, the crowd's roar took an extraordinarily long time to dissipate before they broke into spontaneous singing and dancing. The ongoing celebrations lasted for the next three days and nights across the whole land.

CHAPTER 38

W hile she and Catelyn stood beside Aedyn, during his coronation ceremony, Kinta had noticed a tall, blond, handsome young man. He was just a few years older than herself and stood proudly beside his father, the King of Nantgarw.

She felt the first slight flush of embarrassment colour her face. She had suddenly become aware that Vaalyun openly admired her as well while she stood up there beside her parents. *I'm glad Mama and Misty convinced me to wear this pretty dress, rather than my battle armour, for today's ceremony!* She thought to herself.

Then, she blushed even further when she realised that she thoroughly enjoyed his admiring glances. Almost unconsciously, Kinta stood up straighter and brushed down the front of her dress to remove any creases. Then, she pulled back her shoulders, which emphasised the ample swell of her firm young breasts. They stood up proudly beneath the thin fabric of her new dress.

As a brand-new princess, and without any formal training, Kinta was not entirely sure exactly how she was meant to behave during formal occasions. However, despite the lack of formal training, she continued to covertly admire the young man's handsome face, broad shoulders, narrow waist, and thick muscular arms and legs.

Suddenly, the formalities were over, and the royal guests made their way to the dais to offer their congratulations to the new royal family. Aedyn stepped down from his place on the raised dais. Then, he turned and extended his hand to Catelyn to assist her as she stepped down. Once Catelyn was safely down, Aedyn turned to extend Kinta his hand, only to see a handsome young man had already helped her.

Then, suddenly, Aedyn's hand was grasped firmly by the King of Nantgarw and shaken vigorously. "Congratulations, King Aedyn of Libertas! I am Nyvorlas, your northern neighbour!" he said. "This is my wife, Liluth, and my son Vaalyun is the presumptive one, who took your daughter's hand from under your nose!"

"Thank you, Nyvorlas!" he said and chuckled. Aedyn warmly returned Nyvorlas's firm handshake. "But, please ask Vaalyun to return my daughter's hand!"

Nyvorlas glanced around to where Vaalyun stood and noticed his son still held Kinta's hand. The two of them stared dreamily into each other's eyes. That was until he finally realised that they were the centre of the conversation. Then, Vaalyun quickly dropped Kinta's hand as if it were a hot ember and stepped back.

The two men laughed out loud. The others around them joined in until, eventually, Aedyn regained his composure and turned back to face Nyvorlas. "Thank you, Nyvorlas, for your good wishes!" he said and introduced his family members. "This is my wife Catelyn, daughter Kinta, and our special friend Misty!"

"I don't think I speak out of place, but I do know that I certainly speak for all present. When I tell you how much all Nantgarw are excited by *your* replacement of that bumbling imbecile, Daemon!" enthused Nyvorlas. He leaned forward and conspiratorially spoke as he grasped Aedyn by the upper arm. "And, now Libertas truly has the opportunity to flourish on the global map!"

Suddenly, there was an intense rush of activity as the other royal guests each tried to be the next to offer their congratulations and introductions. In the distraction that this generated, Kinta sensed Vaalyun's acute embarrassment from his hung head and shuffled feet. She reached out and tenderly retook Vaalyun's hand into her own. Then, as she leaned forward, she whispered into his ear. "*When the crowd finally disperses, and the festivities are in full swing, we'll be able to speak together discretely!*"

Instantly, Vaalyun's whole demeanour changed and he stood up straighter. Then his face lit up and glowed. He smiled and squeezed Kinta's hand gently in return. Kinta's heart seemed to skip a beat as she suddenly realised the impact she'd had on the man before her.

Then, when it felt like her heart was going to leap out of her chest, it began to thump so loudly that she thought everyone must surely be able to hear it. Kinta looked down, and her eyes met Misty's. Both girls knew instantly what the other was thinking.

...oooOooo...

Catelyn awoke unusually early in the morning, just before the sun had even peeked in through the large drapes that covered the large floor-to-ceiling windows. It was unusually early, considering the late night of ongoing coronation celebrations they had attended the evening before. However, unusually for her, she was feeling a little nauseous and queasy in the stomach. *I'm sure I didn't eat anything strange, or spicy, last night!* She thought. She kept her eyes closed and turned over onto her back. Then she pulled the covers up loosely around her chin and attempted to go back to sleep.

Then, the sun rose, and bright morning light streamed in through the huge glass windows of the royal palace bedroom. It splashed across the rumpled linen of the large comfortable wooden bed in which they lay. Slowly, she opened her eyes and tried to get her bearings, as she felt a little disoriented. *The last time I remember feeling like this, I was pregnant with Kinta...*

The thought trailed off as Catelyn gently placed both hands on her lower belly. Suddenly, she remembered again that her life was about to take another fantastic twist and turn. Then, she turned her head to look at Aedyn as he slept beside her. She felt a sudden rush of emotion, as she realised just how deep her love was for her husband. *First time round turned out pretty good! Let's hope it turns out alright again!* She thought and smiled to herself. *I think it's time to share my exciting news with the rest of the family!*

Catelyn rolled gently onto her side, lifted her head slightly and placed it onto Aedyn's shoulder. She snuggled up closer to him until he opened one eye. Then he tenderly reached around and put his arm around her shoulders. He pulled her closer and kissed her lightly on the forehead. "Good morning, light of my life!" he asked her sleepily. "Did you sleep well after the celebrations last night?"

"Mmmmm!" was her equally sleepy reply. "However, this morning I don't feel quite so good!"

Aedyn turned his head slightly to face her, with a deep frown etched into his forehead and obvious concern written all over his face. "I hope it's nothing serious?" he asked, as Catelyn smiled and nodded her head.

"It's very serious!" she said and giggled. "You're going to be a Papa again, my sweet, and Kinta will be a big sister!" Aedyn immediately wrapped her in his strong muscular arms and rocked her gently until he could trust himself to speak again. "You've made me the happiest man on earth!" he said and kissed her again. "A new life to share as *we* begin *our* new life!"

Carefully, he sat up and gently lifted Catelyn, placed several large cushions beneath her back for support, then they both sat up in the bed, still cuddled together. Aedyn turned his head toward the massive closed wooden door at the entrance to their bedroom, leaned forward and placed his hand up to his mouth. "Kinta! Misty!" he yelled loudly to get their attention. "Come girls quickly, and we have some exciting news!"

The two girls burst into the room like a sudden summer storm, each determined to be the first to hear the news. They bounded onto the bed and flopped down together onto the covers, and their eyes sparkled. "Tell me! Tell me! Tell me!" they shouted, as each tried to outdo the other.

"We are blessed to be having an addition to our family!" Aedyn announced. He and Catelyn both laughed out loud at the girls' excitement. "Mama and I are going to have another baby!" he said. Then, he leaned back next to Catelyn and placed his arm around her shoulders again.

Kinta crawled up the bed and wriggled and squirmed until she sat between her parents. Then, Misty jumped up onto Kinta's lap to be close. She sat there as her tongue hung out and her tail wagged vigorously.

"Mama is it true?" asked Kinta and her eyes glowed. "How do you know for sure?"

Catelyn chuckled, leaned her head over until it rested lightly on Kinta's head and reached out her hand to touch Kinta's face lovingly before she spoke. "Yes, it's true!" she said gently to Kinta. "And, Mamas just know these things!"

Then, she reached down and ruffled the hair on top of Misty's head, who immediately rolled over to have her belly rubbed. "Oh, Misty!" Catelyn laughed out loud. "I think it's me who should get a belly rub!"

The whole family laughed and cuddled each other as they relaxed and tried to look forward to pleasant memories in the future, rather than the unpleasant memories from their immediate past.

...oooOooo...

In the busy days since Vylaine and Daemon's capture, a lot of changes had taken place in Libertas. Aedyn, Catelyn, Kinta, and Misty settled comfortably into the refurbished royal quarters within the palace, which now included a new nursery for the baby.

Aedyn and Catelyn found it refreshing to stand together upon the battlements of the palace each evening, as the sun set over the mountains. They looked out over the patchwork quilt of tilled fields and vineyards across the valley floor and down to the broad blue hazy line of the Great Southern Ocean on the far horizon.

Catelyn's already swollen abdomen made it difficult for her to comfortably climb the steep stone staircase all the way up to the battlements. But the peaceful time that this allowed her to share with Aedyn made it worth the extra effort involved. Besides, she enjoyed the additional tender assistance that Aedyn provided as he helped her to climb the staircase.

The two sisters, Seraphina and Lorelei, relocated themselves into the temple extension on the side of the palace, which was now two luxury apartments. There they shared the occasional overnight company of Tyson, in their capacity as advisers to the royal family.

Over the past half year, the formerly displaced villagers, whose homes, fortunately, weren't destroyed, have all returned from the rustic cabins in the secret valley, and have again taken up some semblance of ordinary existence. Even the children, for whom every event in their life is just another adventure, whether good or bad, have returned to their education at the regular village schools. The sound of their laughter can be heard as it rings out while they play during class breaks.

The regular weekly sound of the clang of church bells rings out across the valley again, which summoned the villagers to prayer. It signalled the only day of rest for the hard-working rural community and was a welcome addition to the regular timetable of life in the new Libertas.

As the new Lord Chancellor, Laytn was utterly determined to finally bring justice and fairness to the judicial system, for which he had willingly assumed full responsibility and now only answered to King Aedyn.

Today was the first day of former King Daemon's hearing, and Laytn was pleased that a jury was finally selected. Now the citizens of Libertas would get the opportunity to put forward all the evidence of Daemon's cruelty and negligence.

Maeve had made him a hearty breakfast this morning, which the two of them had shared. Now he travelled by coach to Bayville for the hearing.

CHAPTER 39

After the formalities of the coronation ceremony, Kinta and Vaalyun had excused themselves and spent the evening as they walked and whispered together. They had laughed, gasped and been generally astounded at the vast difference in their life experiences up to that point. Particularly the involvement of Kinta in the recent battle for freedom.

But there was one thing of which they were both certain. That was the intense desire to spend more time together in shared experiences, from this point forward. They had gone along together and spoken to both sets of parents. It was agreed that Kinta would visit Vaalyun in the summertime when she accompanied Aedyn and Catelyn to Nantgarw for a civic reception that Nyvorlas and Liluth were to hold in their honour.

Now, the time had come for Aedyn and Catelyn to make the first of their many planned formal visits. Kinta was very excited as she packed her things to join them on this royal visit to Nantgarw. "Misty, I can't believe that we are finally going!" she said. She rubbed her hands together briskly, and her eyes sparkled, but with a far-off look.

Misty stretched herself out on the top of the bed and watched fascinated as Kinta selected various outfits from her wardrobe. She held them up to the light, then held them up to her and swirled around, then placed them in her travel chest if they met her requirements. "I know!" said Misty. "It seems like such a long time since the coronation! You must be looking forward to seeing Vaalyun again soon?"

Kinta stopped and clasped her hands together under her chin. Her eyes seemed to stare off into the distance momentarily before she turned to face Misty. "Oh, Misty, it feels like forever since we last spoke!" she said. "I enjoyed Vaalyun's company, and it feels like we've known each other for our whole lives!"

Kinta turned and looked at her reflection in a large mirror mounted on the wall. She studied her face intently and played with her hair for some minutes as she changed from her hair being up, to her hair being down again, then from having a tight ponytail, to carefree, loose and ruffled. Then, she turned side on to the mirror and slowly, thoughtfully, studied her profile. She pushed out her firm young breasts and pulled in her stomach and buttocks as she turned continuously from side to side. She spent quite some time as she admired the curvaceous contours of her trim young woman's body, and all the while chatted away animatedly to herself and Misty.

"Do you think he'll recognise me again?"

'Will he see me as a woman, or will he think I'm just too young to be taken seriously?"

"Oh, Misty, I hope he still likes me!"

Our young princess is falling in love! Misty thought. She chuckled silently to herself as she smiled and closed her eyes.

...oooOooo...

Madeleine sat down on the couch close beside Ox, lifted one of his massive hands and placed it gently on her lap. Then, she grasped two fingers of his enormous hand between both of her small hands. Since they had moved into their new quarters in the palace, there was so much more room for the three of them.

Because of the height in each room, Ox didn't have to hunch over to miss the ceiling now continually. "Now, what was it that was so important that you needed to tell me immediately?" she asked.

"Aedyn has asked me to accompany the royal family to Nantgarw, as his bodyguard!" Ox said. He turned his massive head and looked lovingly down into Madeleine's eyes. Then he carefully lifted his huge arm and placed it around his petite young wife's shoulders. She continued to hold the fingers on his hand and snuggled up close to his massive body.

Erwyn sat in his comfortable chair near the fireplace. Upon having heard this news, he looked up over the top rim of his glasses as he read his book to listen.

"This means that I will be away for one complete cycle of the moon!" Ox continued. "I wish I could take you with me! I hate having to spend time away from you and Papa! It is my home now!"

Madeleine snuggled up even closer. She squeezed the two fingers of Ox's hand tightly before she spoke. "My darling husband, I will also miss you greatly while you are absent from our lives on your royal bodyguard duties!" she said quietly, then looked up lovingly into Ox's eyes. "I'm very proud of you and all that you have done and love you more than words can express! However, my darling, there is something equally significant I must also tell you!" she continued.

Madeleine carefully lifted Ox's huge hand from around her shoulders and placed it gently upon her belly. She covered it and held it in place with her two hands before she continued. "As much as Aedyn is relying upon you to protect his life while you are away with him, I am counting on you to return quickly to share and protect the miracle of the new little life we have created within me!" she said.

Ox's eyes grew huge, and an enormous grin spread across his face. He struggled to find the words to precisely say what he was thinking. "What...? Am I...? Are you...? Do you mean...?" he asked stammering, incredulous.

Madeleine felt her love for Ox swell within her chest until she didn't feel she could contain it within her body. "Yes, my darling, you're going to be a Papa!" she chuckled. They both turned to look at Erwyn who just glowed, with a tiny tear that trickled down over one cheek.

"Now, I'll be Papa, and you'll be Grandpapa!" said Ox to Erwyn proudly and they all laughed heartily.

...oooOooo...

Laytn lifted the heavy wooden gavel and banged it down loudly on the polished timber block on top of the bench.

"Order in the Court! All present, be seated!" yelled the Sergeant-At-Arms. It immediately prompted a shuffling and rustling of those who complied. "Bring in the prisoner!" Laytn shouted, to compensate for the ongoing noise of movement.

A sudden hush fell over the courtroom, as everyone leaned forward slightly, in anticipation of what was about to happen. A huge collective gasp arose from the crowd, as the heavy solid oaken door in the side wall swung slowly open.

Two heavily armed guards brought Daemon stumbling between them into the courtroom. He appeared to have aged dramatically in the several months since his incarceration followed the revolutionary coup that toppled his reign. This image was amplified with his face unshaven and his hair and beard long, grey, knotted and unkempt.

Slowly, painfully, he shuffled and dragged his bare feet across the polished timber floor, in the massive, restraining metal leg-chains and manacles. He was led to the dock and securely locked into place by the guards.

The strong morning sunlight streamed in through the large plate-glass windows. They were set high up in the walls on either side. The bright golden beams highlighted the tiny motes of dust that floated in the air and illuminated the prisoner's dock like a spotlight.

In his pathetic attempt to maintain some degree of personal dignity, during the initial part of the hearing, Daemon had tried to remain standing. Albeit with his head bowed, and his legs and back bent due to the heavy restraints. The short, heavy, metal chains prevented him from standing fully upright, and he certainly looked like a beaten and broken man. Loud mutters and whispers erupted among the gallery.

Laytn banged the gavel several times loudly, to try to gain control of the room again. "Prisoner, you are charged with treason against the State!" Laytn asked in his best loud officious voice. "How do you plead?"

There was immediate silence as all ears strained to hear the reply. Daemon stood up as tall and straight as the heavy restraints would permit before answering in a soft quavering voice. "Not guilty!"

Catcalls rang out loudly from all around the room, as the outraged citizens took their first opportunity to voice their apparent anger at how their country almost was destroyed at Daemon's hands.

"Hang the traitor!"

"Nah, hanging's too good for him!"

"Give him to the Dark Angels!"

Peals of laughter rang out at each suggestion, and a festive atmosphere again lifted the room. The noise of the gavel rang out across the courtroom and order was slowly restored.

"Bring in the jury!" Layton addressed the Sergeant-at-Arms, who immediately walked briskly across the polished wooden floor of the courtroom. He opened the polished mahogany wooden door behind Laytn's bench, to allow the jurors to enter and file into place.

The eight chosen men and four chosen women slowly shuffled into the room. They nervously took their positions on the twelve padded wooden seats that had been set up in two rows down one wall at the side of the courtroom beside the raised bench and chair upon which sat Laytn.

Once they were all finally into the room, seated and comfortable, having ensured they had each sat in the seat marked with their name, Laytn addressed them. "Ladies and gentlemen of the jury, thank you for being here today!" he said. "Your duty to this court is a matter of national importance! Throughout this trial, you will hear both the prosecution and defence put forward their cases, in the matter of treason by the prisoner before you to the State of Libertas, formerly known as Skargness!"

He continued. "It is your responsibility to determine the guilt or innocence of the prisoner, based entirely upon the evidence presented before you! Members of the jury, are you prepared to swear that you will perform this task to the best of your ability?"

Aartuur, the baker from Bayville, who had been elected as the Chairman of the jury, stood up from his seat at the left-hand end of the front row and answered on their behalf. "We are, Your Lordship!" Aartuur responded in a voice loud enough to be heard above the general hum of conversation in the gallery, and by the massed crowd of citizens outside, who were unable to fit inside the courtroom.

As Aartuur sat slowly back down, Layton banged his gavel again loudly. He waited patiently, as he smiled to himself at how well everything was going until the noise had once again abated before he responded. "Thank you, Mr Chairman!"

Layton then addressed the crowded room. "Members of the public gallery, you are permitted here today, at the benevolence of His Majesty, King Aedyn, to witness justice being done! If by your actions, whether fair or foul, you impede the processes of this court, you will be expelled and barred from further entry!" he continued. "Do I make myself clear?"

An intense hush descended immediately upon the citizens within the courtroom. Laytn could hear his heart beating in his chest, and all movement in the room ceased. Layton looked down at his notes on the bench in front of him, smiled broadly to himself and said out loud, "I'll take that as a resounding '*Yes*'!"

CHAPTER 40

Two short, portly footmen struggled slowly down the final few stone steps at the main entrance to the palace. They dragged the massive weight of the enormous wooden chest behind them but had to admit total defeat when they attempted to lift it onto the roof at the rear of the royal carriage.

Several of the general palace staff, who had gathered at the foot of the stone stairs to farewell Aedyn and the royal family, rushed forward to assist. But, alas, the combined efforts of all couldn't lift the massive weight of the chest. The footmen and staff members now milled around the chest on the ground. They each waved their arms about and discussed various theories, in loud voices, on how they would be able to lift it.

Fortunately, before too long, Ox emerged from inside the palace, as he walked along with the royal family. He immediately noticed the commotion behind the carriage, excused himself and strode down the front stone steps to assist in raising the massive chest. "Stand aside and allow me to lift that!" he shouted, in his deep booming voice. Immediately, the footmen and staff members leapt backwards in fright to allow him through.

Then he stepped forward, carefully placed one of each of his huge hands on either end of the massive chest and hoisted it quickly onto the roof. Then he made his way to the side of the carriage, which had now sagged significantly down at the rear.

Ox carefully opened the gleaming gilded door of the carriage, which now carried the brand-new Royal Arms emblem of the House of Aedyn. Then, he stood stiffly upright to one side. He allowed the royal family to climb in and take their places inside the carriage while he offered his hand to assist them aboard.

He waited until they were each comfortably seated before he closed the door and scrambled up onto the front seat near the driver. It now caused the front of the carriage to settle down much lower onto the springs and lean to one side.

Meanwhile, the two footmen had clambered up and scrambled about on the carriage's roof. Eventually, they managed to get the massive chest moved into its correct place, correctly tied down and secured for the long journey ahead. As they carefully climbed back down the steps onto their footplates at the rear, they were exhausted and breathed a massive sigh of relief and grabbed the handrail, just as the driver cracked his whip.

The carriage moved forward slowly. It gathered speed as it crossed the courtyard. Then, it burst through the already open gates before it raced down the gravel road. It disappeared among the trees in a cloud of dust, closely followed by a highly trained squad of heavily armed and mounted House Guards.

The four occupants were excited to be finally on their way. Their conversation was light and bubbly, with most of the discussion led by Kinta and Misty. Seated up front with the driver, Ox relaxed slightly and settled down into his seat, as he prepared for the long journey to Nantgarw. The timid driver slowly turned his head towards Ox. He nervously smiled as he asked, "Is this your first big coach trip?"

"It certainly is!" Ox nodded as he answered. He leaned back into the padding at the small of his back. "However, I am caught between my excitement for the new experience and concern for the safety of our passengers!"

Ox turned his head and looked back through the gaps in the trees overhead to where Madeleine and Erwyn still stood and waved from the ramparts high up on the top of the royal palace. His eyes became slightly misty, and he choked somewhat as he thought of how much he loved his current and future family. He would miss them while he was absent for the next full cycle of the moon.

Suddenly, the foliage of the trees closed in and covered his view. Ox turned forward again and slumped slightly into the seat. Suddenly, he sat bolt upright and shook his big shaggy head, which caused the carriage to sway alarmingly. "I must be alert for any threat to the royal occupants!" he said aloud, almost to himself.

The driver fought furiously for several minutes to regain control as the carriage swayed, then chuckled and slapped Ox warmly on the upper arm. "My friend, their Majesties are in very safe hands!" the driver said. Then he asked as if trying to reassure himself. "What, with yourself guarding up front here and the twenty-man escort, armed and mounted and riding behind us, nobody will attempt anything ... will they?"

Ox relaxed slightly and turned to face the driver. A cheeky grin spread across his face. "I certainly hope not, or I'll have to use you as cannon fodder to help protect them!" he said. His huge booming chuckle caused the seat to vibrate.

"You wouldn't ... would you?" the driver asked shakily. He turned back to focus on driving the horses.

Ox's chuckle started small but rapidly grew until it became a rumbling thunder of laughter and his whole body rocked back and forth, which caused the carriage to sway like it was a dinghy on the open sea. Kinta suddenly emerged from a front side window and asked the driver, "Mr Driver, is everything alright? We seem to be swaying around a lot, despite the road being smooth!"

The driver swallowed nervously before he answered, "I'm sorry, Princess Kinta! There seems to be a huge disturbance aboard, which I am unable to control!"

"Mr Driver, please inform our huge disturbance that we shall all need motion sickness medication if he doesn't settle!" said Kinta. Her tinkling laughter sounded like a wind chime that blew in a gentle breeze.

Ox turned and leaned right across the driver until he could see Kinta's face as she looked up at him. "I'm sorry, Miss Kinta!" he apologised. "I'm missing my family already and was trying to distract myself at the driver's expense!"

Kinta immediately felt her heart go out to the gentle giant. She was desperately missing Vaalyun, and her face softened before she replied. "Loyal Ox, I thank you for being here with us to provide us with the level of protection that only you can!" she said. "We all feel much safer for having you along!"

"Thank you, Miss Kinta! I will try not to move too much and cause the carriage to sway!" said Ox and shifted uncomfortably in his seat.

"Thank you very much, Ox!" said Kinta and smiled. "We shall stop the carriage in a couple of hours and then we can all stretch our legs!"

Ox straightened up his massive body and settled back into the seat. He glanced around to check his surroundings as the driver gulped and swallowed nervously, his eyes fixed firmly on the road ahead.

Feeling satisfied that she had calmed Ox's disturbances and reassured the driver, Kinta eased herself gently back into the carriage. She settled back into the plush cushioning of the seat and smiled at Mama and Papa. "We're certainly in very safe hands with Ox to protect us!" she said.

Then Misty climbed up onto Kinta's lap and settled herself down comfortably. It didn't take very long after that before their eyes became heavy and both girls began to nod their heads against their chest. They slowly drifted into a light sleep.

"We are indeed blessed with our daughter, Kinta!" said Aedyn. He leaned across and spoke gently to Catelyn. "She's grown up into such a strong, confident young woman so quickly though. It only seems like yesterday she was a little girl!"

Catelyn's eyes misted, and she nodded slowly as the memories flooded back.

...oooOooo...

The thin mountain air slowly grew progressively cooler. The narrow dusty road climbed up through the winding rocky pass and twisted and turned between the snow-covered peaks of the bordering mountain ranges. Shaggy white mountain sheep stopped dead in their tracks and raised their heads in the middle of their mindless, endless migration in search of food. They silently watched the dusty cavalcade pass by before they resumed their endeavours.

Ox's eyes were everywhere. He scoured the cracks and crevices in the steep sides of the pass, as he knew instinctively that this was the ideal setting for bandits to attempt to rob them. Kinta had joined him on the roof of the carriage. She sat armed with her longbow and ready for immediate response to any situation that may arise.

The sun had just begun to set behind the tops of the mountain peaks and the cold evening air had turned violet. Dusk had settled over the ranges when Ox turned his huge shaggy bearded head and spoke over his shoulder. "Miss Kinta, the driver, has advised that we are approaching a Tavern. We should stop here for the night!" he said. "It won't be safe to proceed after dark through these parts!"

"Papa, we are stopping at a Tavern soon!" said Kinta. She gripped the side of the roof and leaned down to speak through the window of the carriage. "Will this be suitable accommodation for tonight?"

"Yes, of course! We've made perfect time today!" Aedyn answered. "Please advise the driver, and we will all enjoy the comforts of the Tavern for tonight!"

The royal carriage and its heavily-armed mounted escort came at speed around a sharp bend, and the Tavern came into view up ahead. It was snuggled up against the rocky backdrop of the cliff face that towered over it. The driver dragged back heavily on the long leather reins and slowed the carriage. Then, he brought it to a rocking halt immediately outside the front door of the Tavern. Welcoming lamp-light spilled out through the opening and beckoned them inside.

Both footmen leapt down from their perch at the rear of the carriage. They hurried to open the doors for the royal passengers. Aedyn and Catelyn alighted and stretched the kinks out of their bodies after the long day's journey cramped into the royal carriage, albeit in relative comfort.

"Mama, Papa, I'll be joining you both shortly!" Kinta yelled down from the roof of the carriage. "We're just going to move the carriage around to the side of the Tavern, so it doesn't block the entrance here!"

"Okay, my darling, we'll order you something to eat for when you come inside then!" replied Catelyn. She and Aedyn turned and made their way inside with Misty, followed by their entire entourage.

"Gee up!" yelled the driver loudly as he flicked the long leather reins. The carriage moved off slowly down to the side of the Tavern. There they parked it before they unhitched the horses and walked them into the undercover shelter in the stables behind the Tavern for the night.

When everything had been unpacked from the royal carriage and was ready to be moved inside, Ox clambered back up onto the roof of the wagon. He snuggled up tightly into a warm blanket where he could guard the wagon against any would-be pilferers.

"Good night, Ox, and thank you for volunteering to be the guard for the royal carriage tonight!" called Kinta over her shoulder. She turned around, rubbed her hands together briskly against the bitter-cold high-altitude night air, then walked back to the front door and made her way inside into the warmth of the Tavern.

"Good night, Miss Kinta!" Ox replied quietly to himself as she disappeared. Then he settled his huge body down on the exposed roof of the royal carriage for the long night's vigil ahead.

As Kinta stepped in through the entrance to the Tavern, she immediately spied Aedyn and Catelyn, along with their entire group of support staff, seated at a large table in the middle of the room. Upon learning the true identity of his guests for the evening, the Tavern owner had called in all staff, even those that were meant to be on a break. He was exceeding even his exceptional service to ensure that his overnight occupants were comfortable and had everything they desired and more.

Catelyn looked up, smiled and waved her hand to show where they were seated. Kinta made her way quickly across the room and joined them. The serving staff almost fell over each other as they attempted to rearrange the seating for the new guest to join the table.

Then, like a swiftly flowing mountain stream, the food began to flow out onto the table. It started to groan under the tremendous weight and servants hurriedly scurried back and forth to and from the kitchen as they carried huge platters of roast meat and mountains of vegetables.

It had been so long since the owner of the Tavern had hosted such VIP guests, he was not going to spare any expense. He was determined to ensure they were pleased with his hospitality tonight, so that they may return themselves or recommend his Tavern to their friends.

When the royal party and the entire entourage had all finished eating, Aedyn stood up from the long trestle table and called the delighted Tavern owner across to the table. "Thank you for this fine spread! We will be retiring to our rooms now!" he said. "Please see that a substantial meal is sent to the man guarding the carriage!"

"It will be as you wish, Your Majesty!" said the Tavern owner.

CHAPTER 41

Misty awoke early in the morning, to the first pale sunbeams that cheekily peeked through the drab curtain-covered windows to herald the new day. She stretched languidly, then rolled slowly and gently over onto her belly, to better survey the sparsely decorated surroundings in the tiny room.

Since Kinta still slept soundly, her slow, gentle breathing caused the warm, heavy covers to rise and fall rhythmically. Her mass of golden-blond curls formed a halo around her head on the soft duck-down stuffed pillow.

The surfaces of all the thin walls were patchy. In some places, they were unpainted and in desperate need of some serious maintenance attention. It was not altogether unusual as they matched the peeled and stained ceiling perfectly.

However, although the connecting door to the bathroom was only barely functional, Misty was pleased to see that the main entrance into the room was soundly constructed. It was made from solid timber beams with a good solid metal lock, which would provide some security if needed.

She wriggled and squiggled her way slowly and carefully up along the bed until she had reached the area of Kinta's warm lower back. There she snuggled up close and waited for Kinta to awaken for the day.

It didn't take long before Kinta's eyes slowly opened. Her long,

lean legs stretched out as she rolled over onto her back, then pushed
down the heavy covers slightly. She stretched her arms and yawned,
then greeted her friend. "Good morning, Misty! Did you sleep well?"

At that, Misty jumped up quickly, then climbed up onto the
bedclothes that still covered Kinta's belly and sat there looking into
her face. "I slept like I was on a cloud!" she replied.

Kinta giggled and stroked her fingertips gently down through the
thick fur on Misty's back before she scratched the base of her spine
where she found it difficult to scratch herself. Misty's tail wagged
vigorously with pleasure at the relief. She eased Misty down off her
stomach and onto the bed before she rolled out and stood up onto the
polished wooden floor with her bare feet. Then, she stretched her arms
up high above her head and tried to come awake properly. "C'mon,
Misty!" she said, "You go and get yourself something to eat! But first,
I'm going into our bathroom next door to relax in a hot bath for a
while!" she continued. "Tell Mama and Papa that I'll be down to eat
with them soon!"

Misty made her way carefully onto the floor and over to the door.
Then, she waited for Kinta to open the door just enough for her to be
able to get through before she slipped out and headed for the dining area.

Kinta peeked out through the small opening into the passageway
to see if anybody else was up and about at this time. But she was
pleasantly surprised to see it empty, and she locked the main door
behind Misty. Then she crossed the small room and opened the thin
wooden dividing door.

She stepped into the even smaller bathroom, which had a full-sized
deep bath along one wall and a large floor-to-ceiling mirror on the
opposite wall. Fortunately, there was a large copper vat of steaming
hot water. It bubbled away already over an enclosed fireplace in one
corner. An equally large barrel of icy cold water had been stored in
another corner.

After she locked the bathroom door behind her and used the
large spoon that was provided, Kinta half-filled the bathtub with
the steaming hot water. Then, she topped it up with cold water and
measured the temperature with her elbow until it was comfortable
for her body.

She slipped out of her warm fleecy pyjamas in readiness for her bath and hung them up behind the door to keep them dry. She was pleasantly surprised to notice her full-length naked reflection in the large mirror on the wall. She rubbed the steamy fog off the mirror with her towel, then stepped back to stand beside the bath.

She turned slowly from side to side to take full advantage of the first real opportunity to study herself properly. Especially some of the physical changes that she had gone through just recently. The first thing that she noticed was her face, neck, and long, lean arms that had been tanned bronze from their constant exposure to the sun. And, her long shapely muscular legs that stretched from the firm rounded white globes of her buttocks down to her petite feet.

She was also pleased to see that her firm young perky breasts were now fully rounded white globes, that stood out proudly from her chest and were tipped with small delicate rose-petal pink nipples. Kinta looked down and watched, fascinated, as she traced her fingertips lightly up across her washboard-flat stomach until the long fingers on her strong hands sensitively cradled her breasts.

Then she gently rolled each sensitive nipple between the index finger and thumb on each hand and was amazed at just how quickly her nipples responded. They instantly became tight and erect, then stood up proudly like small berries on the surface of her firm breasts. She continued to fondle her breasts and nipples gently. It didn't take too long before she began to feel that now familiar warm tingling feeling had started again between her legs.

Kinta glanced up at her reflection in the mirror. She was suddenly attracted to and seemed to consciously notice for the first time, the thick patch of blond curls between her legs. She trailed one hand down across her taut stomach until she ran her fingertips gently through the coarse hair.

She focused her gaze intently on her naked reflection in the mirror, as she sat back onto the edge of the bath. Then, she slowly opened her long, lean legs very wide and carefully studied her flowering womanhood as it seemed to bloom before her very eyes.

Kinta saw that the thick outer lips had parted and revealed a small raised bud of sensitive flesh nestled in the upper folds. Below that was an opening, surrounded by delicate fleshy rose petals, that led deep into her inner depths. She moved her index fingertip slightly down and found the small firm plump bud. She then began to massage gently, which caused herself to gasp involuntarily at the intensity of the pleasurable sensation it created. And, it was making her nipples extremely sensitive to touch.

She remembered her intense enjoyment of the initial raw experience on Misty's horseback, and Kinta continued to stimulate herself briskly between her legs and simultaneously gently fondled her breasts and nipples. But, this time, she was in total control and alternately raised and lowered her tempo. The applied pressure of her fingertip extended the intensely pleasurable experience for as long as she possibly could.

Then, again it happened suddenly without any prior warning, her back arched involuntarily. Her eyes clamped shut tightly, and her whole body shuddered violently in the ongoing spasms of intense sexual orgasmic release. She gritted her teeth and moaned gently.

She finally recovered her composure sufficiently to open her eyes and focus into the mirror again. With the curiosity of new physical exploration, Kinta moved her fingers slowly down into the warm moist opening between her legs. She gently inserted and withdrew the tips of two fingers, and she felt a damp, slippery stickiness on her fingers that had lubricated right down deep into her vagina.

It allowed her two fingers to slide in and out effortlessly as she explored her depths. She was surprised at the small rough ridges she felt on the inner surfaces of her vagina. She made a mental note of the pleasant sensation of fullness and other unique feelings she experienced when her two fingers were fully inserted.

Suddenly, she became aware of how much time had passed and quickly removed her fingers. Kinta swung her legs around into the bath, then plunged in and immersed herself into the warm water. She revelled in the ongoing pleasure as she ran her soft hands over her still aroused naked body.

When she figured she had soaked sufficiently in the steaming hot bath and had thoroughly washed her body and hair, Kinta reluctantly climbed out and patted herself dry with a large luxurious cotton towel.

She spent another couple of personally pleasurable minutes as she admired her naked body's reflection in the mirror again.

Then, she pulled on her travelling clothes in readiness for today's leg of the journey. She unlocked the bathroom door and stepped back out into the bedroom. She quickly packed the last few loose remaining items back into her overnight bag. Then, she threw it onto her back, left the room and headed for the dining area.

When she arrived at the Tavern's dining room, she found Misty, Aedyn, and Catelyn already eating a hearty breakfast at one of the tables. The Tavern owner once again fussed around them and ensured they had plenty.

Kinta quickly crossed the room and joined them. She soon satisfied her own growing teenager's ravenous appetite as she ate from the mountain of hot cooked food already piled onto the table in front of her.

"Good morning, young lady!" Aedyn greeted her. "Misty advised us of your taking a bath!"

"Did you sleep well, sweetheart?"- Catelyn smiled and asked. "Your bath water must have been boiling because your face is still a little flushed?"

"Good morning, Mama! Good morning, Papa!" Kinta replied hastily, between mouthfuls, without looking up. "I slept very well thank you!"

"I see the cool mountain air has done nothing to dampen her appetite!" Aedyn laughed and looked over his shoulder to Catelyn. The four members of the royal party then took the time to finish their meal in comfort. They spent a few minutes and thanked the Tavern owner again for his generous hospitality before they made their way out to the waiting carriage.

The two footmen were waiting, dressed in all their finery as they stood rigidly beside each of the gilded carriage doors to help them to climb in. They also took their overnight baggage to replace it on the roof. When the footmen had safely and securely stowed the overnight luggage back into place on the roof and were safely back on their perch at the rear of the carriage, the driver cracked his whip, and the cavalcade moved off slowly again.

As the chilly morning wore on, eventually the ice-covered mountain roads they were travelling thawed out and began to slope downwards. Soon they emerged from the cold, snowy mountain passes beyond which lay the warmer green valley.

Ahead of them stretched the beautiful rural countryside of Nantgarw. There were vast stretches of tree-covered rolling hills and bubbling snow-melt streams, which reminded them so much of back home in Libertas.

High up on a distant hilltop, and standing out proudly against the crystal-clear blue sky, they could see the magnificent stone castle of the royal palace as it awaited their arrival. Flags and banners flew in the gentle breeze from atop the towers.

Suddenly, Kinta began to get excited as she anticipated finally meeting up with Vaalyun again, after the somewhat extended passage of time since they had first met at the coronation of Aedyn. "Oh, Mama!" she chirped, as she wriggled in her seat with her head out of the window. She attempted to take in every new sight, sound and smell simultaneous. "Finally, we are nearly there!"

Catelyn laughed at her beautiful excited daughter. She fondly remembered being young and in love herself. She had been about Kinta's age when she and Aedyn had first begun to date. "Kinta, my sweet, I know you are excited about seeing Vaalyun again after so long, but you must remember that you are a princess now and there will be civic functions that we will all need to attend!" she said gently. "Especially, when we first arrive!"

"And, your reputation as a hero warrior Princess has already preceded you!" Aedyn added. He inclined his head slightly and indicated out the window.

Kinta immediately turned her head to look out the windows as the countryside rolled by, and soon noticed the crowds of people that lined the road and waved as they passed. "Oh Papa, I see what you mean!" she said and waved back. It immediately created an explosion of noise as the people responded.

"Miss Kinta, it seems you are very popular here already!" said Ox as he leaned down to speak through the window. His booming chuckle was able to be heard over the noise from the crowd.

Suddenly, as they sensed the need to fulfil their unfamiliar royal duty, Aedyn and Catelyn began to smile and wave out of the side windows also, and the heavily-armed soldiers that followed closely behind the royal carriage sat up straighter on their horses. Even the footmen stood rigidly upright on their rear perch.

The carriage passed between the waving masses that lined the footpaths through the narrow cobble-stoned streets of a small village. Then, to ensure that their passing injured nobody lining the narrow streets, the carriage was forced to slow down. The size and noise of the crowds that lined the road increased dramatically.

They were joined in front of their carriage by a troop of mounted Nantgarw Royal House Guards as they exited the village. It ensured they were able to travel unhindered for the remainder of their journey.

Before too much longer, their carriage approached the castle gates, and a loud fanfare of horns was heard as they announced their arrival. It made Aedyn's face flush slightly, and he turned to Catelyn and smiled. "For this experience alone, it was worth the fighting and hardship we have had to endure, in securing the freedom of our country!" he said proudly.

"My sweet, the love and respect I feel for you today is almost too much for my poor heart to contain!" said Catelyn tenderly. She leaned over and placed her hand gently on Aedyn's muscular upper arm and looked up into his eyes. "It's almost ready to overflow!"

"Likewise!" said Aedyn. He gently placed his hand over the top of Catelyn's, then they both turned and waved out the carriage's windows again. Kinta's eyes misted over. She hugged Misty up close to her chest as she realised just how proud she was to be their daughter.

Suddenly, the Libertas royal carriage stopped. The footmen alighted and ran forward to open the doors. Aedyn stepped down and turned to assist Catelyn, Kinta, and Misty, down the steps and onto the red carpet that stretched from their carriage to the main castle entrance.

CHAPTER 42

Laytn banged his highly-polished wooden gavel loudly on the heavy timber benchtop in front of him, to bring the courtroom gallery members back to order again, then turned to face the panel of jurists. "Members of the jury, you've just heard the Defence's closing argument!" he addressed them, then turned to face the Prosecutor. Mr Prosecutor, you may begin to deliver your closing argument!" He sat back to listen carefully and ensure his notes matched the verbal summary about to be given.

"Thank you, Your Lordship!" said the Prosecutor. He stood and addressed the court. Then, the Prosecutor stepped out from behind his desk and sauntered across to face the jury, stopped abruptly and paused for dramatic effect. "Members of the jury, I will only ask that you bear in mind a few simple, yet salient, points, as you ponder the heavy decision you have before you!" he said. He held his arms out wide to include every member of the jury panel seated before him.

He dramatically held up his left hand in front of them, with the index finger extended. Then took the longest path possible to bring his right hand over and count it with his right index finger.

"One! That the prisoner before you had a God-given moral responsibility for the safety, security, and stewardship of the citizens of this country and was therefore derelict in that duty!" he said very loudly and officiously.

He paused again for dramatic effect before he also extended his left middle finger and counted that with his right index finger.

"Two! That the prisoner held a position of power, which could have, and should have, enabled him to protect the rights of the citizens, yet he chose to abdicate that power to a person whose agenda was solely the destruction of our country!" he again said very loudly and officiously.

The Prosecutor then paused again and held up the third finger on his left hand and counted that digit.

"Three! Both points have been adequately proven, beyond any reasonable measure of doubt, by the clear and concise evidence provided by the myriad of witnesses we have called throughout this hearing!" he added, again very loud and self-important.

The Prosecutor then lowered both of his hands down beside his body and courteously dipped his head slightly in deference to the panel of jurists. He turned to address the front bench and bowed very low from the waist. "Your Lordship, and members of the jury, I rest my case!"

The courtroom erupted into absolute chaos as the members of the public gallery hooted and cheered their endorsement of the Prosecutor's summation. It took several more minutes before order was fully restored once again.

Eventually, with much banging of the wooden gavel by Laytn, and lots of shouted threats by the Sergeant-at-Arms, the noise slowly but surely decreased and Laytn could finally address the members of the jury. "Members of the jury, now that you have heard both sides present their case, it is time to retire to your rooms and determine the fate of the prisoner!" he shouted. "You are therefore excused until that decision is made!"

The twelve seated members of the jury stood up as one and turned. Then, they walked gravely out through the side entrance in single file and into their adjoining rooms.

As the solid wooden door closed behind the final juror, Laytn faced the public gallery and addressed the packed courtroom. "Good citizens of Libertas!" he said, by way of introduction. "It has taken three long days of hearing the cases for and against the prisoner in the dock! I understand it has been an exceptionally emotional time for all concerned! Therefore, I thank you all for your patience in bearing true witness that finally justice has been done!"

Laytn then turned his head and addressed the Sergeant-at-Arms, who stood beside his bench after having let out the members of the jury through the side entrance. "Remove the prisoner from the court!" he said. "He will be returned to the dock when the jury has reached its decision!"

The Sergeant-at-Arms moved regimentally to the front of the dock and stood rigidly to attention before he yelled his command out very loud. "Guards! Remove the prisoner from the dock!"

Two heavily-armed guards burst through the door and scurried into the courtroom. They rushed to unlock the manacles and leg-chains from the heavy dock restraints before they shuffled Daemon out through the other side entrance and down the stairs to the cells below.

...oooOooo...

Tyson arrived at the front door of Lorelei's apartment. He knocked gently to announce his arrival, which was punctual as always. Then, he stood back politely to wait for her to open the door for him.

However, several paces further down the entrance passageway wall, the front door to Seraphina's apartment suddenly opened. Lorelei stepped out in her dressing gown and came sashaying up the passage to meet him. After they had kissed, made their mutual greetings and tenderly embraced, Lorelei took him gently by the hand and turned back towards Seraphina's apartment door, and she indicated that he should follow her there. "Come with me!" she said softly and seductively. She pulled on his hand and led him along as she looked back at him and smiled. "There's something important that Sera and I wish to discuss with you!"

Tyson was a little reluctant to go next door as he had anticipated a quiet night of romance at home with Lorelei. Even though it was abundantly evident, she wore nothing underneath the dressing gown, he could see that possibly rapidly slipping away.

As they both entered through the front door into the apartment, Lorelei stopped and turned around. She let go of Tyson's hand, then closed it behind them and pushed the bolt home to lock it securely. Then she took Tyson by the hand again and led him down the long hallway towards the rear of the apartment. It was a little confusing as the sitting room was at the front and that's where he would have expected to meet Sera.

They continued past the entrance to the kitchen and dining area. Then, Lorelei turned down the short passage that leads to the main bedroom, which by now had Tyson completely bamboozled. But he obediently followed along behind as Lorelei continued to guide him around the corner into Seraphina's luxuriously appointed boudoir.

However, he was completely and utterly taken aback though when they finally entered the massive bedroom space. He saw Seraphina as she lay back entirely naked on the bed, with her hand extended out. She asked him to join her there.

He quickly glanced nervously around at Lorelei to see her reaction. Tyson was even further shocked when he saw she had already undone the front of her dressing gown.

She now began to undo the buttons on his shirt while still moving him gently in the direction of the bed. "It's alright, Tyson, my sweet!" she said quietly, as she undid the last of his buttons and removed his shirt. "I'll join you both in a moment when I'm fully undressed as well!"

Then she quickly and very efficiently undid his belt and slipped his pants down for him to remove. He climbed naked onto the bed, still without having spoken a word. Seraphina sat up and welcomed him onto her bed. Her eyes were wide open and fixed hungrily on his enormous penis, which already hung almost to his knees and seemed to be still growing.

Tyson was still a little tentative, but he very much-admired Seraphina's slim, lean figure and small firm breasts. Lorelei shed her dressing gown and hurriedly joined them on the bed. In a simple comparison between the two sisters, Lorelei was about the same height as Seraphina but a little more rounded and curvier. Her larger breasts still retained the firmness of youth.

The huge standout difference between the two girls though was

Seraphina's completely hairless womanhood with large pouting lips. Lorelei's smaller female parts are covered with a thick dark thatch. Finally, Tyson found his voice. "Please don't misunderstand me!" he said. "I'm not complaining, girls! I'm just curious as to why?"

"I love my sister deeply and, after she suffered at the hands of Vylaine, I could see that she was in dire physical need of some serious male attention!" Lorelei said tenderly. She attempted to explain the reasoning behind the unusual arrangement. "So, I offered to share with her the only male I knew I could trust fully and, my darling, that was you!"

"I hope you don't mind, Tyson?" asked Seraphina gently as she reached down and took his enormous male member into both of her hands. She began to gently stroke it, then felt it grow rigid and stand up and throb in her hands.

To help him make up his mind, Lorelei reached down and took his scrotum into both of her hands as well. Then, she began to gently run her fingers over and around the wrinkled sac until it became tight and tucked up firmly under his penis. "You are the only man I know who could satisfy both of us simultaneously!" she said and leaned forward to kiss him passionately on the mouth.

Tyson lay carefully back onto the bed between them. Both women cuddled up close to him and continued stroking with both hands to bring the enormous penis to full erection. Suddenly, Seraphina sat upright. She rose up onto her knees and straddled his thighs. Then, she slowly and methodically wriggled and shuffled forward until she finally squatted over his hips.

Then Lorelei guided the large throbbing head of his rigid penis into place at the already moist opening to Sera's vagina. He slipped easily inside her body. Tyson was shocked at just how wet, and ready Seraphina already was. And, he was then equally surprised as he quickly slid fully home inside her and she settled down and had been impaled onto him.

Seraphina's mind flashed quickly back over her time strapped onto the table in Vylaine's dungeon. Then, the subsequent lonely solo nights of self-induced pleasure in her apartment with the aid of her little carved and polished friend.

After she had ensured that Tyson's mighty phallus was firmly ensconced inside Seraphina, Lorelei gently moved up towards Tyson's shoulders. She raised herself on her knees until she straddled his face. Tyson raised his hands and gently placed them on Lorelei's upper thighs. He tenderly and sensitively traced his fingertips up over the curves of her hips and on up over the ridges of her ribs until he took both her breasts into his hands.

Then Lorelei lowered herself slightly, and he used his tongue to stimulate her erogenous bud. Both women began to embrace. Lorelei gently fondled Seraphina's breasts while they kissed each other passionately on the mouth.

Seraphina began to slowly but regularly raise herself until Tyson only just remained inside her. Then, she would settle slowly back down onto the enormous rock-hard penis until it filled her again.

Although she had become highly aroused and began to get a little breathless, Seraphina decided it was necessary to share deep confidence with both Lorelei and Tyson. "Tyson, if you find it a struggle to keep up the effort for too long, I also have "Mama's Little Helper" to assist us tonight!" she said, between gasps of pleasure. "Although, I must admit, my little carved wooden Pinocchio's nose now comes a very poor second to your perfect pleasure pole!"

Tyson freed up his mouth for a quick comment. "Please don't wear it out, Sera!" he said and chuckled, tongue-in-cheek. "There's plenty to go around for both of you! And, when we finish here tonight, I'm going to marry both of you girls…!"

Although, understandably, the last part was a little muffled and difficult to understand, as his mouth was once again preoccupied. Lorelei wriggled and writhed her hips around and demanded his attention.

Seraphina just chuckled and slowly began to increase the tempo of her plunging ministrations on Tyson's titanic totem.

CHAPTER 43

As they made their way regally along the red carpet, Kinta could see Vaalyun as he stood beside his parents at the top of the stairs. He grinned at her, and her heart gave a little leap as she smiled back, and consciously stopped herself from starting to skip along the carpet.

Following the protocol, she remained a half pace behind her parents until they arrived at the base of the stairs. Then, they made their way up the stairs and, when they finally reached the top landing, Nyvorlas and Liluth formally greeted them. "Welcome to Nantgarw!" said Nyvorlas. "May our two nations remain forever locked in friendship!"

Both families stood together, turned and faced the flags of Nantgarw and Libertas. The flags flew side by side and symbolised the union of the two nations in friendship. Another blaring fanfare of horns marked the end of the official arrival as the two families embraced. They turned together to enter the castle, and Nyvorlas placed his arm around Aedyn's shoulder as they walked. "Tell me, my friend, how was your journey?" he asked. "I hope you didn't suffer anything unpleasant on your way here?"

"On the contrary, our journey here was a most pleasant experience!" Aedyn replied and smiled at his host. "More importantly, we were constantly entertained by the building excitement of Kinta, as we approached Nantgarw!" he added.

Nyvorlas laughed heartily before he replied. "I hear what you're saying!" he chuckled. "We also have had the building of excitement for Vaalyun as the days have passed!"

Following behind the adults, Vaalyun covertly reached for Kinta's hand as they walked so close together that they almost touched from shoulder to ankle. Kinta felt her heart flutter at his touch as she entwined her fingers into Vaalyun's.

He gazed down into her ebony coloured eyes and his breathing felt like it had become stuck in his throat. His heart raced at her nearness, and Vaalyun could smell the sweetness of Kinta's breath. But, when he spoke, the words came very effortlessly. "It has felt like an eternity since we last spoke!" he said quietly. "I've missed you enormously since then, and I'm so glad you're finally here with me!"

Kinta squeezed his hand tenderly and leaned her head lightly against his shoulder. "I've missed you also!" she said softly. "It feels so good to be back together again finally!"

Vaalyun placed his arm around her waist and pulled her nearer. Then, Kinta put her arm around his waist, and the two young lovers walked together as one. "I have so many places to show you and so many things to do together, I don't know where to begin telling you!" he said excitedly.

"I'm so looking forward to sharing these and many more things with you!" said Kinta and squeezed Vaalyun tightly.

The group had arrived at the royal residence. Nyvorlas and Liluth showed them into the royal guest quarters, where they would stay for the duration of their visit. Then, Nyvorlas opened his arms wide, in an expansive gesture, and looked at his royal guests. "If there's anything that you need, or want, you have only to ask, and I shall immediately have it delivered!" he said warmly.

Aedyn smiled and looked warmly back at both Nyvorlas and Liluth before he replied. "My dearest friends, you've made us enormously welcome, and for that we thank you!" he said. "Please, allow us to unpack our things and make ourselves presentable after our long journey, and we will join you again shortly!"

Nyvorlas placed his large hand on Vaalyun's shoulder and steered him gently towards the door. "Come, young man, leave the poor girl to her peace!" he said. His voice showed his deep love for the handsome young man. "They will join us again shortly!"

Vaalyun looked back dejectedly at Kinta as if he were seeing her for the very last time. Kinta raised her hand, smiled a huge smile and wriggled her fingers in a friendly farewell wave. "Go, Vaalyun!" she said and chuckled. "I'll see you when I've changed my clothes and refreshed myself from our travels!"

Vaalyun's face erupted into a huge grin, and he spun on his heels and headed after his parents. "Don't take too long!" he shouted over his shoulder, as he left the room and Kinta giggled.

"I won't!" she shouted after him.

Catelyn smiled and acknowledged inwardly that her baby girl was now definitely a woman. *I really must have the mother-daughter talk with Kinta, and now she is old enough to understand!* She thought. She watched her daughter staring wistfully after Vaalyun's receding back.

As their hosts left the room and closed the doors behind them, Aedyn and Catelyn made their way over to the large comfortable bed. They lay back on the pile of pillows to allow Catelyn to rest up before the night functions began.

"I'm far too excited to be able to lay down and rest!" said Kinta enthusiastically, as she spun around on the spot and giggled. Misty ran around Kinta's legs, and wagged her tail vigorously and puffed, with her tongue hanging out. The two girls eventually both collapsed onto the floor in a giggling heap and stayed there as they chatted quietly together.

Aedyn turned onto his side and spoke quietly to Catelyn as she lay with her eyes closed. "Oh, to be young again!" he said.

Catelyn simply nodded her agreement with his sentiment without having opened her eyes.

...oooOooo...

Once again, Laytn banged his gavel loudly to gain their attention and addressed the vast crowd of citizens filling the courtroom. "Sergeant-at-Arms, please bring in the jury!" he shouted.

"Yes, Your Lordship!" said the Sergeant-at-Arms. He strode

across to open the door and let the members of the jury back into the courtroom.

The jurors ambled in and resumed their seats, under a mutual cloud of gravitas. An expectant hush settled on the room, as all eyes looked for some sign of the possible outcome. However, the jurors all held passive faces and stared straight ahead or looked at Laytn for instructions. "Members of the jury, have you reached a decision?" asked Laytn, as he addressed them in a loud voice.

Aartuur stood and faced Laytn before he replied. "Yes, Your Lordship!" he said. "We have reached a unanimous decision!"

Laytn silently breathed a massive sigh of relief. Then, he sat up straighter in the chair and asked the inevitable question. "In the matter of treason against the State of Libertas, formerly known as Skargness, how do you find the prisoner?" he asked.

An instantly audible sharp intake of breath could immediately be heard. All occupants of the room leaned forward eager to listen to the reply.

"Your Lordship, in the matter of treason against the State, we the members of the jury find the prisoner … guilty, as charged!" Aartuur's voice rang out across the room.

A huge cheer erupted from within the room and from the crowd packed around the area immediately outside the doors. Laytn allowed the excitement to settle naturally, of its own accord, before addressing the courtroom. "Thank you, members of the jury! Your duty has now been done!" he announced. "You are, as a result of this, excused and may re-join the other citizens in the gallery before I pronounce sentence!"

The sound as chairs scraped and people moved played out across the room, as the ex-jurors took their places with the other citizens. Then, when all had again settled, Laytn addressed the dock. "The prisoner will rise!" he said.

Daemon shuffled slowly to his feet and stood with head held high, but shoulders and back slumped, due to the limits of his chain restraints.

Laytn took a couple of calming breaths before he pronounced his sentence. "Prisoner, in respect to the charge of treason against the State of Libertas, formerly known as Skargness, you have been found guilty!" he stated. "Therefore, this court sentences you to five years of incarceration, in solitary confinement, within the cells contained in the city watch-house! Upon completion of this term, you will be exiled from the State of Libertas, never to return, for the term of your natural life!" he concluded. "Sergeant-at-Arms remove the prisoner!"

As the Sergeant-at-Arms unlocked the chains from the dock, the courtroom buzzed with excitement and the citizens of Libertas filed out to spend endless hours as they discussed the inevitable outcome.

Laytn sat back and reflected on just how far they had come since Aedyn's family had joined his band of rebels and provided the leadership necessary to ensure a successful outcome. Then, after several minutes of contemplation, he stood and turned to face the new flag of Libertas.

Then, he bowed his head, and he excused himself from the courtroom and made his way outside into the bright sunshine. The air smelt sweeter, the sun shone warmer, and the sky appeared bluer than when he had entered the courtroom that morning. "Ah, it's a beautiful feeling to have the yoke of oppression finally removed from our nation!" he said out loud, to nobody in particular.

With a renewed spring in his step, Laytn stepped off and made his way back towards the coach depot for the trip home. As he walked along the footpath beside the road, several small family groups were walking in the opposite direction past him.

The women bobbed down in a quick curtsy, and the men raised the brim of their hats in salute as they passed. Layton heard the men explain proudly to their children who he was as their voices became softer with their passing.

He couldn't help standing a little straighter and hold his head up proudly, with a spring in his step as he continued along his path.

CHAPTER 44

A fter they had bathed and dressed in their new formal attire, utterly resplendent in the Libertas Ruler's Crown in preparation for the evening's royal reception, Aedyn and his family made their way out into the passageway outside their room. As they exited the room, two armed guards from the Nantgarw military sprang to attention and held their spears rigidly by their side.

Standing there, waiting in the passageway to meet them, a member of the senior palace staff introduced herself. "Honoured royal guests of King Nyvorlas and Queen Liluth. I am Teyla, Head of the Royal House Staff!" she said. "I have been tasked with escorting you to the Royal Ballroom, where you will be the guests of honour at this evening's formal State Reception! This way please, Your Majesties!" she said.

With that, she bowed politely, turned, and began to walk down the passageway at a carefully measured stride, to allow their royal party to follow discretely behind. As they passed slowly by each closed doorway or intercepting passageway, armed guards snapped to attention and stood rigidly at either side of the opening until they had passed by, then relaxed slightly and returned to their duty.

"Did you ever imagine this, while we were in the rebel camp?" Aedyn turned his head slightly and whispered to Catelyn out of the corner of his mouth. He glanced at Catelyn briefly and saw her shake her head

subtly, without having taken her eyes off Teyla, as they approached the enormous open archway that led into the Royal Ballroom.

When they arrived at the entrance, Teyla stood to one side and allowed them to each pass inside to be met. Standing just inside the doorway was Nyvorlas, Liluth, and Vaalyun, each dressed in their formal attire, complete with medals, ribbons, and sashes.

Also, Nyvorlas and Vaalyun each had a ceremonial sword that hung in a sheath at their side. The burnished gold of their handles and hilts gleamed in the bright lamplights of the ballroom.

Nyvorlas stepped forward and took Catelyn's hand on his arm, then turned and escorted her slowly into the ballroom. Immediately, Aedyn stepped up to Liluth and followed closely behind Nyvorlas, with her hand on his arm.

Finally, Vaalyun stepped forward and held out his arm, and he looked the perfect gentleman as Kinta stepped forward and placed her hand gently upon his arm. The two of them joined the others, and Misty followed closely, as she strutted along behind and her tail wagged like crazy.

The entire royal party strolled down the centre of the ballroom and chatted informally to the sound of loud applause from the other VIPs in attendance. Kinta felt like she was floating as she held Vaalyun's arm, and they traversed the length of the ballroom.

It was beyond her wildest dreams and vivid imagination when she had imagined spending time with Vaalyun on this visit. In her eyes, Vaalyun was the most handsome man in the room, other than Papa, and the two of them made a beautiful couple.

When they had all finally reached the small raised dais, which stood in the centre of the wall at the front of the ballroom, each member of the mixed couples stepped up and turned to stand ramrod-straight as they faced the other guests, who had discretely moved to a point just in front of the dais. Misty stood perfectly still beside Kinta's leg, with only her wagging tail that betrayed her excitement as the applause slowly petered out.

Nyvorlas extended his arms and addressed the assembled VIP guests that stood en masse in front of them. "Distinguished Citizens of Nantgarw, we welcome our royal friends from neighbouring Libertas!

We extend to them our deepest gratitude, for allowing our two great nations to be inextricably bound together in peace with the strongest of ties!" he said. "And, besides, King Aedyn and Queen Catelyn, have graciously allowed Prince Vaalyun to host the Royal Princess Kinta, while they are visiting our nation! For this, we are indebted and ask that anyone who meets them, during their stay, extends to them the same courtesy that you would extend to us!" Nyvorlas continued, then turned to face Aedyn. "And so, on behalf of the nation of Nantgarw, I welcome you!"

The two royal monarchs stepped together and shook hands warmly. A volley of loud applause erupted from the gathered VIPs standing before them and the other members of the royal party standing on the dais.

Kinta reluctantly dragged her eyes momentarily away from Vaalyun just long enough to grin broadly and wink conspiratorially at Misty, whose tail began to wag like it was possessed. The two girls had spoken at length during their journey here, about how they thought they would feel when on show at the formal occasions they were expected to attend.

But neither one had anticipated just how comfortable they would feel and how excited they would be during this extremely public experience. Kinta was so excited that she began to feel a little light-headed and thought she might have even fainted. But she held tightly onto Vaalyun's arm and steadied herself until the slight dizziness had passed. Then she glanced covertly at Vaalyun's face from out of the corner of her eye and could see that he was slightly flushed and kept glancing discretely down at her.

Kinta turned her face slightly toward Vaalyun and smiled sweetly back at him, feeling him stand up a little straighter with pride at having her on his arm.

Sometimes, dreams do come true! She thought.

...oooOooo...

The music eventually ground to a halt, and the last dance was complete, though Vaalyun continued to hold Kinta's hand as they made their way off the dance floor. Kinta's formal gown glittered like fairy lights in the bright lights of the ballroom. Her face glowed from the exertion of having danced all night.

Vaalyun leaned in close, turned his head slightly and whispered into her ear. *"Now that we have finally finished with the formalities, let's go outside and get a breath of fresh air?"* he said softly.

"I'd like that!" Kinta softly replied. She smiled up into his strong, handsome face.

Vaalyun led them quickly out through a side door and across the wide passageway to another door. It let them into a long, winding stone staircase that leads upstairs. "Watch the hem of your dress on these steps!" he said over his shoulder. He held her hand and led her quickly up the stairs. "I don't want you tripping over and injuring yourself!"

Kinta hitched the hem of her gown up with her spare hand and hurried after him. In a couple of minutes, they came out onto the stone flagging of the battlements. Kinta's breath was immediately taken away with the beautiful vista that met her eyes. "Oh Vaalyun, it's gorgeous!" said Kinta. She snuggled up close to him, and Vaalyun placed his arm around Kinta's shoulders and held her close.

Below them, the city lights were like a fairy landscape, a glittering carpet of colour that spread from the castle to the skyline. Above them, the sky was the colour of ebony, and tiny pinpricks of light formed a jewelled canopy overhead. Vaalyun sensed the moment was right and gently turned Kinta to face him. She turned her face up toward his and closed her eyes. Vaalyun placed his hand gently on Kinta's cheek and lowered his face to meet her lips.

As their lips met, Kinta's heart skipped a beat, and her mouth opened slightly with the intense pleasure she felt with her first kiss. Vaalyun's lips tasted warm and sweet, like wild honey, and her tongue went exploring, only to meet his tongue looking for her.

Kinta's legs began to feel like jelly, and her whole body melded with Vaalyun's until they were almost a single being. After what seemed like an eternity, their lips reluctantly parted and they both struggled to regain their breath.

Kinta turned her head slightly, tenderly leaned her face onto

Vaalyun's chest and squeezed him tightly. She listened to his heart beating wildly, as he gently twisted his fingers through her long blond hair. *"I think I've died and gone to Heaven!"* he whispered into her ear.

Kinta nodded her head and squeezed him tighter. *"I don't want this moment ever to finish!"* she whispered in return.

They stood together quietly, unmoving, for several long minutes until, eventually, Vaalyun broke the silence. "Unfortunately, we need to return to the ballroom before we have been missed, and the palace guards begin searching for us!" he said tenderly as he chuckled merrily.

"Yes, you're right!" Kinta responded and giggled along with him.

At that precise moment, she knew that their two lives were now intertwined, and her destiny was determined. Reluctantly, they broke their embrace and turned to head back down the stone staircase arm-in-arm together. As they discretely entered the ballroom again, they were met by Aedyn, Catelyn and Misty exiting to return to their room. Kinta leaned up and kissed Vaalyun on the cheek, said goodnight to him and joined them.

Kinta leaned her head lightly onto Catelyn's shoulder and wrapped her hands tenderly around her mother's arm as they walked along slowly together down the passageway toward their royal guest room. *"Mama, compared to earlier, I haven't felt so good all evening!"* she said quietly.

Catelyn had a genuine look of concern on her face as she gently placed her arm around Kinta's shoulders and supported her tall daughter while they both walked the last few short paces to their door. "I'll have a look when we get inside the room, sweetheart!" she said comfortingly and squeezed Kinta's shoulders lovingly.

Aedyn opened the door for them, and they all entered together. Then, the three girls continued into the bathroom together and closed the door behind them, which left him on his own.

"Now, what seems to be the matter, my sweet?" Catelyn asked gently.

Kinta sat down with some relief on the edge of the bath, then looked up and grimaced as she placed a hand tenderly on her lower abdomen. *"I've had cramps in my lower belly on and off all evening, but I haven't felt like going to the toilet, and I also felt a little dizzy earlier!"* she said quietly.

"Let's get you out of this first!" Catelyn offered. Then she leaned forward and started to undo the many small pearl buttons down the front of Kinta's ball gown. Kinta stood up shakily, and Catelyn finished undoing the many buttons and ties on the beautiful dress. She gently lifted it over Kinta's head and when she had removed it, turned and hung it on the hook behind the door.

Catelyn turned back around to face Kinta. She was mildly surprised by the beautiful, grown-up young woman that stood before her, with firm, round milky-white breasts capped with rose-petal pink nipples, and a thick bush of coarse blond curls nestled in her groin.

However, she recovered her composure quickly. Kinta's affliction was immediately evident and apparent to Catelyn as she noticed the small trace of ruby-red blood that traced its way down the inside of Kinta's leg from the area of her womanhood. "Please, my darling, sit down on the edge of the bath!" Catelyn said as she helped Kinta to sit back down again. "We'll get you into the bath first to clean you up, but then you and I need to have a little chat, as one woman to another!"

Catelyn carefully half-filled the bath with steaming hot water, then slowly and methodically added cold water until she finally managed to get the temperature right by measuring it with the point of her elbow. "Besides, this hot bath will help to ease your stomach cramps and make things a little more comfortable for you!" she said.

She carefully assisted Kinta to step into the steaming hot bathtub. Kinta carefully lowered herself gently down and lay back into the heated water until it came up to her neck and slowly closed her eyes to try and relax. "Mama, I'm more than a little worried about the appearance of that blood and where it's coming from!" she said quietly, without having opened her eyes.

Misty sat down, and Catelyn knelt on the floor next to the bath and leaned over the edge with a washcloth in her hand. "Tonight, my sweet, you are officially a full-grown adult woman!" she said. She started to clean her adult daughter and quietly explain the mysteries of being a woman.

CHAPTER 45

Morning sunlight filtered down through the thick drooping branches and long green leaves of a huge weeping willow tree, on the gently sloping grassy banks of an ornamental stream that flowed through the grounds of the palace gardens. Kinta, Misty, and Vaalyun sat together and whispered on a blanket beneath the tree, as they exchanged ideas about their previous individual plans and began to do their joint projects for the future.

Vaalyun had a genuinely stern look upon his face for quite some time. He slowly and silently mulled over the pros and cons of sharing his concerns, before he eventually turned to confide in Kinta. "I know my parents expect me to be here, to take over their monarchy when they get old and infirm!" he said. "But I want to do something a little more worthwhile with my life before I have been shackled with that responsibility!"

Kinta reached out and tenderly took his strong manly hand in hers and squeezed it gently to reassure him that she knew and correctly understood what he meant.

Misty decided that this was the perfect opportunity to reveal to Vaalyun that she was more than just a fluffy white pet dog. "Vaalyun, there are many, many adventures waiting for you, out there in the big wide world!" she said, quietly with a serious tone. "You just have to be prepared to go out there looking for them!" she continued. "But, unfortunately, they don't always come searching for you!"

After his initial shock, Vaalyun's eyes were still very, very wide as he silently glanced back and forth between Kinta and Misty, trying to process what he thought had just happened quickly.

Maintaining her grip on Vaalyun's hand, Kinta lifted her other hand and placed it on Vaalyun's upper arm. "It's alright, Vaalyun, Misty is my extraordinary friend, and we have shared some exciting adventures already!" said Kinta. "And, you have now been included in the secret that she can speak, but this is just one of her many special talents!"

Vaalyun's look of shocked surprise slowly changed into one of absolute amazement until, eventually, he was able to find his voice again. "Misty, thank you for including me in this confidentiality!" he said. "I have always felt exactly as you have just expressed! But, for some reason, I have always felt the need for someone special to accompany me in the search for these adventures!" he explained.

Misty cocked her head to one side, listened intently and glanced back and forth between Vaalyun and Kinta before she spoke again with a huge grin. "In that case, it seems to me that there is nothing to prevent you from beginning the search now!" she chuckled.

Vaalyun's head suddenly rocked back, and he laughed out loud as his entire body shook with the effort. When he finally regained some degree of composure, he took a deep breath and settled. "You're right!" he said. "And, I now feel completely confident that the three of us, together, could accomplish anything that we set our minds to do! I also feel like a huge weight has lifted from my shoulders, and my true life's purpose is finally revealed!" he continued.

Kinta leaned forward and embraced Vaalyun warmly, remaining in his arms as she looked up into his face with her eyes aglow. "I also feel that way and have done so since we first met!" she said. Vaalyun tenderly placed his hand behind Kinta's head and pulled her face up to his, where their lips met in a passionate kiss.

Misty sat back and felt satisfied that things were turning out correctly. *I think our princess's life is about to change dramatically in the very near future!* she thought, as she discretely watched the two young lovers.

Suddenly, to Kinta's complete surprise, Vaalyun broke away from their tender embrace and stood up. Then, he extended his hand and took Kinta's to help her up from the ground. "Come on, let's go and grab some food to take with us!" he said excitedly. "I'll get the grooms to prepare some horses, and we'll go for a ride!" he continued. "There are some wonderful places I want you to see!"

Kinta climbed slowly to her feet and rubbed her hands together briskly with delight. "Oh goody!" she said. "C'mon Misty, let's go and tell Mama and Papa what we're doing!"

The three of them set off back towards the side entrance to the castle at a brisk walk, excited to be heading off on their first adventure together. When the friends arrived back in the royal residence, Vaalyun excused himself and headed to his room. The two girls went down the passageway to their quarters to find Catelyn.

She and Aedyn were both laying down on the bed in the guest room, resting in preparation for the planned activities later in the day. Kinta climbed up onto the bed and cuddled up to Catelyn, with her head laying on her mother's shoulder.

Catelyn smiled and placed her arm around Kinta's shoulders and squeezed her. Then, she tenderly picked up Kinta's hand and carefully put it gently onto her swollen abdomen. "Kinta, my sweetheart, can you feel the baby moving!" she said, "Today is the first time that's happened!"

"Oh, Mama!" said Kinta, absolutely fascinated, with her eyes wide open. "That feels amazing!"

Catelyn placed her hand tenderly on top of Kinta's and turned to look deeply into her daughter's face. "I want you to share every part of this amazing experience with me, for a couple of reasons!" she said. "Firstly, as a woman yourself, it's important that you know the various stages and changes that pregnancy goes through, so I'll answer any questions you have! But, secondly, as a *young* woman with your whole life in front of you, I want you to see that having a baby is not easy and changes you forever!" she continued.

"Thank you for sharing that amazing experience, Mama!" Kinta said as she listened attentively, then leaned up and kissed Catelyn gently on the cheek. "You are the best Mama on earth! I've just had so much happen to me in such a short time, that I do need some time to mull it all over and process it all!" she said. "However, Vaalyun has asked Misty and me to go riding with him right now, and I wanted to ask you if that would be okay, considering everything?"

"Of course, that's fine, my darling!" Catelyn said gently. "Just don't do anything too vigorous for the next few days!"

Kinta and Misty gently eased their way off the bed and started heading for the door to their room so that they could get changed. When they were about to leave the room, Kinta turned around and winked at her mother. "I think we'll have lots to talk about tonight!" she said conspiratorially.

She and Catelyn both chuckled, and then the girls left.

...oooOooo...

The royal grooms stood patiently as they held the reins of two horses, as Vaalyun, Kinta, and Misty finally emerged from the side entrance to the palace and made their way casually across the courtyard towards the stables. Showing that she had listened carefully to Catelyn, Kinta had wisely opted for a comfortable, loose-fitting cream cotton top, which she fashionably wore out over a pair of dark-brown soft linen pants and ankle-high brown leather boots.

Whereas always the practical male, Vaalyun was wearing a casual riding outfit of long-sleeved white cotton shirt, which he had left open at the neck, and heavy-duty leather trousers that had been tucked into knee-high, polished, black leather boots.

Vaalyun's horse was a huge black stallion named Thunder. As soon as he sighted them walking towards them, he started stamping his feet and calling to attract Vaalyun's attention. The grooms, acting on Vaalyun's explicit instructions, had specially selected a slightly smaller beautiful golden palomino mare named Xanthe for Kinta. She stood quietly, saddled and waiting.

Vaalyun placed his hand carefully under her foot and gently helped Kinta up into the saddle, lifted Misty to sit in front on Kinta's lap, then tightened the cinch strap around Xanthe's girth and adjusted the stirrup lengths to match Kinta's long legs. All the while, Thunder pranced and constantly nudged Vaalyun with his head, too impatient to wait for the ride to begin.

Eventually, Vaalyun turned and took the reins for Xanthe from the groom, passed them over Xanthe's head and gave them to Kinta. Then, finally, he turned and took Thunder's reins from the other groom and vaulted onto his back. "Okay, Thunder! Now it's your turn!" he shouted, pulled back on the reins and caused Thunder to stand up rampant on his hind legs with his front legs pawing the air.

Kinta nudged Xanthe gently with her knees, and they moved off slowly, leaving Vaalyun to bring Thunder under control and follow them out through the open front gates. "C'mon girls! Let's get this show on the road!" said Kinta, her laughter rang out and echoed off the castle walls.

Vaalyun finally gave Thunder his head and went galloping at full speed past them, until they reached the hedge bordering the gardens, which Thunder cleared without slowing at all.

Then, Kinta brought Xanthe up to a canter and followed them out through the open garden gates. "Hey, Misty, I hope Vaalyun comes back to show us where to go!" she said, laughing as the drumming of hooves signalled their return. "Uh oh! Speak of the devil!"

"He must have heard you!" Misty chuckled and looked back over her shoulder and under Kinta's arm to see Vaalyun and Thunder reappear at their side.

For the next couple of hours, Vaalyun proudly pointed out some of Nantgarw's more beautiful, prominent and popular features and places of interest. Then, the countryside slowly became more uphill, and the trail became steeper until they eventually entered a small village sitting on the edge of a ridge, which overlooked a broad, sluggish river below.

Vaalyun quickly dismounted first and took Misty from Kinta. He placed her down carefully onto the ground, then helped Kinta to dismount and tied both the horses to a tree. Then, they all made their way carefully on foot down onto a large flat rock that overlooked the slow-moving river below.

As they stood and quietly admired the panoramic view, Vaalyun reached out toward her and Kinta smiled and took his hand. Then, he extended his other arm and pointed carefully, but precisely, down at the large wooden boat landing platform that sat beside the river far below them.

When he spoke, his voice had a slight tremor of both nervousness and excitement. "Ever since I first came here as a small boy, I have long had plans, to launch a boat from that landing down below and explore this river, as it passes between those two mountains yonder and out into the vast unknown!" he explained and glanced at Kinta to gauge her reaction.

He was much surprised to see her eyes were moist and shone. Her face was aglow with excitement as Kinta reluctantly dragged her eyes away from the river below and turned to face Vaalyun. "Thank you so much for bringing me here and sharing your vision!" she said. "I've truly caught your dream and would like to join you on that adventure!"

Vaalyun exhaled loudly with relief, then drew a long, slow, deep breath before he finally answered. "Kinta, you make me very happy!" he said. "Although I could have and, if necessary, eventually would have gone alone, I've always hoped for someone special to join me on my life's adventure! Now that I have found you, Kinta, marry me and make me the happiest and proudest man on this earth!" said Vaalyun.

Kinta felt her heart skip a beat as she suddenly realised what Vaalyun had just asked and she closed her eyes and took a couple of deep breaths to catch her composure. "Yes, Vaalyun, you make every moment of my life worthwhile!" she finally replied. "I would be honoured to be your wife and will follow you to the very ends of the earth!" Kinta lifted her face and leaned towards Vaalyun, and he leaned down towards her until their lips met in a passionate kiss.

On contact, Kinta's lips felt like they were burning, and she opened her mouth to get some relief. Vaalyun placed his muscular arm around Kinta's shoulders and pulled her in close, as he also opened his mouth and began exploring with his tongue.

Kinta's heart raced and thumped in her chest. Her cheeks had become flushed, and she felt a warm glow that spread deep in the base of her belly. Her whole body seemed to meld completely with his until she could feel the warmth of his skin along the length of her entire body through his clothes.

Then, she felt something unusual happen. Something stirred inside Vaalyun's pants and grew until it prodded her in the lower abdomen. Suddenly, as if to prevent himself from overstepping an invisible boundary, from which there would be no return, Vaalyun breathlessly broke contact, turned and started heading for the horses. "Then it's decided!" said Vaalyun as he clambered up off the rock, carefully rearranged his groin, and held his hand out to help Kinta. "Now we just need to return home and tell our parents!"

Kinta was left a little bewildered at the sudden end to their kiss but turned to see where Misty was and to make sure she didn't fall over the edge of the rock. "C'mon Misty!" she said and turned and took Vaalyun's offered hand. "It's time to head home!"

Once Vaalyun had assisted Kinta and Misty to climb onto Xanthe's back, he leapt up onto Thunder and moved closer until he could lean over and kiss Kinta again. "Thank you, my darling, for agreeing to be my wife, as well as coming here to share my vision with me today!" he said, and they both sat up straight again and turned the horses for home. "Now, we must hasten home to let both of our families know of our decision and to make arrangements for our nuptials before we depart on our journey!"

CHAPTER 46

Kinta was curious about the incident with Vaalyun, that caused him to break away as they had kissed earlier. She spent the rest of the day and evening wondering if it was something she had done or said that had made him suddenly separate from her so quickly.

Next morning, after she sat down and had an extended, leisurely breakfast with her family, she decided to go for a walk alone through the expansive gardens at the rear of the palace to do some thinking.

"Do you want me to come with you?" asked Misty, with concern in her voice.

"No, but thank you for asking!" Kinta replied warmly to her best friend. "I just need time alone to mentally process everything that has happened in the last few days!" She returned to the guest quarters and cleaned her teeth, then made her way downstairs and walked out slowly across the cobblestoned courtyard, and then she continued through the vine-covered archway that leads out to the royal gardens.

As she wandered through the brilliant colours and magnificent blooms of the manicured flower beds, along with the stepping-stone pathways set into closely trimmed grass, Kinta's mind worked overtime. She tried to digest and make sense of the numerous physical changes her body had gone through and the enormous emotional stresses that this had created as she had accustomed herself with this.

Kinta was slowly coming to grips with these changes, along with the excitement of spending quality time with Vaalyun, and then she suddenly recalled the incident with Vaalyun's pants yesterday and was perplexed again as to whether she was responsible.

Deep in thought, and without paying any attention to where she was going as she pondered these profound and perplexing questions, she had wandered deep into the vast expanse of older gardens.

With their tall lush leafy trees and large bushy plants, these garden beds all looked similar and made it difficult to remember the actual path she had followed to get here. So, she figured to find somewhere to wait and let them find her. Kinta spent some time until she saw a flat expanse of lush trimmed grass surrounded by thick beds of bamboo and vines that created a private and shaded natural screened enclosure with a discrete entrance. *It looks like the perfect place that I've been seeking!* She thought.

She decided to use it for her own private space to reflect on what she had achieved so far in her life, as well as what was still hoped to be accomplished in the future, and she lay back on the fresh, lush grass and closed her eyes. Several hours later, she awoke to the sound of Vaalyun calling her name loudly from nearby. "Vaalyun!" she yelled to get his attention. "I'm in here!"

It didn't take long before Vaalyun's head poked through the opening and he smiled broadly at finally having found her. "I've been searching for you everywhere!" he said warmly, but with obvious concern in his voice, and came over to join her by sitting close beside her on the grass. "I was concerned that I might have done something wrong when you didn't come to see me this morning!" he said with a quizzical look on his face.

"I came here to ponder the same question!" Kinta giggled and reached out to place her hand tenderly against his cheek. "Can we just agree to be open in the future and ask each other if we have any real concerns?" she asked, then tilted her head slightly to one side and smiled warmly.

"Of course! That's the sensible thing to do!" Vaalyun replied, "However when I'm near you, I can't think very sensibly! All I can focus on is wanting to please you and be as close to you as possible!" he said.

Kinta turned her head to look directly into Vaalyun's eyes and could see the concern there, so she decided to ask him the question that was causing her the most interest. "Vaalyun, when we were kissing yesterday, on the rock overlooking the river, why did you suddenly break away?" she asked gently. "I honestly thought I had done something wrong and have spent until now trying to decide what that was!"

Vaalyun slowly stood up, turned himself around and sat down carefully again, so he faced Kinta, then placed his hands tenderly on her shoulders and gazed directly into her eyes. "Please let me explain, Kinta, it wasn't you who did anything wrong!" he explained. "I deliberately broke away so that *I* didn't do anything wrong by you! I have grown to love you deeply, even in our short time together, and would never do anything that I thought might hurt you!" he said.

Kinta's eyes became moist, and she felt her heart suddenly swell, and her breathing become quicker with the immense love she felt inside for this honest young man. "Vaalyun, I have loved you dearly since I first saw you and want nothing more than to spend every minute of every day with you!" she said quietly, then almost choked on the words.

Vaalyun pulled her close, and they warmly embraced before Kinta leaned back and looked questioningly into his eyes. "I promise to hold no secret from you from this point forward but would like you to promise me the same thing!" she said as Vaalyun's eyes opened wide and he nodded.

"I promise!" he said gently, with slight trepidation, knowing in his heart where this was going.

Kinta lifted her hand and cupped his chin before leaning forward and kissing him lightly on the lips. "I know that I'm still young and naïve, and you're my first and only love, but please explain what happened in your pants yesterday that caused you to be so worried about hurting me?" she asked, with genuine concern.

Vaalyun briefly pondered this vexing question, but decided, as only a male's logical deduction could, that it would be better, and more comfortable, to bring Kinta's anatomical education up to speed quickly with a practical demonstration. "Do you trust me sufficiently to do as I ask?" he asked her gently.

"Of course!" she replied instantly, but with her brow slightly furrowed with puzzlement as to where this was leading as Vaalyun stood up and offered Kinta his hand to help her stand also.

"Since bushes surround us, and we are unable to be seen by outside eyes, I will demonstrate the cause of my concern from yesterday!" he said, still holding her hand as she stood in front of him. "Please, undo my belt and remove my pants!" he said gently.

Kinta hesitated slightly, looked up into his eyes for reassurance, then reached forward tentatively and did as she was asked, causing Vaalyun's pants to fall immediately to the ground.

Her eyes became wide with amazement when she saw his manhood for the first time as it peeked out of a nest of coarse blond hair and hung down over his wrinkled swollen scrotum.

"This is the first time that I have seen a naked man!" she asked quietly with genuine curiosity. "May I please touch you?"

"Of course!" he said tenderly, "But, please be gentle!"

Kinta's hand started to move slowly forward before she hesitated slightly, then stopped and began carefully undoing the buttons on her dress and allowing it to slip down onto the grass at her feet before she stepped out of it. "No more secrets!" she said shamelessly. "I love you deeply and choose to share my body with you also!" she continued tenderly and stepped closer until she was standing immediately in front of Vaalyun, who had also removed his shirt by now.

Kinta placed both her hands gently onto Vaalyun's chest and felt the rippling muscles underneath the skin. Then, she slowly removed one hand and reached down gently between his legs to take his scrotum into her hand, feeling the contents weighing heavily in her palm. As she glanced down to see where her hand was, she was surprised to see his previously flaccid penis had started to become firmer and grow rapidly in size.

Kinta moved her hand slightly and gently gripped his penis, which caused it to quickly swell and expand enormously, then stand up and become rock-hard as it throbbed in her hand and brought a low moan to Vaalyun's lips. She felt a now familiar glowing tingle begin between her legs as her nipples became erect and stood out on her firm young breasts. Kinta moved her other hand off his chest and grasped

Vaalyun's hand, then raised it and placed it on her already sensitive and highly aroused breasts.

He tenderly kneaded her breast and nipple as he moved his other hand down and ran his fingers gently down across her lower abdomen and through the thick, coarse blond curls between her legs.

Kinta shifted her feet apart slightly and opened her legs to allow his hand to more easily find her womanhood, which was now already moist in anticipation. Vaalyun's fingers probed tenderly between the outer lips and found the sensitive bud he was seeking, which caused Kinta's back to arch slightly and involuntarily and a tremble to begin throughout her body.

She started to move her hand slowly up and down along the length of his penis and felt his body stiffen with pleasure. Then, Vaalyun began to gently but briskly massage her erogenous nerve centre.

Kinta's initial concern had vanished, and she slowly increased the tempo of her hand's ministrations as each had their eyes focused intently on the physical responses of the naked body of their partner. She could feel her body quickly respond and begin to reach a crescendo with the constant sensitive touch of Vaalyun's hand and fingers.

Suddenly, Vaalyun groaned loudly and his back arched. Then, his body suddenly stiffened and spasmed as his penis began to pulse vigorously in her hand and pumped thick, sticky globules of male ejaculate out to run down warmly over her still moving hand.

The sight and first experience of Vaalyun reaching his orgasm, and the constant sensitive ongoing attention he still provided to her needs throughout that, suddenly brought Kinta to a back-arching spasming orgasm herself, which made her legs go to jelly and she leaned into his chest for support.

Kinta gently released her grip on his penis as it once again shrank, shrivelled and contracted, and the two of them collapsed exhausted into each other's arms and supported each other in a tender naked embrace, as they slowly recovered their breath.

After several long minutes, Kinta lifted her face from Vaalyun's chest and bent down to wipe her hand on the grass, then smiled cheekily up as she looked lovingly into his eyes. "See, my darling, you needed not have worried yesterday!" she giggled. "That didn't hurt me a bit!"

Vaalyun smiled back tenderly and then, on an impulse, pulled her in close as he crushed her naked body and sensitive breasts into his hairy muscular chest with his massive arms. "Let's just enjoy this first-time experience, for now, my sweet!" he said, running the fingers on one hand up into her blond hair and cupping her firm buttocks with the other hand, "We can talk about the hurting part later!"

Kinta was quiet for a couple of seconds, then gently raised her face and looked him in the eyes with a quizzical look upon her face.

"You mean there's more?" she asked tenderly. "I can hardly wait for that!" she said, and they both laughed out loud as they began to get dressed.

CHAPTER 47

A fter another fabulous week of sharing each other's company, and one more trip on horseback to admire the vast, slow-moving river of Vaalyun's dreams, it was time for the family to return to Libertas and the affairs of State.

Vaalyun and Kinta had shared their exciting news about their forthcoming marriage, and both families had discussed the details at length as plans were made for the upcoming event.

Aedyn and Nyvorlas had spent considerable time together during this visit, as they developed the outline for a strong alliance between their two countries, and they now both looked forward to bringing it to fruition in the future.

Catelyn and Liluth had talked at length about her upcoming birth and how excited she was at becoming a mother again. However, Liluth had made it abundantly clear that she was going to enjoy that experience vicariously through the birth of any grandchildren in the future.

Standing beside the royal carriage waiting to take them home, Aedyn grasped Nyvorlas by the hand and shook it vigorously in his display of warm friendship. "Nyvorlas, thank you very much for your invitation and generous hospitality over the past couple of weeks!" he said, then added, "Please, feel free to visit us in Libertas at any time!"

"We are about to become family! I believe there will be many such visits over the coming years!" Nyvorlas laughed. Both men chuckled at the thought and turned around to check on their respective family members.

Since it was finally time to go, Catelyn and Liluth embraced warmly as new close friends and held each other's hands as they continued to say their farewells quietly.

Meanwhile, Vaalyun and Kinta were wrapped tightly in each other's arms and whispered little sweet nothings to each other as only lovers can. Misty sat beside their legs and wagged her tail in anticipation of being able to spend more time with Kinta.

Finally, Aedyn turned and opened the carriage door, then stood back to watch as the two footmen scurried around to hold the doors and assist the rest of his family up into the vehicle. "Okay, folks, let's get this return trip started!" he said as the others all began to move towards the open door. He reached out and took Catelyn's hand, and placed an arm around her waist for added support, as she climbed onto the single step and then moved up into the carriage to her seat in the rear.

Aedyn turned back to assist Kinta and Misty, only to find Kinta had gone back to Vaalyun's arms for a final quick kiss goodbye. Misty looked from Kinta to Aedyn and then moved over to take his offer of assistance in climbing into the vehicle.

"C'mon Misty, I'll give you a lift up!" he said, then picked her up and placed her on the front seat where she settled in for the long trip home.

Suddenly, Kinta spun around and ran to the door, then held out her hand for Aedyn to assist her in climbing in as she climbed into the carriage. She sat down on the front seat near the closest window and leaned out, holding out her hand for Vaalyun to take.

Aedyn climbed in and sat down next to Catelyn, smiling at his daughter still staring out the window. "Okay driver let's get moving! We have a long way to go!" he shouted out the window.

There was a single loud crack of the whip, and the carriage began to move slowly forward and gathered speed quickly. Vaalyun ran alongside for a short time but was unable to keep pace as the horses leaned into their harnesses and were soon running strongly.

Kinta leaned out the window and vigorously waved until the figures standing outside the palace were finally too small to see, then she climbed back inside and lifted Misty onto her lap. "Thank you, Mama and Papa, for organising this visit!" she said as she rubbed Misty's coat. "What a fabulous time I've had!"

Aedyn turned his head to look back at Catelyn and obtain a glance of reassurance from her, as only long-married couples can, before turning back to speak with Kinta. "Your Mama and I are very happy for you, sweetheart!" Aedyn said, then reached out his hand and held Kinta's as he gave it a gentle tender squeeze. "Vaalyun is a fine young man from a strong, loving family and will make you a wonderful husband! We have great pride of the young woman that you have grown into, and Libertas will be eternally grateful for your contribution to our future peaceful state!" he said warmly, before rising out of his seat to lean forward and kiss Kinta. "You have our full and unconditional consent and our strongest blessing for your marriage with Vaalyun!"

Kinta was utterly speechless for several minutes before she could process what was said. "Oh, Papa, thank you!" she said as tears welled up into her eyes. "You truly are the best parents in the world!" Kinta grabbed Misty and held her close to her chest in a warm embrace as the tears of joy trickled down her face.

"Misty, did you hear that!" she said between sobs. "We *are* going to be married!"

...oooOooo...

Their return trip began uneventfully. The sun climbed slowly up into the clear blue sky and made for pleasant travelling. The countryside gradually changed as the carriage made its way back across the open farming plains of Nantgarw. Timber plantations progressively replaced cereal crops as the land climbed up into the foothills of the mountains.

"This is such beautiful countryside, isn't it?" observed Kinta. "Nantgarw and Libertas are so very similar in appearance!"

"Yes, you're right!" said Aedyn. "However, it's the direction and leadership by those responsible for managing a country that makes all the difference!"

Catelyn shifted her body until she sat nearer to Aedyn, then leaned her head onto his shoulder and closed her eyes. "After such a long and busy week, I'm going to take a little nap to recover some of my energy for when we get home. I have a feeling that things are going to become quite hectic very quickly after we arrive!"

Aedyn lifted his arm and placed it around Catelyn's shoulders to further support her. She adjusted her position again slightly to rest against his broad chest. "Ah, that feels more comfortable!" she said. Aedyn smiled.

By late afternoon, the carriage had begun its long slow climb as it lumbered up through the foothills. Clouds of dust billowed out from behind the wheels of the gilded carriage and coated the mounted members of the House Guard. The armed riders moved forward and slightly apart until they were alongside the wagon. It gave them some relief from the caking and cloying dust.

Ox increased his level of vigilance as they approached the steep mountain passes through which the dirt road twisted and wound its way. Kinta passed Misty out to Ox through the open side window, and then she climbed out after her. The two girls settled down onto the roof into their familiar role of ensuring the safety and security of their family's travelling party.

"The temperature's beginning to drop again, Ox!" Kinta observed. "We must have already passed through the thermal inversion layer and be on the mountain proper!"

"I think you must be correct, Miss Kinta!" said Ox. "I can also see the early traces of snow drifts beginning to appear along the edges of the road!"

"That will mean another freezing night tonight unless we can reach the halfway Tavern before it becomes too late!" Kinta observed. "Mr Driver, you will need to maintain maximum speed!"

'Yes, Miss Kinta!" replied the driver. He lifted his hand and touched his forelock as a sign of respect. Then, he reached down, picked up his long, leather whip and sent it snaking out across the team, cracking just above the backs of the horses, which spurred them on.

Kinta could feel the slight increase in their speed, but she knew that the horses couldn't maintain this pace for much longer. Sooner or later, they would need to slow down to a gentler pace to retain enough energy to drag their heavy carriage over the mountain passes. "Another thirty minutes at this pace please, Mr Driver, then we will slow down and give the horses some respite?" Kinta requested.

Then she slightly rose until she was crouched lightly on the carriage roof. She held her hand up to shield her vision from the bright sun overhead, then Kinta strained her eyes to gauge the distance that remained until the slope levelled out again slightly. "Make that just fifteen minutes please, Mr Driver! We are closer than I initially thought, and the horses will enjoy the breather!" she said.

"You know that they would run until they dropped if you asked them?" asked Misty. "They have told me that they would do whatever you asked, just to be able to serve you!"

"They are certainly beautiful horses!" Kinta said as she glanced down at the sweat-soaked team straining to pull the carriage over this rise. "We'll give them a well-earned rest again shortly!"

Kinta shifted her gaze to take in Ox's rear profile as he continually scanned the mountain passes that towered over them. She knew that he also was one who was prepared to do whatever has been asked, regardless of the request. Her heart filled with immense gratitude for the loyal people of Libertas, that Mama and Papa would be secure and able to live the rest of their lives in peace.

Suddenly, Misty sat bolt upright and began to stare fixedly at the left-hand rocky overhead slope up ahead. Something had caught her eye. It was an almost imperceptible movement, but she had been astute enough to pick it. "Please, Kinta, ask the driver to stop quickly, but safely?" she requested.

"Mr Driver, stop immediately, without hurting the horses!" Kinta said, loud enough to ensure he heard the demand, but without screeching.

The driver immediately began to drag back on the extended leather lead-reins in his hands and simultaneously applied the handbrake to slow the carriage rapidly. "Whoa there! Easy does it!" he yelled to the team.

Ox had come up to a crouch in his seat, with his right hand lightly resting on the hilt of his massive sword strapped to his back. He was ready to leap down and face whatever they were about to encounter, regardless of the consequences to himself.

"What is it, Kinta?" Aedyn asked out of the open side window of the carriage. "Why have we stopped!"

"I'm not sure yet, Papa!" Kinta responded. "Misty has seen something up ahead, and we will go and check it out now! It's best if you remain in the carriage and help Mama! That will be our safest strategy!"

"Of course, my darling, you're right!" he said. "But, make sure that you take precaution against whatever we face!" *It's not often that a father gets told to stay put, while his daughter runs off to protect him!* He thought, with a sardonic grin. Catelyn continued to snooze.

Kinta picked up Misty and held her close so they could speak softly together. "What did you see, my sweet?" she asked, without taking her eyes off the slope ahead.

"I can't be certain, but I think there is a mountain lion on the ledge above us!" She replied softly, as she gazed intently at the rocky overhead ledge. "It was only the slightest movement that I saw, but I think it was the mountain lion dropping its head to remain unseen as we approached!"

"In that case, I think we need to give that old mountain lion a surprise!" said Kinta. She moved to the edge of the roof and leapt nimbly down onto the road below. Then, she turned and reached up to lift Misty down as well.

The two girls walked towards the rear of the carriage to provide them with a little more room to move. As Kinta walked past the open carriage window, she looked inside and winked at Aedyn who grinned back. Catelyn was still sleeping soundly and resting on his broad chest.

When they arrived at the rear of the carriage, Misty morphed into a giant white honeyeater bird, and Kinta leapt onboard. Misty's wings began to beat at such a fast speed that they became almost invisible. The girls started to levitate up into the air until they were hovering about five paces above the rocky ledge, then they drifted slowly down the road towards where Misty had seen the mountain lion earlier.

It didn't take them long before the sly, sneaky animal came into view, as it hugged the ledge to remain out of sight from the carriage. It was waiting for the transport to pass underneath before it leapt down onto the horses and devoured them as prey. What it hadn't counted on was someone coming up to meet it.

The two girls hovered on the side of the road furthest from the ledge and drifted up until they were directly opposite the mountain lion. It kept itself low but followed them with its eyes as they approached. There was a confused look upon its face.

Kinta slowly removed an arrow from her quiver and notched it into the drawstring of her longbow. She eased back the drawstring until the tip of the shaft sat snuggly beside the body of the longbow. She released the arrow and watched as it struck the soft sandstone ledge beside the mountain lion's head and buried itself into the rock.

Then, there was an instant explosion of fire and noise from the detonating arrow, which caused the mountain lion to leap terrified into the air. Then, it scratched and scampered as it launched itself up the side of the rocky slope to escape this terror.

"Ha ha ha! Terrific shot, Kinta!" Misty laughed. "That poor old mountain lion won't come back down to these parts again for a long time!"

"I think you're right!' chuckled Kinta. "He was just hungry, so I didn't want to hurt him! But a good scare never hurt anyone before!"

With her wings buzzing noisily, Misty drifted back towards the rear of the carriage until they dropped back down onto the road's surface. Then Misty morphed back into herself, and they walked towards the carriage door.

Kinta leaned in through the window and smiled at Catelyn still sound asleep on Aedyn's chest. "When Mama wakes up, let her know that we are now safely moving on and should make our planned stop on time still!"

Aedyn grinned back. "Thank you, sweetheart!"

Then, Kinta and Misty climbed back up onto the roof of the carriage and settled down again. "Thank you, Mr Driver! We're now right to proceed again!" she said.

The driver turned his wide-open, bugged-out eyes towards the front and cracked the whip over the team. "Yes, Ma'am! Thank you, Miss Kinta and Miss Misty!" he said and touched his forelock.

CHAPTER 48

They arrived back home into Libertas Castle late in the afternoon, after a relatively uneventful trip, other than chasing away the hungry mountain lion. However, there was now even greater respect for Kinta by the household staff, some of whom weren't present when she led the revolutionary uprising.

The story of how she and Misty had singlehandedly flown through the air and spirited away the raging beast with their bare hands, had gathered momentum and grown exponentially from the moment they arrived home. Everywhere she and Misty walked now, there were whispers and secret glances as the staff continued to build their legend even further.

Kinta's focus now was preparing for her upcoming wedding with Vaalyun, which was to take place in the next few weeks. She, Misty and Catelyn spent many hours discussing the intricate details and organising the preparations.

Eventually, both girls needed a break and headed out to their secret waterfall for some downtime. They made their way slowly, as they strolled along the tiny, twisting paths through the scrubby bush, chatting away amiably about their recent visit to Vaalyun.

"I was *so* impressed by Vaalyun's story, about his dream to sail off down that sluggish old river, all I wanted to do was go with him right there and then!" mused Kinta. Her memories of the time spent with Vaalyun were still vividly fresh and poignant in her mind.

"I could see that on your face while he was speaking!" said Misty. "My greatest concern was saying goodbye to Mama and Papa, before we both disappeared down that river, never to return!"

Both girls laughed at the recollection. Up ahead through the tangled scrub, the sound of the little waterfall spilling over the ridge, and into the sparkling pool below, made them walk a little faster. They always enjoyed the peace and solitude provided by their little secret hideaway.

"I'm looking forward to our swim today, Misty!" Kinta said. She reached down and picked up Misty, held her close to her chest, then gave her a warm embrace. It was as if she had so much love to offer, and she just needed to share it with everyone.

"Thank you, Kinta. I love you very much also!" Misty said, then leant up and kissed Kinta on the cheek. It prompted Kinta to cuddle her even more.

They rounded the last bend and saw the opening to their secret clearing between the bushy shrubs at the end of the narrow pathway. Kinta felt like a weight had been lifted from her, after the heavy responsibilities she had personally shouldered during the last couple of months. "I can't wait to feel that cooling water splash down on us, Misty!" she said.

Kinta and Misty made their way into the shady grove and found their favourite location under a massive weeping-willow tree. Kinta leaned down and placed Misty on the ground again, which allowed Misty to scurry around, sniff the plants and grass under the tree, then squat and relieve herself.

Kinta smiled at Misty's antics. Then, she walked carefully back around behind the enormous wooden trunk of the weeping-willow tree. After finding a suitable spot, she lifted the bottom of her pretty dress around her waist to keep it dry, squatted down, and relieved herself.

It was always fun to play with the children at the nearby schools on her weekly visits. However, compared to her regular water intake, she drank so much water sharing their make-believe cups of tea, and she spent the remainder of the day relieving herself.

"The water in the pool looks spectacular today, Kinta!" yelled

Misty from out of sight somewhere. Kinta stood and dropped the bottom of her dress down again, then she walked back around to the front of the tree and sat down on the cold, green grass.

"Yes, you're right!" Kinta said. "The water seems to be sparkling even more than usual today!" She closed her eyes and dropped her chin down gently onto her chest. In comparison to her usual carefree existence, there were so many thoughts going around in her mind, and Kinta tried consciously to clear the chaos in her head through meditation.

Eventually, she felt her mind begin to clear and peace settled within her. Now, I can start to focus my thoughts on how my life will progress from here! I need a clear vision for where I'm headed! She thought.

Kinta felt Misty come back and sit down quietly on the grass beside her. She knew from previous experience when she was meditating, she needed to be undisturbed. She glanced down and saw Misty settle her chin down onto her front paws and close her eyes, knowing that Kinta would awaken her when she was ready.

She allowed her clear mind to begin to wander, seeking ideas and inspiration for the adventures she knew lay ahead when she and Vaalyun set off. Random images flittered across the screen of her mind, though seldom staying long enough to leave a permanent imprint.

When her conscious and subconscious mental activity had finally ceased, Kinta opened her eyes and stood. She arched her back and stretched her arms back above her head, flexing her leg muscles and feeling her latent energy begin to flow strongly again. "Okay, Misty! Time for us to have that swim we promised ourselves!" she said. Kinta relaxed and quietly began to undress.

She slowly undid the cloth ties that held the back of her brightly coloured, wrap-around dress together. However, two crystal-clear, vivid images remained etched on her mind. She had seen two very different and contrasting images with clarity during her meditation, and they continued to puzzle her as to their significance.

On the one hand, she had seen vast oceans of raging water, as she had been pounded by howling wind and crashing waves and feared for her life. On the other hand, she had seen the silent, sweeping, sandy desert that stretched as far as the eye could see, and the crushing, oppressive heat caused a searing insatiable thirst. *These two things are so clear, and yet, so much in contrast to one another! What can they mean?* The thoughts persisted and rattled around inside her mind.

Kinta released her pretty dress from her body and hung it from a small wooden knot on a nearby branch in the weeping-willow tree to stay clean and dry. As she stood there, naked and still pondering, Misty realised that something had her friend preoccupied. "Is there something that I can help you with, my sweet?" Misty asked.

In an instant, Kinta appeared to shake her head and clear her mind, then responded in her usual bubbling personality. "No, my precious friend! It's nothing serious with which you need to worry your pretty head!" she chuckled.

Suddenly, Kinta turned and sprinted for the pool, and her lithe, young, naked body wiggled and jiggled as she ran. Misty leapt up and followed her into the water. The two girls dived below the surface, then re-emerged with streams of water running from their faces, laughing and glowing with pure joy.

The stark images that had caused Kinta so much consternation earlier, now lay hidden just below the surface, waiting to resurface when she decided to remember. Until then, her focus needed to be on her forthcoming wedding. The girls spent the remainder of their day, laughing and frolicking in the fresh water, as they relaxed and prepared for the upcoming event.

...oooOooo...

Catelyn looked up from sitting in her armchair when she heard the front door of their royal apartment noisily open, then slam closed again suddenly, and their girly giggles were a clear giveaway that Kinta and Misty had just returned home. She smiled as the two girls appeared around the corner of the room. "Hello, my darlings! Did you both have a nice afternoon?" she asked.

"We both had a great afternoon, thank you Mama!" they both said together in unison, then they started giggling again because of that coincidence. Their joy was infectious, and before long Catelyn was laughing along with them.

"You girls go and get yourselves freshened up, Papa, and I are about to get ready for dinner!" she said. "If you would like to help me get ready, I'll be in our room when you have finished!" The fact that she no longer had to cook or prepare meals herself still seemed foreign to Catelyn, and she was often found in their private kitchen preparing little snacks.

"No worries, Mama! We'll be there soon to help you get dressed!" Kinta said, and the girls hurried off to get cleaned up.

Catelyn's belly was now so swollen with her pregnancy, and she often relied heavily upon Kinta to assist in removing her clothes and getting dressed again when they were leaving their apartment. She enjoyed having guests over for meals, which meant using the large formal dining room. However, it was still a challenge, and she considered it a little inconvenient, currently getting dressed in her condition.

She leaned upon the arms of her lounge chair for support, then struggled into a standing position and began to waddle towards her bedroom. *It must be a boy!* She thought wryly. *Kinta was never this big! And, she never made me feel this uncomfortable!*

Catelyn finally reached the door of her bedroom, opened it and leaned on the door for support. Aedyn suddenly noticed her while he was getting dressed and hurried over to assist her into the room. He took her arm and supported her while she closed the door behind her and made her way slowly and carefully to the edge of the bed and sat down to rest again.

"Will you be right to get ready by yourself?" Aedyn asked gently. "We still have some time to spare, before we need to head to the dining room! I can help you if needed!"

"I should be fine!" Catelyn said. Even as she spoke, their bedroom door burst open, the two girls came bustling into the room, stopped suddenly, then quietly strolled over to join her. "I think my help has just arrived!" she chuckled and smiled up to Aedyn.

Aedyn was initially surprised by the girls' sudden intrusion, and then he burst out laughing. "In that case, I defer to your professional helpers!" he chuckled, bowed low in deference towards the girls, then went back to finishing his final dinner dressing preparations and moved out to the loungeroom.

Catelyn was exhausted. "Sit down here beside me, girls! We'll begin the torture of getting me dressed in a minute!" she chuckled, with a wry smile on her face.

"Oh, Mama! You're so funny tonight!" said Kinta. "By the way, who are we expecting to join us for dinner tonight?"

"Laytn and Maeve are dining with us this evening!" Catelyn replied. "That is if I can still fit into any of my clothes!" She made as if to stand, and instantly the girls were there to assist.

Catelyn waddled over to her dressing room and surveyed the racks of beautiful clothing that hung along the walls. There were evening gowns, ball gowns, and formal dresses of every colour imaginable adorned the space.

"I think this is where I get to say, 'I don't have a thing to wear'!" she chuckled. "Unfortunately, I struggle to fit into any of these beautiful clothes now!"

"Mama, I think I have the solution! Which of these is your favourite?" Kinta asked. Catelyn thought carefully about her selection, then indicated a lovely royal-blue evening gown, which she loved to wear when entertaining guests.

Kinta removed the dress from its location and held it out for Catelyn to wear. "I think you'll find this one comfortable for this evening!" she said and helped Catelyn to begin removing her house dress.

Catelyn dubiously slipped the evening gown over her head but was pleasantly surprised when the dress fitted perfectly, and she looked terrific in her favourite colour. "I'm not even going to ask how that was possible, as this gown ceased to fit me months ago!" she laughed. "Whatever am I going to do, in situations like this, in the next few weeks when you marry Vaalyun?"

Then she suddenly felt a wave of sadness come over her, that she was about to lose her daughter in marriage. However, she quickly recovered and smiled at the two girls.

Since Kinta had already dressed for the evening, the three girls headed out to join Aedyn in the loungeroom, laughing together as they went.

The days flew by and, before she knew, it was time to visit Madeleine for a fitting. As soon as she had found out from Kinta about her betrothal to Vaalyun, Madeleine had immediately volunteered to design and make Kinta's wedding gown.

Kinta and Misty strolled across the courtyard and knocked on the door of Ox and Madeleine's apartment. She was excited to be seeing her wedding gown for the first time, after seeing the amount of time and effort that Madeleine had put into making her gown. And, how beautiful that dress had turned out.

Suddenly, the door opened, and Madeleine appeared. "Come inside! I was expecting you, girls, to turn up today!" Madeleine said, smiling broadly at her two friends. She was showing her pregnancy now but remained quite slender.

"Hi, Madi! Thank you for doing this for me, sweetheart! I'm certain I wouldn't have been able to do it as well myself!" said Kinta. She stepped forward and hugged Madeleine, then turned around to check on Misty. "C'mon Misty, let's go have a look at what Madi has done!" The two girls hurried inside, and Madeleine closed the door behind them.

Madeleine led them down the passageway until they reached the spare room, where she let them inside and closed the door behind them again. "I've been keeping it back here and locked away, so no little sneaky peaking male eyes go snooping! They will get more than enough opportunity to see your dress when you wear it on your special day!" she chuckled.

The two girls laughed. It was always fun to visit Madeleine, and they often came over to keep her company while Ox was away with his many duties. Even Erwyn was kept busy these days, managing the large numbers of busy House Staff for so many official functions in these early days since Aedyn's coronation.

Madeleine ushered them over to the vacant sofa, and they both sat down while she opened the locked cupboard to retrieve the dress. "Oh Madi, I'm so excited to be seeing my wedding dress today, it makes it all seem so much closer! Time seems to have been standing still!" said Kinta with a nervous giggle. She reached down and held Misty closer. Then, Madeleine turned back around and raised the wedding gown up for Kinta to see.

It was stunning! The burnished cream colour of the translucent silk material in the flared skirt, which hung to the floor in layer upon layer, appeared to be suspended slightly above the ground. The gorgeous dress was brilliantly highlighted by the matching colour of the form-fitting bodice from the same material, with hundreds of tiny complementary-coloured freshwater pearls sewn into a swirling pattern all the way around.

Kinta sat with her mouth agape and just stared! Compared to this wedding gown, she had never seen anything so gorgeous in all her life. Her mouth went up and down several times, but no sound appeared. And, she was utterly stunned to think that she would soon be wearing this wedding gown to marry Vaalyun.

"I think you'll find that she likes it, Madi!" said Misty, chuckling as she looked at Kinta's stunned reaction to the incredible vision before her. "You have done an amazing job, Madi! It's breathtakingly beautiful!"

Kinta was finally able to move, and she slowly turned her head slightly to look into Madeleine's eyes. "Madi, my darling, you have excelled!" she said, with her voice slightly quivering and tiny tears forming in her eyes. "I'm certain that there has never been before, nor will ever be again, another dress quite so beautiful, and made with so much love! Thank you, Madi!"

Kinta stood and quickly walked the few paces across the room to join Madeleine, then the two close friends hugged each other warmly in appreciation. They both held their embrace for some time, due to their strong feelings for each other. Finally, Madeleine broke free.

"Okay, Kinta! Let's get you out of those shabby street clothes of yours, and into this wedding gown, before you've grown old and fat and you won't fit into it!" Madeleine said, then burst out laughing at her humour. Kinta and Misty laughed along with her.

"It's a good thing I love you like a sister!" chuckled Kinta, then she began to remove her house dress. She quickly undid the buttons down the front and allowed it to fall around her ankles. Madeleine helped her to step out of it, and she hung it up for later.

Her eyes remained riveted to the slim, athletic figure of Kinta, with her full, rounded breasts, flat stomach, thin waist, curvaceous hips cradling a thick, blond thatch in her groin, and her long, lean limbs. When she finally broke her gaze away, she held out the wedding gown for Kinta to try on.

Kinta took the beautiful dress and carefully stepped into it. She gently lifted the bodice and wriggled her chest slightly to allow her full breasts to fit comfortably into the tight-fitting garment. The bodice modestly covered her chest and left her shoulders and arms free.

However, at the rear, the line of the bodice was raked low and sat just above her waist to highlight the golden tan of bare skin on her exposed back. The attached skirt flared from her hips and accentuated her slim waist. It hung to her ankles but was so full as to make her feet appear invisible. It created the illusion that Kinta was floating in mid-air.

Kina stepped over in front of the massive floor-to-ceiling mirror and spent considerable time as she admired her reflection. She turned slowly from side to side to get a full appreciation of the image she created.

Madeleine produced a hand-held mirror and stepped over beside Kinta. "Please, allow me to hold this small mirror for you, so you can turn around and see the back of your dress?" Madeleine suggested and held the mirror for Kinta to use.

Kinta turned around and used the small mirror to see her reflection in the large mirror, which showed the back of the dress accurately. She was astounded at the delicate, intricate handiwork that Madeleine had completed without any previous fittings. Everything fitted perfectly.

"Madi, you are a genius, my darling!" said Kinta, as she enthused over her reflection. "I have no idea how you managed this creation from just our initial brief discussion! Thank you, for the most incredible wedding dress ever!"

"Kinta, you look stunning, my sweet!" said Misty, her tail wagging busily. "I'm sure Vaalyun will be suitably impressed with his bride!"

"Thank you, to both of you, ladies!" said Kinta, then turned to look directly into Madeleine's eyes. "Madi, please say you'll agree to be my Matron of Honour? I would love to have you beside me on the day, to help me through this ceremony!"

Madeleine's eyes quickly began to get moist, and she dabbed at them to prevent the tears from spilling down her face. "Kinta, thank you, it will be my honour!"

The two close friends embraced again warmly. Suddenly, Madeleine interrupted and stepped away, again acting all bossy. "Now, Miss Kinta, we need to get you out of this wedding dress again, so you don't wreck it, and I have to need to make another!" she chuckled, flitting from side to side and helping Kinta to wriggle out of the close-fitting garment carefully.

When she had removed the dress, Kinta suddenly stopped and appeared deep in thought as she stood there naked. "My only disappointment today, is that Mama was not in any condition to accompany us and see this fitting!" said Kinta. "However, I'm sure Misty and I will do our best to describe it for her tonight!" She stepped over to the cupboard to collect her house dress.

Madeleine sidled up close beside Kinta and whispered conspiratorially into her ear. "Would you like me to sneak it up to your Mama's room tonight so that you can show her in person?" she asked. "I'll just need you to tell me when Aedyn is busy elsewhere!"

Still naked, Kinta squeezed Madeleine tightly to her. "Oh Madi, you are such a thoughtful friend! Thank you so much, my darling!" She quickly separated again and stepped into her house dress, then she pulled it up, placed her arms through the sleeves, and started to fasten the buttons down the front.

Once she had finished dressing, Kinta gave Madeleine a quick farewell kiss on the cheek and turned for the door. "C'mon Misty, we have a busy day ahead of us!" she said back over her shoulder. Misty bounded down off the sofa and followed Kinta out the door.

...oooOooo...

Aedyn reached out and lifted the warm drink to his mouth, sipped carefully on the hot contents, then placed the mug back down again onto the table he and Laytn were seated at for their discussion. He continued to listen carefully as Laytn laid out his plans for establishing a judicial system like those already in place in several other advanced countries.

"Aedyn, I shall need your sanction to establish a department responsible for maintaining peace and order among the populace!" said Laytn. "And, I would like to build smaller courtrooms in the villages to handle lesser crimes!"

"That sounds like a great idea, Laytn!" agreed Aedyn, taking another sip from his drink. "If we speak with Azrael, you may be able to use some of his former soldiers to form your planned department! He is currently working frantically to reduce the previous numbers of our army and would like the opportunity to offer another occupation to these men upon their discharge! He has both officers and enlisted men that he needs to re-train and re-employ in some worthwhile occupations!"

"In that case, I think this may just all work out fine!" said Laytn, smiled and sat back in his chair.

"There is one other important matter that I also need to discuss with you today, Laytn!" Aedyn explained. "Catelyn and I are about to begin a series of State visits to some of our neighbouring countries, and this will leave Libertas without my leadership for extended periods!"

Aedyn sat back in his chair and drew a deep calming breath before he carefully considered how and what he said next. Then, he leaned forward and looked directly into Laytn's eyes. "I have conferred with

Catelyn, Kinta, Seraphina and Lorelei for their opinions, and will be making a royal proclamation tomorrow! I will need your assistance in broadcasting it to ensure its broad dissemination to the entire populace!" Aedyn said, then paused to allow his next statement to have the necessary gravitas. "Whenever I am absent from Libertas on affairs of State, I am making you my deputised Head of State, in my stead, until my return!"

Laytn took a few seconds to collect his thoughts, then stood rigidly to attention before he responded. "Your Majesty, I am eternally indebted to your leadership for having led our country out of the abyss, blight and carnage created by Vylaine! Your compassion and fair-play have been a shining example to the people of Libertas in how we will move forward into a future of peace and prosperity!" He took a deep breath and swallowed, trying to remove the lump in his throat before proceeding. "Thank you, for considering me for this position! I am privileged that you have chosen me, and I will be honoured to represent you, Catelyn, and our country on the global stage!"

"Sit down, Laytn, my loyal friend! I can think of no man more suitable to take the reins of our country while I am absent!" said Aedyn, then smiled and took another sip of his drink.

Laytn visibly relaxed and resumed his seat, although he was still a little flustered. "Thank you again, Aedyn!" he said.

Both men continued their relaxed chat and discussed many different affairs of state over the next few hours.

CHAPTER  50

Finally, the day had arrived for the highly-anticipated royal wedding to take place. Crowds had gathered for the past three days, as they sought their perfect vantage point to see their beautiful princess, Kinta, marry the handsome prince, Vaalyun, from Nantgarw.

The flat, level, cleared area immediately outside Libertas Castle's gates, and the raised wooden platform dais that had initially been prepared for Aedyn's coronation, were again swept down to ensure that they were fit for use by the royal party and their invited guests.

Significant numbers of visitors were expected to attend from both Libertas and Nantgarw, to witness the permanent, peaceful union of their two countries through the marriage of their two favourites.

Food and drink stalls had quickly been erected around the outside of the cleared area, to cater to the needs of those already gathered and expected to arrive today. The sound of festivities and merriment had already begun and could be heard brashly echoing out across the countryside, as a welcoming beacon to guide the masses to the massively planned ceremony.

Vaalyun had arrived late that morning with Nyvorlas and Liluth, and they had taken up temporary residence in the guests' quarters of the castle to dress and prepare for the wedding. A large contingent of their invited official guests had accompanied them from Nantgarw, and they had all travelled together as a convoy over the mountain pass.

This morning, Kinta was seated in the living room of their family's apartment in the castle, with Misty on her lap, as she spoke with Aedyn and Catelyn. Misty enjoyed listening to them reminisce about all the things they had done together while Kinta had grown up from being a little girl.

Kinta had seen Vaalyun, and his parents and their entourage, arrive at the castle earlier and was a little disappointed that she couldn't rush downstairs to greet them.

Instead, she had remained upstairs with her parents and tried to stay calm and relaxed before the commencement of her special ceremony. "Mama and Papa, thank you for being the best parents a girl could possibly have had as I was growing up! You've always provided me with a loving home, and a safe and secure environment, to allow me to grow and become my own person! For this, I am, and will always be, eternally grateful!"

Catelyn was seated with Aedyn on a comfortable sofa. Her eyes finally conceded and allowed tears of joy to spill out and trickle down her face, which she then constantly dabbed at as she tried to dry them. She held Aedyn's hand, who had his arm around her shoulders for support and fought hard to prevent his eyes from tearing up as well.

"Kinta, my darling, Mama and I are so very proud of the strong, independent young woman you have grown to become! We will always remember you as a little girl, always wanting to do everything for yourself!" said Aedyn. "Little Miss Independent, Mama always called you!"

All four laughed at the distant fond memory. Then, Kinta leaned forward and looked into her parents' eyes. "I am most grateful for the two of you having your strength of character, and the confidence, to allow me to marry Vaalyun and head off into the vast unknown on our adventures together!" she said, then leaned back again and relaxed as she saw both their faces smiling.

"Sweetheart, just remember, we will always be here if you need us!" said Catelyn, as she dabbed at her eyes again. "Papa and I have done our part in preparing you for life, whatever it shall bring, but it's entirely up to you in how you live it!"

"Thank you, Mama! That means so much to me!" said Kinta, then noticed Misty still sitting on her lap. "And, Misty!" she hurriedly added and all four laughed again heartily.

...oooOooo...

Madeleine arrived early afternoon and joined Kinta in her room. As Matron of Honour, she was wearing a stunning sapphire-blue gown along similar lines to Kinta's dress.

The dress complimented her huge blue eyes and was made from a light, translucent chiffon material that clung to Madeleine's svelte figure.

Aedyn and Catelyn were in their bedroom dressing, and Misty had joined them to accompany Catelyn downstairs shortly. Kinta was still relaxing.

"Hi, Madi, is it that time already?" Kinta asked, and rose to greet her when Madeleine appeared. "I'm so pleased you agreed to be here with me for today! After all, you're already married, so that makes you an expert in knowing what to do at these things!"

The two girls both laughed. "Yes, Kinta, I may be married! But I'm certainly not considered an expert at looking casual and relaxed in front of the entire population and leaders of two great nations, all gathered together to celebrate my nuptials!" said Madeleine and giggled nervously. "My wedding was held in the middle of the night, with a few special friends!"

"Madi, my darling, both of our weddings will be long remembered fondly by each of us, and both will have achieved the same aim! We will each have found the man of our dreams and be committed to spending the rest of our lives together!" said Kinta, and Madeleine rushed forward and squeezed her tight.

"Oh, Kinta, I just love the way you always see things so simple and straightforward!" said Madeleine, as she continued to hug Kinta tightly. "But I think we had better begin to get you dressed and ready, or neither one of us is going to be very popular if you're late!" she said, then stepped back and surveyed Kinta as she tried to think of what to do first.

"Okay, Madi, make me beautiful!" chuckled Kinta, and held both her arms out for dramatic effect.

"Kinta, you are already beautiful! My role is just to make you presentable!" said Madeleine. The two girls both laughed heartily again.

"Thank you, Madi! And, I will be your willing assistant!" Kinta chuckled, then began to undress from her house dress. When she had removed the clothing and stood naked, she passed the house dress to Madeleine.

Madeleine turned and went to Kinta's wardrobe, and hung the house dress back in the closet. Then, she removed the magnificent wedding gown from the closet and brought it back. She held it out for Kinta, who took the dress and stepped into it. Both girls worked together to lift the wedding gown and carefully adjust it so that Kinta fit comfortably into the tight-fitting garment.

Kinta turned around and looked at herself wearing her wedding gown in the full-length mirror on her wall. "Oh, Madi, it looks even more spectacular today!"

Suddenly, there was a loud knock on Kinta's bedroom door. "Are you dressed and decent?" came Aedyn's voice from behind the door. "I just wish to see you briefly before Mama, and I go downstairs!"

"Of course, Papa!" Kinta called back.

The bedroom door opened slowly. Aedyn tentatively entered wearing his complete royal regalia, glanced around to see where the girls were standing, then made his way to Kinta. He stood in front of her and cast his eyes over his daughter dressed for her wedding. "Kinta, my darling, you look absolutely stunning!"

Then, he reached inside his jacket and removed a magnificent necklace of huge, matching, cream-coloured pearls, which he opened and then clasped and hung around Kinta's neck. Then he stepped back and smiled as he admired his addition. "Sweetheart, this is just a little something that Mama and I wished you to have, to complete your outfit for today, since it is your special day!" he said.

Tears sprang into Kinta's eyes as she placed her hand on the necklace and rushed into Aedyn's arms. "Thank you, Papa! I love you and Mama and will treasure this necklace always!" she sobbed.

Aedyn hugged his daughter tightly. "I know you will, sweetheart!

But now you need to let Madeleine help you be rid of those tears and get you ready to go see your soon-to-be husband!" he chuckled. He released himself from Kinta's embrace and turned, then made his way to the door. "I will be waiting just outside your door to escort you to your wedding!" he called back over his shoulder, then stepped out and closed the door behind him.

Madeleine busied herself with drying Kinta's eyes and dusting her face lightly with powder. Then she brushed and coiffured Kinta's long golden locks into place. Finally, she went to the wardrobe and returned with a waist-length, gossamer-thin, cream-coloured veil, which was attached to a golden tiara that had been inset with cream-coloured freshwater pearls.

"This is just a little gift from Ox, my Papa, and I, also to complement your wedding gown!" said Madeleine and placed the tiara carefully in place on Kinta's head. Then she gave Kinta a little hug and a quick kiss on the cheek, before lowering and putting the front of the veil over Kinta's face.

Kinta was stunned, and momentarily speechless. Finally, she spoke. "Madi, thank you, this is absolutely perfect!" She gave Madeleine a quick hug in return, and the two girls made their way out to join Aedyn.

...oooOooo...

The huge, gilded, royal carriage, drawn by the matching six white horses, slowly pulled to a stop in the clearing at the end of the long, red carpet. Surrounding the carriage's location, and in every available space within eyesight, were literally thousands of people of every age and ilk. There were families and young children, older folks, and single men and women, all pushing and bustling to try and get a glimpse of their favourite princess.

Along either side of the red carpet, official guests and dignitaries had been seated. They now rose as one and stood to welcome the bride. From a raised platform to one side of the assembled throng, three smartly dressed heralds lifted their polished horns and blew a loud fanfare to welcome Kinta.

Seated beside her in the carriage, Aedyn leaned closer to Kinta and whispered into her ear. *"I think this means we're expected to get out and join them! Are you ready for this, my sweet?"*

Kinta whispered back. *"Papa, I have waited my whole life for this moment! My lifelong dreams are about to come true! Please, take me to my husband!"*

Aedyn stood and stepped down from the carriage. He turned around and put out his hand to help Kinta down as she stepped out to join him. Then he stood to her left-hand side, and she placed her hand through his arm.

There was another massive fanfare to signal the commencement of formalities. Alongside the raised dais, an enormous steam-driven organ began to play a bridal marching tune. Kinta glanced up and looked down the entire length of the long, red carpet to where Vaalyun stood at the bottom of the steps leading up to the dais. He was facing her, resplendent in his royal uniform, and winked when he saw she was looking.

Kinta smiled discretely back. She and Aedyn began their long, slow walk, which took them down the red carpet to meet Vaalyun. Along either side, Kinta recognised many of the faces she had fought alongside or met on her visit to Nantgarw. She smiled tenderly back to acknowledge their presence and good-wishes on her special day.

Eventually, they reached Vaalyun's side and halted. Vaalyun leaned closer and whisper to her. *"Kinta, you look stunning, my sweet! My love for you is boundless!"*

"Who gives this woman's hand in matrimony?" Laytn's voice rang out loudly from the top of the dais.

"I do!" Aedyn responded. He leaned forward and kissed Kinta lightly on the cheek through her veil, then turned and made his way back to stand beside Catelyn in the front row.

Vaalyun took Kinta's hand and helped her climb carefully up the few steps to join Laytn on the dais for the ceremony. They stood quietly together, calmly held hands, and listened to Laytn as he took them through the various requirements of legal marriage.

"...Therefore, I pronounce you husband and wife! Vaalyun, you may now kiss your bride!" Laytn concluded.

Vaalyun gently lifted the flimsy veil away from Kinta's face and placed it back over behind her head. Then, he took Kinta lovingly into his arms and kissed her warmly on the mouth, crushing her into his chest. Kinta went into his arms willingly and raised her hands to hold Vaalyun's face while they kissed.

A massive cheer went up from the assembled thousands of voices, the large organ began to play again, and the heralds blasted another huge fanfare simultaneously in celebration.

Vaalyun and Kinta thanked Laytn, then turned and walked arm-in-arm back through the massed crowds to the waiting gilded carriage that would take them to their reception.

Aedyn turned to help Catelyn, but she looked up at him with her eyes wide open and her hands held to her groin. "My waters just broke! We're going to have a baby!" she said.

CHAPTER 51

K inta leaned forward and rested her hands lightly on the stony crenellations of the massive ramparts, as she gazed out across the valley floor. *This is such a beautiful country!* She thought quietly to herself. *We are indeed blessed!*

She looked carefully over the edge and peered down the sheer stone face of the palace, to where the forest below grew up to the base of the mountain, upon which the royal palace perched. Like a jagged scar, that split the picture-perfect image below, a gravel road emerged from the front gates of the castle and vanished among the trees further down the slope.

The gilded royal carriage shone in the early morning sunlight. It kicked up a cloud of dust behind the team of six white horses as it exited the gates and began the downhill run into the trees. Her parents leaned out of the carriage window, then waved over their shoulders, just before being swallowed up by the forest. Kinta got a brief glimpse of her new little brother, Aconis, snuggled up in Catelyn's arms and she smiled broadly. *I have indeed been blessed!* She thought as they disappeared.

Kinta stood up straight, stretched her shoulders back leisurely, and stared out across the patchwork of fields, to where the azure-blue of the Great Southern Ocean blended into the sky on the horizon. *I wonder where we would be now if things had turned out differently?* She asked herself, and a cold shiver suddenly ran up her spine at the thought of some of the possibilities.

Then, she was again suddenly flooded with warmth, as she remembered that she and Misty were about to re-join Vaalyun later today, after another long absence of six weeks from her new husband, to begin their planned lifetime of adventure on the river.

Vaalyun had left immediately after their reception to accompany his parents back to Nantgarw, while Aedyn, Kinta, and Misty had been busy while they assisted Catelyn with her birth. He had spent the past few weeks busily occupied as he purchased, stocked and prepared their vessel in readiness for their impending departure. It would be fantastic being able to catch up with Vaalyun again later today.

Kinta turned and made her way slowly across the cold flagstone floor of the battlements. Then, she headed for the open stone portal of the nearby tower archway, which led to the staircase that would take her back down to her room.

She suddenly became intensely aware of the warm sun on her skin and stopped abruptly, closed her eyes against the brightness and extended her arms, then turned her face up to meet the welcome warmth of its rays.

She was still standing there, motionless like a statue, when Misty came out to join her. "And so, the adventure begins...!" said Misty, with a tremor of obvious excitement in her voice.

Kinta slowly pirouetted on the spot as her tinkling laughter rang out loudly, bounced off the rockface of the mountain behind them and echoed across the palace grounds. "Bring it on!" she shouted, and Misty's tail vigorously wagged as she laughed with joy and ran around Kinta's legs.

To be continued

About the Author

K im Looke grew up in a sleepy little West Australian Wheatbelt town and completed his primary school years at the local State School, but attending high school meant travelling daily by school bus to a neighbouring mining town, eighty kilometres away to finally finish Year Ten.

After fifteen idyllic years in this rural backwater, he left home to join the Royal Australian Air Force in January 1968, where he completed a trade apprenticeship in avionics, and eventually served twenty-six years of full-time service, retiring in December 1993.

In September 1973 he married Joan and, upon his retirement from the RAAF, the family opted to stay in the Hawkesbury region of New South Wales. But, after a decade of stability, they were once again on the move and in December 2002, relocated to South East Queensland where they have now settled.

Printed in the United States
By Bookmasters